BARABBAS

"Now AT THAT FEAST HE [PILATE] RELEASED UNTO THEM ONE PRISONER, WHOM-soever they desired. And there was one named Barabbas, which lay bound with them that had made insurrection with him, who had committed murder in the insurrection. And the multitude crying aloud began to desire him to do as he had ever done unto them. But Pilate answered them, saying, Will ye that I release unto you the King of the Jews? For he knew that the chief priests had delivered him for envy. But the chief priests moved the people, that he should rather release Barabbas unto them. And Pilate answered and said again unto them, What will ye then that I shall do unto him whom ye call the King of the Jews? And they cried out again, Crucify him. And so Pilate, willing to content the people, released Barabbas unto them, and delivered Jesus, when he had scourged him, to be crucified."

—MARK, 15:6-15

"And they had then a notable prisoner named Barabbas."

—MATTHEW, 27:16

"And they cried out all at once saying, Away with this man, and release unto us Barrabbas: (Who for a certain sedition made in the city, and for murder, was cast into prison.)"

—LUKE, 23:18-19

"Then cried they all again, saying, Not this man, but Barabbas. Now Barabbas was a robber."

—JOHN, 18:40

BARABBAS

A Novel of the Time of Jesus

by EMERY BEKESSY

With the Collaboration of
ANDREAS HEMBERGER

Translated from the German
by RICHARD *and* CLARA WINSTON

New York · 1 9 4 6
PRENTICE-HALL, INC.

Copyright, 1946, by

EMERY BEKESSY

Printed in the United States of America

Contents

BARABBAS

1 ❦

Ezra's Flight

A LONG DRAWN-OUT BUGLE CALL GAVE THE SIGNAL FOR REST. IT WAS
the fifth hour and the heat under the thatched roofs of the working
quarters in the west of the Holy City was so unbearable that the arms
of the Roman overseers began to feel limp. The snapping of the
lashes upon the naked backs of the convicts had ceased; the workmen,
dripping with sweat, leaned against the pillars that supported the roof
and greedily gasped in the air that fanned down from the hills. It too
was hot, but at least not so thoroughly saturated with flour dust as the
air all around the mills.

The convicts who were turning millstones in teams of four dropped
to the ground beside the beam to which they were chained. Leaning
their flayed backs against the beam, they stared dull-eyed into space.
They lay motionless where they had slumped to the ground, only their
panting breath indicating that life remained in their beaten, exhausted
bodies. There were two hundred rather young men, most of them
Jews, who were kept busy turning the fifty millstones.

The labor of emptying the grain into the mills, sifting, and filling
the sacks with flour and bran, was done by slaves. The work was just
as grueling, but the slaves were not chained, and now they pressed
past the overseers into the open air to snatch a breath. They would
not wander too far from their place of work; the Roman legionnaires,

1

pacing up and down so that their metal cuirasses rattled and holding their short swords naked in their hands, would see to that.

The two hundred chained men, who were but a small fraction of the thousands of convicts forced to labor for the Roman masters, were by no means criminals—unless it was in itself a crime to be a Jew. Rome was preparing for a new campaign against the Parthians. The preparations entailed great work, and the workers were picked up wherever they could be found. In a city like Jerusalem a fake riot was a ready pretext. Groups of men standing around harmlessly suddenly found themselves surrounded by legionnaires who drove them off like cattle. Anyone who dared to protest was sent to the galleys, if he were not at once nailed to the cross. The rest were sentenced to three, six, or twelve months of forced labor and sent to the mills and quarries or employed in building roads and fortifications. In this way the Romans secured cheap labor; moreover, it was a good method of holding in check the hated, rebellious Jews.

The labor in the grain mills was by far the cruelest. Here not a day passed without a few "convicts'" falling beneath the beam never to rise again. But such an incident was not troublesome: the burial grounds were near by and the overseers simply chained another man to the vacant place along the beam. If there were no new convicts at hand, old ones who had already served their sentence were simply not released.

After half an hour of rest, of dull, exhausted silence which was interrupted only by the panting of the prisoners, the sound of carts rolling over the stony ground outside the mill was heard. The convicts' sole meal of the day was being delivered: a gruel of bran, a little flour and water. Slaves ladled the gruel from huge troughs into clay bowls; others carried the bowls on broad platters into the room, open on three sides, in which the millstones stood, and placed the bowls beside the chained men. But none of the prisoners reached for the food.

"Water!" some of them groaned. "Water!"

The thirst of these exhausted men was a burning torment. But the slaves did not understand what they wanted and answered the groans with kicks. These slaves felt themselves the masters here; it pleased them, downtrodden and beaten as they were, to kick and strike these refractory sons of a despised race.

It was another half hour before the carts with the jugs of water arrived. These were carried around to the prisoners. The parched men poured the lukewarm, opaque, ill-smelling water into their mouths, drank all they were permitted. Then, with trembling fingers, they began eating the gruel in their bowls.

Near Mill XV there was a brief brush between a prisoner and the slave who handed him the jug. The slave had wrenched the jug away from the prisoner's mouth before he had allayed his thirst. The chained man had responded by kicking the slave, an Ethiopian, in the belly. The slave screamed; one of the overseers came up and lashes whistled down upon the prisoner's shoulders. Then the overseer took the man's bowl of gruel and walked away. Not a word had been exchanged. Indeed, there was no point to speech, for the overseer did not understand the language of the country and the prisoner knew no Latin.

Now the whipped man lay on the ground and stared upward. His lips trembled under his curly dark beard, as if they were forming words; his fingers scratched in the sand and clenched into fists; his breath came heavily.

The young man of no more than twenty years who was chained beside him looked at him.

"Ezra, why did you do that? You know very well . . ."

There was no reply to his murmured question. A suppressed moan was wrung from the breast of his mistreated fellow.

"Ezra—I will give you half of my meal. You poor fellow!"

Now Ezra turned his face toward the other. It was pale as death up to the roots of his tangled, dark hair, but his eyes glowed like coals.

"Enough, Jonah—you cannot fill yourself with what you have."

"I can, Ezra. I can well spare half of it. In this heat it is hard to eat at all."

He swiftly gulped down half of his gruel and pushed the bowl toward the man he had called Ezra. But Ezra pushed the bowl back to him.

"You are a kind boy, Jonah. But I do not want it. Do you hear, I do not want to eat. It would soften my hatred for these dogs. I want to go hungry, understand? I want my hatred burned into my gut, so that I will feel it to my last hour."

The youth shook his head.

"But, Ezra," he said gently, "you harm yourself alone."

"That is what I want—don't you understand? The more I suffer the stronger grows my hate. Woe to the dogs when I am free!"

"Woe to the dogs!" repeated the third man in the team of four, who sat on the other side of the beam. And the fourth chimed in, whispering:

"Woe to the dogs!"

A few minutes of silence followed. Then Jonah asked:

"How much longer do you have, Ezra?"

The whipped man drew himself half erect and again leaned his back against the beam.

"I do not count the days," he panted. "Else I would lose my mind. Nor is there any sense to counting. It will never end until I free myself. One day I will break one of their heads and then I will perish chained to this beam—if they do not send me to the galleys first or nail me right to the cross."

"Until I free myself . . ." Jonah murmured softly. His words sounded like a sigh.

Their two fellows on the other side of the beam had turned toward Ezra and were looking at the panting prisoner with amazement. He had let fall a word that had shaken their souls, grown torpid with misery; a word that made their weary eyes sparkle. But only for a brief moment. Then they sank back again and the light in their eyes went out.

"Until I free myself . . ." One of the two, an elderly, frail man, unbelievably gaunt, murmured the word again, as if he were trying to comprehend its meaning. Then he burst out:

"A foolish thought. Here we are chained—surrounded by soldiers —it is mad even to think of it."

The man named Ezra pulled himself to a sitting position. He turned to Jonah.

"Mad? How so? Because none has yet attempted it? That does not prove it is impossible—it proves our cowardice. Why, when we are unchained in the evening and dragged off to our prison, do we not fall upon our oppressors and kill them? Or in the morning when we are driven out here? Two hundred against forty—is that madness? They might kill a hundred of us, but the other hundred will be free and will live!"

"You yourself do not believe that, Ezra," the gaunt man said. "And even if we should succeed—where would we flee? The Romans own the whole world. I tell you, Ezra, it is madness to think of it!"

"And I tell you, Reuben, that you are craven, that you are all craven. The Romans own the whole world, you say? That is not true. They own the world as far as their arrows fly, as far as they can cast their lances, no farther. A few days' march toward the dawn and you come to the end of their might. They do not even venture so far as the rim of the desert."

"The desert! What would we do in the desert? We can just as well die of hunger and thirst here."

"Under the whips of the Gentiles—ah yes! But I tell you, I would a thousand times rather hunger and thirst in the desert and be free than—I do not speak of our own suffering—than endure the sight of these dogs in our Holy City. And I tell you this too: liberation will come to Jerusalem and Judea from the East. Have you heard the name Barabbas?"

Reuben drew in his lips contemptuously.

"Do not speak of him, Ezra. Barabbas—do you ask whether I have heard his name! What would you have of this robber?"

"Robber, robber! You are a fool, Reuben. What else are the Romans? Are they no robbers because they come with cohorts and legions, with lances and swords and arrows? Have they not plundered the entire world? And you call Barabbas a robber! What does he do? Does he rob the poor and defenseless? No, he helps them. And he takes only what he and his men need to live."

"But he takes it from the righteous. And not only does he rob sheep and neat cattle, but also kills the herdsmen when they defend themselves."

"So he does, but why do they defend themselves? Are a few sheep and cattle of their rich master more important to them than the salvation of our people?"

"The salavation, Ezra? You know not whereof you speak."

"I know very well. What else does Barabbas desire but to free Judea of the accursed overlordship. Why else does he gather about him resolute men if not to lead them against the exploiting heathen? I tell you: Barabbas seeks freedom. He will drive these haughty barbarians from the country and make Israel as great and free as she was in the past."

Ezra's dark eyes seemed to be gazing into the remote distance. He had braced his fists against the floor and looked as if he were about to spring to his feet. But as he moved there was a rattling sound from the chain which fettered his powerful arms to the beam of the mill, and his body relaxed.

The gaunt man whom he had addressed as Reuben was silent for a moment. Then he asked softly:

"Do you believe that Barabbas is the Messiah?"

Ezra tossed his head irritably.

"The Messiah! I have heard enough of that! For how many centuries has Israel waited for the Messiah? It is a children's tale that the priests have invented to keep the people quiet. Whenever things go ill for Israel the people are consoled with the promise of the Messiah—who has never come. Always the people freed itself by its own might—and that is the way it will happen now. That is the way it must be, Reuben. We should not place our hopes in the Messiah, but in Barabbas."

Reuben had lowered his head—at a loss for answer. Now the fourth member of the team joined in the murmured conversation. He was a man in the prime of life, tall, powerful, with a long, flowing beard and mild eyes set in a dark countenance.

"Do not speak so lightly of the Messiah, blasphemer. For centuries our fathers have believed in the promise—he will come when the need is greatest. And do you not know that some of the scribes say that the time will soon be fulfilled?"

"It is not my wont to regard what the scribes say, Simon. I am not one of the pious sheep who feed on fine words and quench my thirst with passages from the holy books. I find that it leads nowhere. We need deeds, not words!"

"Perhaps Barabbas is the Messiah after all," Reuben interjected, mainly in order to calm the excited Ezra, who was speaking so loudly that he was attracting the overseers' attention.

The man named Simon took him to task at once.

"Foolishness, Reuben, foolishness. Do you not know that it is written the Messiah must come out of the royal house of our forefather David? Barabbas is but a potter, and it is even said that his mother is a Samaritan woman."

"To me it does not matter whether or not he is the Messiah," Ezra exclaimed. "Barabbas is a hero, like Judas the Maccabean. He will free Israel."

Israel. He lames our fighting spirit. Barabbas holds that view, and he will soon put an end to the nuisance."

"Do you know any more about Barabbas?" Reuben asked, looking askance at Ezra.

"Oh yes, I know a good deal about Barabbas. I was with him and I will join him again. He alone offers salvation. If we had men here . . ."

Ezra was unable to complete the sentence. One of the overseers, noticing the rather loud conversation, strode quickly up to them. Without a word he drew his heavy lash several times across Ezra's shoulders. He also lashed Jonah, Reuben, and Simon and then vanished as rapidly as he had come. This behavior was typical of all intercourse between the overseers and the prisoners. The lash served as a substitute for all speech.

The other prisoners had paid no attention to the incident. Lashes were virtually a matter of course to all of them. Most of them were already sleeping the sleep of exhaustion.

Of the four men who had been punished, only the feeble Reuben uttered a cry of pain; he groaned and whimpered as he rubbed his bony arm which had received the blows when he raised it to protect himself. Ezra clenched his teeth so that they grated and whispered when the overseer was far enough away!

"You will pay for that thousandfold, you dogs!"

But the overseer had achieved his purpose. The conversation stopped. The four now sat or lay as apathetically as the rest of their unhappy fellow-sufferers, enduring the enervating heat of midday until a low horn blast ended their period of painful rest. With leaden, trembling limbs the chained men rose to resume their unendurable labor. Two pushed and two pulled the beam that turned the stone, and the snapping whips of the rested overseers gave the rhythm for the horribly anguished circles the men trod.

From the ninth to the twelfth hour, and then on again until sunset, the unfortunate men dragged their burden, always in the same tight circle. At the end their strained muscles became utterly insensible and there remained only a dull pain throughout their bodies. The sweat ran in streams over the red weals on their naked backs; their heads were hunched between their shoulders and their eyes were half closed. Little that was human was left in these men. A

"I have never heard that the Maccabean was a robber," Simon
torted. "But Barabbas is a robber. The priests say . . ."

"I do not wish to hear what the priests say," Ezra interrupt
"What do they know of us? What do they know of our distre
They sit at table with the heathen and revel . . ."

"That is not true!"

"Not true? Is not the High Priest, Annas, always with th
heathen, with the highest among them, the Procurator?"

"You do not believe that he eats unclean food there?"

"Does that matter? It is enough that he sits with the chief o
these dogs; that is treason to Israel. Unclean food! Is what we are
fed here clean? Is it prepared according to the Law? What nonsense!"

"You are a Sadducee!"

"What if I am? At any rate I do not trouble my head about the
laws. I am concerned with the struggle for Israel's freedom. Will
the priests fight? The scribes who are close friends with the heathen
dogs! No, no, no. But Barabbas fights. And he will bring us
freedom."

"With the few score vagabonds he has in his company?"

"Today there may be a few score, as you say, but tomorrow there
will be thousands and a little later an army capable of anything."

"Who lives by the sword shall perish by the sword," said the youth
at Ezra's side.

"Where is that written?"

"I heard it from a man who lives in Galilee—a Nazarene. He
preaches to the people and has a great following among the poor
folk."

"Ah—you mean that Jesus of Nazareth. Just the one for us! We
have heard him in Jerusalem: Be peaceable, suffer patiently, do good
and even love your enemies—I know the tune. He will get far with
his peacefulness."

"He is like a holy man," Jonah said. "Many consider him a
prophet."

"And many the Messiah," Simon added.

Ezra laughed cynically.

"That one the Messiah! What a mad idea—that he should liberate Israel. He has one thing in his favor: he sometimes lets the
scribes and pharisees hear a bit of the truth. But he is harmful to

few of them fell down, and after they failed to rise in spite of frenzied lashing—because they were dead—they were quickly unchained and dragged off to the near-by burial grounds. Where one of a team fell, the three remaining men for that day had to do the work of four.

The sun vanished below the hills before the horn sounded the end of the working day. The chained men slowed their pace; the mills stood still. Most of the men fell to their knees. They could still have managed to go on walking, but to stand still was beyond their power.

Now the overseers went from one beam to the next and loosened the chains. In groups of four times four the prisoners were delivered over to the guards to be taken to the prison, to the airless, unlit, stinking holes where they could scarcely breathe any better than amid the dust of the mills.

When Ezra, Jonah, Reuben and Simon were unchained from their beam, the overseer gave Ezra a few kicks for good measure. Now they stood alongside one another waiting to be led off. The guards were in no hurry; they seemed to be discussing some matter. As a result the group was unguarded for a moment. Only a moment, but that was enough.

"I'll give Barabbas your regards," Ezra cried in a low voice to his three companions, and before they guessed his intention he had leaped to one side, raced past an overseer whose back was turned to him, and could be seen making off toward the Valley of Hinnom. Obviously he was attempting to reach the area where Pilate's great aqueduct was being built; there he might be able to hide until nightfall.

The flight was discovered the moment it took place. The overseers shouted and surrounded the prisoners, lest others attempt to follow Ezra's bold example. They swung their lashes vigorously upon the rest of the prisoners. The guards called out orders, arrows whistled after the fleeing man, and four armed men began racing after him.

Indescribable excitement raged among the prisoners. Ezra's escape was something so inconceivable, so utterly impossible, that they no longer felt their exhaustion or the lashes of the overseers. But they were trembling with fear that the guards would soon seize the fugitive.

"Ezra ... Ezra ... it is Ezra ..." a few of them whispered. That
was all they could say.

Very few of them knew even the name of this savage man with
the fiery eyes. But each of them felt himself the fugitive; his fate
was their own; their own lives hung upon what was happening on
the slope of the Vale of Hinnom. They disregarded the blows of
the lashes; like madmen all of them thronged out into the open—not
to take flight like Ezra, but to see whether his flight succeeded. Not
until the strengthened guards advanced threateningly toward them
with their swords bared, not until half a dozen of them lay bleeding
on the ground, did they retreat. They had been able to see Ezra
only for the fraction of a second; the four soldiers were pursuing him,
but he was far ahead of them, clambering rapidly up the precipitous
slope that in places was almost sheer cliff. Then the gathering dusk
happily swallowed up him and his pursuers.

The overseers seemed to have given way to a frenzy of savagery.
They struck the prisoners like a herd of cowed sheep until their
arms grew numb. A few of them were foaming at the mouth; others
screamed hoarse curses. The prisoners could not understand the
words, but now that Ezra was out of sight they felt the blows.

In the jailhouse the prisoners were crowded into narrow chambers—so many of them in each cell that there was scarcely room for
them to lie. The air in these holes was indescribable; the masters
saw to it that even at night these convicts would not be refreshed
after their terrible day's labor.

Such was the fate of the lower classes of the Jewish population
under the glorious world dominion of Rome. Every single prisoner
realized the political significance implicit in his personal destiny.
When they asked themselves why they were exploited and abused
more than animals, they could find an answer. Animals, especially
draft animals, had a certain market value, but more than enough
men were available. The material need not be used sparingly, for it
cost nothing.

All that night hundreds of men lay suffering frightfully from thirst,
scarcely breathing, tormented by fever, beside and upon one another;
and crushed together as they were all had but one thought: Had
Ezra succeeded in escaping?

All who were still capable of wishing wished that he had. But
they did not dare to hope it. How could an utterly exhausted man,

hindered by the chain on his arm—how could such a man possibly escape four rested, powerful soldiers? Perhaps the man of the fiery eyes lay on the ground even now, laid low by an arrow; perhaps he had been taken alive. Then he would be crucified; such was the death for slaves.

In the crowded darkness the beaten, enslaved bodies moaned in torment, the torment of enslaved and beaten souls.

2

Pilate Knows What to Do

THE LATE AFTERNOON SUN CAST ITS SEARING, PITILESS RAYS DOWN upon the palace of Herod, which now served as the residence of the Procurator.   Valerius Gratus, the predecessor of the present Procurator, had remodeled this dark, sinister fortress which had been erected by Herod the Great into a building more fitting for a Roman to occupy.   The Roman architects had made such cunning alterations that the palace became an endurable residence even in the heat of summer.   Partitions were torn down and high, wide windows were installed in the massive walls to admit the cool sea breeze from the Mediterranean to the west.   Outside staircases led from the street into the spacious chambers of the palace, which gave a view out over the western and northern portions of the city.   The dark wooden paneling of the rooms had been replaced by white marble.

The visitor who did not look out upon the neighborhood of the residence might have thought himself in one of those Roman palaces that had made the City of Seven Hills a wonder of the world.   But one glance at the tower and the temple which reared far above city and palace, one glance at the narrow streets lined with almost windowless houses, one glance at the naked summit of Golgotha with its crosses on which hung dead men—would sweep away the spectator's illusion that this palace lay on the bank of the Tiber.   The

Procurator's palace was only an airy island of light amid the dark, clumsy structures of the Jewish capital.

In one of the front rooms of the palace, which had been transformed into a white, high and bright, columned hall—this was the room in which the business affairs of the procuracy were conducted— sat two men facing one another. They were very unlike in appearance.

The Procurator, Pontius Pilate, a man in his early forties, lay rather than sat among the particolored cushions of his wide settle. Over a thin undergarment of white linen he wore the purple-fringed toga of the imperial governor, the representative of the Roman Emperor, of the master of the world. And the predominant note in the Procurator's face was that of pride. The large, gray eyes flashed commandingly under dark brows; around the finely-molded, voluptuous mouth tiny wrinkles of superiority quivered during the conversation; the resonant, decisive tone of his voice betrayed the man accustomed to giving orders. The smooth-shaven face with its aquiline nose was well shaped; the hair, cut rather short, fell in waves around forehead and temples. All in all, this was an imperial Roman face whose vigor seemed diminished only by a trace of sluggishness. The very white and somewhat too fleshy hand held a handkerchief with which the Procurator now and again dried his perspiring forehead. On his feet he wore fine leather sandals; his body, insofar as it could be seen beneath the flowing garments, gave an impression of strength that was, however, tending toward fat.

His companion was a wholly different sort of man. He, too, was in his forties, but his long hair and curly beard was already shot through with gray, which contrasted sharply with the deep black of its original color. Under dark, bushy eyebrows glowed a pair of dark-brown eyes that bespoke flexibility and cleverness, and a fleshy, hooked nose projected mightily above the thick beard under which his lips were wholly concealed. The clothing which covered the man's rather frail body was the Jewish costume of the day: a dark, embroidered undergarment which fell down to his sandals and was gathered around the waist by a leather girdle. Over this was a crimson upper garment which hung loosely around the man's thin shoulders. This he kept tugging back on his shoulders with a nervous movement whenever it threatened to fall off as a result of the vigorous gestures of his hands.

This man was Joseph the Sadducee, called after his birthplace Joseph of Arimathea.

The language in which the Sadducee and the Procurator conversed was Greek—at that time the social language of both educated Romans and educated Jews as well as the language of philosophers and those who wished to be considered philosophers.

The Procurator had leaned back against the cushions and let his right hand, which held the handkerchief, dangle down so that it almost touched the marble floor.

"No, Joseph," he said in rather weary voice, "I have not felt at ease here for a single moment. You who know Rome and Athens will understand that. I cannot see why anyone would wish to live here who could live somewhere else. Why at least do you not go to Caesarea or Alexandria?"

A trace of a smile passed across Joseph's stern features.

"You forget, Procurator, that Jerusalem is my home, the home of my parents and grandparents."

The Procurator gestured agreement.

"You are right—I forgot that for a moment. I prefer to forget utterly that the only man in this place with whom one can have a sensible conversation calls this dreary town his home. Just look out there—isn't it dreadful? Don't you feel the oppressive barbarian obstinacy in that tower? Don't you feel that the gloom of that temple smothers every pleasant thought in the bud? Ah, Rome, ah, Hellas! I was ill-advised, Joseph, when I let myself be persuaded to leave my Latium and accept the ungrateful task of representing Augustus in this harsh land. I have said it before: it was no happy hour."

"Feelings of happiness or unhappiness are governed least by the place one happens to be," Joseph retorted. "A man bears his emotions with him."

Pilate disregarded this. As so often in conversations with Joseph, he was bent upon venting his spleen against Jerusalem.

"And the climate, Joseph, the climate! In winter the cold that pours down from the snow-covered peak of Lebanon is scarcely endurable; and in summer the heat makes it a fiery furnace. Add to that these people—sinister, stubborn, taciturn, adhering to a barbarian cult, devoted to repulsive customs."

"You do not speak kindly of my people, Procurator."

Pilate made a gesture of appeasement.

"I am sorry, I keep forgetting that you count yourself one of this nation. But in all earnest, Joseph, what have you, who are half Roman, and what is more half Greek—what have you to do fundamentally with these people?"

Joseph gazed gravely at the Procurator.

"A man becomes all the more conscious of belonging to his own people as the misery of that people increases, your excellency."

The Procurator sat up. The haughty line around his mouth deepened.

"Do you mean by that, Joseph, that you Jews have been made miserable by us, by the Romans?"

"Yes, I mean that, your excellency. You have permitted me to speak openly with you. And so I say to you: Your rule is one of the factors that make us miserable, Procurator. It lies heavily upon us."

"To be ruled by others is never easily endured, Joseph—that I will admit. But you do not seem to know how Rome has treated other subject peoples. Please recall the fate of Carthage . . ."

"Rome had reason for her wrath toward Carthage," Joseph said softly. "But the Jews have never harmed her in any way."

"That is true, my friend. And for that very reason the Hebrews enjoy an exceptional place among the vassals of Rome. When I came here, Augustus said emphatically to me: The manners and customs of this people must be respected unconditionally. Where else do we do that? We have erected temples for our own soldiers outside of the city in order not to offend the religious feelings of the Hebrews. Hebrews do the cooking for Hebrew prisoners because you have these insane dietary laws. Where else do we show such consideration?"

Joseph was not eager to irritate the Procurator. He might have reminded him that this "exceptional position" had been won through hard fighting. Was it not Pilate himself who had begun his governorship by transferring the main camp of his army from Caesarea to Jerusalem and planting the standard with the image of Divine Caesar in the center of the Holy City? Not one of his predecessors had dared attempt such desecration of the Holy City. Was it not Pilate himself who had suddenly arrested the Jewish ambassadors to Caesarea on the fifth day of negotiations for the removal of the idolatrous image from the city—arrested them simply because they were ready to die rather than permit the continued desecration of the city? No, Pilate had never understood the Jews. Tiberius Caesar himself had had to intervene in order to bring Pilate to his senses. But, of course, that was more than six years ago; it could not be denied that since then Pilate had learned a great deal. Not the least part of his knowledge had been acquired from him, Joseph himself. What was the use of recalling the dead past?

However, Joseph could not refrain from making a single remark. "The people," he said, "are not sensible of this consideration. You ought, my lord, to have a little more contact with the people." "Am I not in contact with your people, Joseph? Have I not tried to come to a peaceful agreement with the influential leaders among your people? And what have I achieved? Little more than politeness, and that half-hearted. Your so-called high priest, Caiphas, is insufferably arrogant and his father-in-law, Annas, the real head of the temple and the synhedrion, tells me every time he sees me that his son is at Augustus' court and enjoys the special favor of the Emperor. Sometimes this arrogance is more than I can bear. And then you tell me that we Romans make the Jewish people miserable and unhappy and that I have no contact with the people. Shall I doubt your friendship also, Joseph?"

Pilate had talked himself into a rage. But such frank discussions with the Procurator seemed to Joseph too important for him to let the questions and accusations go unanswered.

"You misunderstand me, your excellency," he said calmly. "It may be that you do treat the Jews better than other subject peoples. But the lower classes, who come into direct contact with the garrison, complain bitterly about the soldiers' harshness. In the prisons and the workhouses that you have erected Jews are abused and often beaten to death."

"Insubordinate criminals are nowhere anointed with fragrant oil," Pilate objected.

"That may be," Joseph replied. "It would all be very well were the punishment somewhat related to acts which you could call insubordinate and criminal. But these men are treated like slaves and worse than slaves. I do not reproach you, lord, because I do not believe such to be your intention. I merely desire you to understand that your overlordship makes us Jews more miserable than we are by nature."

"By nature—what do you mean by that?"

"You do not know our people's history, lord—or if you do, you know but the surface. You have based your judgment of it upon the mockeries that are told about us in the oratorical schools of Athens and Rome. I admit that many of our traits may seem ridiculous to foreigners, especially the fact that we shut ourselves off from all who are not of our race. But the reason for that is to be found in our religion, in a religion that is for us both our blessing and our heaviest burden. It is a religion that binds us intimately together and yet is the fundamental reason for our inward conflicts."

Pilate shook his head.

"I do not understand that—you must explain it more fully to me, Joseph."

"Gladly, your excellency. You know that our religion recognizes only one God. According to our sacred books, this one God made a covenant with our forefathers: they agreed for themselves and in the name of all their descendants to reverence Him alone. In return they were to be that God's chosen people, out of whom, when the time was fulfilled, salvation for the entire world would come—salvation of the whole human race."

The Procurator laughed.

"Salvation for the world—as if the world needed salvation! And that is to come from you Jews! I suppose you dream of a Jewish world empire, Joseph?"

"That is how we have interpreted our sacred books, lord."

"What are they, your sacred books?"

"They are the writings of blessed men whom we call prophets because they possessed the gift of foretelling the future."

"Aha, we have such men too, my dear Joseph."

"Yes. But yours prophesy from the intestines of animals, or the flight of birds, or in an intoxication from vapors that becloud the mind."

"And yours?"

"From the spirit of God, Procurator."

"And do you really believe that, Joseph? I thought you were an enlightened man."

Joseph of Arimathea fell silent for a moment. With his handkerchief he wiped away the perspiration that was beaded thickly upon his white forehead. He had let himself be carried away in his zeal;

now he suddenly became aware of the cutting scorn in the Procurator's face. Slowly, somewhat hesitantly, he continued:

"This faith, lord, is born with one; it is the heritage of generations.
I belong to the Sadducee sect, which the orthodox Pharisees consider heretic. But we, too, believe in the one true God and we, too,
believe in the revealed word of our prophets."

"Very well. That I can understand," said Pilate with a mocking
smile. "I even find it a good deal more comfortable to have only
'one God to cling to. With us a man is constantly afraid of offend-
ing one when he sacrifices to another. I will gladly give you our
whole Olympus if you want it, Joseph. However, I'm afraid I would
not know what to do with your Jehovah. From all that I have heard
of him he is much too harsh and uncompromising for me. Our gods
are willing to talk things over . . ."

Joseph disregarded the mockery.

"Yes—our God is a harsh God. A God without pity for those
who oppose Him. Our people have often been made to feel how
hard it is to be chosen by Him, for He has punished us for every mis-
step we made, for every failure to cleave to Him. Consider, lord,
what it means to struggle for a thousand years and more between the
obligation we have undertaken and our inborn evil inclinations.
Frequently—all too frequently—we failed in this struggle and at once
we were made to feel His heavy hand. From here you can see out
beyond the Vale of Hinnom where stand the remains of a temple to
Moloch, and in Jerusalem, the Holy City itself, temples were erected
to foreign idols. In his old age even the great King Solomon gave
way to idolatry and had temples erected to the gods of his concubines
beside the Temple of the Lord. What was the result of this mis-
step? The only true God turned His face away from Israel and gave
Israel up to the might of her foes. The Babylonians came, the Assyrians; Antiochus ranged through the land with fire and sword, and
more than once the heathens leveled the Temple of Jerusalem to
the ground. But through disaster and sorrow, through misery and
bondage, the people of Israel passed inwardly unscathed, and in its
sorest straits it remembered its mission and returned to Jehovah.
And the God forgave them. He led our fathers out of Babylonia
and out of Egypt, He humiliated Israel's foes—He kept the covenant
He had made with our forefathers. And that is why . . ."

Joseph did not finish the sentence. He had forgotten who his companion was; when the Procurator burst into shrill laughter Joseph suddenly realized that he had been about to proclaim his hopes for liberation to the very man who was tyrannizing his people.

"And that is why," Pilate laughingly added, "you expect your God to drive the Romans from the country and make the nation of Israel a world power even greater than Rome. Please, do not contradict me, Joseph—you are making a fool of yourself. It does not surprise me that your high priests believe it, and perhaps even your puppet king, Herod. It is their business to believe it or to pretend that they believe it. But you, Joseph, who with your own eyes have seen Rome in all her power and glory—can you really believe that a handful of Jews could seriously endanger such an empire? A few bandits against the Roman legions? Barabbas against our generals?"

Joseph raised his head. Forthrightly, his eyes met the Procurator's mocking glance.

"Why do you mention that name, lord? What does this desert thief have to do with the dreams of our people?"

"Desert thief? Either you are not being frank with me, Joseph, or you don't know what is going on. I assume the latter.

"I do not want you to think that I'm being hoodwinked. To all seeming Barabbas may be merely a desert thief who ranges the countryside accompanied by a few fellow bandits, extorting money from his own countrymen, stealing the shepherds' livelihood, and now and then killing a few people who defend themselves. Of course Barabbas does all that. But have you no eyes in your head, Joseph? Have you never seen a Jew wearing the two intertwined triangles—the 'Star of David' I believe it is called. They are followers of this 'desert thief' of whom you speak with such contempt. Do desert thieves have followers who parade insignia? No, my dear Joseph, Barabbas is no ordinary bandit. Let me tell you, there are a good many of your countrymen who consider Barabbas the liberator of Israel."

"If that is so, lord, why do you not have the man captured?"

Pilate laughed.

"Why should I? It is not the way of the Romans to make a mountain out of a molehill. Is it not sufficient to know what the man's intentions are? Taking him too seriously would be the act that would really set up his movement. In fact, I will admit to you,

Joseph, that I consider such a man highly useful to us. We could have arrested him long ago, but we do not care to. A small, innocuous popular movement like his suits us very well."

"I do not understand, Procurator."

"It is really quite simple, Joseph. We are not interested in maintaining a sluggish peace in Judea and Samaria and the surrounding countryside. What would we do with people that sat modestly and peacefully at the feet of their priests and lawgivers, pursued their crafts and their agriculture and quietly paid the taxes we imposed? Power must prove itself constantly; otherwise it grows feeble and is not respected. We need a bit of rebelliousness now and then, my friend, in order to demonstrate our power. I am telling you the honest truth when I say that it is far more advantageous to us for there to be a lump of sourdough to ferment the sodden masses of the people. We will always see to it that the ferment does not get out of hand. Barabbas is sourdough—that is why we let your 'liberator' go about unmolested. The petty uprisings he occasionally starts offer us a good opportunity to clamp down somewhat, to conscript the laborers we need, and to prove to you that Rome does not sleep."

Joseph of Arimathea was once more sitting with lowered head. His restless hands lay in his lap, tightly clasped, as if they were chained like the Jewish nation. But he refrained from betraying his surging emotions to the Procurator. From the square of Gabatha came the bleating of sheep as they were driven past and other sounds, the muted noises of the city. In deep, gurgling tones a *tuba* sang out upon the Temple Mount, proclaiming the approach of sunset.

Pilate looked at his silent, introspective companion with a glance of mingled mockery and pity. Then, endeavoring to give a softer tone to his metallic voice, he said:

"Have I annihilated your cherished hopes, my poor friend?"

Joseph lifted his right hand in a gesture of abnegation.

"Certainly not, Procurator. Barabbas is but a fool, even though he cloaks himself with nationalistic sentiments. Only fools would expect anything from him. To my belief the liberation of Israel will not be accomplished by force, but by the spirit."

Pilate leaned forward, his face revealing keen interest.

"Now you have said it, Joseph! By the spirit. The Greeks succeeded in conquering us Romans by the spirit. I confess it without any shame, for after all we subjugated the Greeks by force of arms. When we did that we were, more or less, still barbarians. Have the Greeks become Romans? Not at all. But we Romans of today make it a point of honor to be Greeks. The spirit of Hellas has overcome us. We no longer speak the language of Cicero and Caesar, but that of Plato; and it is one of our chief ambitions to speak it well. Even now we two are conversing in that language, Joseph— Is that not astonishing, when you consider it? The vanquished have conquered their conquerors by their language—by their spirit. But, Joseph, do not forget that they were Greeks! Can the Hebrew language, which you seem to cough up out of your bellies, be compared with the music of Greek? Have you a Homer, a Plato, a Sophocles, a Euripides, a Socrates?"

Joseph looked squarely into the Procurator's eyes.

"I might say to you, my lord: We have a Solomon, who was a great poet; we have our sacred books that speak lofty words of eternal truth and wisdom. But when I said 'by the spirit' I had something else in mind. Perhaps I should have said, 'by the heart.' "

Pilate smiled.

"You know, Joseph, that I am a man of reason. I don't think much of the heart."

"I suspect that, my lord. But let me explain what I mean. A year ago, when I was in Galilee, I had a remarkable experience. A young scribe, the son of an artisan, was traveling from place to place accompanied by a number of followers of all ages, preaching the fulfilment of the Law and healing the sick. I have seen blind men who were made to see by his works—mark you, my lord, by his works alone! I saw deaf men to whom he had restored the gift of hearing; lame men who rose and walked at his word. Moreover—the man's teachings were even more remarkable than these things.

"You do not know our religious laws, Procurator. There are a tremendous number of them—even knowing them all is difficult, let alone obeying them. This man who, I was told, comes from Nazareth, teaches that there is only one Law: Love God, thy Lord. And a second: Love thy neighbor as thyself. He preaches gentleness and peaceableness. He says when the priests drive away him and his adherents: Do good to those who hate you; pray for those who persecute you. He asks men to love one another like brothers. He asks the rich to give their possessions to the poor. He teaches men not to desire but rather to despise earthly goods; he rejects all property, lives on bread and the little his followers give him. That may all sound confused and full of contradictions—one must see the man, one must hear him, to grasp how clear and simple and beautiful all that is, to understand how his teachings affect the poor above all, the lower classes. He is a remarkably handsome man, this Nazarene. His language is simple and yet winged, because it is inspired by an idea that seems to me a grandiose one: the idea of brotherly love among all men. When one considers the implications of that idea, Procurator—I don't know, but it seems to me greater than Plato's ideas. Equality of all men before God and among themselves—is that not a vast, a tremendous thought?"

During Joseph's last words the Procurator had risen. Now he stepped close to the Sadducee who had talked himself into a fever of ardor. Twilight began to fill the high, wide room.

"A tremendous idea, you say? Perhaps. But a slave's idea. Equality of all men—what would that mean to us? To the Romans, for example? Our power—and all power, I think—rests precisely upon the fact that there is no equality among men. We, who are above others—are we voluntarily to give that up? What foolishness. To remain above—yes, and to climb higher if possible—that is the thing! And there can only be an 'above' when there is also a 'below.' "

"Is that so terribly important, Procurator?" The question passed gently, rather hesitantly, across Joseph's lips.

"I do not understand you, Joseph. Do you feel an urge to part with your goods? Or to tear up the acknowledgments of indebtedness that you keep in your chests? My dear boy, what ludicrous fantasies you pursue. What is this man you speak of but a beggar who tramps about the country spreading the dreams of a beggar? Who are his followers but the unpropertied rabble? You yourself have said that his doctrines influence only the poor, the lower classes . . ."

As he repeated Joseph's words Pilate seemed to grasp their significance for the first time. He interrupted himself and mused for a while before he spoke again.

"Yes, but such beggars' dreams are dangerous. They arouse desires in the lower orders. Such ideas are far more dangerous than those of Barabbas. We shall have to keep an eye on this remarkable preacher of a new doctrine lest he drive the multitude out of their senses . . ."

Joseph was following the shifting currents of Pilate's thought. He determined to make sure of his suspicions.

"Do you think, Procurator," he asked, "that conditions as they now are can last?"

"How do you mean that?"

"I mean, will there remain forever on the one hand a possessing upper class which can permit itself the most extravagant luxuries, on the other hand a multitude of the poor, the downtrodden, who are no more than slaves of the limited number of the wealthy and who are treated like beasts. You reminded me, Procurator, that I have seen Rome and Athens. Not only did I see them, but I tried to understand what I saw. What was that? Why, I saw what unspeakable rottenness has poisoned the body politic; I saw what a horrible cancer are those who you say are 'above.' The disease has not yet run its course in our country; we are a nation of herdsmen and peasants, of artisans and merchants. Forgive me if I offend you, Procurator—but I can see that our nation receives little good from Rome. Our wealthy men, our powerful men, have begun to imitate yours in extravagance, in pride, in the mistreatment of their dependents. But what if the slaves, the disinherited, should some day refuse to bear their yoke any longer?"

Pilate raised his right hand in a gesture of deprecation.

"Crosses will take care of such matters, my friend. Do not forget what we did to Spartacus and his men. Moreover—those are dangerous thoughts, Joseph. The man from Nazareth seems to have addled your sound mind. Believe me, it is better not to consider such matters. I myself am not pleased by everything that is done in Rome; but nothing in the world achieves perfection. You must admit that it is pleasanter for a few to enjoy satisfaction and a full life than for the entire human race to mourn. What a dull, grey, monotonous world that would be if all men were equal. Don't you agree?"

Again Joseph lowered his massive head. With weary, dull gaze he looked out into the rapidly advancing darkness.

"I don't know, Procurator. But it appears to me that misery is so vast not only among us, but throughout the world, that it cannot possibly go on. And that in truth 'the time is fulfilled,' as our prophets say."

"And that therefore the liberator must come," Pilate added scornfully. "The Messiah—you see, I know your word for it. But gently, my friend. We will . . ."

The Procurator did not finish his sentence, for a clarion call suddenly rang within the confines of the now dark room. The call was answered by a second and a third from farther away. The Procurator listened for a moment; then he stepped to one of the marble tables, grasped a small metal hammer and struck thrice upon a silver salver.

The centurion on guard in the atrium entered swiftly, stood still two paces from the Procurator, and raised his right hand in salute.

"What has happened?" Pilate asked.

"A prisoner has escaped."

"From where?"

"From the fifteenth mill."

"Details?"

"None as yet, Procurator. The man is being pursued."

"Have the century that was on guard sent to the border by forced marches this very night, and on half rations. A hundred lashes to the overseer of the prisoners. If he survives let him be chained to the mill in the escaped prisoner's place. If anyone is found to have aided the escape—the cross. Clear?"

"Very well, Procurator."

"What measures have been taken?"

"Three centuries are in pursuit of the fugitive."

"Idiots! Three hundred men to pursue a single wretched prisoner. Recall them! Rather to let the fellow go altogether and round up a substitute instead. One thing more: the convicts on Mill XV will receive no food or water tomorrow. That will cure them of any urge to leave. And now let us have light."

The Procurator waved his hand and the centurion departed.

Joseph of Arimathea had risen to his feet.

"You are harsh, Procurator, very harsh," he said unsteadily.

A number of youthful slaves brought in burning lamps and fastened them to the wall. By the light, Pilate stared at his guest in astonishment.

"Harsh? What do you mean. I mete out only proper punishments. Am I to reward the men for failing in their duties?"

"But the prisoners? How are they guilty?"

"Perhaps they are, perhaps not. They were probably with him in spirit at least. For that they must pay. I am extremely mild. Valerius Gratus would have had the prisoners, the guards, and the overseers all immured. I might send every second man to the galleys, or crucify every fifth. But I have no liking for grand gestures. And this heat is so enervating. I have heard that your religion forbids food and drink at certain times in any case. The men on Mill XV can imagine that tomorrow is one of their fast days, for all I care. Incidentally, how about dining with me?"

"Permit me to take my leave, Procurator," said Joseph, settling his cloak about his shoulders.

"Are you going so soon?"

"I am expected at home, lord."

"And besides you prefer not to eat with me," Pilate said with a smile. "I don't mind. I had forgotten that your laws forbid it. Although, I must say, it surprises me that a man of your culture should adhere to these superstitions. Farewell, Joseph, and thank you for the visit. Come soon; you are always welcome here. But next time we will discuss more interesting matters. Are you acquainted with Plato's *Symposium*?"

"Certainly, your excellency."

"Reread it before you come again. I would like to hear your views on some of Socrates' theses. And now once more, farewell!"

Joseph crossed his arms over his breast in the oriental fashion, bowed low before the Procurator, who had accompanied him to the door, and then slowly descended the outside staircase into the darkness of the summer night.

From the Temple Mount there once more sounded the gurgling note of the tuba. From the Akra, the lower city, came the scattered barking of dogs. The streets were deserted. In the center of the city Joseph passed the Hippodrome, which the Romans had built. Muted by the thick stone blocks, there could be heard the hungry roar of the wild beasts that Pilate had imported for his games. And Joseph could not forbear to think that of all the beasts of the earth the worst was man when he held power.

Why, he wondered, why?

And as he strode over the irregular paving-stones toward his home, his thoughts turned to the man from Nazareth . . .

3 ❧

Blind Eliazar

IT WAS AN HOUR BEFORE DAWN. THE CRESCENT MOON HUNG PALLIDLY upon the western horizon, the sparkling starlight was already dimming, and in the east a milky ribbon had fluttered gently down upon the desert sands. The contours of the massive grey boulders were delineated by this light. The great rocks lay scattered about the desert as if a giant hand had destroyed a proud, man-made structure, brushing the rubble carelessly aside and letting it lie where it fell.

No trees grew here, nor shrubs, nor grass. This was the desert.

A keen wind blew from the east with the coolness of dawn, bearing along a fine, feathery-light powder of atomized stone that for millennia had served the wind as a plaything, lightly taken up and lightly cast away. It bore this dust westward for countless miles, sheathing leaves and flowers, trees, shrubs and grass in a layer of grey dust that had the odor and taste of death. No twitter of birds sounded here, no bleating of sheep or lowing of cattle; the only sounds were the hungry howl of the jackal and the angry barking of the desert fox when his prey escaped him.

A man limped through this gloom and void—Ezra, the fugitive. His filthy garment hung raggedly about his body; he lifted his blistered feet only with the greatest effort; his bloodshot eyes peered into the semi-darkness, seeking landmarks amid the confused heaps of boulders. For five days, or rather five nights, he had traveled from

26

Jerusalem to the desert, sustained by the hope of finding the man who alone could save him—Barabbas. He alone offered bread to the hungry, freedom to the enslaved, vengeance to the abused.

But why, why was there no one in sight? Already the eastern sky was flaring red; soon the sun's first rays would break upon the sea of sand. This was the time when Barabbas and his men set out on their raids to the west.

Ezra reached the region of great boulders. He stood still and listened. Had Barabbas, in the four weeks of his absence, changed his camp, or had he and his men been captured by the hated Romans? This thought, to which Ezra had given no consideration until this moment, assailed him all at once. His mind reeled and he sank suddenly to his knees and then stretched out on the sand. He was utterly exhausted by his flight; he was half starved and had gone more than twelve hours without a drop of water, and his tortured brain could no longer endure any disappointment. If he did not find Barabbas at once, he was lost. He would lie here until death came, and after death the jackals.

Day broke.

A stone's throw from the prostrate Ezra an old man crept out from under a boulder, knelt down in the sand with his face toward the rising sun and began to pray aloud. He was dressed in a kind of caftan of sheepskin which in many places had its fleece completely rubbed away. Under a cap of hide long strands of gray hair hung down over his neck and his bearded face.

The man dipped his hands into the sand as if he were washing; he touched his brow, lips and breast and then, bobbing up and down, continued his worship.

Ezra saw him. He raised himself somewhat and called out: "Eliazar! Eliazar!"

The man showed no signs of having heard until his prayers were finished. Then he turned, still kneeling, and asked:

"Who is there?"

Ezra, now also kneeling, held out his arms toward the man. Eliazar arose and approached with uncertain steps.

"Who are you who call me by name? The Lord has weakened my sight—I cannot make out who you are."

"I am Ezra of Jericho. Where is Barabbas—where are the others? Have you water and bread for me?"

"You ask many things at once, Ezra. I can give you drink, and food as well. Come. Barabbas and the men went away three days ago, down to the Jordan. Whence come you?"

"From the Holy City. I am fleeing—from the Romans. For five days I have had no more than a few morsels to eat."

"Come," the old man repeated. He took Ezra's hand and led the stumbling fugitive to the rocks out of which he had come to make his morning devotions. A low, narrow passage led into a small cave—Eliazar's dwelling-place, which he shared with his mountain goats. There was a bed of hides in one corner; leather water skins, clay pottery and utensils were scattered about the floor. From under a slab of stone Eliazar fetched a large clay pot of goat's milk and handed it to Ezra who took it without a word and drained it dry. Then he broke a hunk of bread in two and gave Ezra the larger part. With a haftless knife he cut a large piece from a side of dried meat that hung on the wall.

"You must pound it between two stones," he said. "It is too hard for the teeth as it is. Water I cannot give you until I have taken the goats down to the spring. I will bring back a skin of water if you do not wish to go with me. Or would you rather come? It is far to the spring."

Ezra chewed silently at the bread, which seemed of the consistency of granite. Then he dropped down upon the hides.

"Sleep," he murmured. "I must sleep."

"As you like."

Eliazar untied the thong that held the goats to a post and paying no further attention to his guest, who was already asleep, departed with the animals at his heels. A crude, narrow path led through the chaos of boulders toward the north where, surrounded by a wall of rock on all sides, a small spring formed a pond. In a narrow area around this pond grew green grass and low bushes. The stumps of a few trees showed that palms as well had once grown here; these had been felled because they might have betrayed this spot of life in the midst of the rocky waste. The spring was an hour's fast walk from the place where Barabbas and his men usually camped; they kept their distance because at night the water attracted wild beasts. The band preferred to fetch their water, and old Eliazar, frail and half blind as he was, had to walk this long way every day, for only

near the spring could the goats find feed. He usually spent the day
at the spring, returning toward sundown.

Ezra sat waiting for him at the entrance to his cave. The long
sleep had refreshed him, but he was again hungry. And since he did
not wish to take Eliazar's bread and meat without asking, he had impatiently awaited the old man's return.

"You have been gone long, Eliazar."

"The grass by the spring is so sparse and the bushes so dry that
the goats must feed all day to fill themselves. And they must fill
themselves or they will give no milk."

Once more Eliazar gave Ezra bread and meat, and some cheese as
well. Then he milked the goats and proffered some of the fresh,
warm milk.

"You must tell me what happened to you in the Holy City, Ezra.
I always hoped to see the Temple again, but now that will never be.
My eyes grow weaker every day; soon I shall probably be wholly
blind. And if Barabbas does not return . . ."

"What has happened to Barabbas?"

"I told you, he has taken his men to the Jordan. Three days
since."

"But why should he go to the Jordan? If they seize him there,
they will certainly turn him over to the Romans."

The old man nodded agreement.

"That is what I said. But you know his stubborn will. When he
had made up his mind, he will not be swerved. At the Jordan there
is a man—a very wise and pious man, they say—who has great influence among the people. He has healed the sick and can bring the
dead to life."

"You mean Jesus, the Nazarene?"

"Yes—that is what they call him. Barabbas has gone to him because of his power over the people. He wishes to see what there is
in the man, he says. If they marched together and had all the people
behind them, he does not think it would be difficult to raise a rebellion against the Romans. And since this Jesus is supposed to be
such a worker of wonders—but I am not sure any of the tales are
true. I have often thought, if only he could restore the light of my
eyes! But how could I ever make the journey to the Jordan or to
Galilee?"

Ezra sat silent, staring into the darkness. All his limbs still ached;

his blistered feet were as painful as the sores on his wrists where the chains had been clamped. He had managed to break the rings around his hands during the five days the sores had festered. Tomorrow, he thought, I will go to the spring with Eliazar and bathe my hands and feet. Barabbas will probably return in a few days.

"Have our men had good fortune recently?" he asked the old man, who had already stretched out on the floor of the cave.

"Good fortune . . . well, yes. They have taken the contributions from the herdsmen and a few devout people have sent money from the Holy City. Barabbas intends to use the money to obtain better arms for the men. He has sent Judah to the Holy City to recruit. You know Judah—he is cunning and a fine speaker. In the last few weeks the number of our followers has greatly increased, Barabbas says, and if he succeeds in winning over this Nazarene, perhaps the day will soon dawn . . . you know what I mean."

"The day of vengeance," Ezra muttered between his teeth.

"They did not treat you very well, did they, Ezra?"

"To put it mildly. The evening after my arrival I stood in the Akra with a number of young men and spoke of Barabbas's plans. Suddenly we were surrounded by soldiers and arrested. They threw us into a hole where we could scarcely breathe, and the following morning, off we went to the mills. They are frightful, Eliazar—never was a beast abused as are the men of Israel in those mills. But that is good . . ."

"Good? How so?" Eliazar demanded.

"Because there a man learns to hate. Anyone who spends even a few weeks in the mills accumulates enough hatred—fierce, burning hatred—to last him his whole lifetime. If only the scribes and the rich men might have that experience, might feel what it is like to be chained to a beam, to perish from thirst and to be lashed until the skin bursts!"

His eyes glowed in the darkness and his whole body trembled with the memory of his sufferings.

"And how did you escape?"

"I can scarcely remember any more. I simply ran away one night as we were being led back to the prison. I have always been a good runner and somehow they did not catch me. A whole century pursued me, the arrows whistled around me, but I was the faster. In any case they would never have caught me alive. I had made up my mind rather to hide in the lepers' caves than to let those hangmen seize me. I would rather live an outcast, rather see my living body rot slowly away, than be the slave of those dogs. But they did not even come close."

"Did anyone help you?"

"No. Night fell swiftly, and beyond the aqueduct they are building—but, of course, you know nothing about that. I was able to hide and break my chains by pounding them between stones. Then I set out for here. And now here I am and Barabbas and his men are gone. Who knows whether they will ever return . . ."

Eliazar raised his head.

"Why should they not return? Do you believe that the struggle will begin so soon?"

For a long time Ezra did not speak. His martyred body, the festering wounds tormented him and made him disconsolate.

"I have heard something of this Nazarene," he said at last. "The Galileans can speak of nothing else. But I do not like the tales I heard. Let him heal the sick if he must—although we have enough healthy men to . . . But that is what wins him his following, so we cannot quarrel with it. What irritates me is the meekness of the man, Eliazar. Naturally we must keep to the laws as far as possible— I admit that. But what does he mean by: 'Love your enemies. Do good to those who hate you and persecute you!' Can we expect to free Israel with phrases like that? Are we to love the Romans? They say he preaches love—what good is that to us? I don't understand why Barabbas has decided to curry favor with him. He wishes to join the man, you say? Can fire and water join? I think Barabbas was ill-advised to make this journey to the Jordan. Do you agree?"

"I don't know, Ezra—I cannot judge except by what I hear. Some of the men were full of enthusiasm, especially Judah. I think it was he who persuaded Barabbas to go to the Nazarene."

"Judah, Judah! He is a dreamer with the wildest fancies running through his head. Incidentally, it was a mistake to send him to the Holy City. He can speak well, of course—even with scribes. But what is the good of talk? Are we Greeks? We do not need men of fine words, but men-at-arms, men with iron fists, men who will fight to the last drop of blood. Such men Judah will not find in Jerusalem, nor Barabbas at the Jordan, worshipping at the feet of this preacher."

Eliazar did not reply. Weary from the heat of the day and his long walks, he stretched out on the floor and soon fell asleep. Ezra, who felt choked by the stale air of the cave and the odor of goat droppings, got up and went outside.

The cool night air refreshed him. He sat down on a stone near the entrance to the cave. The stars shone brilliantly in the desert sky, and low on the western horizon gleamed the silvery crescent of the moon. In the distance sounded the hoarse bark of a jackal that had been driven by hunger to the fringes of the desert. Nocturnal birds whirred through the air.

Ezra groaned heavily. His heart was filled with the desolation, the hopelessness of the desert . . .

4 ✠

"What Are Your Aims, Barabbas?"

ALONG THE FOOTPATH THAT LED FROM MAGDALA TO TIBERIAS WALKED a group of men absorbed in conversation. It was the late forenoon; the sun stood high above the hills and a fresh breeze from the lake shook the leaves of the olive trees so that they glittered like silver tinsel.

"And I tell you," exclaimed one of the men, who wore the frontlet of the chief rabbi of a synagogue, "it is fraud and deception. They say he has been in Egypt; perhaps he learned such things from the idolators of that land. The idiot masses cry, 'Miracle, miracle!' but I tell you he has the help of the devil. Unless it is all . . ."

"You think it is chicanery, rabbi," said an old man with white hair and beard, "and so did we think. But all of us saw Lazarus dead; we were present when he was laid to rest in the grotto . . ."

"That proves nothing, Michaeas, nothing at all," the rabbi interrupted violently. "It has happened before that a man appeared dead and awoke again after hours, even after days."

"Perhaps this Nazarene is really one of the prophets," the old man insisted obstinately. "In any case he is something out of the ordinary. His speech, his behavior, are not those of ordinary human beings."

"He is an impostor, I tell you, a magician who ought to be stoned.

33

Out of the ordinary indeed. In what way, may I ask? His father was an artisan in Nazareth, a carpenter. What arrogance the man has, traveling about the country with his following and inciting the people against the scribes, against all the authorities. Do you know what he called the elders in Capernaum? 'Generation of vipers.' What right has he to preach such things? Who gave him permission. He denies the law—speaks of the Temple like a Samaritan!"

The old man whom the rabbi had called Michaeas shook his head. A few of the younger men in the group muttered their disagreement with the rabbi. They themselves were artisans, and it incensed them to hear their handicrafts spoken of so contemptuously.

"I do not know, rabbi," the old man said. "Of course, you may be right, for you must know the law. But I do not think him arrogant at all. He is the soul of modesty; whenever the people wish to honor him, he withdraws. And as far as the elders of Capernaum are concerned, you yourself have never spoken well of them. When you see this Nazarene and hear him speak—there is something about him—I cannot express it. Perhaps I should say, there is light where he is. It feels good to be in his presence."

The rabbi's eyes flashed angrily.

"Then stay with him—all of you stay with him, if the company of runaway fishermen, publicans, Roman mercenaries, heathen and public women is more pleasing to you than that of the righteous! Have you all gone out of your heads? Does not the kind of following he attracts give you cause for anxiety?"

"They are all poor people to be sure, but quite honorable," one young man protested hotly.

The rabbi was about to retort with equal vehemence, but there was an interruption. Several men, who had apparently crept forth from the rock formations that lined the sides of the path, stepped out and blocked the way. They were stout fellows, but somewhat raggedly dressed and none of them wore an overly friendly expression. One of them who was a head taller than any of his comrades, a man with a fierce face framed in curly hair and beard, stood in the center of the path and looked at the group from Tiberias with a mocking smile. He was a man of about forty. Half concealed under his clothing was a short sword, and in his hand he held a massive walking stick that seemed well adapted for use as a bludgeon.

His handkerchief was pinned to his clothing by a pin, the head of which was shaped into the Star of David. His companions, who were similarly armed, bore this same insigne.

"Peace!" the man said in a low, harsh voice. As he spoke, more and more ragged, armed men appeared from behind the rocks.

"Peace be with you!" the rabbi replied. His voice trembled slightly, for this sudden throng of armed men seemed to bode ill. "What do you want of us?"

The stalwart leader knocked his walking stick against the ground.

"It is well that you ask, rabbi—we will come to an understanding all the sooner. It is not our wont to make long speeches. Must I introduce myself? I am Barabbas. I do not know whether you have heard of me, but it would surprise me if you have not. I am the man who will free Israel from the yoke of the accursed heathen. I demand support from all true-believing Israelites. Do you wish to make a voluntary contribution of the money and valuables you carry with you?"

"This is robbery," the chief rabbi screeched, holding his hand on the pocket of his caftan.

The black-haired giant laughed.

"I believe you are the chief rabbi of the synagogue of Tiberias, but a wise man you are not, else you would not use words so loosely. I said 'voluntary contribution.' For a good cause. Or are you against the salvation of Israel?"

"I have only a few shekels with me—and most of these men with me are poor . . ."

"I find it boring, rabbi, to observe how you wealthy men always seek to hide behind the poor. Those who are poor will give nothing; the others will give what they have with them. But give quickly; we have no time to waste on you. Here—throw your money and your jewels on my handkerchief."

Barabbas's companions had by now completely surrounded the group from Tiberias. The "voluntary" gifts of money and valuables were swiftly deposited on the handkerchief, and when the number of coins seemed insufficient to these queer saviors of Israel, their hands swiftly searched the pockets of their victims. Besides coins of silver and copper and a few rings, a number of articles of clothing also changed owners.

"You may go," Barabbas said, when the collection was completed.

"But one thing more. I want to know where I can find Jesus the Nazarene."

The chief rabbi, whom this sudden assault had uttedly distracted, suddenly pricked up his ears.

"Why do you wish to meet the man?" he demanded, taking a step toward Barabbas.

"That is none of your business," the robber said rudely. "Tell me where I can find him and then go to the devil."

The chief rabbi persisted.

"Listen, Barabbas. You have taken all we had with us—but it was not very much. The community of Tiberias would gladly give ten times as much if you would drive this Jesus and his followers out of our neighborhood, and do it so thoroughly that they would never return. What do you think?"

"I would not consider playing the bloodhound for you. If you want to be rid of him, drive him away yourselves. But I am over-joyed to hear that the community of Tiberias is so prosperous and will be able to make further contributions to our nation's cause. Now speak: Where can I find this man from Nazareth who appears so troublesome to you?"

"He is probably near Magdala, the estate owned by Lazarus," the rabbi replied crossly.

"Who is this Lazarus?"

"A very rich man who will be happy to meet you," the rabbi replied spitefully.

"Whether he is happy or not is none of your business. Now get out of here."

With an imperious gesture he waved the whole group away, and the men from Tiberias continued on their way. When they had vanished around a turn in the path, Barabbas spoke to his men.

"Let us go to Magdala to visit this Lazarus who will be so happy to see us."

The men laughed and the little band set off down the path toward Magdala.

The stately white villa that crowned a small slope sat squarely in the center of the broad lands of Lazarus and his sisters, Martha and Mary of Bethania. Lazarus, Abdias' son, sat in the shade of the house, facing his friend, Joseph of Arimathea, who had come from Jerusalem for the funeral and so had been present at the raising of Lazarus.

Lazarus' face still bore traces of the severe illness through which he had passed. His handsome, finely molded features were faintly overcast by an inward weariness and his dark eyes seemed to be gazing into immeasurable distances. The calm manner of this man, who despite the gray hair on his temples could be little more than thirty, contrasted oddly with his friend's animation. Joseph's hands and shoulders were in constant motion; again and again his eyes passed across Lazarus' face, though not without shyness.

The conversation had been halting and desultory for some time. Obviously Joseph wanted to ask Lazarus a question, but had not yet summoned up the courage. Now he composed himself, placed his nervous hands on his knees, cleared his throat and at last said:

"I have been wanting to ask you whether you have any memory of the time when . . . when you . . ."

"When I was dead," Lazarus completed the sentence for him. He fell silent for a moment. "Believe me, that question has concerned me almost every moment since, but I have found no answer to it."

"Do you remember anything at all?" Joseph of Arimathea pressed him.

"Remember?" Lazarus repeated in a soft, pensive voice. "Memory it is not. It is rather like a premonition within me that something, something utterly tremendous happened to me. But it cannot be grasped clearly in thought, still less in words. One thing, however, seems to me beyond doubt: even though my body was dead, something of me continued to live, although in a wholly different form and under conditions that I cannot describe because my mind cannot grasp them. When I attempted to say anything about it, I suddenly feel an emptiness within my mind; the only thought I have is the certainty that I cannot speak. And it seems to me that it is not wise to brood about it. If the Creator desired man to know what lay beyond the portal of death, He would have revealed it to us. I have returned through that portal and I accept the fact with humility and thankfulness."

"You must understand, Lazarus, how terribly important this is to me. We Sadducees deny that the human soul lives on after death. From the hints you have given me—am I to judge that we are mistaken?"

"You are mistaken, Joseph—that is certain. It is my unshakable conviction that my soul did not die with my body."

Joseph bowed his head and did not reply for some time.

"I believe you, Lazarus," he said at last. And raising his eyes he added:

"But what do you think of Jesus of Nazareth?"

"Can any man give life?" Lazarus countered.

"I do not think so."

"Certainly not. He can only take it away. The gift of life is God's alone. And that is why I believe that Jesus of Nazareth is the son of God; he is the Messiah who was promised to our people."

The words rang like a solemn confession of faith through the garden which lay bathed in the afternoon sunlight. It was a quiet, peaceful scene. Larks rose blithely toward the blue sky and in the distance the laborers could be heard singing in the vineyards. Joseph had risen from his seat and now stood leaning over Lazarus. The man who had returned from the grave sat with closed eyes in his comfortable chair.

"You have given speech, Lazarus, to what I have dimly felt ever since I first saw and heard him, months ago. The time is fulfilled— the Lord has sent his son to us to be the Saviour of our people. What happiness to be granted the grace of living in these times, to share in the great event that our ancestors longed for over many centuries with all the ardor in their hearts! I can scarcely grasp the joy of it. But how, Lazarus, how will our redemption take place? Do you believe that what was meant was merely the liberation of our people from the yoke of the Romans?"

"Once I believed that, Joseph, my friend. Today I think differently. For think you: when God gave to Adam and Eve, who had fallen in sin, the promise of redemption, there existed neither Israel nor Rome. There were only men. Therefore the promise must apply to all, to all men. To the heathen as well. To liberate our nation from the yoke of Rome would not require the incarnation of the son of God! What could such a liberation mean? The nation of Israel has been free for long periods in the past—but was it then redeemed? To ask is to answer. You have heard him, the Messiah —he is no man of violence nor of war, like the hero Judah. And if I interpret his words correctly, he means his work of redemption in a purely spiritual sense: redemption from sin, reconciliation with

God. Moreover, does he preach only to the orthodox Jews? Not at all. That is one of the chief reproaches of the scribes—that he wishes to let the pagans and even public women share in the grace of the All Highest. He never asks his followers: Are you indeed a son of Israel? His redemption will embrace all mankind, and it will be a redemption of the spirit, not of the flesh."

"What about his close followers—his disciples—is that what they believe?"

"His disciples are simple men, mostly pious Jews who still feel the needs of their bodies more than those of their soul. What they expect above all is the liberation of Israel through him. Perhaps some of them would fall away from him were not the force of his personality and his words irresistible to all men of good will."

"How then do you think the Messiah will accomplish the salvation of mankind?"

"Through the Word and through the Deed!"

"Yet you said, Lazarus, that the Nazarene was not a man of deeds."

"In the sense that the deed means an act of violence, certainly not. I cannot really explain to you just what I mean and how I came to understand this—I have some vague inkling of a monstrous, incredible sacrifice that will bring about the redemption."

At that moment the bailiff of the estate went up to the friends and murmured a few words to Lazarus.

"What say you? Strangers? How many?"

"Some twenty, lord. And armed. They look like robbers, and I believe that is what they are. Their leader calls himself Barabbas."

"If you have heard aright, Manasseh, they are robbers indeed," Joseph interjected. "This Barabbas is well known on the edge of the desert. It surprises me that he should venture so far."

"What do they want?" Lazarus asked.

"They want to stay the night here," the bailiff replied.

"Magdala is not an inn. But I will not have it said that I turned away travel-weary men. Have straw spread in one of the barns and slaughter a sheep. Twenty men, you say? Two sheep, then, if you think necessary. But the men must behave themselves and above all not molest any of the women."

"The man they call Barabbas wishes to speak with the Master."

Lazarus and Joseph shot each other a glance of surprise. Were even the bandits of Israel coming to sit at the feet of the Master?

"That is not for me to arrange," Lazarus said, "but I will tell the Master. Do you know where he is right now?"

"He has gone to the lake with the disciples and some of the people. But they will probably return by evening. Martha has sent a messenger to ask him to sup with us."

Lazarus nodded and the bailiff withdrew.

"That is very curious," Joseph remarked, "very curious indeed. This Barabbas is a scoundrel. He steals, demands tribute, and even murders occasionally when he encounters resistance. There are many others of his kidney, of course, but he has developed a method of his own that simple people find very attractive, I fear. He claims that all the evil he does is simply in order to free Israel from her oppressors. In Jerusalem he even imposes taxes on the wealthy for that cause. He and his men wear the Star of David as a badge, and more and more people are wearing it, especially among the youths. All his followers talk big. Naturally, the Romans laugh at them. They could long ago have arrested him and his men, but they prefer to exploit the unrest he stirs up for their own purposes. It enables them to oppress Israel all the more. What can the man want of the Master?"

Lazarus could suggest no answer. From the farm buildings could be heard a good deal of noise. Sheep bleated and chickens cackled. Then came a few sharp words, and the noise abated suddenly. Obviously the uninvited guests were trying to behave with as much gentility as they possessed.

While the two men sat silently, a young woman with somewhat sharp but rather handsome features stepped out of the house. She had rolled up the sleeves of her dress and was drying her hands on a white dustcloth. Apparently she had just come from cooking at the hearth.

"Pleasant guests!" she said to Lazarus. "I am not exactly overjoyed, brother."

"I am sorry to inconvenience you, Martha, but I thought it best to take in these men peaceably. They will look after themselves, I think."

"But think of all the disturbance. And, of course, Mary is again not here."

"So much the better. I think it well if you women keep out of sight of these guests. The maids as well! Our guests are not highly praised for good breeding. By the way, where is Mary?"

"I suppose she has gone to the Sea with the Master and the others. Naturally she never considers how I am left behind to work my fingers to the bone."

"You should not scold her on that account, Martha. She can do no better than to listen to the Master's words."

Martha smiled.

"What about the work, my dear brother?"

As he so often did these days, Lazarus looked off into the distance. Almost whispering he said:

"It seems to me that the work is not the most important thing. Were I not so weak and tired, but there is work to be done also. What would the Master and his disciples eat if no one saw to the cooking?"

"According to what we have heard of the miracle of the bread," said Joseph of Arimathea, "neither he nor his disciples would go hungry. Nevertheless, it is good that someone does take pains, for the Master cannot be asked to perform miracles all the time. Moreover, we humble men are here—and I must confess that I am very curious to see what Martha has prepared for our supper."

"Roast lamb, chicken and fruit," Martha said proudly, visibly pleased that at least one of the men showed interest in her labors.

"You may also send wine to the uninvited guests," Lazarus said. "But not too much; we would not have them grow sportive."

"I have already seen to that, and chosen a small vat. It is somewhat sharp, but nevertheless a good wine. I rather think those men will not have spoiled palates."

"Your sister thinks of everything," said Joseph of Arimathea with a smile of approval. He lowered his voice and resumed the conversation on a note of gravity. "There are twenty of the men—and armed. Will your servants be able to control them if they should prove unruly?"

"We outnumber them four to one," Lazarus said. "But I hope it will not be necessary. I am troubled more by the question of what they want with the Master."

Lazarus did not remain in doubt for long. The leader of the "guests," Barabbas, strode toward them with heavy tread.

"I am seeking the master of this house," he said in a low voice, with a gesture of salutation.

"Peace be unto you!" Lazarus replied. "I am he."

"Peace! I have asked hospitality for myself and my men, Lazarus of Bethania, and it has been vouchsafed me in your name."

"You are welcome. You call yourself Barabbas, I understand?"

"I am Barabbas. We have been given two sheep and bread and beds for the night . . ."

"You will also receive a vat of wine and fruit. I wish to stress that this hospitality is neither a tribute nor a sign of weakness. But I assume your men will make no trouble."

"They will not. I thank you, Lazarus of Bethania. Because you have been kind to us I will tell you why we have come. We wish to see Jesus of Nazareth, who is said to be a prophet, to perform miracles and to have raised you from the dead."

"It is as you say, Barabbas. What do you want of the Master, Barabbas, and what do your armed men want?"

"That is not easy to say, Lazarus. I myself am not certain. We have heard that this man has a great following and that there are great multitudes in Israel who hearken to his words. If his aims should prove the same as ours, perhaps it would be possible—perhaps it would be well—if we joined forces."

"What are your aims, Barabbas?"

"The liberation of Israel."

"And you want to accomplish it by violence?" asked Joseph of Arimathea, fixing Barabbas with his penetrating gaze.

Barabbas countered with an amazed question of his own: "How else?"

At the moment Joseph of Arimathea could think of no answer that the bandit could possibly understand. Nervously, he tugged at his light jacket, and for a moment deep silence prevailed. With a suspicious glance at the guest Martha returned to the house.

"You must speak with the Master himself about that, Barabbas," Lazarus observed after a brief pause. "We care only that you do not behave in an unfriendly fashion to him. The Rabbi is a guest in this house; we have cause to be unendingly grateful to him and we love and honor him as do all who know him."

Barabbas replied with great earnestness:

"I have not come with any hostile intent. On the contrary. I do not know, Lazarus, whether you know of my work."

Lazarus nodded. He was disinclined to quarrel with the man, at least until he had heard what he had to say. Barabbas continued:

"I may boast of a considerable number of followers. I think that number is growing daily. But what is needful if the movement is to achieve its goal is unanimity among the entire people . . ."

Barabbas did not finish his explanation. Through the garden, where the olive trees were already casting long shadows, a man slowly approached them. His long white garment seemed to illuminate the shadows, as though a light were approaching through the gathering dusk.

He was of medium height. The white headcloth that served as a shield against the sun had slipped down upon his neck, revealing wavy brown hair, parted in the middle, that flowed down around his shoulders. Beneath his high, white brow gleamed a pair of golden-brown eyes, and the face was framed within a thick brown beard that fell in a natural part under the chin. He might have been in his early thirties, but his features had something of the grace of a youth, and yet also something of the dignity of an old man. There was a sternness in this face, but it was belied by the gentle eyes which seemed to bespeak infinite kindliness.

He was followed by some two dozen people of varying ages, most of whom appeared to be artisans. A few women with children were in the group.

The man went up to the three who sat near the house.

"Peace be unto you!" he said in a soft, resonant voice, crossing his arms over his breast in the usual salutation.

"Peace!" Lazarus and Joseph replied. Barabbas took a step backward and looked with astonished eyes at the man, who had turned his gaze upon the robber.

"Greetings unto you, Barabbas, son of Ezekiel. I thank you for coming."

"Greetings, rabbi!" Barabbas replied in a choked voice. He crossed his massive, ungainly arms over his broad chest and lowered his eyes before the luminous gaze of the other. "I see that you know me."

"The children of Israel speak often of you, and not good alone. You have come to speak with me, and I rejoice in that. Come!"

He nodded to Barabbas and slowly walked past him, between the dwelling and the farm building, toward a low slope. Lazarus and Joseph followed him with their eyes. Those who had just come from the lake also watched, and a few of Barabbas's band appeared, curiously regarding the man with whom their leader wished to negotiate.

Barabbas stood still for a moment in indecision. Then he turned abruptly and strode after the man from Nazareth.

5

"Think Not that I Am Come to Destroy the Law"

To THE EAST, AS FAR AS THE EYE COULD SEE, SPREAD THE DARK GREEN surface of the Sea of Galilee, surrounded by the silver sheen of olive groves from which black cypresses rose like pillars into the slowly darkening sky. Clouds fringed with red and gold hung over the Sea, birds fluttered above the water, and in the distance could be heard the lowing of cattle and the bleating of sheep.

Jesus slowly ascended the hill, followed by Barabbas, who remained a few steps behind and wondered all the while that he had submitted so easily to the will of another.

By a rocky outcropping that thrust forth from the fruitful soil to form a sort of bench, Jesus stood still.

"Sit down with me here, Barabbas; you have come a long way and must be tired," he said in a soft voice.

Barabbas the robber sat down beside Jesus of Nazareth, whom many considered a prophet and many something greater than that. A curious feeling of embarassment that Barabbas had never yet experienced with any man hindered him from saying what he had intended. He felt as if this Jesus of Nazareth saw through him at once; as if all his thoughts were laid bare.

Jesus spoke:

"You have come, Barabbas, son of Ezekiel, to tempt me. I have already been tempted by Satan, after fasting forty days and forty nights, and he promised me all the kingdoms of this world and all its glory. You, too, come with a great promise, I know. You promise that you will free Israel of the alien rule if I follow you."

Discountenanced, Barabbas shifted his position. Was the man going to anticipate all he had to say? He groped for a reply, but before he could find the right words Jesus continued:

"You promise that to all who follow you. But your desire, Barabbas, is to drive away the Romans only that you may set your own foot upon the people's necks. Selfishness has hardened your heart and tainted your hands with blood. It is an evil way that you go, evil for you and for all who follow you. Cease, Barabbas, cease!"

The reproaches were harsh, indeed, and Barabbas would have retorted with all the harshness of his character were it not for the infinite gentleness of the man's resonant voice, for the ring of sorrow in his tone. Barabbas felt that the man pitied him. But he had not come to Jesus of Nazareth for pity; he had come to reach an understanding. And so he replied defiantly:

"I do not deny, rabbi, that I am a man of violence. But were not Joshua and David and Gideon and Judas the Maccabean, the heroes of our nation who made Israel great and free—were they not also men of violence? Do you condemn them also?"

"I have not come to condemn, but to forgive, Barabbas. I say to you: Woe unto them who use violence."

"What else but violence can be understood by those who use violence to enslave our people? You do not know, rabbi, how great my movement has already grown. There are influential people in the Holy City, and in other places as well, who agree with our ends and means and who support us. Great doings are in the making, rabbi—a struggle for liberation such as even the history of our people scarcely records. I am no scribe and read the scrolls with difficulty. But in the Holy City they say that the time is ripe and that the promise to our fathers must soon be fulfilled."

"What promise do you mean?"

"That the Lord will make our enemies our footstool."

Jesus placed his hand on Barabbas' shoulder. Like a child's frail hand the white, thin hand lay on the giant's broad shoulder. And yet Barabbas felt as if this hand clutched him so tightly that he could not move until he was released.

"Your footstool, you mean, O Barabbas. You err, and those who encourage you in your error do ill indeed. For look you, it is not the power and glory of earth that the Father has prepared for the nation of Israel. The kingdom that has been made ready for Israel is not a kingdom of violence nor of arms, but the kingdom of right-eousness and peace. But how should righteousness and peace arise out of violence? How love out of hate? For in your heart I see hatred and darkness. You, O Barabbas, are not the instrument that the Father will employ to bring redemption unto Israel."

Barabbas slid along the rocky seat to free his shoulder from the touch of the hand. He was breathing heavily and could not summon up enough presumption for more than a few words.

"Are you that instrument?" he asked.

"If I should say yes, you would not believe. For your heart is hardened and your ear deaf to all that does not serve your love of self. What you do is not for the sake of Israel but for your own sake. Your God is Barabbas and your aim is vengeance and power. My aim is forgiveness and humility. Am I then so little known that there can be one man in Judea and Galilee who thinks there is any com-mon ground between your aims and mine?"

Barabbas stood up. This conversation with Jesus of Nazareth did not at all fit in with his preconceived notions. Before he had had the opportunity to speak at all of the "community of aims" which had led him to undertake this visit, the other had shut the door on all collaboration.

"Then you despise me, Jesus, son of Joseph?" he asked with un-concealed bitterness.

Once more the hand rested upon his shoulder.

"Far be it from me to do that, Barabbas—I despise no man, for the worst among men are but in error. And it is to embrace the errant with my love that I have come; not to condemn them but to lead them back to the Way of the Father. I do not despise you, Barabbas—I love you. That is why I would break the shell of pride and self-love that has encased your heart, so that your heart may once more become good and humble and pleasing to the Father. You believe you are chosen to liberate Israel. You have made yourself the first among your followers and imagine therefore that you are the first. But I say to you: The last shall be first and the first shall be last. For many are called but few are chosen. None can be first who is last in the law."

"Do you not yourself teach disrespect for the law?"

"I am not come to destroy the law, but to fulfil it, O Barabbas. To give it new meaning."

"Yet you have replaced the ten commandments of Moses by two?"

"I have summed up the ten commandments in two—Whosoever loveth the Father out of a full heart and whosoever loveth his neighbor as himself, fulfils all that the law demands of him. But Barabbas: Do you love the Father out of a full heart? Do you love your neighbor whom you kill when he does not surrender what you demand of him?"

Once more Barabbas felt the blood surging in his veins. He wanted to give way to the fury that he always felt whenever he was reproached for his killings. He knew that he was commonly called "Barabbas the Robber" and deeply resented the name. The Nazarene refrained from saying "robber," but the word hung in the air. For a time they stood facing one another, eyes locked, the frail white hand clinging to his. And it appeared that the touch of this hand assuaged his fury. But Barabbas felt that he must say something in his own defense.

"What else can I do, Master, when they do not freely give me the wherewithal to appease my hunger. You charge me harshly with the evils I may have committed while in great need. Wherever the power of the foreigners reaches, I and my men are despised. Our home is in the desert—a parched home that has nothing, nothing at all to give its children. We took of the wealth of others, more fortunate than ourselves in order not to starve. But is not my struggle in behalf of all the people? Is not the struggle for their liberation a great service to Israel?"

Jesus sat down on the rock with signs of weariness. Barabbas remained standing.

"We are talking in circles, Barabbas," Jesus said. "The children of violence always find excuses for the evil deeds of their hands. What you do is not for the sake of Israel, but for your own sake. For I say unto you: Desist from violence; by repentance wash your hands of the blood you have shed. Do you think the Father would have need of you if He had wished to save Israel from this trial?

Wherefore will it profit you if you cast down the whole world and the Father in Heaven must cast you out?"

Since the beginning of their conversation the dusk had given way to night. From the black sky shone the transcendent light of a multitude of stars. Scattered clouds still gleamed brightly above the Sea of Galilee. But the light that appeared to flow out of Jesus of Nazareth, who sat quietly and almost without stirring upon the gray rock, seemed brighter than all the light of the heavens.

Barabbas stood with lowered head, gazing bleakly down upon Jesus. He was very sensitive to the urgency of the Nazarene's appeal to him, and dimly he was aware that what he said was right. But his whole soul passionately rebelled at making such an admission. Were all his ambitious dreams to dissolve into nothingness because of the words of this scribe? Was he to relinquish his personality, his power, his will and acknowledge himself no more than a petty, contemptible robber? No—it was not going to be that easy—Barabbas, son of Ezekiel, was not the man for resignation.

It was true, he had not created his movement out of love for Israel. Certainly he had no reason to love Israel—above all not the rich and powerful men of Israel. The fact of his origin would have justified the question: what is Israel to him, or he to Israel? His mother had come from Samaria and the Samaritans were considered semi-pagan. They were the oldest sect among the Jews, but they rejected all the later books of the Old Testament and their ruined temple on Mount Gerisim was as sacred to them as Jerusalem to the Jews. But these Samaritans had never quite freed themselves from Judaism. Did not the high priests and their supporters claim that this man from Nazareth was a Samaritan and therefore an emissary of the devil?

Clearly, Barabbas had no reason to love Israel. After a childhood filled with privation, rejection and abuse, he had learned in his young manhood what it meant to be virtually an outcast, a man who was distrusted and valued as little more than a slave. Despised by the Jews, by the Roman soldiers, kicked about and lashed until his back was bloody, one day he had committed the act that decided his destiny. In a moment of uncontrollable rage he had smashed in the skull of a soldier of Caesar. Fleeing to the edge of the desert, he had gathered about him a few fellows of similar temper and become the leader of a gang of bandits. Later it occurred to him to mask his illegal activities in a way that would give him a certain status among the children of Israel. The liberation of Israel from foreign rule—that slogan struck fire wherever it fell, for the nation was like dry tinder. The poorest classes of the population suffered frightfully under the ferrule of Rome. It was from their ranks that the masters of the country took the labor for their mills and workshops. And anyone who had once panted under the lashes of the Roman overseers was steeped in hatred for the foreigners.

There were other allies. Among the prosperous citizens and even among the priests of the Temple there were a good many persons who considered a violent rebellion against the rule of the foreigners both possible and necessary. These persons were not repelled by the fact that the leader of this movement was no pure-blooded Jew and was moreover a robber and murderer. They contributed money to him; and in Jerusalem and the other cities that suffered under the arrogant Romans the number of wearers of the metal badge shaped like the Star of David grew steadily.

The growth of his movement worked an inward change in Barabbas himself. The idea of liberating Israel from foreign rule, which had originally been merely a cunning slogan, rooted itself strongly in the mind of this man of vaulting ambition. In his dreams he saw himself making footstools not only of the conquered Romans, but of the former leaders of Israel as well . . . Was he now to abandon all this because the man of Nazareth so desired? Barabbas realized the power that dwelt in this man's words and in his personality. But that was all the more reason for his obstinate temperament to resist Jesus of Nazareth, to stamp out all his better impulses. How could he have ever considered winning this fellow over to his cause?

"You do not know, Jesus of Nazareth, how great is the power that I already have," he said at last.

"Had you a hundred legions, Barabbas, you would achieve nothing."

"You are for the Romans, the enemies of Israel!"

"I have not come to be either for or against any nation, Barabbas. I have come to bring about the reconciliation between the Father and mankind."

"What do I care for mankind? I care for our sufferings, our misery. The hunger of the outcasts, the pain and torment of the prisoners, the shameful deaths that are inflicted upon hundreds and thousands of us by the base whims of the oppressors. Have you no heart for all these wretches?"

Jesus' voice trembled slightly as he replied:

"Why think you, Barabbas, that I do not sorrow for my poor brethren? But if a man do harm to his soul, that is worse than all sufferings of the body. You desire liberation—from the rule of the Romans? But I say to you: Those who enslave the body are not the worst enemies of Israel, but those who slay the soul. What help would it be for Israel were she to shake off the yoke that oppresses the body yet could not free herself from the slavery of sin?"

"Sin . . . sin . . . I have heard that tale before," Barabbas replied, some of his anger edging into his voice. "Remember the man who preached and baptized at the Jordan, John, son of Zacharias. He, too, called for repentance from sin and conversion—and you know what he accomplished. Of course, you know—all Israel knows that Herod had his head cut off. And you, Jesus of Nazareth, will suffer the same fate if you can do no more than preach repentance of sin. It is said that you can heal the sick by the touch of your hand, and even that you have raised the dead to life. If you are such a great magician, why will you not place your ability at the service of your people? He who can heal can also kill . . . But I remember hearing that you healed the servant of a Roman captain. How could you do that? You must bring death down upon all Romans, and all Roman hirelings!"

Jesus stretched out his hand toward Barabbas. The hand seemed to glow in the starlight.

"Love your enemies— Do good to them that hate you."

Barabbas took a step backward. In the course of his long speech he had become excited, and somewhat enraged, but he sobered instantly.

"If that is what you think, rabbi . . ."

"It is your duty to the Father in Heaven for you also to think and to act in this way and no other."

"Then I have nothing further to say to you, rabbi. I am sorry that I believed for a single moment in the possibility of a union between us that would be helpful to Israel. Now I see that you are a foe of Israel, a foe of your own people. There can be no community of purpose between you and me because there can be no community between fire and water."

Barabbas turned to go.

Jesus of Nazareth rose to his feet. It was with sorrowful eyes that he looked upon the defiant man.

"You go, Barabbas, son of Ezekiel, and I cannot hold you, although I know that you do not regard my words . . ."

"No," Barabbas interrupted, "that I do not, for your words are those of a milksop, of a foe of Israel."

". . . that you do not regard my words—which is not well for you or your companions. The way of violence leads to ruin, now and forever. I will pray for you to my Father. And when my hour comes, you will be near me, Barabbas."

Barabbas had not turned while Jesus spoke. Now he strode off down the hill without one word further. He had heard what the Nazarene said, but no sooner did the words impinge upon him than he brushed them aside; his soul was filled with rage and hatred.

Jesus of Nazareth stood watching him for a while, pain and grief mingling in his look.

A voice rang out of the darkness.

"Master!"

"It is you, Simon? How come you hither?"

"I saw you go up here with the robber, and you stayed so long that I became afraid for you. This Barabbas is a man of violence. I followed and heard you speaking and waited, ready at hand to help you if he should attack you."

As he spoke the man approached closer, until he stood before Jesus. Jesus of Nazareth smiled.

"I thank you, Simon, son of Jonas. Where are the others?"

"They are below in the house of Lazarus, waiting for you to bless their bread. All are very tired."

"Come then, Simon."

Jesus placed his left hand upon the man's shoulder. Simon was somewhat smaller than he, but he was a stocky, solidly-built fellow. Together they slowly descended toward Lazarus' house. Above the Sea the red half moon was rising, glowing in the bright azure of the sky and casting a ruddy light over the rolling land, over the cultivated fields, the olive trees and the black terebinths that slumbered in the peace of the summer night.

In Lazarus' farmyard was a good deal of bustling. The uninvited guests from the desert had lit campfires to roast their two sheep.

They lay around the fires, with the vat of wine among them, waiting with unconcealed impatience for their supper.

Barabbas had sat down at some distance from his men. He looked blackly at Jesus and his disciples as the two entered the yard. His men fell silent as Jesus passed them, but their hostility, with which obviously their leader had infected them, was unmistakable. Barabbas had not given his men a lengthy account of the interview; he had merely informed them brusquely that an alliance with Jesus of Nazareth was unthinkable: the man was a stupid dreamer who was not interested in national liberation.

This news produced a change in his followers' attitude toward Lazarus. They no longer felt it necessary to check their wildness and lustiness or to keep the peace. A few minutes ago, before Jesus and his disciple came by, they had behaved noisily, shouted insults at the servants and obscenities at the maids. Their wanton conduct was checked only momentarily by the appearance of the Master.

In order to avoid incidents, Lazarus had ordered the manservants to withdraw to the house. He, Joseph of Arimathea, and the disciples who never parted from Jesus waited in the great hall. The folk from the vicinity who had accompanied Jesus to the estate—most of them women and children—had been fed and soon after dark they had set out for their homes.

The great hall was fairly well illuminated by oil lamps hanging from the ceiling and the wooden walls. As Jesus entered, Lazarus, Joseph, and the disciples rose from their seats on the long benches that lined the walls. Lazarus stepped forward to greet the Master.

"Peace be unto you!" Jesus said, raising his arms.

"Peace!" the others replied.

Lazarus led Jesus to the upper end of the long table that stood in the center of the hall. On the white linen tablecloth lay fresh loaves of bread beside earthenware plates. Metal cups shone in the flickering light of the lamps. Along the table stood high stools—the Roman custom of lying down at table had not yet penetrated to Galilee.

Jesus of Nazareth sat down and held out his hands in blessing over the bread that lay before him. There was a moment of silent prayer. Then the supper began. Maids brought in great steaming bowls of food, manservants went from place to place pouring wine into the cups from their huge, earthenware jugs.

To the right of Jesus sat Joseph of Arimathea, to his left Lazarus. Jesus appeared to be lost in thought. He ate little and sipped the wine only once. The rest of the company conversed in low tones—in the presence of the Master every meal became a kind of solemn ritual. Beside Joseph of Arimathea sat Judas, the son of Simon of Karioth, one of Jesus' constant companions and most zealous followers. A small, dark-complexioned man, his sprightliness contrasted with the pleasant heaviness that characterized most of the others, for, taken as individuals, the disciples seemed to be distinguished by little else than their touching devotion to the Master. Judas Iscariot was rather more a man of the world than these others, who for the most part had never traveled beyond Galilee. He had worked for some time in Caesarea and in the coastal cities, and his eager curiosity and alert mind had enabled him to make the most of his opportunities—unlike the others, he had formed a view of the world and liked to talk about it, especially in the presence of the Master. The conclusion he had drawn from his experiences was that the time had come for Israel to win her merited place in the world at the head of all the nations of the earth. Less loving and humble than, say, Simon or John or Andrew, he was wise in the ways of the world and knew how to tally the contributions that flowed into the little community. He had become, virtually by default, the cashier and financial secretary of the group.

The remains of the meal were removed. Jesus spoke a brief prayer of thanks while he and the others washed their hands. He seemed on the point of leaving them, and since all wished to have the Master with them a little longer, Joseph of Arimathea addressed him.

"You have had a long conference with this fellow Barabbas, Master. From his behavior since, it would seem that he did not obtain what he wanted," Joseph said.

"You are right, Joseph. His is a mistaken way which cannot be my own."

There was a moment of silence in the hall.

Judas Iscariot turned his flashing eyes toward Jesus.

"But the goal he has set for himself is a great one," he said. "And his followers are many."

"It is the destiny of those who use violence to die by violence," Jesus said quietly. "It is not the meaning of the bond that the Father sealed with Abraham that ambitious men who crave glory are to arm themselves and set up a kingdom of violence instead of the kingdom of righteousness and love."

Judas spoke passionately.

"Do not the Scriptures say: 'I will make thy enemies thy footstool'?"

Jesus smiled.

"That is the same passage that Barabbas cited. But I say to you, Judas, son of Simon, that it is not good to interpret the scriptures according to what you desire."

"In any case," Joseph of Arimathea remarked, "what Barabbas aims for is utterly impossible. Any really serious attempt at revolt would be drowned in blood by the Roman legions."

Judas Iscariot turned to Joseph.

"What can hirelings of a rotting empire do against the spirit and indomitable courage of a people that has been hounded to desperation. I, too, do not believe that this Barabbas is the man who has been called to lead Israel out of the shameful state in which she has languished so long. But someone must come to fulfil the promise!"

His eyes, filled with a harsh light, sought those of the Master— but did not find them.

In the silence that followed Judas' outburst all heard the thump of a heavy stone against the door of the house. The disciples, with Simon in the van, sprang to their feet and made toward the door. But Lazarus, who had remained sitting, as had the Master and Joseph of Arimathea, called out to them in his thin, reedy voice:

"No need of that. The servants are ready and well armed in case the men out there venture an assault."

The disciples lingered uncertainly by the door. Outside the noise and vituperation swelled. Once more a stone thumped against the door.

Jesus of Nazareth rose to his feet.

"I do not wish the peace of this night and this house to be troubled," he said. "I want no blood spilled here." And he walked quietly toward the door through the group of his friends, pushed back the bolt and stepped outside.

In front of the house it was almost as bright as day. Barabbas' men had stirred up the fires over which they had roasted the sheep, so that these cast a spangled glow over the yard, and the bright moon lit all the dark spaces between. The men were standing some twenty paces from the door of the house. Some had unsheathed their swords; others were hefting clubs in their hands; still others had supplied themselves with stones. Barabbas himself was not among them; he sat by a fire to one side, staring crossly into the leaping flames.

The doorway of the house was a few steps above the ground level. When Jesus appeared at the top of the flight of stairs, he stood in the full light of the moon. And once more it seemed as if a glow, an aura radiated from him. He descended these steps and remained standing at the bottom with his arms raised, palms outspread, his gaze resting earnestly upon Barabbas' men.

They had fallen silent the moment Jesus emerged. And now something quite remarkable took place. Those who held stones in their hands let them drop, the men who stood with raised clubs lowered them, and the others sheathed their swords. A few moments of dead silence ensued. Then the men began shifting backwards; silently they retreated into the shadow of the barns. Barabbas himself remained seated by the fire, but he covered his face with his hands as if to shield his eyes against a light that was too painfully blinding.

Jesus said not a word. Behind him in the doorway stood the disciples who had hastened to follow him, intent on protecting him against attack. They had seen at once that no protection was necessary; as if driven by some superior force, the unruly men had retreated. It can scarcely be said that the disciples were astonished at the Master's power over these men. To restrain this band of robbers by a glance or a gesture was by far less miraculous than the raising of Lazarus or the healing of the blind, the halt and the leprous.

When the men had retreated quite out of sight, Jesus turned again, ascended the steps and re-entered the hall. Judas Iscariot's eyes glistened as Jesus passed and he murmured softly to Joseph of Arimathea:

"If the Master so wished, he could drive the Romans into the sea by his will alone."

Joseph did not reply. He had been more deeply moved by the miracle than the disciples, for what had happened was not a commonplace to him.

Jesus sat down on one of the benches along the wall. Lazarus, Joseph, and the disciples grouped themselves around him. Mary, called the Magdalene, who had entered the hall, sat down on a footstool at the Master's feet. Martha stood in the doorway that led to the kitchen. All waited for Jesus to speak.

He was silent for a long time. His gaze seemed turned inward, he had lowered his head and his hands lay motionless on the white linen of his garment. At last he began to speak in a low voice:

"The day will come, and it is not far off, when you will all be wroth with the son of man, for he is not sent to be sickle, but corn . . ."

But they did not understand him.

By the following morning Barabbas and his men were gone.

6 🗲

Barabbas—King, Messiah . . .

BARABBAS STRODE ALONG AT THE HEAD OF HIS MEN, CROSS AND TACI-
turn as he had been ever since they left Magdala. They had been
following the left bank of the Jordan for three days' marches. Obviously Barabbas intended to turn east toward the desert once more.
His men were glad of that, for they felt unsafe in this thickly settled
region. If they should chance to meet up with the Roman soldiers
who circulated through the country in small detachments to keep
order, their journey to Magdala and the remarkable man of Nazareth
might really come to an ill end.

The remarkable man of Nazareth!

They did not at all understand why they had retreated from a
single man that night, why they had dropped their stones and lowered
their clubs and swords. By common consent they avoided discussing
it with one another, and as yet Barabbas had not even mentioned
the incident. For him, who was considerably cleverer than his men,
it was a significant and depressing matter. He could not help recogniz-
ing that the man of Nazareth possessed a more-than-human power
which simply deprived his opponents of their will.

Was he a prophet? Barabbas had no high regard for prophets. He
had been reared in the observance of the outward forms of Judaism,
but deep religious feeling had always been foreign to his nature.

When he began his career as a bandit, he had also dropped the outward forms. He paid little attention to the dietary laws; he kept the Sabbath only when it was convenient; and he and his band had long since forgotten the prescribed prayers and ceremonial washings. They were Jews by birth but no longer by faith.

In the long hours of silence Barabbas wrestled with the question of what position he must take toward this man. At last he felt that he had come to the proper analysis. He decided that Jesus of Nazareth was no prophet but a magician who shammed great piety. His pose was such that the priests could not reasonably take action against him; it also gave him a hold over the simple folk. There was a whisper within Barabbas' mind that this estimate did not correspond with what he had seen, but the robber leader firmly repressed any idea that the Nazarene's mission was a great, religious one. The "magician" he could hate wholeheartedly; he could contend with him man to man and deride his childish theory of revolution.

Barabbas had to admit that he was greatly chagrined at his failure to win Jesus over to his cause. And he resented the fact all Galilee rang with the man's fame, while little attention was paid to himself and his group. These men of Galilee, these rough peasants with strong arms and ready fists, would have been valuable, extremely valuable, in his movement. But now they were bubbling with enthusiasm for the miracles of that magician; what was worse, they were letting him teach them a curious sort of patient piety. Barabbas realized that there was no hope of inciting rebellion among these praying, psalm-singing peasants, artisans, and fishermen.

Barabbas struck his gigantic walking-stick vigorously against the ground. He carried his stick in his right hand, and it was to this that he owed his nickname, "the man with the club." In his bitterness he seriously considered whether he might not have done better to act on his quick impulse and send the estate at Magdala up in flames. But—would that have been possible while the "miracle worker" was staying there? And should anything have happened to that magician, the populace would have been so indignant that he and his men could hardly have escaped with their lives.

Evening was drawing near. From the wooded top of Mount Gilead a cool wind blew down upon them.

Barabbas stood still and with his left hand wiped the sweat from his frowning forehead. The road had brought him and his band to the vicinity of one of the many streams that fed the Jordan from the surrounding hills. Somewhere in front of them would be the city of Pella. The stream flowed out of a rocky declivity; therefore there would be caves near by where they could find shelter for the night.

"We will camp here tonight," Barabbas said curtly to his men, who had stood still when he did. "Look for a cave."

"We need more than that," said one young, savage-looking fellow. "What else?"

"We have eaten nothing today and our pouches are empty."

"Then look around until you find something. There must be herds in the vicinity."

"What will we pay with?" the young bandit asked with a grin.

"With your club," Barabbas replied. "But be as tactful as you can about it."

Barabbas did not elaborate, but his men knew well that he did not like it to be said that "Israel's savior" made a practice of murdering the children of Israel.

A few of the men, led by the young fellow who had spoken out, began clambering up the slope to the left of the road. Others followed the brook down its ravine looking for a cave. Barabbas walked a few steps from the road and threw himself down on the stony ground. A few of the older members of his band followed his example.

They heard the men who were looking for a cave call out to one another. Then they fell silent and only the rustling of the stream and the singing of the wind in the trees were audible.

From the south a man came toward them walking very slowly. His gait expressed utter exhaustion, and from the manner in which he sought cover behind the bushes that lined the road and spied out the path ahead of him, it was clear that this weary traveler was anxious to avoid meeting up with other men.

Barabbas caught sight of him first. He let him come quite close. Then he recognized the man, for he exclaimed in amazement:

"Ezra!"

The man stood still in affright, but as soon as he recognized Barabbas an expression of pleasure lit up his haggard face.

"Barabbas!" he cried. "I was beginning to fear I would never find you again."

Barabbas embraced the man with sincere gladness.

"Where have you come from, Ezra?"

"From the camp. I went there looking for you, but Eliazar told me that you had gone off to this prophet, Jesus of Nazareth . . ."

Barabbas frowned.

"Do you too call him a prophet? I'll have none of that. Did the Roman dogs release you?"

Ezra laughed scornfully.

"Release me? No, they did not dream of doing that. I escaped. Just in time or they would have beaten me to death."

Barabbas gave him a glance of admiration and respect.

"You escaped! I have always thought highly of you, Ezra—but that you were able to bring that off . . ."

"Sooner or later they would have beaten me to death or sent me to the galleys or crucified me. I preferred the uncertain death to the certain one. There was a very slight chance and I took it."

"Were you badly mistreated, Ezra?" Barabbas asked sympathetically.

Ezra did not reply in words to this question. He threw off his sleeveless upper garment and showed the wounds and scars on his back. Then he showed the still purulent sores on his ankles and wrists. The men who had lain down near their leader had come up; they uttered cries of horror and indignation at the sight.

"Frightful!" Barabbas said. All the blood had drained out of his face. Perhaps he was moved not so much by his sympathy for Ezra as by his hatred for Ezra's oppressors.

"But now that I have found you all is well," Ezra said, drawing on his clothing. And then, as if to ward off any more expressions of compassion, he said, "Have you anything to eat? I am starved." He sat down on the ground beside Barabbas.

"You will be fed," Barabbas said. Since he had eaten almost nothing at Magdala, his men had saved his portion and placed it in his pouch. There was still some bread and meat left, both dried out and scarcely edible. Barabbas handed this to Ezra, who devoured it ravenously.

"Now tell us about it," Barabbas commanded when Ezra had finished.

Ezra narrated his adventures from the day he had been arrested by the Roman legionaries to the morning he had arrived, half dead, at old Eliazar's camp. For three days he had enjoyed the old man's hospitality, but then the waiting became too much for him. He had realized that he would be running the risk of recapture by roving detachments of soldiers, but he had felt that he had to seek out Barabbas. What would have been the sense of escaping if not to find the leader?

"For there is no salvation except with you, Barabbas," Ezra concluded his tale. "Only as long as I am with you can I be certain that every blow they mete out to a Jew will be repaid thousandfold."

Barabbas nodded, his vanity flattered. After the snub the Nazarene had given him such adulation was especially welcome. Unconsciously—or perhaps consciously—he adopted a pose. Affectedly, he placed his hand on Ezra's shoulder just as Jesus of Nazareth had placed his hand on his own shoulder. For a moment he was keenly aware that his own hand was strong and hairy.

"We will take frightful revenge, Ezra, when the day comes. And you will do much to make that day come soon. You will show your wounds and your scars. It will be a poor Jew who will not be roused against those beasts by such a sight."

There was a moment of silence. Barabbas was not a very gifted speaker; only too often had his men heard this promise of The Day when all Israel would rise up against the Romans. Then Ezra said:

"I do not know whether you have heard that Judah has arrived in camp. He came the day I left."

"I have been on the road since then," Barabbas said. "Did he tell you what he accomplished in the Holy City?"

"He brought a good deal of money and promises of much more. Above all, he had news that you should have known before you traipsed off after this prophet. Soon all will be up with Jesus of Nazareth. The priesthood is hostile to him and will destroy him because he is a demagogue and a blasphemer. They intend to bring him to trial. Have you seen him, Barabbas?"

Barabbas hesitated before he replied:

"I have seen him and spoken with him."

"What do you think of the man?"

"The priests are right about him, but in another sense. He is a demagogue, that is quite true, because he preaches gentleness and patience and commands his followers to love even their enemies— which means the Romans as well. I couldn't say whether or not he is a blasphemer. You know I don't trouble my head about religious matters. But he is a remarkable magician. He has healed many sick people and even raised the dead. All Galilee is talking about him; his following is tremendous. It is unfortunate that the man is on the wrong track—we could have made good use of him . . ."

As Barabbas spoke a malignant expression passed across Ezra's face. His eyes smouldered. In a hoarse voice he cried out:

"Love your enemies—yes, I have heard the same tune. It won't get us far. Hate, unrelenting hate, that's the thing for us. If we don't kill every Roman that falls into our hands, we are done for."

This outburst was highly gratifying to Barabbas. It provided a convenient opportunity for him to wipe out the impression of weakness which his men must have received from the encounter with Jesus of Nazareth. Ordinarily he avoided discussing his plans before his men. But now he thought it best to let his little band hear his answer to their unspoken questions.

"You are right, Ezra," he said, "right as can be. For the present we will rid ourselves of the smaller detachments of oppressors, of the half centuries that roam the countryside. Then, we'll time the uprising; it will break out simultaneously in the Holy City and all other places where the Romans hold fortified positions. In a few days Israel will be free. And not a Roman will be left to carry the news of the annihilation of the legions and the officials and of all the uncircumcised to the accursed city on the Tiber. Not a single one!"

Barabbas fell silent, his chest heaving. Ezra and the rest of the band had listened to his words in a transport of enthusiasm. Not only had he relieved himself by giving vent to his rage, but he had the satisfaction of knowing that he had restored his followers' confidence in him. The momentary weakness at Magdala would be forgotten, was already forgotten.

Dusk was falling by the time the men returned who had gone upstream in search of shelter. They had found a place and led Barabbas, Ezra, and the rest through the underbrush to a large cave. A bright campfire was already burning in front of it. One man remained behind to guide the group who had gone off to requisition food. He did not have long to wait; a few moments later the young fellow and his comrades returned. They were carrying three sheep that they had already slaughtered, and bread and cheese as well. The men were conducted to the cave where the others were impatiently awaiting them. The stolen sheep were swiftly skinned and quartered and hung over the coals of the fire, while the bread and cheese were equally distributed. The weary, hungry men waited avidly for the meat to be done.

But before they were able to begin their meal five men armed with heavy cudgels stepped into the circle of light cast by the fire. Huge fellows clothed in sheepskins, with tangled hair and beards, they appeared even more dangerous than Barabbas' band of robbers.

"There they are, the jackals," the biggest of the men cried. "Strike away!"

Before they could attack Barabbas rose to confront them with bared short sword.

"What do you want? Who are you?"

"We want the sheep you stole from us."

"There they are, roasting. Take them away," Barabbas said calmly.

In the meantime his companions had sprung to their feet and grasped their weapons. Faced with four times their own number, the shepherds lost some of their aggressiveness. Their leader addressed Barabbas in quieter tones:

"You broke into our fold and took away our sheep. Besides that, you took all the bread we had in our tent and our whole store of cheese. That is robbery!"

Barabbas laughed.

"Perhaps it is. Do you know who I am?"

"No."

"Perhaps you have heard my name. I am Barabbas."

The leader of the shepherds fell silent. He and his companions lowered their cudgels.

"I see that my name is not unknown in these parts," Barabbas said complacently.

"You are the scourge of all the shepherds between the Jordan and the desert," the herdsman murmured. He appeared to be on the point of turning and fleeing.

"Well spoken, my friend," Barabbas said. "But you exaggerate. I am friendly with many shepherds, extremely friendly. They gladly let me have a few sheep now and then, and in return they enjoy my protection. But—even if I were really the scourge of the shepherds, do you know who would be to blame?"

The shepherd shook his shaggy mane. Barabbas felt tempted to try his oratorical powers on these men. After all, what else did that fellow Jesus of Nazareth do but talk and talk? And he won adherents by his talk. Once more Barabbas put on an oratorical pose.

"The oppressors of our people are to blame, for they compel me and my men to live the life of fugitives and robbers. And all of us whom you see here will meet the death of slaves on the cross should we fall into the hands of the Romans. That is why we must avoid the cities and the great highways; that is why we are forced to take whatever food comes our way. We are fighting for liberty, and because of our fight we are hunted unrelentingly. And yet you would complain because you have lost a few sheep and a few loaves of bread."

The shepherd was not overmuch impressed by this speech.

"My lord," he said, "we must replace the sheep. They do not belong to us. And the bread and cheese you took from us was our whole stock of food for a week. We are as hungry as you."

Barabbas reached into his pouch.

"I will pay you for the sheep. Here is the money. Bread you can obtain more easily than we, since we must avoid the towns."

He gave the shepherd leader a few silver coins which more than compensated for the theft.

"And if you are hungry you can eat with us," he added.

"My lord, we are Samaritans," the shepherd said. His manner had become very humble. "You will not want to eat with us."

Barabbas laughed.

"What do we care? Do you think it matters to us whether you go to the Temple in Jerusalem or pray to God upon a mountain? You, like us, are poor, oppressed, downtrodden human beings who suffer under the yoke of the enemy. Do the Romans distinguish between Jews and Samaritans? Would you deny that Samaritans as well labor in the galleys, the mills, and the workshops, and that many Samaritans have ended on the cross?"

"No, lord, we do not deny that."

"There you are: we belong together by rights. Sit down here, eat with us, and some day you will fight at our side and help to exterminate the accursed race who would snatch away the very air we breathe."

The leader of the shepherds still hesitated. But Barabbas gave him no time for reflection.

"Would you see," he went on, "how the oppressors treat the men of our people? Ezra—come here. Show them your back. Do you see those sores? Do you see the scars the lash has left? Such is the fate of all of us—and yours as well. And it will grow worse unless all of us rise—every man of us, the people of Judea and Galilee and Samaria—to destroy these murderers and free the country that is the mother of us all!"

Barabbas had reckoned wisely; the display of Ezra's wounds did not fail in their effect. The shepherds looked, and then they sat down to share the supper. Barabbas' men began cutting up the roasted sheep with their sharp knives and gobbling down the hot meat.

While they were eating, the shepherd leader turned to Barabbas.

"You spoke of liberation, Barabbas. Do you know that there is a prophet in Galilee whom many believe will free our country?"

Barabbas frowned darkly. How long was this to go on? Would he run afoul of this man from Nazareth everywhere?

"I have heard of him," he replied harshly. "I have even spoken with him. It is stupid, childish to expect anything of that man. He is nothing but a soft-brained scribe, a wide-eyed dreamer. Do you know that he requires his followers to love even their enemies. Can you do that—love your enemies?"

The shepherd gazed pensively into the fire.

"I don't think I could . . ." he said. "But he must be a very devout rabbi and a good man. Some of us heard him at Jacob's Well, and they say he does not despise the Samaritans although he is an orthodox Jew. He has healed many of the sick, and consoled those who came to him in sorrow."

Barabbas felt within himself a driving ambition unlike anything he had ever experienced before. He had to win these men away from the Nazarene. How could he hope to succeed with others if he were unable to persuade these simple folk? But he was sensitive enough to realize that the man's faith was too strongly rooted to be shaken by simple invective or by challenging the power of Jesus.

"I do not deny his piety," he said, weighing his words carefully, "nor the miracles he performs. I myself saw the man he raised from the dead. There is no doubt that he is a great sorcerer. We cannot help respecting his miraculous powers. But, my friend, his teachings are utterly worthless. Such teachings will never free us from the Roman yoke. And you do want to be freed, do you not?"

"Certainly, lord."

"There you are. That is why there can be no common ground between him and us. But you people can work together with us. You are strong, brave men with marrow in your bones—like all men who have not yet grown soft in the towns. With a few thousand men like yourselves on our side the last hour of foreign rule would soon be here. What do you think about that?"

The shepherd chewed a chunk of underdone meat and stared thoughtfully into space.

"Perhaps you are right, Barabbas—perhaps. I rather think that we Samaritans could help you drive out the Romans. But—well, I keep asking myself what we would gain by it. If the Romans were driven out—you say it could be done and maybe you are right—where are we? We would still be the 'unclean'—you Jews would go right on despising us. We would still be Samaritans whom you avoid like lepers."

Barabbas felt that now was the time to employ one of his strongest weapons.

"Do you know my birth?" he asked the shepherds.

"No, lord."

"Listen, then. My father was a Jew; my mother came from Samaria. My father refused to put her away when the priests ordered him to. And what happened? Nothing at all. Today, whenever I send a message to the high priest, he receives it in spite of my mother's birth. And he answers me in spite of the fact that I am only half a Jew. That is all nonsense—it is the man that counts, not where he happens to be born or who his parents are. If our struggle succeeds—and it must—there will no longer be any difference between Jews and Samaritans. I can guarantee that—I who am both Jew and Samaritan!" He paused and then added: "Provided, of course, that the Samaritans take part in the struggle for freedom."

Stubbornly, the shepherd continued to present his objections.

"So you say, Barabbas, and I already believe you mean what you say. But—will you have the power to carry it out?"

The shepherd had touched upon a subject that Barabbas was not eager to discuss. All too frequently the question came up among his

own men: Is not Barabbas merely a tool? Will he not do the rough
toil in order that others may enjoy the fruits? After all, he was only
a simple fellow, a robber who could scarcely read and write.

It was with undue emphasis that Barabbas replied to the shepherd's question:

"Do you think I am going to do all the work and then surrender
the power? Am I to be the liberator of our country and then abandon my followers and the people to the scribes and pharisees, or to
the high priests, or to the rich who care little for the people's misery
and sit at table with the filthy foreigners?—What is your name?"

"Jehudah."

"I say to you, Jehudah: When Moses led the Israelites out of
Egypt, it was he who gave them their laws. When Barabbas has
freed our homeland and cleared out the Romans, it will be he who
rules and not the high priests or the king's courtiers. And it will be
he who makes the laws. Do you realize what that means? We will
not have to endure the arrogance of the pharisees, the priests, and
the rich men who now sit in Jerusalem and stuff their bellies. There
will be no differences between Jews or Samaritans. We will have
freed the country and we will arrange things to suit ourselves, not the
scribblers and the Talmudists. I will have the Scriptures burned, so
that no memory of them will remain!"

The shepherd cast a curious, somewhat roguish look at the bandit
leader. Perhaps it amused him to hear such lofty ambitions from
the lips of this despised fugitive who sat before him in tattered,
filthy clothing.

"So you want to be king, O Barabbas," he murmured after a time,
brushing his long hair from his face.

Barabbas laughed.

"King? Why not? I would not be the first to rise from highwayman to the throne. But, once more I tell you, that depends upon
the people. And upon liberation. When we are free, we can arrange our affairs to suit ourselves. But in order to be free we must
be united, Jehudah—we must be like one man. Do you think the
Samaritans can be persuaded to make common cause with us?"

Silently the shepherd gazed into the embers of the fire.

"Why not?" he said at last. He paused again. "But tell me,
Barabbas—are you the Messiah who is so talked about among you
Jews?"

"What put that into your head?"

"Why, it is the Messiah who will save Israel, according to your prophets."

So many ideas were racing through Barabbas' mind that it was difficult for him to answer.

"Messiah, you say? Oh yes, the Talmudists call the liberator of Israel by that name. But it seems to me it really is just another word for liberator."

"Then you would be the Messiah after all?" the shepherd demanded.

"If you want to see it that way, perhaps."

"There are some among us who believe that this Jesus of Nazareth is the Messiah."

Barabbas' laughter blared raucously into the stillness of the night.

"I can't help laughing, Jehudah. If Messiah means liberator—and in my opinion that is what it means—then this Jesus is the last man in the world to be called by that name. He will never drive a single Roman from the country—not a single one, I tell you."

Calmly, the shepherd cleaned his knife on the wool of his sheep-skin, placed it in its sheath and rose. His men did likewise.

"We will go now and look after our flocks," he said. "Do you wish us to tell our friends of your words, Barabbas?"

"Your friends and all your countrymen. Give them greetings from me who am half Samaritan. You will hear more of me. I'll send messengers to you when the time is ripe. Perhaps I will even come to your city to speak to your men. Let there be peace between us!"

"Peace!" the shepherd replied curtly, and he and his men disappeared beyond the small circle of light cast by the fire.

Their departure was followed by silence within and without the cave. Some of the men had already withdrawn to the interior of the cave; others were lying or sitting by the entrance, finishing their supper. Bits of unburnt wood crackled in the embers. A night-owl cried out near by.

"Why didn't you pay them off with a sound beating?" asked the young man who had led the raid on the shepherds' flocks.

"Fool!" Barabbas replied. "Would you have us make enemies everywhere?"

"Do you think these people can be depended on?" the young man asked.

"At least they're more dependable than the educated rabble in Jerusalem . . ."

The young robber could think of no reply to this. He went to the back of the cave to sleep.

Barabbas remained where he was in front of the fire, staring into the embers. The road he had to travel was beginning to take shape. He must win the peasants, the shepherds, the artisans, and the fishermen. All the solid, sturdy men of Judea, Galilee, and Samaria he must gather around himself. Then the rabble of the towns would fall all over themselves to get into his camp.

He envisioned the revolt swelling like a mighty wave, hurling itself against the hateful foreigners. But also against the high priests, the scribes, and the propertied classes. And he, Barabbas, son of Ezekiel and the Samaritan woman, was the liberator, the savior.

"King"—the shepherd had said. "Messiah . . ." Well, why not? One who had the strength within himself to liberate his nation also had the strength to govern it. What had Saul, son of Kish, been before he took up the crown? A shepherd. And David? Also a shepherd. He thought of Samuel, who had anointed Saul and David with holy oil. And then his thoughts drifted from the prophet of the past to the man of Nazareth . . . But this Jesus was no Samuel! It was depressing to think of him—it appeared scarcely possible not to think of him.

"King! Messiah!"

Barabbas struggled with himself to repress the memory of the Nazarene; for the recollection hindered his ambitious daydreams. In the end he succeeded: the only voice that continued to ring in his ears was that of the shepherd. From all sides, in a mighty crescendo, he heard the words:

"King! Messiah!"

In the distance a jackal howled . . .

7 ✗

The Star of David

THE PROCURATOR PACED RAPIDLY BACK AND FORTH IN A ROOM WHOSE walls were adorned with brilliant tapestries. Burning lamps hung from the ceiling, giving forth a sharp but not unpleasant aroma that mingled with the smoke from the pan of glowing coals. For the season was late autumn and the Procurator, accustomed to the hot Italian sun, was easily chilled.

The young female slave, Chloe, went from one pan of coals to the next, shaking fresh charcoal and sweet-scented resin upon the coals.

Upon one of the couches, wrapped in blankets and skins, lay Claudia, the Governor's wife, holding her hands over the smoking pan that stood near the couch. She watched her husband, whose face plainly revealed his extreme irritation, as he strode restlessly about the chamber. Claudia appeared to be several years older than her husband; her dark hair was already shot through with many traces of white. There was nobility in the cut of her face and in her alert eyes; her stainless features were those of a woman at once aristocratic and kindly.

"You are out of temper, Pilate," she said in a resonant remarkably low voice, speaking the language of their native city of Rome.

The Procurator interrupted his pacing and stood still before her couch.

"Yes, I am in bad temper. Does it surprise you, Claudia? These people are unbearable. This country is unbearable. This cold is unbearable. I am unbearable. Do you know what I mean? Does it never occur to you that now, at this very hour, the sun shines warmly upon the green hills of Latium, while here an icy wind from Lebanon freezes us to the marrow of our bones. I wish I had never seen the coasts of Asia. I wish I had never heard of this black city and these black-hearted people who hate me and whom I despise, who do everything they can to undermine my rule and my reputation."

"Have you had bad news, Pilate?" Claudia asked.

"Oh yes, in addition to everything else I have had nothing but bad news. This robber, Barabbas, is making trouble. Barabbas here and Barabbas there. His following seems to grow daily. There has been another attack on a half century in the vicinity of the city. It was wiped out. And, of course, it was Barabbas, or his followers."

"If you are sure of that, Pilate, why do you not have the man captured?"

"As a troublemaker and rebel against the Roman Empire? No, I don't want to do that. There is no rebellion—there must not be. I don't want it said in Rome— Oh, what is the use of explaining all this? You don't understand. I wish I were somewhere else."

"It was by your own choice that you went to Asia," Claudia said crossly.

"You've reminded me of that time and again, Claudia. Let us have it out right now. I admit it was by my own choice. But it was also by your choice. If you had not wanted it, would you and your family have done everything imaginable to get this post for me? Did I know what I was going to find here? I admit I was tempted by the power. I was ambitious to rule, to be virtually king in a country so rich in treasures, over a nation so rich in story. Did not you and your family concur in that ambition? And now? Where are the treasures of the country? Where are the people? What are they? Disgusting, simply disgusting."

"You have had your pleasures here now and then, Pilate," Claudia said. A faint smile flickered over her face, the smile of a woman conscious of her maturity.

The Procurator made a gesture of impatience, well knowing to what Claudia was referring. He resumed his pacing. After a brief silence Claudia said:

"I had a visitor today."

Pilate looked at her indifferently and did not inquire who the visitor was.

"Aren't you at all interested in my visitor?"

"Yes, of course. But it is not my habit to question you about your visitors."

"It was Mary of Magdala."

"It's a long time since she last visited, Claudia."

"She and her brother and her sister Martha came back from Galilee three weeks ago."

"Do you object to her sending her regards to me?" Pilate asked with some annoyance.

"Certainly not, Pilate—what are you thinking of? It is just that she seemed altogether changed . . ."

"What do you mean by that?"

Claudia supported herself on her elbow. Her face showed deep concern.

"I'll speak quite frankly with you, Pilate. I know you take a great deal of interest in this girl. She is very lovely and clever. And you know that I am not jealous. Moreover, I don't know how far things have gone between the two of you. Quite frankly, I am very fond of the girl. She seems to me too good for a mistress . . . and you would not be able to take her as your wife."

Pilate bit his thin lips and continued his restless pacing. His brow had turned crimson and the blue vein that ran across it above the base of his nose had swollen mightily. To the slave, Chloe, who was still tending the pans of coals, he spoke harshly:

"Go now—let that be. It gives no warmth anyway and makes the air stifling. I will call you when I need you."

Eyes wide with fright, the girl left the room.

"What were you trying to tell me a moment ago, Claudia?" Pilate asked.

"I think, Pilate, that you will have to give up Mary of Magdala."

"I have paid small attentions to her, that is all. If they annoy you, I will see that it doesn't happen again . . ."

"I am not annoyed, Pilate, not in the least. I mean what I said— I am very fond of the girl. But there is no sense in it. I am proud of you and should not like to see my husband in the role of a rejected suitor. Mary of Magdala's mind has turned to other things. Did anyone tell you that her brother Lazarus had died?"

Pilate waved his hand in irritable disbelief.

"Forgive me, Claudia, but that is nonsense. If a man is dead, he's dead. He must have been simply in a swoon. Yes, I have heard about it. A centurion who was in Capernaum told me about it. The whole thing is incredible. The coolest Roman minds seem to go mad in this country. Awakening the dead—what nonsense!"

"You ought to hear what Joseph says about that, Pilate. He was present at the raising of Lazarus."

"Then he, too, was deluded. This Joshuah or Jesus or whatever his name is seems to be a very clever magician."

"They say he is a prophet . . ."

"A prophet! What is there to being a prophet? We too have our soothsayers, but we don't make such a fuss about them. Every cultured man knows that these *haruspices* are deceivers."

"It is mean of you to say that. Think of the Oracle of Delphi and the sanctuaries of Apollo in Italy!"

The discussion was making Pilate uncomfortable.

"Let us drop the subject," he said. "You women are always being taken in by anything singular. Anything you cannot explain seems miraculous and supernatural to you. What has all this to do with the supposed change in Mary of Magdala?"

"A great deal, Pilate, a great deal. All these things have made a profound impression on Mary. As I said, she is completely changed. She no longer uses cosmetics; her nails are not painted; she no longer wears silk. To look at her now, she is a common maid of Magdala, and that is all she wants to be. I like her better this way, but I don't know whether you . . ."

"I repeat, Claudia, that you are exaggerating my interest in Mary. But if this fellow Jesus has turned her head, I intend to turn it back for her."

"You will see her when she comes again. But don't be surprised if she talks more about this prophet, Jesus of Nazareth, than about the things that interest you. She told me a great deal about him. And I must admit, she made me very curious about the man.

"Of course," Pilate said. "Because he doesn't work at a respectable trade, is a good talker, makes a stir, and in addition is fairly good looking, you are curious about him. I am not. Such people are dangerous; they stir up trouble in confused minds. Especially in the minds of women. You said yourself that Mary is changed. And yet she is a clever and cultured girl, speaks Greek as if she had been born in Attica and knows Plato by heart. It is time something was done about the mischief this Nazarene is causing . . ."

"You will not do anything against this man, Pilate," Claudia said.

"Why not?"

"For two excellent reasons. It would be beneath your dignity to get rid of a man who—forgive me, I mean it only in the spiritual sense—who might be considered your rival. Besides that the man is dear to all your Jewish friends."

"Dear to all my Jewish friends!" Pilate repeated in vexation. "Do any of my Jewish friends care a whit about me any more?"

At this moment a legionary entered the chamber and stood facing his chief with raised arm.

"What is it?" the Procurator asked.

"Joseph of Arimathea wishes to pay his respects to the Procurator."

"Send him right in—he is very welcome."

The legionary vanished. Joseph entered almost immediately. With arms crossed over his breast he bowed low before the Governor and Claudia, who sat up, and said in Greek:

"Peace!"

"Welcome, Joseph," the Procurator cried, going up to the visitor. "You come on the sandals of Mercury. I was just complaining that you have given me up completely. Have you come for any special reason?"

"No—and then again yes, Procurator. The main reason for my coming was to see you. But I also wanted to discuss with you a certain matter which I think important. But there is no hurry about that. If I am inconveniencing you, I'll be glad to wait for a more favorable time . . . What I have to say is not very pleasant."

"Not at all, not at all, Joseph. I am in such a wretched mood right now that nothing could make it worse. Tell me straight out what is troubling you."

Joseph of Arimathea took a seat and began at once.

"Are you aware, Procurator, that the movement of this robber Barabbas, whom we once discussed, has been growing and growing?"

"Yes, certainly. Claudia and I were just talking about it. These bandits are becoming more and more troublesome. Only yesterday his men slaughtered a half a century again."

"I guess you also know that this robber's following in the city is increasing constantly, even in the middle and upper classes of the Jewish populace . . ."

Pilate interrupted him.

"I know that by now every tenth man is wearing the badge with the Star of David. My men aren't blind, Joseph. And now, of course, you intend to ask what I am going to do about it, don't you?"

"Yes, that is the second reason for my calling on you, Procurator. Please don't think that I am meddling in your affairs—far be it from me to do that. But this movement is now beginning to be dangerous to us, too. Barabbas' men have come to the point of attacking Israelites who don't agree with them."

"Have they done any injury to you?"

"I did not wish to mention that. They have stolen hundreds of sheep and cattle from me—that I could stand. They have killed three of my shepherds—that is a good deal worse. But such things have happened to many landowners. Yesterday the Sanhedrin began to take the matter up."

The Procurator burst into loud laughter.

"The Sanhedrin? That's priceless. Next, I suppose, the High Priest Caiphas or his father-in-law will come to me in person to call my attention to the fact that Roman rule in this country is menaced. Or have they entrusted this delicate question to you?"

"You don't seem to take the whole matter very seriously, Procurator," Joseph said, his fingers toying nervously with the heavy cloth of his dark woolen mantle.

"I take it as a joke, which it is. I don't mean that personally, Joseph. I am sorry that the robbers have caused you trouble. But why don't you protect yourselves against them? None of you have ever failed to protect your own interests, and you have often rejected my proffered protection."

"Procurator, it is not we but you who are facing a rebellion. Controlling bandits might be our own affair. But I repeat, this is rebellion!"

"There we disagree," the Governor said, his narrow mouth curved in a faint smile. "You see the beginnings of a rebellion against Rome—I see ordinary banditry and ordinary killing. To me Barabbas is and will remain a leader of bandits and murderers, and I will execute him and his men as bandits and murderers, not as rebels against Rome."

"I remember our last conversation about Barabbas. I fear, Procurator, that you want to see nothing but bandits and murderers . . ."

"You are my good friend, Joseph of Arimathea. I'll speak frankly with you—no rebellion exists, not the whisper of a rebellion can exist in any province that I govern. I cannot afford it. Am I to have them say of me in Rome: You are a poor governor; you cannot even keep peace in your province? Do you understand, my good Joseph?"

The Arimathean nodded.

"I understand. That is what people call politics. But, of course, that will not prevent you from capturing and sentencing these—let us say, these ordinary bandits and murderers."

"Certainly not, Joseph. But you will admit that I have to catch them first. Or shall I make a fool of myself by honoring your Barabbas as a soldier and sentencing him in contumaciam?"

"Certainly you ought to be able to lay your hands on a mere robber and murderer?" Joseph asked, with a touch of irony in his voice.

"Your sarcasm is hardly appropriate, Joseph," Pilate said. "He is not easy to catch, particularly since your people protect him against us. My legionaries thought they had him several times, and each time he got away only because your people were in league with him."

"You punished them cruelly, Procurator."

"Cruelly? Here you are asking me to take energetic measures against Barabbas. Very well, I understand that. And then there are people among you who give aid and comfort to this robber and murderer. I get some of them and send them to the workshops instead of to the galleys or the cross. Do you call that cruelty? On the contrary, Joseph, I think I am far too mild with your countrymen, and they repay me with ingratitude."

"The workshops are horrible."

The Procurator shrugged.

"But the cross and the galleys are deathly. I did not set up the workshops nor build the mills. They are institutions of the Roman Empire. You know that; we ought not to have to discuss it. And besides, I have the feeling that you are somehow trying to trick me with this Barabbas affair."

"What do you mean, Procurator?"

Pontius Pilate adopted the tone of a prosecuting attorney.

"What about this man Jesus of Nazareth?" he asked.

Joseph of Arimathea reacted to the question as if it were a blow in the face. Jesus of Nazareth—mentioned in the same breath with the outcast Barabbas, the robber and murderer. It seemed like blasphemy to him. He saw the Procurator's hard eyes fixed challengingly upon him and felt his own face blench.

"I do not see what your question has to do with the subject of our discussion, Procurator," he said, after a brief hesitation.

"Permit me to explain it to you. I am fairly well informed about the things that went on in Galilee this past summer. My intelligence service is not as inefficient as you seem to think. I am aware that this man Jesus of Nazareth has an extraordinarily large following among the lower classes. And he also has many adherents among the well-to-do and cultured people. In fact he has a larger following than Barabbas. Yet you come to me and accuse the robber of open rebellion—but say not a word to me about Jesus. To put it moderately, Joseph, that strikes me as suspicious, highly suspicious. It seems to me you want to divert my attention to Barabbas so that I will overlook Jesus. Won't you answer me now with the same candor with which I've spoken to you?"

Joseph of Arimathea felt suddenly quite calm. The Procurator, he realized, was unwilling to see rebellion anywhere and therefore saw it everywhere.

"I don't think, Procurator, that I have ever given you reason to doubt my candor."

"That is very true, Joseph. Our friendship is based upon mutual frankness. Well, then, what have you to reply to my question?"

"That you are altogether mistaken if you believe for a moment that Jesus of Nazareth is inciting the people against Roman rule. On the contrary, he preaches patience, gentleness, peaceableness. Has anyone reported to you a single case in which his followers were provoked into an act of violence?"

"No. You are right about that. But isn't it also true that his followers have repeatedly wanted to proclaim him king?"

"Yes, that is true. But you must have heard that he has always stopped such attempts. Undoubtedly there are a good many among his multitude of followers who also hope that he will bring about the material liberation of Israel . . ."

"There you are!" Pilate exclaimed. "That's just it. Perhaps he himself has no thought of rebellion—but it's bad enough if his followers expect it of him. Some day they will force him to do it. The masses have a damnably stubborn will of their own, Joseph."

Joseph shook his head quietly.

"Nothing is impossible, Joseph. In any case, I cannot sanction it when a man in my province holds such power over thousands of people, even if he has no intention of abusing that power."

Joseph eyed the Procurator anxiously.

"But you cannot condemn this righteous man because there are fools among his followers?"

"Of course, I can—in fact I must."

"That would be a grave injustice, Procurator."

"Possibly. But it would also be intelligent. Such things must be torn up by the root."

"But he is the root of no sort of evil," Joseph of Arimathea protested. "You ought to know him, Procurator."

"I have a premonition that we will meet one of these days to talk things over. We had a little conversation about him once before, and at the time you declared yourself for him. Since then you have probably seen him in Galilee. Are you still so enthusiastic about him?"

"Enthusiastic, Procurator? That isn't the right word. I believe in him. He is the purest, holiest man I have ever seen upon this earth."

As he spoke these words Joseph lowered his voice, as if it were a confession directed more to himself than to the Governor. The Procurator stood before him, still shaking his head. But Claudia, who had listened silently to the conversation, spoke up:

"Do you hear that, Pilate? Joseph says the same thing. I ought to say, Joseph," she continued, turning to him, "that just before you came we were speaking about him. Mary of Magdala visited me. She goes even further—she thinks he is the Son of God and the Messiah who has been promised to the Jews!"

"Noble Claudia, that is also my belief," said Joseph.

Pilate resumed his pacing. There was a deep furrow etched into his forehead. After a while he said:

"I suppose you were present, Joseph, when he raised Mary's brother from the dead?"

"Yes, I witnessed that miracle. And I have seen many other things that were no less miraculous."

"I do not understand," Pilate said, shaking his head, "how cultured persons can believe such nonsense. You must have seen Egyptian sorcerers, Joseph? I saw one in Caesarea who had himself buried alive, remained in the ground all day and then was 'resurrected.' It occurred to no one to think of him as a god or as the son of a god because he could do this."

"Because everyone knew it was Egyptian mummery, Procurator. But Lazarus of Magdala was dead when he was placed in his tomb, and after four days Jesus brought him back to life. And the lepers from whom the leprosy fell like scales at a word from him were not hired tricksters but people I know. These feats are not mummery or sorcery; they are supernatural powers—divine powers."

Pilate's lips curved in a sneer.

"One must be a Jew to believe that," he said. "Or a woman," he added, glancing at Claudia. "What I would like to know is what Lazarus of Magdala has to say himself about his coming back to life. If it is true that you Jews have an immortal soul, that soul must know what happened to it during the time the body was dead. Didn't you ask him about that?"

"Of course, I did. But he cannot answer. He remembers nothing."

The Procurator laughed.

"There you are. Lazarus' soul must have slumbered during these four days. Yet it was certainly a rare opportunity to learn something about the state after death. No, my dear Joseph, you cannot come to a philosopher with such stories. What kind of man is Lazarus, anyway?"

"He has been my friend since childhood."

"Has he ever left his native land?"

"No. He is a quiet scholar. Even in his youth he spent a great deal of his time studying the Sacred Writings. But he also knows the languages and letters of the West. Mary is his pupil, and you will have to admit that she has learned a great deal."

"That makes it all the more remarkable that in spite of her learning she should be susceptible to the influence of this—as you call him—this Messiah. But that is scarcely surprising after all when men like you . . . forgive me, I don't want to offend you, Joseph. But I simply don't understand it . . . I cannot understand it. Could I get a chance to see Lazarus?"

"He leads a life of retirement, Procurator. Besides, he is rather sickly and only comes to Jerusalem when he is going to the Temple."

"Too bad. I would have liked to talk with him. But perhaps it is just as well if I don't. My questions would probably strike him as insulting. Has he any other sisters besides Mary?"

"Yes, one," Joseph replied. "Her name is Martha, and she spends most of her time running the household, which is rather large."

"I take it that the three are rich?"

"No, rich isn't the right word for it. We landowners are not rich, none of us. We pay taxes to the Emperor, to Herod in Galilee, to the Temple, and last but not least for the poor, as the law requires. Even in times of good crops not much is left over. The rich men are the merchants and money-changers. No one looks into their coffers and they have contrived to make a good business out of Judea's being subject to Roman rule."

"But you do have tremendous herds, Joseph."

"Tremendous is an exaggeration, Procurator. Your garrison sees to it that they don't grow too large. And then there are Barabbas and his men. But I do not complain—I have what I need, and that is enough for me."

Pilate began pacing again, and for a time no one spoke. The heavy air, saturated with pungent odors, was soporific, and, unlike the Procurator, Joseph of Arimathea found the room almost unbearably hot.

"Why have you never taken a wife, Joseph?" the Procurator asked abruptly, stopping before Joseph.

The Arimathean laughed with a touch of embarrassment. Only a Roman would ask such a question. While the Israelites did not shut up their wives and keep them from the public view, they kept their domestic affairs to themselves. For this reason the question struck Joseph as both barbarian and discourteous.

"I never did get around to it," he replied, avoiding the Procurator's eyes. "As you know, I spent a good many years abroad. And now— now I am past the age when men in our country usually marry."

"I suppose you are very choosey, Joseph. In any case, you should marry a Greek woman. All of you ought to take your wives from the West, to cure you of your provinciality."

"The Law does not permit it, Procurator."

The Procurator waved his hand angrily.

"The Law, the Law, nothing but the Law. If I thought your Jesus

of Nazareth would make an end of this Law of yours, I would welcome him."

"He has not come to destroy the Law, but to fulfil it," Joseph
said slowly and emphatically. He rose. It was time for him to go.
"Permit me to take my leave, Procurator. May I assume that you
intend to do nothing about Barabbas?"

"I did not say that, Joseph. I will not take action against Barabbas
the rebel. But I will send Barabbas the robber and murderer to the
galleys or have him crucified—assuming I can lay my hands on him."

Joseph bowed, bade goodbye to Claudia and the Procurator, who
did not attempt to stay him, and was led out by a legionary.

The brisk, cold air felt refreshing to him. He descended the
brightly-lit outside staircase of the palace and groped his way slowly
through the tangle of narrow alleys in almost complete darkness until
he reached his town house. The interview with the Procurator had
scarcely been very satisfying. The sort of "politics" the Procurator
indulged in was dangerous to the welfare of Israel. It amounted
virtually to giving Barabbas free sanction to commit robbery and
murder. How curiously this attitude contrasted with Pilate's sharp-
ness toward Jesus of Nazareth. What were the real reasons, Joseph
wondered.

The scribes, of course, and the priests of all degrees looked with
extreme suspicion upon the miracles and other activities of the Nazarene. That was easy to understand. They were wrestling for the
soul of the masses. The more his influence over the masses rose, the
more their own sank. But why should the Governor be so concerned? The Master's teachings did not matter to him. And how
shortsighted of him to think that anything the Sanhedrin would do
would be to the interest of the Nazarene.

A growing sense of anxiety took possession of Joseph. He felt
afraid for the Master, afraid of the dark forces that seemed to be
uniting against him. Barabbas, the scribes and the Governor were
becoming allies in this, even though they fought among themselves.

He came up to the door of his town house and rapped the knocker
against the heavy door, once, twice, thrice. The doorkeeper came
and opened. He bore in his hand a small, flickering lamp whose
feeble light cast ghostly shadows on the walls as Joseph preceded him
into the house. There was an uncanny atmosphere in this huge,
vacant, ancient house, and Joseph felt a loneliness unlike anything

he had ever experienced. He thought of the question the Procurator had asked him: Why had he never married? He thought of the tenderness he had once felt toward Mary of Magdala, and which he had repressed because, though she was his friend's sister, her unrestrained behavior was not to his liking. He thought of Martha who would have made so splendid a housewife to him, and who perhaps was still waiting for him to make his suit. Perhaps it would have been well to marry, perhaps it would . . . But now—now great things were in the air; unrest pervaded Israel . . . It was best to bear the burden of the times alone.

Joseph of Arimathea scarcely noticed when the doorkeeper brought him his supper. He was an elderly fellow who had been in Joseph's service for many years and served as caretaker of the town house. Joseph was standing at the window, gazing up at the unclouded sky and musing deeply when the doorkeeper spoke to him:

"Are you, too, seeking the star, lord?" he asked.

Joseph looked at him in astonishment.

"What star?"

"People say there is a new star in the sky. Many call it the Star of David. It is said to have been seen in the time of King David— and never since."

"What sort of people are talking about this new star?" Joseph asked sharply.

The man replied somewhat uncertainly:

"Followers of Barabbas . . ."

"Are you another of them?"

"No, lord. But many people believe he will free Israel."

"Barabbas is a robber, and there is no new star in the sky," Joseph snapped, dismissing the servant.

He ate his supper and then went to a large closet where hundreds of parchment scrolls were stored. Here were the spiritual treasures of his own people and of the civilized West. For a while he stood indecisively before the closet. What should he choose tonight? The Greeks? The Romans? No, all of them seemed shallow, even the loftiest among them, Plato. He took up the scroll containing the Song of Solomon, then replaced it. What did he want with poetry now? What did he want of all these books with their dark prophecies, now that the fulfilment was before him!

"David's Star in the sky . . ." Joseph of Arimathea understood what the doorkeeper had meant by that. It had come to this—even his own servants were reminding him that people believed in Barabbas' star. What blindness, what madness!

He closed the closet, sat down and summoned up the figure of Jesus of Nazareth to his mind's eye. He mused over every word he had heard from his lips, listened again to everything Jesus had said. And he absorbed these sayings, not with the critical faculty of his mind but with the believing humility of his heart . . .

8

A Deal

ABOUT THE SAME TIME THAT JOSEPH OF ARIMATHEA WAS RETURNING
to his town house, a small band of men crept through the alleyways
of the Acra, the Lower City. They cautiously avoided entering
broader avenues where, even during the night, Roman legionaries
went about with torches and closely examined everyone who had not
yet retired to his home. Through narrow passageways, past tumble-
down buildings, they at last reached the Temple Mount. They
paused before the house of the priest Nathaniel, who was said to be
the familiar and confidant of Annas, the high priest.

They knocked on the door in a peculiar manner. It opened at
once for them and they were led into a large chamber, partitioned
by tapestries, which was fairly well lighted by odorous, smoking lamps.

Nathaniel, son of Eliud, priest of the first degree, was waiting for
them. He was a tall, gaunt man with a vulture's face, greying hair
and beard and remarkably bright, mild eyes beneath bushy brows
that met over his sharp nose.

"Peace!" the priest said as the men entered the room.

"Peace!" the leader replied carelessly. There were almost a dozen
of the men, all tall, powerful fellows. After the exchange of greetings they removed their cloaks and the kerchiefs that had concealed
the greater part of their faces. They were wearing the Star of David.

Nathaniel the priest also had the badge with the Star of David fastened to his tunic.

The leader who had saluted the priest was Barabbas.

"We have accepted your invitation, rabbi," he began, "although it is not without danger for us to enter the Holy City."

"I thank you, Barabbas. Sit down. You all must be weary and hungry."

"We are, rabbi. But first I would like to know whether the information you sent me was correct. I was told that the high priest was vitally interested in our movement and that it would not be altogether impossible for the entire priesthood to enter into some sort of alliance with me. Have I understood the message aright?"

"Quite right, Barabbas. That was what I meant. But before we confer let us sup. It is not well to negotiate on empty stomachs."

Barabbas and his men laughed. They sat down at a long table, the priest and Barabbas opposite one another. Each seemed to want the other to begin the discussion. During the meal they talked about the weather or were silent. At last Barabbas made up his mind to speak out.

"There is no sense beating about the bush, rabbi. I want to know what is asked of me and what offered me? I know perfectly well that the priesthood does not intend to support my movement for love of me."

"You are right, Barabbas," Nathaniel replied. "There are certain conditions. But first I must ask you a question. How large is your following in Judea?"

Barabbas was prepared for the question. He replied with quiet certitude:

"There are about thirty thousand in Judea and Galilee, and some eight thousand in Samaria."

The priest frowned when Barabbas mentioned Samaria.

"The high priest is displeased that you have permitted Samaritans to enter your movement. In the eyes of devout Israelites they are no better than the gentiles. But we shall discuss that later. You mean thirty thousand men who wear your badge. Of course not all of them would be trained warriors?"

Barabbas smiled scornfully.

"You ought to know, Rabbi Nathaniel—you, too, are wearing the badge. No, not all of them can fight. Among the Israelites not more than half. The other half—forgive me, rabbi—are camp-followers. It is different with the Samaritans. Almost all of them can handle weapons in a fight."

"Do you believe that you and your men are ready to strike?"

"No," Barabbas replied coldly. "The legionaries are better armed. We must be able to make up our lack of arms by numerical superiority. At the moment we cannot do that. But I am convinced that the number of fit fighters would double if the priesthood were to side with us. Then we would be strong enough to begin the struggle."

"Good. Who will lead the fighters?"

Barabbas looked at the priest in amazement.

"Who but me, rabbi?"

Rabbi Nathaniel shook his head. His fingers toyed with the small metal badge that he wore on his breast.

"You are a brave and resolute man, Barabbas, but you yourself must admit that you are not a general. At any rate you have not yet had the opportunity to show that you are, have you?"

"If you have a single tried and tested general among the priests, Rabbi Nathaniel," Barabbas replied angrily, "one who has already won great battles, give me his name. I am ready to take orders from such a man. But I have yet to hear of one such."

The priest appeared very eager to placate Barabbas.

"I did not mean to offend you, Barabbas. Perhaps you really do have the traits of a general and have not yet had a chance to show them in your encounters with shepherds and small detachments of Roman soldiers . . ."

"I have shown that I can sense where and when the biggest success can be won with the smallest means. Our history proves that this sense is two-thirds of a general's gift."

"I don't deny that, Barabbas. Intuition is certainly important. Nor do I mean to assert that there are any great generals to be found in the priesthood. But it seems to us that the magic of a name often means more than military ability."

"Have you been thinking of any particular person?" Barabbas asked.

"Yes. We have our eye on a descendant of the Maccabean, the priest of the third degree, Juda ben Jacob. He, too, has never done

any fighting, but you know what associations a Maccabean brings
to mind."

Barabbas reflected for a moment. Then he said:

"I don't feel that it is especially important what front you put
up. What counts is who exercises the real power."

"I quite agree, Barabbas, I quite agree. Let us shelve this question
as well for a time. What is more important for us to know is what
you intend to do if the rebellion succeeds?"

Barabbas remained thoughtfully silent for a moment, his eyes
fixed inquiringly on the rabbi's vulturelike features. Then he said
slowly, emphasizing every word:

"Rabbi Nathaniel, that is a difficult question to answer. We cannot now foresee how it will all turn out. You understand, do you
not, that the ones who will really fight and bleed and die are those
that have nothing?"

"I believe everyone will give his utmost . . ." the priest replied.

"His utmost!" Barabbas interrupted impatiently. "The others
will lend money and arms and words and perhaps influence, and will
take no risks at all. Do you imagine, rabbi, that after winning the
victory my soldiers will let themselves be pushed aside, put back in
their places? Do you think they will stand for poverty any more?
Or do you expect me to return to the desert after the battle is ended?
I will answer your question by asking one. What do you, what does
the priesthood, what does the high priest think will happen after the
victory?"

Rabbi Nathaniel kept his eyes on the floor as he replied.

"You know the history of Israel," he began. "It is certainly no
secret to you that our nation was happiest during the times when the
high priest was also the king and judge of the people. Decadence
began when the office of high priest was separated from that of
king. Israel suffered more under the kings than from foreign wars."

Barabbas again interrupted him impatiently.

"Forgive me, rabbi, but I have not come here for a lesson in Israel's
history."

"Be patient, Barabbas. What I am saying is pertinent to the
object of our discussion. You asked a question and I am trying to
answer it."

"Make it brief, rabbi."

"Very well. I wanted to say that the people had to atone for the sins of the kings. For what concerned Israel most of all was not the nation's affairs with its neighbors, but its relationship with God. And it was in this respect that the kings heaped great blame upon themselves. I need not speak of the present state of the kingdom in Israel. You can all see that for yourselves."

"What are you getting at, rabbi?" Barabbas interrupted once more.

"That the priesthood is not smitten with longing for a new king. To put it plainly: If the priesthood as a whole is to take part in your movement, to support it both with money and through its influence over the people, it does so only on condition that after the victory all the power of Israel will once more be vested in the high priest, so that Israel will again have a priest-king as in the happy days of yore."

Barabbas rose.

"I thank you, Rabbi Nathaniel," he said. "You have given me a plain answer. I like honesty. At least I now know where we stand. For us the battle and death—for you the power. When all the fighting is happily over, we can go quietly back to our desert. I think we will go back right now."

With every sign of sincere fear that Barabbas really intended to break off the negotiations, Rabbi Nathaniel urged him to remain and listen to further explanation.

"You completely misunderstand me, Barabbas—or rather, you did not let me finish what I had to say. Naturally the priesthood has no intention of being ungrateful. The high priest as king would need an army in the future. In fact, he would need a very strong one to defend the country against fresh attacks from outside. Why should not the heroes who won Israel's freedom compose this army? And why should not the leader of these heroes continue to lead his army. Thus the high priest will be the heart of Israel; the leader of the army will be the strong right arm of the nation. Doesn't this tempt you, Barabbas?"

Barabbas was silent. He felt his comrades' eyes fixed fiercely upon him. This offer of Rabbi Nathaniel's, which seemed obviously made in the name of his superiors, was certainly tempting to a man who had been eking out a living as a robber and a fugitive, and it was probably no less tempting to his men. But the name of Juda ben

Jacob, the Maccabean, had roused Barabbas' suspicions. The rabbi's oily phrases did not deceive him; the priests wanted not only the power but the military glory to accrue to one of their own.

A faint smile passed across Barabbas' face. Rabbi Nathaniel perceived it but did not know what to make of it. Barabbas was thinking: Did the priests really believe it would be so easy to thrust aside the actual leader of a rebellion? And as for the prattle about the priest-king—the real ruler, once the victory had been won, would be not "the heart" but "the arm." The real holder of power would be the man who controlled the armed forces. Was Rabbi Nathaniel so foolish as not to realize this, or did he have other plans? To be sure, it sometimes happened that victorious generals died suddenly after a victory. Barabbas cast a hasty glance at his companions. Ezra was sitting closest to him. On him, and on all the others in his entourage, he could always rely.

Rabbi Nathaniel was waiting for his answer. He would agree, Barabbas thought, agree for the present. His movement needed money and arms; otherwise it might soon break up and his forces dwindle. He was on the point of replying when he suddenly saw the tapestry near the table move slightly.

Treachery?

In two strides he reached the tapestry and wrenched it aside. Then he stood still, nonplussed.

An old man sat before him in a tall chair, a very old man with white beard and hair, white, purple-edged priestly vestments and a curious cap adorned on either side with a plump horn. The old man did not move. His small, red-lidded eyes stared sharply at the face of the robber who stood before him, one hand holding back the hanging.

"What are you doing, Barabbas?" Rabbi Nathaniel cried. "How dare you . . ."

The old man raised his white, fleshless hand with its tangle of prominent blue veins.

"Let be, Rabbi Nathaniel," he said in a hard and curiously youthful voice. "It is quite all right. Why should not Barabbas know that I have been attending this conference?"

Barabbas removed his hand from the tapestry, crossed his arms over his breast, and bowed low, saying:

"Peace be with you!"

"Peace," the old man replied. "Have you decided, O Barabbas, to answer the question that Rabbi Nathaniel has put to you—on my orders? Or would you prefer to confer with your comrades first?"

For a moment there was utter silence in the room. Barabbas felt the eyes of Rabbi Nathaniel and his companions upon him, as well as the piercing gaze of the high priest. Before him, immovable as the Law itself, sat the old man in his sacred vestments, waiting. The air in the room seemed almost unbreathable.

This was the decisive moment, Barabbas sensed. Upon it everything depended. He knew that this opportunity would never return; he had to agree, no matter what hidden thoughts the priests might have about the matter.

"I will give you my answer at once, O high priest," said Barabbas, his voice sounding thick.

"Well then?" the high priest said urgently.

"It is the cause that matters to me and my men, the liberation of Israel from foreign rule. What happens after the victory, whether there is a kingdom or a priest-kingdom, does not seem important to us. Though, of course, we naturally do not want to be simply pushed aside after the victory."

The old man did not reply, but his searching glance never wavered from Barabbas' face. Barabbas continued:

"Rabbi Nathaniel said that we should remain the arm, the arm for the defense of Israel. We agree to that. If the high priest wishes to be the heart of Israel—we have no objection."

The resonant voice of the high priest rang out again.

"You spoke before of some fifteen thousand fighters, Barabbas. Were you thinking only of the Israelites or did you include the Samaritans who are willing to take part in the rebellion?"

"I have said—with the Samaritans we are many more."

"It does not please me to have Samaritans fighting side by side with Israelites, Barabbas."

"They will suffer the blows of the Romans as well as our own men, and they are brave fighters. We cannot do without them."

"Perhaps that is true—for fighting. But afterwards, Barabbas? One must always think of the future. You cannot fail to see that it is impossible to have a half or a good third of Israel's army consist of unbelievers. It simply will not do."

Barabbas almost shrank back from the cold light that gleamed in the old man's eyes as he spoke. It was like the glare of a viper as it tenses for the fatal strike.

"It is open to question whether after the battle the Samaritans might not prefer to return to their isolation," Barabbas said, strongly stressing the word "isolation." "The Samaritans love their liberty above all. I do not think the majority of them would particularly care to remain in Jerusalem as the 'arm' of the high priest."

The old man appeared to consider for a moment.

"You speak to me of returning, O Barabbas," he said, his voice hard. "It seems to me it would not be good if they returned. Do you understand me?"

Barabbas understood. So that was it! The Samaritans were unwelcome but they would be permitted to lend a hand. And then— then they would not be allowed to return. Even the hardened Barabbas shuddered at the thought. He had never worried overmuch about human lives and was willing to sacrifice everything for his ends. But this grey-bearded old man in the vestments of the high priest, the man who ought to be the most reverenced person in Israel, was hinting to him that he was to betray and sacrifice his comrades in arms. Barabbas was horrified. He asked himself whether there were any sense in dealing with such partners, whether it would not be better for him, for his own life, if he were to call a halt to it all and give up his plans.

But then he told himself that there was no turning back, neither for himself nor for his men. If the movement, lacking money and arms, should disintegrate, he would once more be nothing but an ordinary criminal, a robber and murderer, whom the Romans together with the priesthood would soon harry to death. That could not, must not be. And yet he could not answer. He looked around, cast a searching glance at his comrades. They too had understood. And he could see clearly by their expressions that they had no special love for the Samaritans and did not see why the negotiations should break down on account of the Samaritans.

Barabbas nodded silently.

"Good," the hard voice pronounced. "There is no need to say much about that. There are affairs which are not advanced one whit by talking at length about them ... One more thing, Barabbas. Have you heard of Jesus of Nazareth who has been teaching up in Galilee and also in Samaria and has already come into Judea, even into the Holy City?"

"Yes," Barabbas replied. "I have heard of him and seen him. He has a large following."

"Yes. Among the lower classes. He is in or way. We in Jerusalem would not mourn if he should suddenly vanish."

"He is a great magician," Barabbas said.

"Do not believe such folly, Barabbas. There are no magicians. Let us be clear about this—his doctrine that it is better to suffer wrongs than to do wrong, his preaching of patient suffering, is dangerous to your plans."

"I agree."

"Good. Then we need not discuss the matter any more. I assume this nuisance will soon cease. Do you understand?"

Again Barabbas only nodded silently.

"Then we are agreed on the end, Barabbas. The only remaining question is as to the means. What do you need?"

"Arms and money. Arms above all, but money also. Several thousand men must be provided for, training camps must be set up . . ."

"Rabbi Nathaniel will discuss these matters with you," said the high priest, as if unwilling to enter into the details. "Just one more question. When do you think you will be ready to rise in open rebellion?"

"That depends on the means I am supplied with. If the quantity and quality are good enough, we will be ready by this coming summer."

"Good."

The old man rose. He was by no means as frail as he seemed while sitting immobile in his chair. With swift, springy movements he gathered up his priestly vestments and while Barabbas and his men stood with crossed arms and bowed heads, he raised his hand as if in blessing and went out through a door in the paneled wall which opened before him. He was followed by Rabbi Nathaniel.

Barabbas and his men were left alone. They were silent for a moment. Most of them seemed somewhat downcast. One man asked softly:

"Who was that?"

"The High Priest Annas," Ezra replied, also in a whisper. Then he leaned over to whisper in Barabbas' ear, "Why did you agree to all these conditions?"

"You know, Ezra. Because we can still do as we please. Israel's arm will be stronger than the heart."

Some of the men laughed.

"And what about the Samaritans?" asked Ezra.

"What do you think I am?" Barabbas replied. "Doesn't the man know that I myself am half Samaritan?"

The entry of Rabbi Nathaniel put an end to the whispered conversation. They took their seats again and the rabbi spoke.

"One of the conditions, Barabbas, is that that the pact made between the priesthood and yourself must under no circumstances be revealed or even hinted at," Nathaniel said.

"It would be against our own interests to reveal it."

"No one must know even that any negotiations took place—and, of course, it must never be told that the High Priest Annas himself took part in these negotiations."

"I will vouch for myself and all my men here."

"The priesthood would energetically disclaim the faintest rumors about an understanding between us," Rabbi Nathaniel stressed.

"And you would certainly be believed in preference to us."

But after these strictures Rabbi Nathaniel dropped his air of pettiness. The priests could not, of course, supply arms, but there were people in the Temple who had excellent connections and would see to it that Barabbas was given whatever he needed. Ample funds were also promised and a part-payment was handed over at once. This made a good impression on Barabbas' men. Barabbas was perfectly well aware that the silver coins from the Temple treasury were never full weight, but he accepted this simply as a fact.

It was nearing midnight when Barabbas and his men left Rabbi Nathaniel's home. On the way back they were no less cautious than they had been before, but they had no dangerous encounters. Their quarters were an old, half-ruined shelter in the Lower City. They did not dare to leave the city during the night, for the gates were too well watched by Roman guards and it would be too perilous to try to scale the walls in the darkness.

Barabbas and Ezra sat up after the others had lain down to sleep. Ezra appeared to be in excellent humor.

"You've made a remarkable deal tonight, Barabbas," he said. "I have been wondering which party has taken advantage of the other."

Barabbas laughed.

"All these frightfully clever people who have stuffed themselves with all the knowledge on earth are great fools, Ezra. Do you remember the night you met us when we were returning from Magdala? Remember that Samaritan shepherd who was certainly no learned man? He asked, 'So you want to be king, Barabbas?' That fellow understood what a man does with power when he has it."

"Do you really believe they can make use of us and then get rid of us?" Ezra asked.

"They believe it. That is what comes of their filthy arrogance. They imagine they are so wise and so important that their old God himself, up above the clouds or on top of the mountains, can't help doing everything they want. What fools!"

"And they also want to get Jesus of Nazareth out of the way. What do you intend to do about that, Barabbas?"

Barabbas reflected for a moment. Before his mind's eyes rose the figure of the man in the white garment. He could almost feel Jesus' gentle eyes looking questioningly at him. After a brief pause he said:

"What do we care about the Nazarene? He is not harming us. The patient sufferers can follow him for all we care. They would be no good as fighters in any case. If the priests are bothered by him, why don't they take him into court?"

"It would be hard to cook up any charge against the man."

"They'll figure something out," said Barabbas. "He has made too many enemies among the wealthy. Almost as many as I have . . ."

Ezra's curly beard bobbed with his silent laughter.

In the distance a shrill scream sounded.

"What's that?" Barabbas demanded suspiciously.

"We are near the prison," Ezra said. "It isn't surprising that a man should scream. His sores must be painful. I know it all only too well."

Barabbas and Ezra relapsed into a gloomy silence.

9 ❧

"Be Ye Therefore Merciful,
As Your Father Also Is Merciful..."

IT HAD SNOWED DURING THE NIGHT. SNOW COVERED THE STREETS OF the Holy City—an extraordinary sight even in a harsh winter. The old men passed shivering through the narrow streets, but the boys rejoiced. They shouted and sported and threw snowballs at one another as children will anywhere in the world, wherever snow appears.

Joseph of Arimathea intended to spend the Sabbath with his friends in Bethany. He had left his house early in the morning and walked swiftly across the city. After he passed through the old wall near the Temple Mount he saw before him, gathered on the broad suburban street, virtually all the children of Jerusalem jubilantly engaging in sham battles. It was noisier than it ordinarily was on the high holidays, when the Israelites poured into the city from all the surrounding countryside; and the merriment was of a kind that only festive children can provide. Huge gangs of them fought one another, and the white snowballs, which were already smudged by dirty little hands, filled the air like hailstones.

Joseph noticed that the battles were not altogether sham. On one side, he saw, the boys wore the Star of David. He looked more closely at them. These boys were the attackers while the others did little more than defend themselves. The trouble had even seeped down to the children, Joseph thought. Where would it end? Suddenly all his pleasure in the children's jubilation drained out of him and in a dismal mood he walked down the street, keeping close to the houses in order not to be hit by the snowballs.

From the direction of the Tower of Antonia came a Roman cohort, marching in drill-ground step. The legionaries with their bare arms and knees were a rather pitiful-looking lot; they wore sour expressions and their noses and limbs were blue with cold. Men from southern Italy, the light frost must have felt bitterly cold to them.

The moment the cohort came in sight of the snowball fight among the boys stopped instantly. They formed straggling, silent lines on both sides of the street, all their merriment chilled by the sight of the Romans' battle insignia and the naked sword of the leader of the cohort.

Joseph of Arimathea stood still by the steps of a house as the legionaries approached. He too felt oppressed by the sight of the occupation troops. Suddenly, from the midst of a dense group of boys whom the cohort was just then passing, Joseph saw a huge snowball fly through the air and hit the leader squarely in the face.

What followed took place with uncanny speed. The leader, a centurion, shook the wet snow from his face and at once his sword lashed out at a boy who stood closest to him. A scream—the boys scattered in all directions—and the street was deserted. Deserted but for the boy who lay motionless on the ground, his blood reddening the snow, and the cohort which had halted at the centurion's command, and Joseph who stood by the entrance to the house as if numbed.

The centurion gave a low-voiced command and at once Joseph was surrounded by legionaries. The centurion confronted him.

"You will follow us. If you show any resistance, we will cut you down. You are the ringleader of this band of boys. March!"

"You are mistaken, centurion," Joseph said quietly. "I was merely passing here by chance. Moreover, you will not take me prisoner."

He took from his pocket a small thin shield which bore an eagle and the Procurator's name. It was a sort of pass issued to the Procurator's particular friends.

"Who are you?" the centurion asked, obviously impressed by the shield.

"I am Joseph of Arimathea and, as you see, one of the Procurator's friends."

"You saw what happened here?"

"Yes, I saw it."

"You saw that I was attacked."

"By a child—with a snowball."

"No matter."

"Was it necessary for you to kill him?"

"It was necessary."

"And one who was innocent besides?"

"That doesn't matter. We have orders to preserve the dignity of the legionaries with all the means at our command. You will bear witness for me as to what actually happened."

The centurion did not wait for an answer. He snapped out a command and the cohort reformed and marched off again, tramping heavily upon the soft snow.

Beside the motionless boy knelt a poorly dressed woman, sobbing softly. Joseph of Arimathea went up to her. The boy had a deep gash in his shoulder. The woman had laid it bare and was trying to bind it with a rag of linen that she had torn from her kerchief.

"Is the boy yours?" Joseph asked.

The woman merely nodded.

Joseph examined the wound.

"It isn't fatal," he said. "You will keep your child." He bound the boy's arm with a clean linen cloth that he had with him. The boy stirred slightly.

"You are very poor?" Joseph asked the woman.

"I am a widow and have three other children," she said wearily.

"I am Joseph of Arimathea. You may come to me three days from now and I will see that you are given flour and oil. Take the boy to a priest and have his wound treated properly. Here is money for that. But be sure to go to the priest—it is not far from here to the Temple."

The woman looked up at him wide-eyed as he handed her the money. A momentary flicker of radiance passed over her careworn features.

"May the Eternal repay you for what you have done for us," she said simply and, taking her child to her arms, went toward the Temple with him.

By now a few people had come into the street and were staring at the red splotch of blood upon the snow.

Joseph of Arimathea walked on. His pleasure in the brightness of the day and the clear, cold air had fled. The misery of Israel lay like a weight upon his shoulders, bowing him down. He felt sharply that his disquiet did not spring solely from the roughness of the Roman soldier, nor from the sight of the child's blood and the poverty of his mother. There was some other cause for his uneasiness. Suddenly he realized what it was. The boy had been wearing the Star of David.

"The Barabbas Youth," he murmured to himself. "Poor children . . ." To what condition had these poor, downtrodden people been brought that they should expect salvation from a robber!

In Bethany he found Lazarus and his two sisters in a mood of joyous excitement. They had heard that the Master would be coming to Jerusalem in the spring and were looking forward happily to the time.

"He will stay with us," Martha said, obviously already thinking of how she would serve the Master.

"And he intends to teach in the Temple," Lazarus remarked. "He will challenge the priests and they will be unable to contradict his teachings."

"He will console the poor and heal the sick," Mary said, her large dark eyes glowing with inner light.

"I am afraid he will not be able to convince the priests," Joseph said. "They do not want to be convinced. And I am not sure it will be good for him to challenge them. I am afraid they are planning to harm him in every way they can."

"You have no love for the priests," Lazarus interjected. "But who has ever been able to resist him?"

"I hope events will prove you right, Lazarus, my friend," Joseph replied in a troubled voice.

"You are out of sorts and pessimistic. We are full of hope and rejoicing. May I ask what has happened to put you in such low spirits?"

The Arimathean recounted his experience of the morning, and his narrative visibly shocked the three. All of them had become accustomed to violence, but it was something else for a poor, innocent child to be struck down because it happened to be standing within reach of a legionary.

"The Eternal will not abandon his people forever," Lazarus said in an attempt at consolation. But his words awakened no echo in Joseph's breast, and neither of his sisters ventured to second him.

They were sitting in depressed silence when the door opened suddenly and a powerful man strode into the large room. A blast of cold air momentarily dampened the heat from the pans of coals.

"Peace!" he said curtly and threw back the hood of his cloak so that his bearded face could be seen.

The man was Barabbas.

Lazarus and Joseph arose and gazed with astonishment on the man whom they had last seen that evening in Magdala.

"You are very daring, Barabbas!" Lazarus said. "To venture so close to the city . . ."

The man made a gesture of deprecation.

"I am running no risk at all. My men are guarding all the roads into the town. They know where I am."

"And what brings you to us?" Lazarus asked.

"You remember who I am—I can see that from your concern for my safety. You may also know that I seldom make pleas—I usually demand what I want. Nevertheless—I have come to you with a plea. One of my men—a man I am particularly fond of—has been badly wounded. He received a dangerous wound in a brush with some Roman soldiers and is suffering a great deal. We have no camp near by where we could shelter him and treat him. To bring him to safety we would have to travel a great distance and he would probably not survive it. Therefore, Lazarus, I ask your permission to shelter the man on your grounds. We do not need much, but in this cold the man must have a roof over his head or he will die. Perhaps in one of your stables . . ."

Lazarus raised his hand to stop the man.

"The poor fellow is welcome. Have him brought in. We will not have him put in a stable but take care of him here in the house. What we can do to ease him will be done gladly."

"Thank you, Lazarus. That is more than I wanted to ask. I will have a man left with him to take care of him."

"That will not be necessary, Barabbas. We will gladly tend him and he shall lack for nothing."

"Thank you. And may I occasionally inquire after him? I am very concerned about the man."

"Certainly. But for your and our own safety do it at night. And have the man brought in at once. My sister Martha will see to it that he is given good quarters."

Martha had already left the room.

Barabbas had turned to go but remained hesitantly for a moment.

"There is one more thing I wanted to say, Lazarus . . . It is even kinder of you to do this favor because I know you are not in sympathy with our cause, perhaps even hostile to it."

"That has nothing to do with our helping a poor fellow who is in need. We help our enemies also."

Barabbas cast a look of embarrassment at Lazarus.

"I know that is what Rabbi Jesus preaches . . ." he said.

"Yes," Lazarus replied. "And he teaches that we should be merciful as our Father also is merciful to us."

"Well—it was about Jesus of Nazareth that I wanted to speak to you. In return for your kindness. I know you think highly of him. Warn him. The priests have set a price on his head. There are likely to be plenty of men who would be glad to earn it. I don't know where he is at present, but perhaps you know and can send him a warning. It is a deadly serious matter . . . The Temple has a long arm."

"Thank you, Barabbas. Has the Master anything to fear from your men?"

Barabbas considered for a moment.

"No," he said finally, "not from us. We are not precisely hostile to him, though we cannot be his friends either. He does a great deal for the poor. It's too bad that we could not come to an agreement that time I spoke to him at your home. And also too bad, Lazarus, that you and I are enemies."

Lazarus took a step toward Barabbas.

"I am not your enemy, Barabbas. I am no man's enemy."

"But you are against us, and your guest . . ." He cast an unfriendly glance at Joseph of Arimathea. "He is a friend of the Procurator and therefore our enemy."

"You don't know the whole story," Joseph spoke up.

"That may be. But an Israelite who frequents the house of Israel's oppressor is our enemy. You are Lazarus' guest and he is doing us a great favor, so I don't want to quarrel with you here. In any case there is no sense in argument. You would confuse anyone with your oily, learned tongue. I will have the wounded man brought in as soon as it grows dark."

"In spite of the Sabbath?" Lazarus asked.

"If your mercy is so great, Lazarus, it probably will not adjourn for the Sabbath," Barabbas replied harshly.

"You are right, Barabbas." There was a note of shame in Lazarus' voice.

"Peace!" Barabbas said, bowing curtly, and he strode out as swiftly as he had entered.

"A remarkable man," Mary said.

"A murderer and a crackbrain to boot," Joseph replied.

"A poor wretch who walks in error, Joseph," Lazarus said. "We are not his judges. Had he been better treated as a boy he would probably have turned out much better. It is said he was a talented potter . . ."

"He and his movement might well bring a terrible calamity down upon Israel," Joseph said. "I have been meditating a great deal about that terrible incident this morning, wondering whether it is really best to endure everything without defending oneself. But how shameful to see the idea of rebellion embodied in a robber. And what are we against the Romans, against the mighty Empire that controls the whole world. People in Rome would scarcely find it worth mentioning to one another should Israel be crushed beneath the tread of the marching legionaries . . ."

Lazarus, Mary, and their guest sat for a while in silence, immersed in mournful thoughts about the future of their nation.

"Do you believe," Mary at last broke the silence, "that the Master is in any real danger, Joseph?"

"Alas, I cannot help believing it, Mary. The priests hate him—at least most of them do. There would be little point to their seizing him and bringing him to trial because the Sanhedrin has no power to execute a death sentence. They would have to go to the Procurator and he, if only to annoy them, would not agree. That is all the more reason for thinking that they will try to get rid of him in some other way . . ."

Lazarus looked at his friend in horror.

"Do you really think, Joseph, that the priests and Barabbas . . ."

"I know it. There are followers of Barabbas among the priests. Without help from the priesthood Barabbas' movement would have collapsed long ago."

"But you yourself heard that Barabbas does not want to do harm to the Master?"

"I find it hard to trust the man. And besides, a movement that depends so largely upon money from the powerful and on the ambitions of one man is incalculable. If the priesthood some day decides to pinch the purse, Barabbas will do what they ask of him. He or one of his men . . ."

"But I cannot believe it, Joseph. The servants of the Lord, who stand next to his altar, cannot possibly plan crimes," Lazarus said.

Joseph shrugged.

"You know well, Lazarus, that serving God has become a thing for show in Israel. The priesthood want to secure their power by every means at their command. Perhaps they even believe they will be pleasing God if they get rid of the Master."

Lazarus was at a loss, but his sister spoke up.

"They will not be able to harm him. He who can command the winds and the sea, whom Death must obey, cannot be touched by the malice of his enemies."

Mary's eyes burned and her whole body quivered.

"May your prophecy prove correct, Mary," Joseph said.

After dark two of Barabbas' men brought in a rude stretcher on which lay the wounded man. The men had come by way of the garden to avoid detection and had knocked at the rear door.

Mary had prepared a small room for the sick man. Here he was laid upon white linen. The poor fellow was deathly pale, as if all the blood had drained out of him, and apparently unconscious. An arrow had pierced deeply into the right side of his chest and in addition he had a deep sword-cut on his back.

Joseph of Arimathea, who was an excellent physician, cleaned the wounds as best he could and bandaged them. The two men asked whether they might come to ask about the wounded man every day after dark. Lazarus gave them permission and learned from them that the man's name was Ezra.

The Arimathean pricked up his ears as he heard this name. He recalled an escaped prisoner of the same name and at once realized the significance of the many scars that covered the man's body. But he said nothing about his conjectures; he had no desire to alarm Lazarus and his sisters. For while it was dangerous enough to lend aid to one of Barabbas' fellows, it was in the eyes of the Romans a great crime to shelter an escaped prisoner.

"Is he very bad?" asked Martha, who had been helping Joseph treat the man's wounds.

"Very," Joseph said. "His lung is injured and in addition he has obviously lost a great deal of blood. He must have a strong constitution to have survived at all."

"It is too bad the Master is not here," Martha said. "He would save the poor fellow."

Joseph did not reply. Something in him rebelled against this acceptance of Jesus of Nazareth's ability to work miracles as if it were a matter of course, something that had become a part of everyday life.

He, Lazarus and the sisters shared the vigil over the wounded man, who was running a high fever. Ezra could not move, but his bony fingers twitched and quivered on the white linen and from his racked, parted lips came incomprehensible sounds which would not form into words.

Joseph of Arimathea and Lazarus, who were both as well acquainted with medicine as were all the cultivated laymen of the time, discussed what means they could use to soothe and quiet the invalid, if not to save him. Lazarus produced some bark which he had received from India; this he steeped in water and boiled, and forced Ezra to drink the essence, which was rather difficult since the wounded man resisted and could swallow only with the greatest difficulty. Joseph also renewed the bandage frequently and placed some salve on the wounds. Probably the priests, who in those days alone practiced medicine, could not have done much more.

Toward morning, while Joseph was sitting with him, the wounded man grew quieter and the fever seemed to recede somewhat. At dawn Lazarus appeared to relieve his guest.

"Have you forgotten, Lazarus, that today is the Sabbath?" the Arimathean asked with a faint smile.

"Your Sabbath as well," Lazarus replied.

"We Sadducees are not so strict about it as you Pharisees."

Lazarus placed his hand upon his friend's shoulder.

"Do you not think it remarkable that both of us have the letter of the law in our blood and it was necessary for Barabbas the robber to remind us of the Master's teachings. Joseph, my friend, we must still impress it more deeply on our hearts that love is greater than the law . . ."

Joseph nodded and went to his room to rest for an hour.

The following morning when he returned to Jerusalem the snow was completely gone. The wind was blowing from the sea, laden with warm air.

Lazarus and his sisters did not have an easy time caring for Ezra. The more his condition improved and his periods of consciousness lengthened, the harder it was to keep him quiet. Only Martha, the most resolute of the three, was able to make him lie still. He did not speak, he asked for nothing and gave thanks for nothing that was done for him. His restless eyes glared suspiciously at these strangers who cared for him so faithfully. He was like a captive desert animal, feeling above all his captivity.

During Ezra's convalescence Barabbas had sent his men every night to ask about the man. In the middle of the week he came himself, disguised as he had been the first time, and Martha led him to the room where Ezra lay. Mary was sitting with him and had just finished feeding him some broth when Barabbas entered. After a murmured greeting the robber went up to the bed.

"Do you know me, Ezra?"

The sick man nodded, more with his eyes than his head which he could scarcely move.

"I can see you are much better and that you are being given good care here, Ezra. You will get better quickly. The camp is waiting for you and I, too. It will please you to hear that not one of the Roman dogs who attacked us escaped with his life."

Ezra closed his eyes, but a trace of color appeared in his pallid features.

"Why should he be glad to hear that men have been killed?" Mary asked softly.

Barabbas looked at her in amazement.

"They are our deadly foes, the men I am speaking of."

"Do you not know what the Master says: 'Love your enemies, bless them that curse you, do good to them that hate you, and pray for them which despitefully use you, and persecute you'?"

Barabbas frowned. He was obviously restraining himself with difficulty from shouting at the girl.

"Listen to me, Mary of Magdala," he said in a tense voice. "Let us get one thing clear. I am grateful to you and your brother and sister for saving Ezra's life and I mean to show my gratitude. But as for anything else—there is a whole world between us. If you imagine you can make a business out of your kindness and convert me to the beliefs of your Jesus of Nazareth, you're on the wrong path."

The words sounded harsher than Barabbas had intended. This girl was charming and beautiful; he was really grateful to her and her brother and sister for taking care of Ezra and he did not want to offend them. But whether it was the rudeness of his nature which could not be held back or whether he did not want to appear soft-hearted in Ezra's presence, something forced him to speak harshly. Also it angered him to feel himself stumbling over this message of patient suffering every time he met these people.

Mary of Magdala, however, did not appear to have taken offence. She said smilingly:

"We are not caring for your comrade in order to be thanked, Barabbas, but for the sake of the love our Master teaches. You can see that his teachings work out to your advantage. But conversion? No, not we, only your own conscience can convert you. And are you not already on the way to conversion? You receive love in this house and wish to be thankful for it. Is not love the strongest weapon, O Barabbas?"

"For women, perhaps. But battle is more fitting for men—not for us the word but the deed. Are we to win Israel's freedom by loving the Romans?"

"I say to you, Barabbas," Mary replied softly, "true freedom is to be found only in Him!"

Barabbas could not help smiling. This chit of a girl with her shining eyes was trying to tell him where freedom was to be found. He was susceptible to feminine beauty and it seemed more suitable to him to pay homage to Mary's beauty than to continue this embarrassing dispute with her.

"You are beautiful as the Rose of Sharon, Mary, and good as an angel. But we will not agree about this and it is better not to discuss it. May I ask you to leave me alone with Ezra for a few minutes?"

Mary went out.

“They are very kind to you, Ezra,” Barabbas said.

Ezra nodded.

“Yes. Still—I would like to leave as soon as it is possible,” he whispered.

“How are you feeling?”

“I am still very weak. But past the crisis, I know. I heard them saying so. And they thanked God for it—here at my bedside.” And straining himself to the utmost, almost screaming, Ezra added: “Get me out of this house, Barabbas, get me out of this house . . .”

Barabbas understood what was passing through Ezra’s mind. He tried to divert him.

“I won’t leave you here a moment longer than is necessary. But now and in your present condition you can’t go out. Don’t worry about anything. Our army is growing and you will soon be fighting at our side again.”

“Get me out of this house . . . I can’t stand it here any longer . . . I’m afraid of their kindness . . .”

Panting, Ezra let his head sink back on the pillow. Weariness overwhelmed him; Barabbas saw that he was falling asleep. Deeply moved, he stood at the bedside for a few minutes looking down at the sleeping man. Ezra’s face, which had been contorted while he spoke, was relaxed in sleep.

“Afraid of kindness . . .” Barabbas murmured to himself. “That is the danger . . .” He shook himself and straightened up. “We will not be overcome by it, Ezra . . .”

He brushed his big hand over Ezra’s hot brow and with heavy tread strode out of the room.

10

"Whosoever Liveth and Believeth in Me Shall Never Die"

SLOWLY THE GLOOMY, UNPLEASANT DAYS OF WINTER PASSED. PIERCING cold alternated sharply with damp warmth from the sea. Heavy downpours of rain made the roads almost impassable, even in the vicinity of the capital. But in spite of the poor communications rumors reached even to the house of Lazarus in Bethany of a defeat of the Roman troops on the Syrian border, and of heavy reinforcements being sent from Italy.

Joseph of Arimathea, who visited at least once a week, had heard a great deal about these matters. Bethany was not more than fifteen miles from Jerusalem, but the roads were so bad that Lazarus was grateful to his friend for making the uncomfortable journey so often. Joseph reported that the Procurator was extremely irritated and in an altogether unpleasant mood; even in Jerusalem he had begun tightening the reins. Scarcely a day passed without his arresting a number of persons on some pretext and sentencing them to forced labor. The cries of the flayed and beaten sounded incessantly from the workshops and the prisons. People scarcely ever ventured into the streets for fear they would be corralled like cattle. The Roman soldiers were now going about in full centuries, for smaller troops had been repeatedly attacked—the attackers had ventured as far as the very gates of the city—and killed to the last man. The Romans knew very well who the attackers were but so far they had not succeeded in capturing a single one of Barabbas' bands, which were now growing ever more numerous and brutal in Judea itself. Their tactics were always the same—a swift, unexpected assault from ambush, a bloody slaughter of the surprised soldiers, and immediate flight. It was fairly obvious that occasionally Barabbas' men were being sheltered by the populace or aided in their flight.

On one of these dark, rainy nights there was a loud knocking on the back door of Lazarus' house in Bethany. Lazarus himself opened and found himself confronted by Barabbas, who was holding the reins of two mules.

"Peace be with you!" Lazarus said, but Barabbas did not reply to the greeting.

"I've come to get Ezra," he murmured swiftly.

"But Ezra isn't fit yet—it might mean his death to move him."

"His death will be much more certain if he stays here, Lazarus. He must leave at once. I have heard that he was betrayed to the Romans; someone has informed them that he is in this house. Perhaps the Procurator's men are already on their way to capture him. You understand—it will be much better for you, too, if he is not found here. Bring him quickly—quickly."

Lazarus was about to rush up the stairs, but apparently Ezra had heard for he met his host halfway. His face was white and his hands quivered as he clutched the banister to support himself.

Barabbas called from the doorway:

"There is great danger, Ezra. Can you hold on and ride?"

"If I must I can," Ezra said. "Let's go."

"But you must be dressed more warmly, Ezra!" Lazarus cried and hurried to find a woolen coat. When he returned with it Barabbas was already busy helping Ezra mount the mule. Barabbas took the coat from him and threw it over Ezra's shoulders.

"I have no time now to thank you, Lazarus," said Barabbas. "Nor has Ezra. Perhaps a time will come soon when we will be able to thank you and yours with something else than words."

A moment later the pair had disappeared into the darkness. Lazarus closed the door and went back into the house. Not until then did he realize that not only Ezra was in danger, but he himself and his sisters. "Betrayed to the Romans—perhaps the Procurator's men are already on their way . . ." Barabbas had said. What did it mean? A cold sweat broke out on Lazarus' forehead.

His sister Martha, a lamp in her hand, came out of her room.

"What has happened?" she asked.

"Ezra is gone."

"Run away?"

"Yes and no. Barabbas came for him. He says someone has informed the Romans that a fugitive was being sheltered here."

Martha turned pale. She placed the lamp on a bench in the hallway.

"This may get us into trouble, Lazarus."

"It can't be helped, Martha."

"No?" she said. "Perhaps it can."

She picked up her lamp again and went upstairs to Ezra's sickroom. Lazarus heard her working and knew she was trying to wipe out all traces of Ezra's presence.

Dawn had not yet broken when the loud tramp of horses' hoofs sounded outside and a moment later the knocker thudded heavily against the wooden planks of the front door. When the door was opened a half dozen Roman soldiers thrust their way in. The leader said that he wished to speak with the head of the house.

"We are seeking an escaped criminal who has been staying in this house for weeks. The house is surrounded on all sides. You had best give him up voluntarily."

Lazarus replied in Latin:

"There is no criminal and no fugitive in this house."

The leader, an elderly man, made a gesture of contempt.

"We'll find him." He turned to his men. "Guard this man."

Two of the men stepped toward Lazarus and forced him back into the room. The leader left with the others and began searching the house. They were very thorough about it; it was broad daylight before the leader returned, visibly angry and disappointed.

"The bird has flown," he said. "But you are responsible to me," he said to Lazarus. "You will come with us."

"Shall we tie him up?" asked one of Lazarus' guards.

"No. But if he makes the slightest effort to escape—you know what to do."

"May I take leave of my sisters?" Lazarus asked.

"Only in my presence. Your sisters too are under suspicion, and the entire household. I am leaving six men behind to guard the house and the servants until the Procurator decides what is to be done with you all."

Lazarus said goodbye to his sisters. Martha remained calm and resolute.

"It will only be a matter of a few hours, Lazarus," she said consolingly. "Have no fear."

"I am not at all afraid," Lazarus said quietly. "The will of the Lord be done."

Mary wept.

"I will go to see the Procurator," she said.

The soldiers placed Lazarus in their midst. He was ordered to mount one of the horses and the group rode at a sharp pace toward the Holy City. The streets through which they passed were deserted. When they reached the Governor's palace, Lazarus was at once thrown into a prison cell.

Martha quickly won the goodwill of the six guards by serving them all an excellent breakfast. She provided one of the household's better wines and the soldiers applied themselves eagerly to it. These legionaries were by no means spoiled and felt extraordinarily comfortable in Lazarus' house. The oldest of them attempted to console the sisters.

"You don't have to worry too much about it," he said, somewhat drunkenly. "He may well get away with the galleys. If he's very lucky it may only be a couple of years at forced labor."

"If only Joseph were here!" Mary sighed.

Joseph, however, usually came on the weekend and they could hardly expect him sooner. Martha plied her domestic virtues so busily upon the leader of the guard that she finally persuaded him to ride to Jerusalem with Mary that afternoon. She pointed out to him that Mary was friendly with the Procurator and his wife and that they had an influential friend in Jerusalem, Joseph of Arimathea, who also enjoyed the Procurator's favor; the Procurator would certainly praise the soldier, perhaps even have him promoted, if he did something for his friends. This last convinced the man.

Joseph of Arimathea was terribly shocked when Mary appeared at his house, accompanied by the soldier, and recounted the events of the morning. He wondered whether he ought not to advise Mary

and Martha to flee to Galilee, for he felt that both the sisters were
gravely endangered. If Pilate passed judgment in this case as he had
been wont to do of late, Lazarus would surely receive the cross and
the sisters imprisonment for life.

"But what about the soldiers?" Mary asked.

"I could manage to trick them."

Mary realized that Joseph intended to sacrifice himself for his
friends. She gave him a look of gratitude and said:

"No, Joseph, you must not do that. And Lazarus comes first.
Are we to leave him to his fate merely to save ourselves?"

For a moment Joseph wondered whether he might not call in
Barabbas in order to be quit of the soldiers. He somehow felt that
the man would be ready to demonstrate his gratitude toward the
sisters. But he did not voice his thoughts, and he realized that Mary
would refuse to think of herself as long as her brother remained in
danger. He finally decided that there was nothing else to do but
intercede personally by going to Pilate; at least he could try to persuade him to act mildly.

He, Mary, and the soldier set out for the palace.

It was late afternoon before the Procurator recalled that the arrest
of Lazarus had been reported to him. He sent for the prisoner.

Lazarus looked pale and ill when he was brought in to Pilate. He
had been freezing in the unheated prison cell and had been given
nothing to eat.

Pilate looked at him in silence for a while. Then he said:

"So you are Lazarus of Bethany, Mary's brother."

"I am he, Procurator."

"It is not long since I said to your friend Joseph that I would like
to see you. My wish has been fulfilled—but hardly in a fashion very
pleasant for you. I cannot deny that I would rather have seen you
here as my guest than my prisoner. Do you know with what you
are charged?"

"I would prefer to hear the accusation from you yourself, Procurator," Lazarus said softly.

"You shall. The escaped criminal Ezra, a robber and murderer,
was present in your house. He was not found there but I have not
the slightest doubt that you have sheltered him. I have the testimony of a very highly respected person as to the truth of this accu-

sation. There is no use in your denying it, Lazarus of Bethany."

"I do not deny it, Procurator," Lazarus said quietly, speaking in Greek as had the Procurator.

Pilate gave him a look of astonishment that bordered on dismay.

"Then you admit that you sheltered an evildoer who escaped from one of the workshops and has been sought for months?"

"I admit it."

The Governor was silent for a moment. The man's unabashed confession had thrown him off balance. Finally he asked:

"And naturally your two sisters knew all about it?"

"I beg permission not to answer this question," said Lazarus. "I am speaking only for myself and not for my sisters."

"It seems to me you are speaking not for but against yourself. But that is your affair. Are you aware that on the basis of your confession I can pass the same sentence upon you that has been decreed for the man you concealed—death?"

Lazarus bowed his head and said submissively:

"I know that, O Procurator. My life is in my lord's hands."

"Are you asking for mercy, Lazarus?"

"For my sisters' sake, Procurator."

The Procurator, who up to now had been sitting, stood up and began his customary rapid pacing of the room. Incredible man, he was thinking, wholly inexplicable. Why had he not said—I did not know that the man was a fugitive? Why did he not, since he had already so incomprehensibly confessed, ask for mercy? The charge was not any too sound; the fugitive had not been found in his house; he had been told at once that there was only one witness against him. And why had he not referred to Mary and to his friend Joseph? Jove, these Jews! What kind of men were they? He would never understand them. Always, in all things, they behaved differently from other men.

"Do you admit that you have acted wrongly, Lazarus?"

"In your eyes what I have done may be wrong, Procurator. But in the eyes of God I have done what was right. For the law commands me to be merciful toward those that suffer. The man was on the point of death when they brought him to me. You may look upon him as a criminal condemned to death, but to me he was a poor unfortunate whom I had to pity."

Pilate was unable to explain to himself why he was still trying to throw a lifeline to this man who insisted on drowning himself. But he said:

"Then you did not know that he was an escaped prisoner when he was brought to you."

"Not at the time," Lazarus said quietly. "But I found out later."

Pilate was becoming more and more interested in this man who apparently wished to place no obstacles in the way of a death sentence.

"And nevertheless you did not turn him in?"

Lazarus bowed his head and did not reply. Pilate continued his interrogation.

"The man recovered under your care."

"He recovered."

"And where is he now?"

"He left suddenly last night, with one of his comrades who came for him."

"He knew that we were on his track. How did he know?"

"His comrade told him. How he knew I cannot say."

Pilate reflected for a moment. He wanted to ask whether this comrade was Barabbas. But the question would have decided the man's fate, and Pilate realized that Lazarus would not lie. He asked another question instead.

"Have you any suspicion who betrayed you to us?"

"None, Procurator."

"Then I will tell you. It was the chief rabbi of the Bethany synagogue. He is your enemy, I take it?"

"I have never harmed him in any way."

"But you are an adherent of the man of Nazareth who is said to have raised you from the dead. Is it true that he did?"

"It is so, Procurator. I know it."

"How can you say that? Did you know anything about yourself while you were dead?"

Lazarus hesitated a moment.

"My body was dead but not my soul."

"Oh yes, your body. You Jews also have a soul that does not die with the body. Don't you believe in death at all? Aren't you afraid of it?"

"The Master says: 'He that believeth in me, though he were dead, yet shall he live. And whosoever liveth and believeth in me shall never die.' "

This, Pilate felt, was his answer. This was the answer to all the questions he had asked himself about this man's strange behavior.

"That is one kind of philosophy, Lazarus," he said.

"It is faith, O Procurator."

"I should have liked to discuss these matters with you some time, for you are a learned man. But now you stand before me as an evil-doer and it is my duty . . ."

Pilate did not finish the sentence. He heard footsteps behind him and turned around angrily. It was Claudia who had come in.

"You know, Claudia, that I do not wish to be disturbed," he said sharply. But his wife went up to him.

"I know," she said, "and I do not do this ordinarily. But in this case—I know that you are questioning Lazarus. His sister Mary has just come and Joseph of Arimathea with her. They ask to be heard as witnesses."

"It is not my wont to refuse to hear witnesses," Pilate said somewhat irritably. "Send them in."

A few moments later Mary and Joseph entered.

"I am sorry," Pilate said after the exchange of greetings, "that our present meeting has not a pleasanter cause. Lazarus freely confesses that he sheltered the criminal and fugitive Ezra in his house. I am very much afraid, Mary, that I shall also have to proceed against you and your sister. The case is one of free confession—is there anything I can do about it?"

"There is, Procurator," Joseph said in a quiet, controlled voice.

"Is there really? I would be curious to hear your reasons, Joseph. I assume that you have come here to defend your friend Lazarus. But I am not yet sure whether you too will have to be brought to trial along with him. Perhaps you were an accessory to the crime?"

"You speak of a crime, Procurator, but I see none. I believe you are in error," Joseph replied.

"I asked you a question."

"Certainly. I will answer that question too. Yes—I knew about the matter. I was in Bethany that evening when a man wounded unto death was brought into Lazarus' house. To refuse him entry meant to kill him. It was not written on his brow that he was a fugitive, a man who had escaped from your mills. Though you know, Procurator, what I think of your mills."

Pilate waved his hand as if to dismiss the matter.

"This does not seem to be the proper time to discuss our punitive system," he said.

"Certainly not, Procurator. I merely wanted to indicate that in Israel not everyone who flees from a mill can be considered a criminal. In any case neither Lazarus nor his sisters knew that he was a fugitive. The man was taken care of for pity's sake. And, O Procurator, I swear this to you—none of us thought that by an act of mercy the great Roman Empire would be harmed."

"And did you not know by any chance that the man was one of Barabbas' men?" Pilate asked mockingly.

Joseph's eyes flashed. He felt that Pilate was asking his question as a trap, but he was glad of it. It was a trap only for the Procurator, he felt.

"Of course, Procurator, of course we knew that. But I recall having heard you express the opinion that though Barabbas might be a robber you were not particularly interested in capturing him or his men. We thought it was no crime that he was a Barabbas man, for you do not look upon such adherence as a crime. The man fled last night without being aided or abetted by Lazarus and his sisters—none of us is responsible for his flight. The core of the matter is still this—that no one knew the man was a fugitive and hunted by your soldiers."

The Procurator, who had listened attentively to the Arimathean's words, laughed aloud.

"Splendid, Joseph, splendid. You ought to speak on the Rostra in Rome or in the market at Athens. You deal very cleverly with the logic of Roman law. What you say about Barabbas particularly tickles me. You pin me down to my own words and I cannot deny them. You are able to prove to me that Lazarus and his sisters deserve not punishment but my approval. May I ask what you think should be done now? You know I have a weakness for good oratorical performances . . ."

The Arimathean was somewhat disturbed by Pilate's merriment. He knew that the Procurator could pass death sentences with a smile. And besides his conscience troubled him a little. He had not spoken any frank untruths, but he had concealed the fact that he had little doubt about Ezra's origins. Moreover, he knew perfectly well why Pilate wished to make no fuss about Barabbas; the Procurator had confided his motives to Joseph. Nevertheless, Joseph of Arimathea was more a man of the world than Lazarus; he was not so thoroughly imbued with the teachings of the Master that he could not think of his personal rescue and that of his friends. And so he decided to continue the sophistry along the lines on which he had begun.

"I am no sort of orator, Procurator," he said. "But I believe I am right in saying that a fundamental principle of Roman law holds that where there is no crime there can be no criminals. Since the charge against Lazarus has proved unfounded, it seems to me that that ends the matter."

Pilate was silent for a moment. He seemed highly amused. A Roman to the core, it was flattering to him that Joseph should invoke Roman law. Moreover, the accusation had been brought by the chief rabbi of the Bethany synagogue. What reason did he have to do this Jew a favor? Buried in his mind was also the unacknowledged thought that Mary was present and had not yet spoken. But he did not want Joseph to win so easily.

"You make the matter sound simpler than it actually is," Pilate said smilingly. "It isn't as clear as all that. I am considering whether I can dispense with the cross and reduce the sentence to the galleys. But you have brought another witness who has not yet spoken up. What have you to say, Mary?"

Mary, who had been standing somewhat timidly beside Joseph, raised her head and looked squarely into the Prosecutor's smiling face. She felt that a great deal depended on what she said to Pilate.

"About the legal dispute I understand nothing, Procurator, and can say nothing," she said simply. "We obeyed the law by taking in and tending him—this I am sure of."

"The law . . . the law . . . what law?" Pilate demanded.

"The law that the Master teaches us," Mary replied calmly.

"The Master—I suppose you mean this Jesus of Nazareth—your prophet—your Messiah! The man who practices magic on the dead."

"The Son of God!" Mary cried.

Pilate seemed momentarily surprised at this exclamation. Then, with a sarcastic smile playing around his lips, he said:

"The Son of God who wanders through the countryside as a

beggar. A curious Son of God indeed. You do not demand much of your gods. Up to now you've got along with just one—now, it seems, he has acquired a son. At least we Romans make emperors into gods. Among your people the lowest vagrant wins such an honor it appears."

"You may mock, Pilate," said Mary. "But if you had ever seen him . . ."

The Procurator interrupted her with a wave of his hand.

"Do not express such a wish, Mary," he said. "It might not turn out well for him if I had occasion to see him. Calling on the name of your—master, if you will, does not get around the fact that your brother has made a confession." He turned to Lazarus. "Why did you do that?"

"It is forbidden to tell lies," Lazarus replied.

"Who forbids it? Your law? If that is so I must say that on the whole it is scarcely obeyed. Lies are common coinage in Jerusalem—perhaps more than elsewhere. You knew what risk you were running, Lazarus. How could you be so incautious as to speak the truth? For my part I must admire the laws of your old high priests. All they demand is a few lambs for the Temple from someone who has committed a wrong and the wrong is at once undone. Why didn't you do the same, Lazarus?"

"Because the Master abhors lying," Lazarus replied stubbornly.

"The Master—again the Master! Incidentally—" Pilate cast a penetrating glance at Joseph—"it would be worth while knowing whether there are any links between this Master and the followers of Barabbas. Do you know anything about that, Joseph?"

"There is no connection at all between Jesus and Barabbas," Joseph responded. "On the contrary, there can be no greater contradiction than that between Jesus and Barabbas. Jesus is the man of patience, Barabbas the man of violence. Water and fire are not more opposed."

"Then it seems strange to me that this man Ezra should have been brought to Lazarus' house, of all places, when it is well known that he is a follower of Jesus."

"Men prize in others qualities they do not have themselves, Procurator. When Ezra was brought to Lazarus' house those who brought him probably did so because it is so well known that Lazarus lives by the teachings of the Master."

Pilate was by now eager to put an end to the matter. But it was hard for him to beat a retreat.

"You have a good answer to everything, Joseph," he said. "But I wonder whether your arguments would impress the chief rabbi of the Bethany synagogue? Or the high priest Annas, who certainly has heard about the affair and who has a son at the court of Augustus? You see, there are many things a Procurator must consider if he wants no trouble with Rome."

"Be merciful, Procurator!" Mary pleaded, raising her hands imploringly.

Pilate looked at her for a long while—a look that made her cast down her eyes.

"I might let your brother go," he said, "and keep you here as a hostage." When the girl shrank back in fright, Pilate added: "Under Claudia's supervision, of course."

Claudia gave him a glance full of amazement. Pilate felt that he had got himself into an uncomfortable position. He decided at last to abandon the whole affair.

"It is repulsive to me," he said, "to make capital out of Lazarus' idiotic implication of himself. Ezra was not found in your home and I accept the testimony of Joseph and Mary. You did not know that the man was an escaped prisoner. It is my finding that the charge against you, Lazarus, was brought unjustly—you are free. And I will have the accuser whipped—that will be a salutary lesson for him and his friend, the high priest. Are you satisfied with my verdict, Lazarus."

"Lord, I thank you for showing grace to me and my house," said Lazarus. "But I also ask mercy for the man who accused me. Do not punish him."

"But he is your enemy, Lazarus."

"That he may be, but I am not his enemy. I plead for him, O Procurator. Your mercy will only be perfect if you spare him as well. Joseph, Mary—help me plead!"

Pilate looked at Lazarus and at the imploring hands of Mary and Joseph. Then he turned away irritably.

"What kind of people are you!" he exclaimed. "I believe you would let yourself be whipped, Lazarus, in place of the man who wished to send you to the cross. Or wouldn't you?"

"Yes, Procurator, if by doing so I could serve him," Lazarus said quietly.

A deep furrow cut across the Procurator's high forehead and his thin lips curled in bafflement. His eyes met Mary's beseeching gaze.

"This is beyond my comprehension," he said. "The informer will be imprisoned for a few days—that much I owe to myself and to justice and to the prestige of Rome. Go now, Lazarus, you are free. I hope, Joseph, that you will visit me more often. There are many things I should like to discuss with you. And you, Mary, remember that you are always welcome in my house and do not, in your enthusiasm for the man from Nazareth, altogether forget your old friends. Don't thank me. Peace be with you."

As Lazarus, Mary, and Joseph left, dusk was falling in the chamber. Pilate remained standing in the back of the room. The gathering twilight made his pale face seem lighter than usual. He did not notice when Claudia silently slipped out of the room.

"The Master, the Master . . ." he was murmuring to himself.

He felt that he had suffered a defeat.

11

"... Neither in This Mountain Nor Yet at Jerusalem ..."

BARABBAS, EZRA, AND ONE COMPANION HAD, IN THEIR FLIGHT, ALREADY left the inhabited regions behind and were nearing their camp. It was early morning of the sixth day since Barabbas had rescued Ezra from Bethany, and there was a brisk wind blowing across the plain, which already seemed lightly mantled in fresh green. In the northeast sharp prongs of the Hauran Mountain Range gashed the bright horizon. Outcroppings of stone increased in frequency—evidence that they were nearing the desert.

Ezra had stood up very well under the strain of riding. In fact, the open air seemed to do him more good than the tenderest care in Lazarus' house. With Lazarus' cloak drawn tightly around his shoulders he sat hunched upon his mule and his weakness was scarcely noticeable until he had to dismount. Barabbas did everything possible to make the strenuous flight easier for the sick man. He cared for Ezra like a brother, and Ezra could scarcely have been happier than he now that their long ride was approaching its end.

They were entering a land where grass no longer grew. The hoofs of the mules crunched into sand, and before them stretched wind-driven billows of sand extending as far as they could see, the plain broken only by the boulders strewn here and there like islands in a yellow sea.

"It will be over soon, Ezra," Barabbas said encouragingly. "Then you can rest."

Ezra nodded.

"Are you sure, Barabbas," he asked, "that the soldier who wounded me really didn't escape?"

He had already put this question to Barabbas well over a dozen times.

"Positive," Barabbas said. "I killed him myself."

"Too bad."

"Why too bad, Ezra?"

"I would have liked to lay my hands on him."

"You will have enough Roman soldiers to lay your hands on," said Barabbas.

Ezra shook his head discontentedly.

"But not that one. He is dead. It's not the same thing, Barabbas, to kill others in his stead. Vengeance is real only when you get the man who has injured you, the same man."

"Your wound is avenged. By death."

"You avenged it, not I. And death—that isn't the worst thing that can happen to a man. I should like to have kept him alive and treated him as I was treated in the workshops . . ."

They were now drawing near to one of those islands of boulders where Barabbas and his men had set up headquarters. The natural caves in this tangled mass of rock, supplemented by light tents, formed the camp in which the army of rebels was to assemble. A part of it was already gathered here. They lived with the herds on which they depended for food; the animals pastured on the near-by plain and on the oases which, surrounded by rocks, could not be seen from outside. To the detachments of Roman soldiers that occasionally appeared in the vicinity these men seemed merely nomadic shepherds like many others, and aroused no suspicion.

The men in camp had already caught sight of the newcomers. A large number of men came running toward them and Barabbas and Ezra were greeted noisily.

"Where is Joel?" Barabbas asked when the tumult subsided.

The man to whom Barabbas had addressed this question appeared to be somewhat embarrassed.

"In the camp," he said. "There has been a little . . . quarrel. Joel will probably tell you about it."

He sounded somewhat defiant. Joel was the man who on Barabbas' return from Magdala had led the little band that took three sheep from the Samaritan shepherds. Barabbas had shown him favor because of his energetic temperament and in his absence had appointed Joel his deputy.

"A quarrel—what does that mean? With whom?"

"With the Samaritans. They would not take orders from Joel and have gone off."

"Where are they?"

"Away. They went back to Samaria. Today is the fifth day since they left the camp. They took their arms with them and also the animals that were assigned to them."

Barabbas had turned pale. His teeth dug deep into his lower lip.

"You stand there and tell me this as if it didn't matter at all," he shouted at the speaker, who had moved a good distance away from Barrabas' mule.

Barabbas leapt from the saddle, threw the reins to one of the men and strode ahead. The man who had spoken to him tried to keep pace with him.

"As a matter of fact we were all glad about it, Barabbas," he said. "We were glad to see all those heathen clear out. They wanted to sit at the same table with believers. You ought not blame Joel. He did what all the Israelites in camp wanted to have done . . ."

Barabbas did not reply, but the look he gave the man shut the fellow up.

At the entrance to the camp Joel stepped forward, at the head of a band of men who were crowded behind him in the narrow path between two walls of rock. The young man looked defiantly at Barabbas, but he raised his hand and spoke the formula of greeting, in which he was joined by the men behind him.

"You don't seem to have been in too much of a hurry to greet me, Joel," Barabbas said, to all appearances quite calm. "It seems you prefer to have others inform me of what has happened in my absence."

Joel shrugged.

"I am not to blame. It had to happen. We should never have taken in those Samaritan dogs."

"You think so, do you? 'We should'—that means I should never have taken them in, doesn't it? You take it on yourself to decide that my orders are wrong, do you? And while I am gone you drive away my best men—yes, my best men!"

"I didn't drive them away," the young man said stubbornly.

"Didn't you? But you and all the rest of you treated them so shabbily that they left of their own accord. Do you know what this means?"

Joel and the others were silent.

"I'll tell you. It means that it will be impossible for us to strike this summer. We are too weak. You fools—don't you know that we need every man, every arm?" He turned to Joel again. "Dogs, you say? 'Samaritan dogs'? You son of a she-dog, you speak of yourself."

Joel smiled, a tight-lipped smile.

At once Barabbas' fist flashed toward him and struck the young man between the eyes. Without a sound, Joel crumbled to the ground. Barabbas stood, his clenched fist still raised, looking at the men who stood before him. An angry murmur arose for a moment, but died out immediately. The men saw their leader's eyes and shrank back.

"Take him to his tent," Barabbas said, pointing to the unconscious Joel. "And from now on Judah commands the camp in my absence."

Without another word, he strode through the lane that opened before him into the interior of the camp. Ezra followed slowly, leaning on their companion's arm, while Joel was carried back.

Barabbas took a few trusted men to the cave where he lived and heard the details about the dispute between the Israelites and the Samaritans. He swiftly realized that in their judgment and treatment of the Samaritans his men had been guided by traditional prejudices. The Samaritans had felt offended because the majority of the Israelites treated them as heathen, as unclean creatures.

"How did open hostilities break out?" Barabbas asked.

"They were dissatisfied with the distribution of meat-animals," one of the men replied. "The Samaritan leader complained, a dispute arose and Joel hit the Samaritan hard. After that the Samaritans gathered around their leader and left."

Barabbas sat in silence for a while, mulling over the problem. He was both personally affronted at this breach of his authority and worried because his plans were imperiled by it. He knew these men acknowledged his leadership only because they feared his physical strength and because they expected to reap advantage from the success of his plans. Otherwise—otherwise they considered him, the half-Jew, no better than a gentile. He could actually trust only a few dozen men who had been with him from the beginning. And even those, as the example of Joel demonstrated, were not absolutely trustworthy. The realization of this fact was more depressing to Barabbas than the loss of nine hundred Samaritans and the probability that from now on Samaritans would no longer join his army. Barabbas was clever enough to realize that insubordination in his own camp constituted his greatest danger. He resolved to nip it in the bud.

For the present he retired into his cave with Ezra alone and held no further conversations with any of his men. He was waiting for Judah's return. Judah, a small, agile man with an ugly but intelligent face, was one of Barabbas' most trusted followers. He was not so much a warrior as the orator of Barabbas' movement. It was Judah who had painted his banditry in nationalistic colors and who had first given form to Barabbas' confused ambitions. Judah had started and built up the movement in Jerusalem and other cities. He also administered Barabbas' financial affairs, receiving the contributions from the priests and the wealthier among the laiety and seeing to the needs of the constantly growing army.

When Judah entered Barabbas' skin-lined cave, he saw the leader sitting beside the bed that he had arranged for Ezra.

"You sent for me, Barabbas," he said abruptly, without troubling to exchange greetings. "I already know the story of the Samaritans' quitting. How stupid of Joel to push things so far."

"Stupid? It was criminal! How could you permit such things to happen?"

"It was you who gave the command to Joel when you left," said Judah without a trace of reproach in his voice.

"And couldn't you do anything to stop him?"

"No. He and his followers were like madmen. I tried hard enough to show them how much we needed the Samaritans. But it was no use."

"Well, what do you advise now, Judah?"

Judah was evidently prepared for this question, for he answered without hesitation:

"You have two possibilities, Barabbas. Either you can accept the Samaritans' departure as an unalterable fact and base the movement in the future exclusively on Israelites, or you can punish with the greatest severity the men who made trouble with the Samaritans against your express wish. If you make mincemeat of Joel and perhaps four or five of his lieutenants, we shall have peace in the camp."

Barabbas stared gloomily at the wall of the cave.

"Which of these two recourses would you take?" he asked finally.

Judah had a keen mind and a coldly cruel disposition. Barabbas had little doubt what his answer would be.

"Do you ask that seriously, Barabbas? You yourself know that we simply can't spare the Samaritans. And purging the movement of future traitors can only be useful to us."

"Traitors?" Barabbas queried.

"There is no other name for them. It is treason merely to undermine your prestige. If Joel and his men succeed in their first rebellion against your authority, it may soon come to a point where you will have nothing more to say. Either you enforce your will right now or we had best break up at once."

Barabbas did not reply immediately. In his heart he was convinced that Judah was right and that he must act with extreme severity. He himself did not know why he was hesitating now at shedding blood. True, he had a weakness for comrades who had shared perils and miseries with him and it oppressed him to have some of them killed now, of all times, when a better future loomed before them all. But that was not it. There flashed through his mind the memory of the scene that night in Magdala, when the man of Nazareth had tamed his raging men by his mere presence. Why had he himself no such gift, he wondered.

But it was this very memory that forced him to overcome his irresoluteness and give Judah a decisive answer.

"You are right, Judah," he said. "Call the lieutenants to a meeting. Have Joel come too. I cannot kill all who agree with him, but he and his closest lieutenants must die. Give a few dependable men the necessary instructions. Let them enter at a sign from you and make away with Joel and those you pick out. I will take care of some of them myself . . ."

Judah rose and left, highly pleased at the leader's decision. Ezra, who had listened attentively to the conversation, looked up at Barabbas with shining eyes.

"This is the way I love you, Barabbas," he said. "Death to the traitors!"

But that was not to be.

A few moments after he had left Judah returned again in breathless excitement.

"Joel is gone, and three of his lieutenants as well," he cried to Barabbas. "I have given orders for them to be pursued and brought back dead or alive."

Barabbas sprang to his feet, but when he spoke his tone was extremely calm.

"How long have they been gone?"

"More than two hours. And on our best mules."

"Barabbas smiled.

"I would not have expected them to take the worst. Naturally they won't be caught. And it is just as well. What sort of impression has their flight made on the rest?"

"A very bad one, as far as I can see. The men are outraged."

"I thought so. In that case they have done us a service by fleeing."

"Suppose they betray us?" Judah asked excitedly.

"I don't think they'll be so stupid. Joel knows perfectly well that the Romans would crucify him even if he did them the favor of betraying us. No—I'll hear no objections, Judah. I am very pleased with the way this affair has turned out. I'll address the men later. Then we will try to patch up the dispute with the Samaritans. Go now and assemble the men."

Judah seemed on the point of saying something, but he apparently thought better of it, for he turned to go.

"One more thing," Barabbas called after him. "Find out whether blind Eliazar has some fresh goat milk for Ezra. He is still very weak."

Judah nodded and left. A curious man, this Barabbas, he mused. A few minutes ago he was ready to order a blood bath and now he thinks of goat milk for Ezra.

An hour later Barabbas appeared before his men, who had gathered, some twelve hundred strong, in the open square that was used for mass meetings.

Barabbas, ordinarily a rather poor speaker, was in splendid form. Speaking calmly but forcefully, he showed his men how foolish it had been to offend the Samaritans and thus weaken the movement so that the date of final victory over the Romans would have to be postponed indefinitely. Did they want to go on living for years like savage, hunted beasts? That they did not. Joel and his men had passed judgment on themselves by their flight. If they fled to the Romans, or fell into the enemy's hands, their death was assured. The Romans loved treachery but always crucified the traitors. Only under his, Barabbas', protection were they assured of safety, and the victory would bring rich rewards for them all. Were they agreed that he should try to persuade the Samaritans to return?

"Bring the Samaritans back!" they shouted from all sides. "Curses on Joel!"

They shouted loudest who had earlier behaved worst toward the Samaritans.

The following day Barabbas left the camp and rode westward unaccompanied. He had installed Judah as commander-in-chief during his absence and provided him with a powerful, resolute bodyguard so that he would be able to command respect. The men who had ridden out in pursuit of Joel and his companions had returned during the night; they had lost the trail of the fugitives.

A warm wind from the west blew in his face as he rode. It was a splendid day, with the promise of spring in the air; the sun shone from an unspotted azure sky. Birds shot up into the crystal air and the plain lay like a smooth, bright-green mat before him.

Barabbas had no eyes for the splendors of awakening spring. He did not like this flat plain where there was no place to hide; and he was too immersed in his thoughts to notice the day—gloomy thoughts of burning ambition, impatience, dissatisfaction with the slow progress of his plans. His patrons in Jerusalem kept their hands tightly on the purse strings, doled out with much bargaining the sums he needed for provisioning and arming his men, plagued him about the Samaritans and pressed him to do something about the man from Nazareth. "Better for one man to die than a whole nation," Annas, the high priest, had said in reference to Jesus. Rabbi Nathaniel had reported the words to Barabbas. Why did the high priest consider this harmless crackpot so dangerous, Barabbas wondered. And he answered his own question: it was because of the strength within the man. He remembered again how the man had stood with radiant countenance at the door of Lazarus' house, casting a spell upon himself and his comrades with his eyes alone.

The sun was at zenith when Barabbas arrived at a nomad camp whose dwellers had known him for years. He found them in a state of great excitement. The departing Samaritans had robbed them of a large number of sheep, and last night Joel and his three companions had passed by, eaten and drunk, and suddenly ridden off without paying.

Barabbas placated the people and promised to pay them for the sheep.

"Do you know what direction the four men took?" Barabbas asked one of the shepherds, for he had no desire to meet up with them.

"We followed them until nightfall but they escaped us; they must have ridden due south," he was told.

Barabbas rode on, pleased by what he had heard. He had reasoned that Joel and his men would scarcely have ridden toward Samaria, where they would not have received a very friendly reception. He need not worry about meeting them.

By evening he had left the flat plain and come into a region where the ground rose and fell slightly. In the distance a few scattered hills could be seen. Under wretched olive trees stood a few miserable huts whose inhabitants wrenched a hard living from the land. These people, too, were friends of Barabbas and had often sheltered him. Here, too, he was given some valuable information.

"Take care, Barabbas," one of his friends told him. "A big detachment of Roman soldiers passed by today headed north."

Barabbas learned that the soldiers were part of a scouting expedition; there were many of these always roaming the country. But what particularly interested him was the news that the soldiers had had two Jewish prisoners with them.

"Was Joel one of them?" he asked, for the people were well acquainted with Joel and his other more important lieutenants.

"No," an old shepherd replied. "But the two were your men. I've seen them with you."

This convinced Barabbas that two of Joel's companions had fallen into the hands of the Romans. What had happened to Joel and the other lieutenant? Had they succeeded in making their escape or were they dead? He was quite sure that Joel did not intend to make common cause with the Romans. But if not with the Romans, with whom?

Mulling over this unpleasant problem, Barabbas continued his ride.

Toward nine in the evening Barabbas on his exhausted mule neared Jacob's Well, not far from the Samaritan city of Shechem. The Samaritans gave all the places in their valley names reminiscent of the age of the patriarchs; this well they considered to be Jacob's gift to Joseph.

The sun lay warm and bright upon the meadows that spread out between the city and Mount Gerizim, the herds pastured upon the undulating land, the men and women labored in the fields and the gentle wind bore the fragrance of the germinating earth and the sound of merry singing.

Barabbas had bound his kerchief around his head so as to conceal his face. To the cries of greeting from shepherds and toilers in the fields he replied by waving without stopping. It was the custom of the country to greet all passers-by.

He reached the well. Heaps of stones lay scattered about, probably the remains of an ancient building which centuries earlier had sheltered travelers who visited the well. Since the building of the city of Shechem the shelter, no longer of use, had fallen into ruins. Now the stones served as seats for the women of Shechem who rested after drawing water from the deep well—water that was not only sweet and fresh, but a curative for many ills.

Barabbas was about to pass by when his eyes fell upon the figure of a man who sat by the well; a man in a red undergarment and a white cloak which fell about him in loose folds. The sun gleamed upon his fair brow and was reflected from his eyes, which were directed at a woman crouching near by. Beside the woman stood a clay jug.

Barabbas recognized the man. It was Jesus of Nazareth.

The thought passed through him like a flash: now he could do what the priests were demanding of him. There was not a soul in sight beside the woman with the jug, from which she had apparently offered the Nazarene water. With one blow the man the priests hated and who had turned so many men away from him would be done for.

Barabbas reined in his mule and dismounted. Neither the man nor the woman paid any attention to him. They were absorbed in their conversation. Barabbas wanted to hear what Jesus would say to the Samaritan woman. He knew that Jesus, too, associated with Samaritans; but it seemed strange even to him that this Jew should not mind drinking from the "unclean" jug of a Samaritan woman. Barabbas pretended he was about to draw water from the well and, sitting down on a stone behind the well, eavesdropped.

The woman was speaking.

"Lord, our fathers worshipped on this mountain, but you say we must worship in Jerusalem."

The man from Nazareth replied:

"Woman, believe me, the hour cometh when you shall neither on this mountain, nor yet at Jerusalem, worship the Father, but in that place where the true worshippers shall worship the Father in spirit and in truth."

The voice sounded gentle and kindly, but it seemed to Barabbas he had heard a thunderclap. What did it mean? What was the man saying? He, Barabbas, did not care overmuch about Jerusalem, nor was he particularly concerned about Mount Gerizim which his mother so loved. But if the people were to believe in Israel's promised power and glory, how could they do so if they were told that their faith was no more rooted in Jerusalem than it was in the gentiles' Mount Gerizim, or any other place in this world? What, in any case, was this faith? Did it not mean that Israel was God's chosen people, destined to rule over other nations and be free in its own land? What else was the meaning of the belief in the Messiah who was claimed by many to be this man at the well, and by many others to be himself, Barabbas? What promise was the liberator of Israel to fulfil if not the promise of Israel's future empire?

Not a thought, not an emotion was stirred up in Barabbas' untrained mind and unsoftened heart with regard to the latter place which the Nazarene had named. All Barabbas understood was: It will not be in Jerusalem. He did not know why these words had aroused such turbulent feelings in him. Then a sudden insight dawned upon him.

What the man of Nazareth had said meant no more nor less than that he recognized no historical tradition, no native land; that, therefore, he denied the right of the priests, and the right of Barabbas and his movement, to derive from the law and the prophets a promise that Israel would have great power.

Now Barabbas suddenly understood why the high priests hated this man so passionately, why they believed it was better for one man to die than a whole nation. And now he understood why there could never be any agreement between Jesus of Nazareth and himself.

What he, Barabbas, promised the people was the creation by combat and violence of a new Israel on this sacred soil. What he, Jesus of Nazareth, promised was renunciation of a new Israel—renunciation through patient suffering and humility which would never be rewarded upon this earth.

Barabbas stared grimly into the depths of the well. His first excitement over the initially incomprehensible words of Jesus of Nazareth had given way to a feeling of profound depression. Could not these words also be interpreted as a prophecy that all his striving and all his ambitions would come to nought? Since Barabbas considered Jesus if not a prophet at least a sorcerer and soothsayer, what the man had said made Barabbas thoroughly uncomfortable.

He wondered for a moment whether he ought not to go up to Jesus and demand an explanation of his words. Curiously enough, the thought of harming the man had quite receded. Jesus still sat, peaceful and silent, beside the well, his hand held in blessing above the head of the Samaritan woman.

"The day draws nigh its end, woman, and I have still far to go. Peace be with you!" Barabbas heard Jesus say. Then he saw the Nazarene rise.

From the hills sounded the bells of the lead animals in the herds and through the air shrilled the jubilant cry of the swallows flying northwest. Barabbas saw a band of men approaching the well from the direction of Shechem.

Why am I letting him go? Barabbas asked himself. Why am I unwilling to win the reward that the high priest and the Pharisees have set upon his head? Is it because the Samaritans are approaching? Could I tell them I have killed a defenseless man who spoke kindly words to a Samaritan woman and drank the water she offered?

Jesus passed by the well and caught sight of the man with the kerchief covering his face.

"Peace be with you!" Jesus said to Barabbas, and walked on in the direction of the city of Samaria.

Barabbas turned abruptly toward Jesus and appeared to be on the point of hastening after him or calling to him. But then he shook himself, stamped his foot and wrenched his gaze away from the bright figure that moved like a light down the brown, dusty road.

12 ✠

Betrayal

THE MEN ON THE ROAD FROM SHECHEM WERE CLOSER BY NOW. Barabbas recognized the shepherd Eliud heading the group of about two dozen. Eliud had been the leader of the Samaritans in his camp. The men wore swords under their short cloaks and made a fairly warlike impression.

Barabbas laid his hand on his own short sword, which he also wore beneath his cloak.

"Have you come to us as friend or foe?" Eliud called out, slowing his pace and neglecting to exchange the formula of greeting with Barabbas.

Barabbas walked toward him. Now more than ever he was determined to win back the Samaritans. He imagined that the woman from Samaria with whom Jesus had spoken would be returning to that city and would certainly bring there only a good report of the Nazarene. A woman's enthusiasm could do a great deal of harm; Barabbas was afraid that the Nazarene's words might completely tame the rebellious spirit of the Samaritans. And so he answered them with the utmost cordiality.

"Have I ever shown myself your foe, Eliud?"

Eliud stood still and faced him, looking Barabbas up and down with alert suspicion. But his reply was not unfriendly.

"No, not you. You never seemed an enemy of ours." He emphasized the "you."

"Then why do you ask?" Barabbas responded. "How should I be coming as an enemy, since I have come alone?"

Eliud shrugged.

"How do we know whether your men are not hiding in ambush at this very moment?"

"That is foolish, Eliud. If either of us had reason for suspicion it would be I. Will you tell me, Eliud, why you and your men suddenly left the camp?"

The men gathered around Eliud and some of them circled behind Barabbas to block off the road.

"Yes, I will tell you, Barabbas. We could not longer stand the high-handed snobbery of your Israelites. We came to you to join in the common struggle against the Romans. We trusted you. But we did not come to take insults and act like slaves for the Israelites. We love our liberty no less than the Israelites, and we have no intention of exchanging the Roman yoke for the Israelite yoke."

"Take it easy, Eliud," Barabbas remonstrated. "I don't want anything of the sort, as you well know. It was very hasty of you to go off without waiting for my return. If, as you say, you trusted me, you should have known that I would never have permitted you to be insulted."

One of Eliud's men said hotly:

"Joel is your own deputy."

Barabbas turned to the man.

"He was, he is not any more. I am sorry I was mistaken in the man."

Barabbas would have preferred to evade the question of what had happened to Joel. By now he was ashamed that he had not punished Joel's disobedience instantly and instead had given the man time to escape. But Eliud came to the point at once.

"What happened to Joel?" he asked. "If you thought so much of us, you must have avenged us."

"I would have done so, Eliud—you can be sure of that. But when I returned Joel and two of his men fled the camp. What has happened to him since I don't know. But I have restored order in the camp—you may rest assured. You should have waited for my return."

"We didn't know when you were coming back. And we told ourselves: If it's like this before the battle when we're still needed, what will it be like when the battle is over and the Romans have been driven out. Then the Israelites will really begin to remind us that they consider us 'unclean' and 'filthy dogs.' "

"And has it never occurred to you that I won't stand for that, Eliud? That I—belong more to you than to the others?"

Eliud was neither surprised nor suspicious of this statement. He liked Barabbas and was sorry to have broken with him.

"We thought of that, Barabbas," he replied. "As I said, we trusted you. But we are not deaf and blind. Do you know what your men think of you, with few exceptions? To most of them you are nothing but a half Jew whom they obey because you have a powerful fist and because they can't agree on who is to take your place."

Barabbas knew the man spoke shrewdly, but he did not want to—he could not—admit the truth of it.

"Perhaps Joel and his men thought so," he said. "But now the camp is purged of those jackals."

Eliud shook his head.

"No, Barabbas, it isn't only a matter of Joel and his few followers. Do you know that some of your men are in league with the priests in Jerusalem? And that the priests are setting others against you?"

"That isn't true!" Barabbas snarled.

Eliud preserved an unruffled calm.

"Have you ever known me to lie?" he asked. "Let me tell you, Barabbas—some of your own men mistrust you, and the priests who are supplying you with money and arms haven't any intention of letting you take power."

Barabbas turned pale and a quiver of rage and fear passed through his huge frame. Was Eliud telling the truth? Were the priests already preparing to stab him in the back? And was it possible that his own men were allying themselves with the priests?"

"Which of my men are in league with the priests?" he asked hoarsely.

Eliud gave him a number of names. Joel headed the list.

Barabbas swallowed this information silently. Now that he had admitted the thought to his mind he was convinced that Eliud spoke the truth. So his own men were betraying him! And the priests—probably they were all ready to install that grandson of the

Maccabean in his place. For a moment it seemed to him that he hated the priests a hundred times more furiously than he did the Roman oppressors; he felt that it was more necessary to exterminate these fork-tongued adders than to kill off the legionaries. Such confusion raged behind his bronzed brow that he could not fix on a single distinct thought. It was as if some evil force had suddenly annihilated all his shining projects. The world rocked giddily around him.

A sudden whistle startled him out of his downcast brooding. Danger?

Down the road along which he had come trotted a small band of mounted men. His keen eyes recognized them at once as Romans.

"Legionaries!" Eliud cried out. "Hide, Barabbas, or you are lost. Climb down into the well—there is a ladder—over there on the other side. Hurry, before they see you!"

"What about you?" Barabbas asked tonelessly. He looked around with a resolute expression.

"Us? Leave that to us. We are just peaceful inhabitants of Shechem. Hurry—hide."

Crouching, Barabbas ran to the other side of the well where the ruins of the ancient building hid him from the sight of the Romans. He clambered swiftly over the brink and vanished into the depths of the well. He had moved almost mechanically, with the feeling that this attempt to escape was utterly vain.

The Roman detachment approached swiftly. It was only six or seven men strong, clearly one of those small detachments that roamed through the countryside to keep order.

The Romans had approached to within some thirty paces when Eliud perceived another man in the center of the mounted legionaries: Joel. He sat on a mule with his hands tied behind his back. Barabbas, peering over the edge of the well, saw him also. So Joel, too, had fallen into the hands of the Romans. Undoubtedly his two comrades had been picked up by another small detachment like this one. The Samaritans outnumbered the legionaries. If it came to a fight he would be saved, Barabbas reflected.

Just before the well the leader reined in his horse and turned to Joel. "Is he among these men?" he asked in Latin.

"No," Joel answered wearily. He seemed utterly exhausted; his forehead was clotted with dried blood.

"Then speak to these men and ask them," the leader, a decurion, ordered.

"There's no use," Joel said in laborious Latin. "I know these men. They are friends of his. They've been in his camp and are his own soldiers. They won't tell you anything—the best thing to do is to cut these dogs down."

The decurion surveyed the situation. The group of Samaritans was three times larger than his detachment and he knew these men were good fighters. He was not at all anxious to attack or be attacked.

"We aren't interested in these men," he said. "Anyway, how do I know you aren't lying? Ask them about Barabbas!"

With his knees Joel guided his mule forward and spoke to Eliud. "Barabbas passed this way," he said. "Will you tell us where to find him? Speak up—no harm will come to you. I told the decurion you are no longer with Barabbas."

"You lie, you desert-wolf!" Eliud cried. "I know enough of their tongue to understand what you said to the soldiers."

Meanwhile the legionaries had dismounted and were leading their horses to the stone trough to which Barabbas' mule was still tied. Obviously they intended to water their horses, and would certainly discover Barabbas hiding in the well. But Barabbas recognized the danger and forestalled them. With one great leap he sprang to Eliud's side and cried out to the Samaritans in a thunderous voice: "Cut them down!"

As if seized by frenzy, the Samaritans fell upon the completely surprised legionaries with flashing swords and swinging clubs. The uneven battle was soon over. The Romans fell where they stood. The decurion alone defended himself desperately until the blow of a club knocked him down and a sword finished him off.

Joel, as surprised as the Romans by the assault, suddenly saw his captors lying dead on the ground and was overcome by panic. He realized at once that it was much worse for him to fall into the hands of Barabbas and the angry Samaritans. From the Romans he could have hoped for mercy if he had succeeded in turning Barabbas over to them. The Samaritans and Barabbas would show no mercy to a traitor.

He urged his mule away, trying to escape. But he was unlucky; the mule stepped into a hole in the ground, stumbled, reared up and threw Joel, who was handicapped by his fettered hands, from the saddle.

A moment later the Samaritans fell upon him, pulled him to his feet and dragged him over to the well.

Barabbas glared furiously at the man. Unconsciously the thought ran through his mind that he was now at the same spot where the man of Nazareth had sat a short time before. What would he do in my place? Barabbas asked himself. Forgive? What had he said that time in Magdala? "Woe unto them that use violence?" What a ridiculous idea, Barabbas thought. Where would he be now, where would the Samaritans be, if they had not used violence? Had Joel hesitated to use it?

He felt more sure of his course.

"Traitor!" he said curtly to Joel. "Have you anything to say to me?"

Joel did not reply. He stared defiantly at Barabbas. His teeth had dug into his lower lip so that a thin stream of blood was flowing down into his beard.

Barabbas gave a sign to the Samaritan standing closest to Joel. The next moment the man's heavy club thudded down upon Joel's head. Joel fell without a sound.

"So all traitors must end," Barabbas said. And then he added, "And all Romans."

He felt certain that he had won the Samaritans back to his cause.

13 𝕏

"O Jerusalem, Jerusalem,
Which Killest the Prophets..."

IN THE HOME OF CAIAPHAS, THE HIGH PRIEST, THE PRIESTS OF THE
first degree had gathered for a conference under the chairmanship of
old Annas. The alleged purpose of the conference was to discuss
preparations for the Passover Feast; and some of the more ingenuous
priests wondered why they were taking this trouble since all the arrangements were a matter of old routine. In reality Caiaphas had
convoked the priests in order to discuss with them two important
points, or rather two personalities: Jesus of Nazareth and Barabbas.

The Passover problems were settled rapidly. Then Caiaphas said:
"Rabbi Nathaniel will give us a report on the movement of Barabbas ben Ezekiel."

The alliance between Barabbas and the priesthood had been in
force for a good many weeks. The inner circle of priests around
Caiaphas knew about the recent events in the camp. Reports were
confused on what had happened in Samaria and the priests did not
yet know of Joel's fate. According to one report Barabbas, after having defeated a Roman detachment, was busy arming the Samaritans
for the uprising. According to another report he was hiding in the
vicinity of Jericho, staying at the home of a woman who had run
away from her husband.

"According to all I have heard," Rabbi Nathaniel said, "the movement which at first seemed so promising to us has suffered a severe setback. Our informers in the camp report that Judah, whom Barabbas placed in supreme command, has not been able to establish his authority. There is only a small minority under the leadership of a man named Ezra who still cling to Barabbas. The majority want a new leader."

Caiaphas raised his hand. A grim crease stood out on the brow of the huge, dark-complexioned, uncouth man, and his low voice was tense with suppressed excitement as he spoke.

"It was a mistake from the first to tolerate this Barabbas as the head of the movement," he said. "The fact that he is a robber and a murderer does not disturb me—God-fearing men cannot be used for this work. But his mother was a Samaritan; that is why he should not lead Israelite warriors. The money we have given him has therefore been wasted. I suggest that we withdraw all support from this movement. If it is true that he is hiding with some woman in Jericho, the best thing to do would be to put the Romans on his trail. We must see to it that the man disappears."

Rabbi Nathaniel cast a questioning glance at old Annas. It was he, after all, who had given his blessing to the alliance with Barabbas. Had he changed his mind since then?

Annas signed to Nathaniel to continue his report.

"You are all well aware," Nathaniel said, "that from the beginning the Maccabean, Juda ben Jacob, was suggested as the head of the movement. I would recommend that we return to that plan. I doubt whether we can afford to drop Barabbas just yet. Another split in the movement might endanger the success of the uprising as a whole."

Caiaphas interrupted him.

"You say yourself, Rabbi Nathaniel, that the majority are demanding a new leader. Good. If the high priests and the priests of the first degree here assembled should decide that the movement as such ought to receive our continued support, I cannot do anything about that. But about the nomination of Juda ben Jacob as the new leader— I know him and I don't think much of him. He refers continually to his great forefathers but he himself has not yet done anything at all. The fact that he makes a great deal of money by exploiting the laborers in his glass workshops does not qualify him as a leader of an uprising. And a warrior he certainly is not. If we choose him, we should have to give him an adjutant who knows something about military matters. Do you have any in mind?"

Annas raised his wan face with its fringe of white beard. He indicated by a slight gesture of his hand that he wanted to speak. And the priests knew that Caiaphas' opinion would not count at all if his father-in-law disagreed. They waited eagerly.

"I am in favor of our giving continued support to the movement," Annas said in the clear, resolute voice that so belied his age. "And I am against turning Barabbas over to the Romans. I have seen Barabbas myself and spoken with him. I was by no means displeased with what I saw. He is a good fighter and above all a man. The fact that he has a Samaritan mother simply impels him to be more Israelitish than the Jews. And if we are to provide Juda ben Jacob with a good military adviser, which I have had in mind right along—why not Barabbas? I know no one who would be better fitted for that task. How do we gain if the Romans crucify him? Certainly he is of more value to us living than dead. Consider that."

"It is, then, your opinion, revered father-in-law, that we ought to get in touch with Barabbas?" Caiaphas asked, returning to the question at hand.

"I think that is the only way if the money we have donated is not to be thrown away entirely," Annas said sternly.

For a moment there was dead silence in the huge conference room. Then Zebulon, priest of the first degree, raised his withered, trembling hand to indicate that he wanted to speak. Zebulon had passed his hundredth year; he could move about only with the aid of two walking-sticks and was held in great respect, especially by the older members of the priesthood. He was a very pious man and one of pure heart, one of the few men in this group in whom there was no falsehood.

In his high, quavering voice that broke frequently from emotion he began to speak:

"For the first time I am hearing about things that fill me with horror. Revolt? A robber and murderer at the head? And the priesthood is supporting this uprising? The man has been given money by us? And High Priest Caiaphas speaks of having the man killed? What has this to do with our service in the Temple, with the service of the All Highest? What are we getting into? I am an old man and my eyes have seen much—at the end of my days shall they yet have to see the priests of the Lord walking in the paths of evil-doing? I warn you . . ."

Annas interrupted the old man.

"Rabbi Zebulon," he said sharply, "you are speaking of matters with which you are unfamiliar. We are discussing the necessity for the people of Israel to throw off the alien rule, to free themselves from the yoke of the pagans. That, Rabbi Zebulon, will not be accomplished solely by prayers and by sacrifices at the altar of the Lord, but by deeds. The Lord does not see the instrument; He sees only the will. What could be more pleasing to Him than the struggle for the liberation of His chosen people? Evildoing, you say? In the struggle for liberty there is no such thing as evildoing. Deeds that we would otherwise shun are sanctified by the goal."

The assembled priests listened with bated breath to this dispute between the two old men. All of them felt that the conflict was not one of words alone, that Annas was defending above all the prestige of his "family of high priests." It had been seventeen years since Annas, son of Seth, had last held office, but they all continued to call him "high priest" and to bow to his will in all important matters concerning Judaism. Five of his sons in succession had held the office of high priest and now his son-in-law held it. No one had ever before dared to question Annas' word or to attack his prestige.

Rabbi Zebulon seemed aware of the importance of his role. During the high priest's speech he had been shaking his head vigorously and as soon as Annas finished he replied:

"Tell me, Annas, in what Scriptures is that written? Shall we no longer obey the word of God, that vengeance is His? Piety and zeal in the service of the Lord alone can bring us salvation, not the bloody hands of hired murderers and robbers."

Annas waved his hand as though to brush away Rabbi Zebulon's objections.

"By fasting and praying," he said, "by burnt offerings and sacrifices we will not drive the enemies of our nation from the land. Who has eyes to see must recognize that the alien rule, the rule of these heathens, means not only physical oppression but makes the people waver in their loyalty to the law. The Lord's people are menaced by two great perils, perils that may destroy them. The source of one of these perils is the Romans . . ."

"Is our religion no longer respected?" Rabbi Zebulon interrupted in his high voice.

Annas looked frostily at the old man.

"Our religion is still respected because the Emperor in Rome is a gentle man. But is our service to God to depend on the mood of a man far off in the west? How do we know that his successor will not place accursed heathen idols in our Temple? How do we know that they will not compel us to bring sacrifices to these idols? Do we not already have Israelites, even here in the Holy City, who have made their peace with the foe of the people and of Israel's God? The gates will be thrown wide to heresy if we do nothing against this Roman plague. There is only one salvation for Israel—and that in battle. But for battle we need warriors. That is why I favor the warrior Barabbas. It is written, 'Your enemies will fall before you by the sword.' Barabbas must be the sword of Israel."

Annas paused briefly at this point, not so much to give Rabbi Zebulon the opportunity to reply as to determine the sentiments of the other priests. Some of them were looking toward Rabbi Zebulon, but the majority had their eyes on Annas and were nodding agreement. Clearly, Annas had the priests on his side and could expect further opposition only from the aged rabbi.

Rabbi Zebulon said:

"It is written that our enemies shall fall by the sword. But only, 'if ye walk in my statutes and keep my commandments and do them.' It is not keeping the commandments to hire murderers. You say, Annas, that those in Rome may try to lay impious hands on our religion. Has that not been tried before and is it not the greatest triumph of our people that countless numbers of them have borne testimony with their blood to their reverence for the one true God?"

High Priest Caiaphas sensed that the debate was on the point of degenerating into bickering over scriptural interpretation, and he knew that such arguments could go on forever. He wanted the conference to keep to the practical questions and therefore intervened in the discussion.

"All honor to your piety and your zeal, Rabbi Zebulon," he said, "but there are matters that are foreign to your unworldly way of thought. My father-in-law mentioned that the Romans were but one of the two perils confronting our nation. May I ask him to explain what the second peril is?"

Annas at once perceived the adroitness of his son-in-law's maneuver. "The second peril may well be the gravest," he said. "It is Jesus of Nazareth."

The priests shifted excitedly in their seats. It was obvious that while they might be divided in their opinions of Barabbas, they were almost of one mind with regard to Jesus of Nazareth. But Rabbi Zebulon spoke up once more.

"What do you have against this righteous man?" he cried, his cracked voice breaking with intensity.

"Do you indeed call him righteous, Rabbi Zebulon?" Annas replied acidly. "Well, it is good that you reveal your thoughts. I know that you are not the only one among the priests of the Temple who has a weakness for this charlatan, this blasphemer, this corrupter of the people. I have heard that you have been thoroughly instructed in his seditious doctrines."

"I do not deny it," Rabbi Zebulon said. "I know his teachings well. And I find no fault in them."

Caiaphas' diversionary tactics had apparently succeeded. Rabbi Zebulon had been driven from attack to defense. Annas took advantage of the opportunity.

"Has God completely taken away your senses, Rabbi Zebulon?" he berated the older man. "I tell you this, Rabbi Zebulon: this man of Nazareth is more dangerous than the gentiles, more dangerous than that vain man in the palace of Herod the Great, more dangerous than the Imperator at Rome. His teachings are nothing but blasphemy of the All Highest. Does he not call himself His son? Does he not speak despitefully of the Temple and of the sacrifices we offer up? Does he not turn the people away from us? Does he not break the Sabbath and go about with gentiles and public sinners? Indeed I need not here recount all the crimes that this man in his blindness has committed—we know them well."

"You lie, high priest!" Rabbi Zebulon exclaimed, his weary old eyes flashing with indignation.

A wave of suppressed excitement passed through the assemblage. High Priest Annas let his outstretched arm drop to the table; Caiaphas tensed as if he were on the point of leaping to his feet and falling upon the aged priest. Annas held his hand on his son-in-law's arm.

"Let be," he said quietly. "I choose not to have heard this outburst of an old man who has lost his mind."

At the lower end of the table a murmur of disapproval was heard. Some of the priests were indignant at this insult to Annas; others apparently did not approve of the manner in which Annas had offended the revered old man. The high priest's eyes were fiery, but he had himself well under control. Quietly, as if he had not been interrupted at all, he continued:

"We know of the crimes of this man, and therefore he must be put out of the way."

"Is it a crime," Rabbi Zebulon interjected once more, "to raise the dead and to heal the leprous and the palsied?"

"It is a crime when it is done for the purpose of convincing the people that the priests of the Eternal are not as powerful as he is. And it is a crime to tell men their sins will be forgiven them. The man has forfeited his life because he threatens the purity of the faith and the binding force of the law. Already all of Galilee is running after him; his following numbers thousands. He is coming to the Holy City for the Passover. This, I tell you, will be the opportunity to put an end to the confusion he has been sowing these past three years."

Rabbi Zebulon raised himself painfully out of his seat. With both hands on the table to support him, he cried:

"Do you intend to kill him?"

Annas replied with unbroken calm:

"Kill him? We do not kill, Rabbi Zebulon. You ought to know that. We will simply see to it that his mischief-making is stopped. It will probably strike the Procurator as fairly important to learn that this man pretends to be the king of the Jews."

With more strength than his frail body seemed capable of, Rabbi Zebulon pushed away the chair that stood behind him and gripped his two walking-sticks.

"I see that I went astray when I came to this assemblage. I have fallen in with conspirators, with murderers, who persecute a righteous man who is a prophet such as Israel has never had before." And raising his voice the old man cried out: "O Jerusalem, Jerusalem, which killest the prophets . . ."

His voice died down in a long moan. Turning, he slowly hobbled from the room without another word. His wooden sandals and two walking-sticks clacked noisily on the stone floor of the room.

Three of the priests who had been sitting at the lower end of the table followed him silently.

After a while Caiaphas snarled:

"He ought to be taken out to the Vale of Josaphat and stoned!"

With a scornful smile Annas replied:

"That would be giving him too much importance. We are fortunate in knowing who is with us and who against us. Now let us return to the subject of Jesus ben Joseph." He turned to the other priests. "I suppose we agree on what must be done. For some unknown reason no one has as yet turned up who could get rid of him without a stir. Barabbas has disappointed me in this respect . . ."

Rabbi Nathaniel raised his hand.

"I know one of the men who is always with him. It is a nephew of mine upon whom I have some influence. A clever young fellow— I've never understood why he runs around after this sorcerer. Perhaps he might be used to good purpose."

"Good," Annas said. "But it would be better, Rabbi Nathaniel, if you make the arrangements through some intermediary who is not directly connected with the Temple."

High Priest Caiaphas glanced irritably at his father-in-law.

"I don't understand this eternal caution," he said. "Why can't we try him right out in the open? His crimes against the law are well known. Isn't it enough that he has gone so far as to revoke the Ten Commandments and has tried to replace them by two? I am convinced the Sanhedrin would sentence him to death for that alone."

"Certainly," Annas replied with an ironic smile. "And what then? What happens after we sentence him to death?"

"Why, then he will be executed."

"Do you think so? What about the Procurator? I'll tell you what will happen. That Roman would let the Nazarene go free if only to annoy us, assuming he had no other reason."

"He would let the man who calls himself king of the Jews go free?"

"I am not at all sure the Procurator would take such idle boasting seriously. It seems to me too risky and uncertain a way to go about

it. I think the best solution would be to rid ourselves of the Nazarene as inconspicuously as possible. What do you think, Rabbi
Simon ben Zacharias?"

The man who had been addressed, a priest in the prime of life,
raised his head and turned toward the white-haired high priest.

"I agree that this method would be simpler and more convenient
but, I fear, not effective. If he should vanish inconspicuously, that
will not be the end of his teachings. His adherents will attempt to
carry out what he has started. Moreover, he will have successors.
Our people are always overready to take false prophets to their hearts.
I have always been in favor of sticking to legal methods. That
makes an impression on the people. Let us try Jesus ben Joseph in
a fully public trial and condemn him. That will surely have a chill-
ing effect upon his followers."

"If only we succeed in condemning him!" Annas exclaimed.

Rabbi Simon ben Zacharias smiled briefly.

"I imagine the high priest has persuaded the Procurator to agree in
matters far more difficult than a death sentence upon a man whom
the Romans care nothing about."

Flattered, the aged priest shrugged his shoulders.

"That may be," he said. "For the present we will wait and see
how things turn out. There is no great hurry—although I should
like to settle this affair before the Passover. Let us return to the
more urgent question of Barabbas. We ought to locate the man and
find out what his plans are. Rabbi Nathaniel, can you get in touch
with him?"

Rabbi Nathaniel nodded.

"That should not be difficult if he is in Jericho. It will be harder
if he is hiding out in Samaria. As far as his plans are concerned, I
am not anxious to ask him personally about them. The man is
quick tempered and unpredictable. By now he must have learned
that we had intended to clip his wings. What am I to offer him to
placate him?"

"What we have already offered him: the high command at the
side of Juda ben Jacob and on condition that he stops recruiting
Samaritans," Annas replied.

Rabbi Nathaniel considered.

"And what if he doesn't agree to that?" he asked after a moment.

"Then we will see to it that he does not stir up any more trouble.

That will not be too difficult—his men are far less loyal to him than the fools who run after that conjurer from Nazareth. Incidentally, I have had Juda ben Jacob come here so that we can form some opinion of him. The question of Barabbas is linked up with him. Let us speak to him first."

With his bony fingers the high priest knocked on a metal disc which was suspended from the paneled ceiling within reach of his hand. A moment later Juda ben Jacob was led into the conference room.

He paused at the door, a man of about thirty, of medium height, with a brown beard and rather undistinguished features. His dress was very elegant and expensive, he wore large rings on his fingers and tinkling bracelets of pure gold. His hair and beard glistened with sweet-smelling oil. Arms crossed over his chest, he bowed low.

"Peace be with you!" he greeted them in a rather high, unmasculine voice.

"Peace!" Annas said. "Step closer, Juda ben Jacob of the noble race of the Maccabeans. I need not tell you why we have asked you to come here—we have just been discussing the matter."

Juda ben Jacob bowed agreement. The high priest was not very well impressed by him. It was known that he had amassed great wealth by manufacturing colored glass, that he had married a woman of good family and had four children—really very modest attributes for the future liberator of Israel. But after all he was merely being asked to lend his name to the movement, or rather the name of his famous ancestors. And perhaps there was more to the man than his appearance indicated. Under the proper circumstances his name would make more of an impression on the masses than the name of David, which the Nazarene's followers often invoked. The Maccabeans were still a living tradition while David was long since dead. Such were the priest's thoughts while Juda ben Jacob glanced at the priests and Annas prepared to question the man. At last the high priest spoke again:

"I take it that you are ready to place yourself at the head of Israel's warriors to restore the liberty of Israel?"

"I am ready, high priest," Juda ben Jacob answered with assurance.

"Very well. I assume, Juda ben Jacob, that you have drawn up a plan. Will you outline it to the priests here assembled?"

Juda ben Jacob cleared his throat before he began what was obviously a well-prepared address. When he spoke his language was rather flowery, but it bore the unmistakable marks of deep conviction.

"I am no soldier and am not familiar with the art of war. But our forefathers were also not warriors when they conquered the land of Canaan. Joshua was no warrior, nor Gideon, and if I may mention my glorious forebears, neither was Juda Maccabi a professional soldier. But the arm of the children of Israel is guided by our faith in the One and Only and our strength and heroism is in the Covenant that He sealed with our fathers. Although we have not learned to wield the sword, to shoot arrows straight to the hearts of our enemies—the Eternal is always with us as He was with our fathers and He will confer victory upon His people, no matter how strong and how numerous are our enemies. Therefore I have said yes without hesitation when I was called upon to set myself at the head of the movement which is to bring freedom to Israel."

Annas sensed that the priests were growing restless under this loquacity.

"Your plan?" he asked sharply.

"I am coming to it. I am ready to depart for the camp today, at once. A hundred servants are ready to leave with me; a hundred mules laden with two months' supplies for a thousand men will leave the city by obscure paths. The servants will lead them in small groups to the northeast. I am prepared to devote my not-inconsiderable fortune to the cause of the rebellion. My gifts to the cadre army of Israel and my readiness for sacrifice will, I believe, strengthen their fighting spirit and help prepare them for the hour when they, with the entire nation behind them, will strike against the oppressors."

"Are you content with the part we have assigned to Barabbas ben Ezekiel as your military commander?" the high priest queried.

"I do not know Barabbas, your reverence, but I rely on your judgment. I am ready to accept advice from Barabbas, the former leader of the movement, in all military matters, and after the victory has been won I will place the army unconditionally at the disposal of the high priest."

To these firm assurances Juda ben Jacob added a declaration of his unqualified respect for the priesthood and closed by appealing to the Eternal to bestow swift and decisive victory upon the arms of Israel.

On the whole the grandson of the Maccabean had made a favorable impression upon the assembled priests. The idea of his appearing in Barabbas' camp laden with rich gifts and provisions for two months struck them as highly intelligent; they themselves had not been overgenerous with the army during the recent past. What would the next steps be? That was his affair. And Rabbi Nathaniel would take care of Barabbas.

Juda ben Jacob was congratulated heartily and basked in the praise that was heaped upon him. The profitable sale of colored glass from his factories had not satisfied his soaring ambition and he was strongly drawn by the lure of fame. Juda ben Jacob had always believed that the glorious name he bore would some day destine him to tasks befitting it . . . And now, with spring beginning, a journey into the desert would not involve any special hardships. He did not feel that Barabbas or his men would prove dangerous, for in his experience all men could be won over with money and gifts. And so Juda ben Jacob, grandson of the great Maccabean, dreamed of victory, honor, and fame.

That same evening the Procurator was carefully informed as to the number of Juda ben Jacob's men and the contents of the packs with which the mules were laden, and, of course, the purpose of the journey.

This conspiracy of the priests with Juda ben Jacob, the glass manufacturer, seemed to him one of the best jokes he had heard in a long time. The Procurator laughed long and heartily.

14 𝔁

"Miriam . . . Miriam . . ."

RABBI NATHANIEL, PRIEST OF THE FIRST DEGREE, RODE ALONG THE highway that led from Jerusalem to Jericho. In accordance with the decision of the conference Rabbi Nathaniel had sent a messenger to Barabbas, after learning definitely that Barabbas was staying at the home of his mistress in Jericho. Barabbas had rudely turned the messenger away, telling him that he no longer intended to have anything to do with the priests. The messenger did not dare to repeat all the curses Barabbas had hurled at the priesthood. All that Nathaniel had been able to gather was that Barabbas had no objection if the priests wished to free Israel from the Romans. Let them go ahead and do it—apparently they had already found their liberator in Juda ben Jacob, the grandson of the Maccabean. Undoubtedly, Barabbas had sneered, this great hero would succeed in driving the enemy from the land with weapons of glass.

After receiving this reply Rabbi Nathaniel had reluctantly decided to interview Barabbas personally. He felt his mission to be a highly unpleasant one, but there was no help for it—unless Barabbas were reconciled the entire movement would fade away.

Like Barabbas on his journey some time before, Rabbi Nathaniel had no eyes for the emerald green of spring in the hills to his left, for the burgeoning of the whole broad valley of the Jordan, nor ears for the myriad voices of awakening life. Gloomily staring at the track ahead of him, he spurred on his mule. He wanted to get this unpleasant task over with as quickly as possible and return to the Holy City.

He regretted having let himself become involved in this whole affair. What would it profit him if Israel should be freed of her oppressors? Annas and his son-in-law would reap the rewards, for the family of high priests would then become the royal family. But he, Nathaniel, was not in line to become a high priest. He would still be required to labor for others and those others, all interrelated by blood or marriage, would share the profits. He had always been an outsider who was inevitably assigned the more disagreeable affairs of Temple politics. Of course it was something to be a priest of the first degree, but he had worked hard and bitterly to earn this status and now he could not possibly advance any further.

A large group of people was moving down the road toward him. They were all men with pilgrim's staves in their hands and small bundles slung over their backs. They walked slowly, with the heavy tread of men who are accustomed to hard toil, and while they walked they seemed to be listening to a man in a white cloak who walked in their midst. Apparently they were planning to arrive early in the Holy City in order to obtain good quarters for the coming Passover feast.

The band of pilgrims doubtless came from Jericho, whither Rabbi Nathaniel was bound. Around this time Jews from all parts of the country, and even from abroad, were making pilgrimages to Jerusalem for the Passover and he would not have especially marked these men had not the man in the white cloak drawn his eyes with compelling force. Rabbi Nathaniel could not explain to himself what it was about the man that so attracted him—whether it was his extraordinary pallor or the strange purity of his features. Whatever it was, the rabbi had the feeling that a light radiated from this man and bathed all his dust-covered companions of the road.

Who is this man? Rabbi Nathaniel wondered, a peculiar feeling of disquiet stealing over him. Almost unconsciously he struck his mule with the lash he held in his right hand, as if he were anxious to escape rapidly from this discomfiting presence. But the mule, unused to such abuse, made a sudden leap to one side and the priest, who was in any case no practiced rider, went sailing into the middle of the road, struck his head against a stone and lay unconscious.

When he opened his eyes again he saw that one of the pilgrim
band was holding the reins of his mule while another was trying to
raise him to a sitting position. His forehead was bleeding slightly.
"Peace, Rabbi Nathaniel," said the man who was helping him.
"Your mule threw you, but you are only shaken up a bit."

"Peace!" the rabbi replied somewhat dazedly. His head was
throbbing and he found it hard to remain upright. He was on the
point of thanking the man for his aid and asking him how he knew
his name when his eyes fell upon the crowd surrounding the man in
the white cloak. There were more of them than Rabbi Nathaniel
had realized and there were women as well as men. They were assembled in a semicircle around the white-cloaked one who was bending over two old men who sat by the roadside with hands stretched
imploringly toward him. The men were shouting rather than speaking and Rabbi Nathaniel, who was scarcely thirty paces away, heard
them clearly. They were crying:

"O Lord, thou Son of David, pity us!"

Now Rabbi Nathaniel recognized the man in the white cloak, and
at the same time he realized why he had tried to whip up his mule.
The man was Jesus of Nazareth.

Recognition was followed by amazement. Then the man was actually venturing to enter Jerusalem, Rabbi Nathaniel thought. Was
it rashness or ignorance that was leading him to the city where his
most powerful enemies were entrenched? Certainly this small band
of poor, weaponless men and women could offer him no protection.
Was he unaware of the dangers awaiting him in Jerusalem, or did he
think himself possessed of such supernatural powers that he could
defy these dangers? And what did the beggars by the road want of
him?

This was the very question that Jesus of Nazareth was asking them
at that moment.

"What do you wish me to do for you?" he asked in a tone ringing
with deeply felt sympathy.

"Lord, let our eyes be opened!" the old men screeched.

A murmur ran through the Nazarene's following and some of the
men ordered the beggars to hold their tongues. It was then that
Rabbi Nathaniel perceived that both men were blind. What instantly followed made the rabbi tremble. Jesus of Nazareth touched
their eyes lightly with his finger-tips and the blind men were given

sight! They leapt to their feet, cried out for joy, embraced one another and stared at the crowd and at the sun, until the others admonished them to accept the miracle with humility and reverence and to join their company. The two blind men who had regained their sight attached themselves to the band of pilgrims and the group set off down the road once more. Jesus of Nazareth, silent and buried in thought, walked at the head.

Rabbi Nathaniel started out of his speechless amazement when the man who was holding his mule addressed him.

"Do you not want to follow him, Rabbi Nathaniel?" the man asked.

Utterly preoccupied, Rabbi Nathaniel took the reins and without replying to the man clambered hastily into the saddle. He felt that he must flee; he dare not remain a moment longer in the vicinity of Jesus and his followers.

He suddenly recalled that the man who had helped him had addressed him by name. Of course, there were many who knew him whom he did not know. But now the Nazarene's adherents would undoubtedly assert that Rabbi Nathaniel, priest of the first degree, had been a witness of one of the Nazarene's "miracles." If there were a trial, he might even be asked to testify. Would he be able to deny what he had seen with his own eyes? Or would he tell the truth and thus incur the rage of the high priest?

Rabbi Nathaniel did not believe in miracles; his rational turn of mind could not accept them. At the same time he did believe in sorcery. He had often seen sorcerers and they had performed astonishing feats. He tried to banish his doubts by assuring himself that he had witnessed a piece of trickery, of extremely clever sorcery. "First he put a spell of blindness on the men," he thought, "and then, of course, it was not hard to take it away." But something within him resisted this easy solution; something told him that he, rabbi and priest of the first degree, ought to have gone up to the man Jesus ben Joseph and said to him: "You have given two wretched old men the sight of their eyes; that was a good deed." But then he would have to add: "Go not to Jerusalem—you will be brought to trial!"

He repressed this thought before it could take definite form. The incident had not diminished his grudge against the Nazarene; if anything the rancor had grown and become more personal. It angered him that circumstances had conspired to thrust him, the exalted priest, into appearing as a witness in behalf of this son of an ordinary artisan, a man who ran about the country in the company of public sinners. Moreover, he began to fear this man with his sorcerer's arts more than ever. He began speculating whether some charge against the Nazarene could not be worked out on the basis of this very incident. He looked around once more, but Jesus and his company had already vanished around a turn in the road.

"Forward!" Rabbi Nathaniel thought, and whipped up his mule once more, this time making sure that he was seated firmly and clinging tightly to the reins. "The faster I settle things with Barabbas, the sooner I will return to Jerusalem. And then this matter of the Nazarene must be put in order once and for all."

It was evening by the time Rabbi Nathaniel arrived in Jericho. He rode to the house of the chief rabbi who was a friend of his and learned that Jesus, to the great annoyance of the Jericho Pharisees, had remained in the city three days and had preached there. The Pharisees had wished to arrest him but the sentiment of the populace was so strongly in his favor that they had not wanted to run the risk.

Rabbi Nathaniel said nothing about his encounter with the Nazarene. As if to reassure himself, he spoke violently against Jesus' "agitation" and gave the chief rabbi to understand that the high priests did not intend to let it go on much longer.

After dark Nathaniel set out to find Barabbas. The home of the woman with whom Barabbas was staying was in a somewhat disreputable suburb where Samaritans and other unbelievers dwelt. Rabbi Nathaniel entered the ramshackle house with some trepidation. Barabbas was totally unpredictable and the priest was troubled lest he might lose his temper. Moreover, it offended Nathaniel's dignity to be seen in such low surroundings.

The woman, whose name was Miriam and who was a native of Jericho, led the priest into a dimly-lit room which contained no furniture but a wide bed and a few stools. Rabbi Nathaniel looked closely at Barabbas' mistress as she walked ahead of him. He knew that she had left her husband and was therefore guilty of adultery, a crime punishable by death according to the law. He was careful to keep the prescribed distance of seven steps between them—a difficult achievement in this tiny room. The woman was aware of his efforts and smiled scornfully. And the priest saw that she was extremely beautiful—a wanton beauty that well suited Barabbas' untamed strength.

A few moments later Barabbas entered. He was accompanied by a gaunt, sickly looking man who inspected the rabbi suspiciously and then, without a word of greeting, sat down on the floor in a corner of the room as if his only purpose was to be a witness of the conversation. Rabbi Nathaniel thought he had seen the man in Barabbas' entourage at the time they had held the conference in his home.

"Rabbi Nathaniel," Barabbas said, "you seem to have left Jerusalem before your messenger returned."

"On the contrary, Barabbas. I know what you told my messenger. That is why I have come. I cannot believe you really intended, even for a moment, to abandon the movement which you yourself created. I would have to hear that with my own ears to believe it. Is the liberation of Israel a matter that depends on your whims and humors?"

Barabbas lost his temper at once.

"Whims, you say? I marvel at your cheek, Rabbi Nathaniel. Do you see that man in the corner? He is my friend Ezra—my deputy in the camp. He came in person, sick as he is, because he was afraid I would not believe a messenger if he sent one. He was afraid I would refuse to credit the news that the new leader has arrived in camp."

Rabbi Nathaniel knew very well what Barabbas meant.

"Aha, you mean the arrival of Juda ben Jacob, don't you?" he said. "Is it that which has so infuriated you that you are willing to abandon the great cause? I hope at least that Juda ben Jacob did not arrive empty-handed?"

Barabbas burst into raucous laughter.

"Oh no, he didn't come empty-handed. I understand my men had a good deal of fun unpacking the presents this new leader brought with him. Just imagine how grateful they were for the woolen underclothes which their new leader seems to think absolutely indispensable for the liberation of Israel. And think of how inspired they were by the thought that those who distinguished themselves in battle would receive the Star of David molded in yellow glass! How I wish I had been there when this Juda ben Jacob of the house of Maccabi, with his oiliness and his honeyed words, introduced him-

self to my men—my men, mind you—as their new commander. It
must have been a precious sight. But in all seriousness, Rabbi Nathaniel, did you people in Jerusalem ever really think I intended to
be pushed aside by this idiotic pip-squeak?"

Rabbi Nathaniel was skilled in conducting thorny and unpleasant
negotiations. Part of his success rested in his faculty for agreeing
with his opponent on minor points. In this case it was not at all
hard for him since he himself had no very high opinion of Juda ben
Jacob. He produced a hearty laugh.

"That's precious, Barabbas, the woolen underwear and the glass
medals," he said. "But why should a man with your sense of humor
lose his temper over a fool like Juda ben Jacob? Didn't you understand what we meant when we proposed that Juda ben Jacob was to
be a figurehead?"

"I think I understood perfectly, Rabbi Nathaniel," Barabbas replied bitterly.

"I don't think you did, Barabbas. Just be reasonable for a moment. You know that the priesthood supplied you with means to
recruit and equip men in larger numbers. But the sources of our
funds in Jerusalem are not inexhaustible. Juda ben Jacob is rich,
very rich as you know, and he has a famous name that will influence
the people. His money and his name will provide you with the
means for building up the movement on a really generous scale.
Those are advantages you ought to make use of for the sake of the
cause, aren't they—even if your vanity suffers a little. What do you
want of us? You might well have resented it if we had sent you a
capable man of action, experienced in war. But this gilded nut-
shell—you see how frank I am being with you—this puppet cannot
harm your prestige or diminish your power. The more he makes
himself ridiculous before your men, the more your own prestige will
rise."

"Fine words," Barabbas retorted. "I don't intend to get involved
in a battle of words with you, Rabbi Nathaniel, for I have no doubt
I would lose. By sending us this glassmaker you have made mock
of the whole movement. You will have to swallow your own brew.
For my part, Rabbi Nathaniel, I'm not playing any longer."

"May I remind you, Barabbas, that we made a deal. Juda ben
Jacob's role was included in that deal—in fact, we made it a condition of the support we were to send you. In an honest bargain you

have to take the good with the bad. And you must admit that the priesthood has the right to have at least one agent of its own in the camp."

That was more than Barabbas could endure. In uncontrollable rage he seized a stool that stood near him and hurled it so violently against the wall that it broke in pieces. He began to growl like a wounded animal.

"I've had enough," he shouted. "Agent in the camp! You had enough of them while I was still there, didn't you? I know how much has been reported to Jerusalem behind my back. Didn't you pay Joel and his crew to stir up trouble in the camp? Do you think I'm blind and don't know what you're trying to do? You need me and my weight in the fighting—then you'll get rid of me at your pleasure, maybe along with the Samaritans whom the high priest intends to use for a while, until he has them slaughtered like sheep. You call me a robber and a murderer—what are you with your piety and righteousness? Do you think I'm a sacrificial lamb like this Jesus of Nazareth? Get out of here, Rabbi Nathaniel; go back to your high priest and tell him I will have nothing more to do with you. Let your smooth glassmaker play the soldier and leader; for my part he can have the men who feel happy in his woolen underwear. My men will know what to do. That is my last word—get out!"

Rabbi Nathaniel was thoroughly disconcerted. Why had Barabbas mentioned the Nazarene? Why had he said he was not blind? How much did he now of what the priests intended? The thought that the Nazarene was already on his way to Jerusalem while he, Nathaniel, was suffering another defeat at the hands of Barabbas, drove from his mind his intended line of argument. He cast a penetrating glance at Barabbas and said:

"You forget, Barabbas, that the arm of the priesthood is long. It reaches farther than the brink of the desert."

"Are you threatening me, rabbi?"

"I am not threatening; I am just stating a fact. The priesthood trusted you and supplied you with money. Now if you disappoint us . . ."

Barabbas was about to reply angrily when he suddenly heard a peculiar, sharp rapping at the door. Instantly Ezra sprang to his feet, pulled open a sliding partition in the wooden wall, and before Rabbi Nathaniel realized what was happening Ezra and Barabbas

had vanished into the chamber behind the wall and the panel was
back in its place.

While this was happening in the room loud outcries and hard
blows against the front door of the house could be heard. There
was a sound of splintering wood, rough male voices and the scream
of a woman. Then the door was flung open and a number of Roman
soldiers, torches in hand, rushed into the room. Rabbi Nathaniel,
blinded by the sudden light, felt them seize his hands and the next
moment he was bound with stout leather thongs. A torchbearer
thrust his torch close to the rabbi's face and a young centurion
stepped up to him and examined him closely.

"Who are you?" he asked in the Aramaic tongue. "You are certainly not Barabbas?"

Rabbi Nathaniel replied in Greek:

"I am the priest Nathaniel of Jerusalem."

The centurion showed his surprise.

"What are you doing here?" he asked, also speaking Greek.

"That is none of your business," Nathaniel said haughtily. "I am
not Barabbas, as you see. Why have you tied me up?"

Disregarding his question, the centurion said:

"You'll learn what is my business, my friend. Where is Barabbas?
He must have been here a moment ago."

"He went out through the wall there," Rabbi Nathaniel replied,
pointing to the edge of the partition.

"But there's no door there!"

"The panel can be moved."

The centurion snapped an order to his soldiers. A moment later
the boards had been torn aside, revealing a dark, gaping hole.

"After him!" the centurion shouted, and three of the soldiers with
torches dashed into the opening. They returned at once to report
that it was merely an exit that passed under a scaffolding to the
street. The centurion rushed out of the house. He could be heard
issuing orders; there was the tramp of searching soldiers and the
whinnying of horses, then another outcry and the faint whimpering
of a woman. Then the centurion returned to the room where Rabbi
Nathaniel still stood with bound hands, guarded by four soldiers.

"Do you know where Barabbas has fled to?" the centurion demanded of the priest.

"No," Rabbi Nathaniel said emphatically.

Two of the soldiers seized his right and left arms and squeezed the muscles of his biceps so hard that the rabbi screamed with pain.

The centurion laughed.

"You are extremely sensitive, Rabbi Nathaniel, or whatever your real name is," he said mockingly. "But we have a good many other methods for making stubborn men talk."

"I don't know anything—I don't know where Barabbas has gone. I just arrived this evening. I insist that you untie my hands."

The centurion seemed puzzled.

"A queer fish you seem to be," he said. "So you claim to be a priest from Jerusalem?"

"Yes, a priest of the first degree, if you know what that signifies."

"You don't say? A real big shot, I see. And you come here to meet Barabbas, the murderer and robber! Fine company you keep. Good thing I caught you, incidentally, since Barabbas seems to have got away again. I look forward to escorting you to Jerusalem. The Procurator will open his eyes when I tell him we didn't get Barabbas but someone who seems to be one of his accomplices—the reverend priest of the first degree, Rabbi Nathaniel!"

"I forbid you, centurion, to call me an accomplice of Barabbas. You will pay for this slander!"

"You forbid? You forbid, do you?" the centurion sneered, stepping closer to the prisoner. He glared at him for a moment and then spat in his face.

"Will you tell me, you dog of an Israelite, why you came here to meet Barabbas?"

"I wanted to persuade him to better his ways," the rabbi said. Nothing else occurred to him; he answered merely to save himself further humiliation.

The centurion doubled over with laughter.

"Do tell! So you wanted to convert Barabbas by fine words? Barabbas! My dear rabbi, I'm just a plain soldier but don't think me a stupid boy. I consider that insulting. I'm not going to waste any more time on you—you're coming along. You can tell your jokes to the Procurator. He'll see to it that you explain what you were doing here."

"You have no right to arrest me!" Rabbi Nathaniel cried, but as he spoke he felt the powerful grip of the soldiers twisting his arms and, moaning, he fell to his knees.

Again the centurion stepped up close to him and said sharply:

"Perhaps I have not the right—but I have the might. And by the gods, if I hear another word from you that displeases me, I'll have you whipped until you lose what little sense you have. Now march! Take him out and tie him to one of the pack-horses—and you don't need to be gentle about it. This weak-kneed servant of Jehovah will find out what it means to be a Roman captive."

Rabbi Nathaniel was seized by the shoulders and propelled violently down the narrow hallway that led from the room to the street.

In front of the shack, surrounded by soliders and with fettered hands, Miriam cowered on the ground. She was deathly pale; her mouth was distorted with pain and her parted lips revealed small, sharp teeth. From her large, dark eyes blazed undaunted hatred.

"Well?" the centurion asked one of the soldiers.

"The woman won't talk," the soldier replied irritably, and gave the cowering woman a brutal kick in the ribs so that she collapsed completely.

"Have you tickled the soles of her feet?" the centurion demanded.

In lieu of answering the soldier pointed to the woman's feet, which were swollen and covered with blood.

"She doesn't seem to feel any pain."

"This damned Jewish obstinacy," the centurion murmured under his breath.

Meanwhile the men who had set out in pursuit of Barabbas returned. They had seen no sign of him. Infuriated, the centurion began to swear at his lieutenant, a decurion. Then he called to the rest of his men:

"Finish up here. I don't want a stick of this hole left standing."

What he meant was swiftly made clear. The torchbearers set fire to the hut at several places. The red flames licked up the walls to the thatched roof and in a few moments the flames were leaping high into the air. Miriam, who had been lying on the ground, rose to her knees and gazed at the burning hut with a tormented expression. A flock of stunned doves fluttered up from the burning roof. From the tiny adjoining stable, which now also began to burn, came the bleating of sheep and the terrified cries of goats.

Miriam uttered a wild scream and sprang to her bleeding feet. She raised her fettered hands and stood panting with anguish, staring into the shifting glow of the fire. "My goats," she screamed, "my goats!"

"What does she want?" the centurion asked the rabbi.

"Her goats," the rabbi translated, shouting to make himself heard over the crackle of the fire.

The centurion laughed loudly.

"Go and get them!" he shouted at Miriam.

As if she had understood him, she rushed toward the burning stable and disappeared, with hands still bound, into the flames. Rabbi Nathaniel, who was certainly not given to emotion, felt his heart stop. The centurion alone seemed to be immeasurably pleased. When the hut and stable suddenly caved in and the whole scene became merely a mass of flame and smoke, he clapped his hands as if he had been watching a fascinating comedy.

Then his hands suddenly went to his throat and the centurion fell to the ground as if struck by lightning. A gurgling sound, accompanied by a stream of dark blood, issued from his mouth. An arrow had pierced his throat; more than a hand's breadth of the point showed through the other side of his neck.

The soldiers burst into shouts, but the decurion whom the centurion had scolded at once took command and restored discipline. He sent half the soldiers swarming out after the sniper; the other half he ordered to withdraw from the light of the burning house so that they would not be exposed to further attacks.

In the street in front of the house, brilliantly illuminated by the flames, lay the dying centurion. His youth fought against death, but in vain; the shot had been too well aimed.

Rabbi Nathaniel had sat down on the ground near the dying man and was staring dully into space. The monstrous happenings of this night had beclouded his mind. It seemed to him that all this was unreal; it must be a fearful nightmare from which he hoped he would awaken at any moment.

Slowly the fire burned down to the ground.

The cries of the agonized animals in the stable had ceased with the collapse of the building. Now the flames completed their horrible work.

After a while—Rabbi Nathaniel could not have said whether it was hours or moments later—the soldiers returned from their search for the centurion's assassin. They had found nothing.

One of the legionaries suggested setting fire to the neighboring shacks.

The decurion shook his grey head.

"Enough for tonight," he said. "We will go now."

The soldiers made a rough bier out of a ladder and fastened the centurion's body to it. They tied the bier crosswise over the packs of two pack-horses.

"What about him?" a soldier asked, pointing to the priest.

"Put him on a horse," the decurion ordered.

Rabbi Nathaniel did not protest when he was lifted roughly to the saddle of one of the horses. He sat awkwardly with bound hands and with no stirrups for his feet, but scarcely feeling his physical and mental misery.

The soldiers rode off with one dead man and one prisoner in their midst. Behind them the glow of the embers slowly died away and was lost in the darkness of the night.

Upon a cliff, high above the scene of the tragedy, lay Barabbas with Ezra at his side. He saw the soldiers moving away, resembling with their torches a glowing serpent crawling slowly along the valley road and disappearing at last.

"She is dead," Barabbas said, his teeth chattering in spite of the warmth.

"She is avenged," Ezra said.

"No, no . . . she is not avenged. She will not be avenged until the last Roman in this land dies like that dog who drove her into the flames. Not until then, Miriam, not until then!" And in a voice so low that not even Ezra could hear him, he added, "If I do not do it, others will. There must be avengers."

The stars shone down upon them out of the clear sky.

From the valley the smell of smoke arose, mingled with the fragrance of burgeoning almond trees.

"We must get away, Barabbas," Ezra said. "They will soon be right on our heels."

Barabbas did not reply. From his smouldering eyes a tear fell hot and heavy as boiling lead.

"Miriam . . . Miriam . . ." he whispered bitterly.

15

"A Fugitive and a Vagabond"

THROUGH THE SPRING NIGHT TWO WEARY TRAVELERS WALKED ALONG the road to Samaria. The two were Barabbas and Ezra. During the days they crawled into secret caves or hid out at the huts of friendly shepherds and at night they continued their westward journey; for the road to the east, to the desert, was barred to them—first by the detachments of Roman soldiers and then by the hostile priests who were perhaps even more dangerous than the Romans. The legionaries could be evaded, but one could never know what the priests were up to. Treachery was worse than open combat.

When they reached the vicinity of Shechem they saw in the bright moonlight the stonework of Jacob's Well lying off to their left. To the right they saw the charred places where houses had been burned to the ground. The Romans had taken their revenge for the assault on the legionaries and had killed all the inhabitants they found and burned down their houses. The town of Shechem itself had to pay a heavy indemnity and in addition supply a hundred young men for six months to the Roman workshops. Half of the young men had been rounded up at once. They had been led off in chains like criminals—and who could say how many of them would ever see their homes again?

Barabbas and Ezra had already learned of this act of Roman justice. They had heard the story while traveling, and now they saw that the shepherds' tales had been in no wise exaggerated. Everywhere they saw traces of burning, killing and destruction. Dogs wandered like the shades of the damned through the night, vainly seeking their masters and their homes.

"Let us rest here," Barabbas said.

They went to the well and sat down in the shadow of the old wall, after making sure they were alone. Barabbas covered his face as if he intended to sleep. But that was not it. He wanted to blot out from his sight the signs of the horrors that had been committed here. He felt responsible for them and this feeling disturbed him. Ezra, on the other hand, seemed to wish to impress this awesome scene of desolation on his mind; it was like balm to his hate-filled soul.

"The seed is sprouting, Barabbas," he said. "Now if the people of Samaria do not rise like one man, they are craven hounds who deserve nothing better than to be slaves of the Romans forever. But they will rise. The time is ripe!"

Barabbas made a gesture of discouragement.

"They will not rise. And I scarcely know why they should . . ."

"Barabbas!" Ezra's outcry rang with horror.

Often since he had been a follower of Barabbas Ezra had been witness to his leader's moods of doubt and despair. The fortunes of the movement were reflected in those moods which alternated between rage and fury and a profound melancholy. But never before had Barabbas expressed doubt of the ultimate goals of his movement; never before had he wondered what they were really fighting for. Was not the liberation of Israel the greatest of causes? Ezra tried to reassure himself that Barabbas was thinking only of the Samaritans, whom the Israelites considered wholly apart from themselves.

"You think ill of the Samaritans," Ezra said.

Barabbas let the kerchief slip down from his face and said harshly:

"Of the Samaritans? They are not the worst. But how little reason they have to be eager to fight for Israel's sake. With few exceptions—you among them—I have a bad opinion of all men. I am wondering whether life was not best for me when I made my way by my own strength of arm, in the days when it never occurred to me to be the liberator of Israel."

"Do you intend to give up the fight, Barabbas?" Ezra asked in dismay.

"I don't say that. But I am sick of being betrayed. I hate the

Romans like poison. But I hate the priests no less. And I hate myself for ever getting involved with them. It doesn't work to pretend to be fighting for freedom and to take money from men who mean only their own power when they talk of freedom. I reckoned wrong. It doesn't add up. I thought I would betray—and I was betrayed myself."

"Whatever you did, Barabbas, you did it for the sake of the people," Ezra said.

Barabbas laughed hoarsely.

"So I wanted to believe. But haven't the people betrayed me? Even those who stayed in camp—didn't I hold them by fear and threats? And how many of them have since gone over to this idiot Juda ben Jacob? The people have to have liberty forced down their throats. And you can't tell the people you are fighting for liberty because they don't know what that means."

"What else should we tell the people?" Ezra asked bitterly.

"I don't know. But certainly not all the fine words that Judah thought up to build the movement. From now on all I shall say will be: You can rob and kill and enrich yourselves at the expense of others. You ought to defeat the Romans not because they take away your freedom but because you can make slaves of them for yourselves. That is simple enough; they'll understand that."

Ezra did not reply. He sat for a long time staring blankly into the darkness. The bitterness in Barabbas' voice was so evident that he could not doubt his sincerity. And it was just this that seemed to him worst of all, worse than anything he had previously experienced or suffered. It tormented him to see this man laying himself bare—this man in whom he had believed more fervently than he believed in God. This was not Barabbas the savior of Israel, the Messiah; this was the robber and murderer that most of the people of Israel called him. And he himself was nothing but a murderer's henchman. No, that could not be, must not be. He sighed heavily as he prepared to answer Barabbas.

"You speak in bitterness, Barabbas," he said. "You have suffered a great deal, had many disappointments, and have also the sorrow of Miriam's death. But do not take away from me and all the poor fellows who follow you our faith in you—we have nothing else."

With a tenderness that was not usual with him, Barabbas placed his hand on Ezra's shoulder.

"Forgive me, Ezra—I didn't want to hurt you. Certainly I am speaking in bitterness—how can I help it? But I am also seeing things much more clearly. You need not despair. We will continue the struggle, but we must start afresh."

Barabbas himself did not believe what he was saying, but Ezra wanted to believe him. It did not occur to Ezra to wonder how they were going to begin afresh without the Samaritans, without the aid and arms of the priesthood, with dissension in their own camp and with a Barabbas who denied his mission. All Ezra heard was the promise that they would go on fighting.

"Let us go on," Ezra said, as if he wished to hurry Barabbas away from this scene of his embittered despair.

It was nearly morning when they reached Samaria. When they came in sight of the walls of the fortified city they turned off to the right. They did not dare to attempt to gain admission through one of the main gates and so they climbed Mount Hebal and from there crept through a tangle of rocks and crumpled walls into the still sleeping city.

Ezra, who knew his way about here much better than Barabbas, led the latter through tiny, refuse-strewn alleys to a shed that covered the entrance to the back part of a rather large house. This house belonged to a brother of Eliud who, with his companions, had completely disappeared since the incident at Jacob's Well. Barabbas and Ezra felt certain they would find him here.

In the gloomy interior of the house they first came across an old woman who seemed to be cleaning and sweeping. She was quite deaf and appeared not at all surprised by this visit so early in the morning. She at once went to fetch Manasseh, the master of the house, who closely resembled his brother Eliud.

"Who are you?" he demanded in a none-too-friendly tone.

"I am Barabbas and this is Ezra. Perhaps our names are familiar to you?"

Manasseh took a step back.

"More familiar than I like," he said brusquely. "I am not pleased to have you set foot in my house. Wherever you come, killing and burning and ruin follow you."

Barabbas was too weary to be angered.

"Where is Eliud?" he asked curtly.

"My brother is not here, nor his companions. It is too dangerous here. Only yesterday the foreign dogs searched my house from top to bottom and I had to spend words and money freely to keep them from burning the house to the ground. Your presence here places me in the same danger again."

"Then you are driving us away—or do you intend to turn us over to the Romans?" Barabbas said tonelessly.

"Far be it from me to refuse you hospitality," Manasseh said, offended but also visibly moved by Barabbas' downcast manner. "Rest yourselves," he added. "You will be supplied with food and drink to the best of our ability. During the day I will hide you in the cellar."

"Will you tell us where we can find Eliud?" Barabbas asked.

"I will do more than that for you. After nightfall I will lead you to Mount Gerizim. There is a ruined temple there dating from the time the heathen still lived in Samaria and worshipped Baal. Under this temple there are a great many caves and galleries. Eliud and his men have found shelter there. You will be safe there and I will supply you with necessities."

"I thank you, Manasseh," Barabbas said. "You are a worthy brother of Eliud."

Manasseh shook his head.

"I wish Eliud had never got mixed up with you. Since the Romans took their revenge in Shechem no Samaritan wishes to hear another word about rebellion or uprising. They curse Eliud and the few men who have stuck by him—they would stone him if they could find him. Our priests tell us no good will come to us from the Israelites."

Barabbas was at a loss for answer. The sorrow in his eyes was so evident that Manasseh was moved to a feeble apology.

"You must understand me, Barabbas," he said. "I am a poor man; I own nothing but these bare walls, a few acres of vineyard and some sheep. I need not tell you what would happen to me if you were found here. The Roman police have announced that to shelter you is punishable by death. And there are plenty of people in Samaria who would like to earn the reward that has been placed on your head . . ."

"I understand very well, Manasseh," Barabbas said in a low voice. "Come then."

They were given food and drink and then they slept for a few hours. During the day only the faintest light penetrated, apparently through a crack in the floor above, into the damp, dark cellar. It was so little that when they awoke they could barely see one another. Buried in thought, neither of the two men spoke much. What was the next step? What would happen to them next? They brooded silently without coming to any definite answer. Ezra was attached to Barabbas with all the love of his lonely existence; he had based his whole life on his leader. Oscillating between fear and doubt that they would ever succeed in mustering their rebellion and driving out the Romans, he repeatedly found excuses for Barabbas' changed attitude. How could a man who desired to achieve great things and was always tripped up by petty misfortunes preserve his faith in human beings? But Barabbas would do it; he was the only one who had the courage and who towered far above all others, Ezra thought. In spite of all disappointments and failures he would complete the task of liberation.

Barabbas was vainly trying to recollect when his faith in the possibility of a rebellion had first been shaken. For it seemed to him fairly certain that he no longer really believed. When had it begun? Was it the day when he returned to camp to find that a great part of his followers had fallen away from him? Was it just this past week after the frightful experience in Jericho?

Unable to answer this question, he began tormenting himself by examining his life. Where was the mistake? He could see one turning point. The first murder he had committed, the killing of the Pharisee, had decided the course of his existence; everything else was a result of that. Coolly and without self-recrimination, Barabbas came to this conclusion. To be sure, it had been a Jew whom he killed; it was a "fratricide" as the Scriptures called it. But what sort of "brother" was it who had refused him bread to allay his hunger and in addition had reviled him, calling him a half Jew, a gentile? No, he had been perfectly justified in killing the man. But since then had he not been fleeing the consequences of that murder?

Barabbas seldom thought of the Scriptures; he had never paid much attention to them. But as if in answer to his verdict of "Not guilty" the Scriptural words haunted his ear: "A fugitive and a vagabond shalt thou be on the earth"—the words the Lord had spoken to Cain. No, no, Barabbas thought, Cain had been right. Was not everything that was done in the world done by violence? Did not everything rest upon the right of the strong?

The image of the Nazarene rose to his mind. For a moment a surge of hatred passed through him when he recalled his meetings with Rabbi Jesus in Magdala and at Jacob's Well. Damnation take this weakling who was misleading Israel, persuading the people to bear their lot with patience and not to rise in revolt! He was turning the people away from the cause. And what had he said: "Do you think the Father would have need of you if He had wished to save Israel from this trial?"

But if He does not need me, Barabbas thought, does He need you, pale shadow of a man, charlatan, and sorcerer? Ah, but I am envious, Barabbas told himself, and once again he racked his brains to find an answer to the question of why people followed the Nazarene and fell away from him. "A fugitive and a vagabond . . ." resounded in his ear again; but he drove away the thought that he himself was responsible for his defeat. He must set about it differently and things would turn out all right.

Ezra was growing impatient. For a long time he had been lying on his back staring into the darkness. Finally he asked:

"What will we do, Barabbas, when we get out of this hole?"

"We will go to the hiding place on Mount Gerizim. I've heard about the place; there are supposed to be caverns that lead deep into the mountain. We will be safe there, Ezra."

"Safe, safe! I don't care whether or not I'm safe. That doesn't matter to me. What are your plans, Barabbas? That's what counts, that alone."

Barabbas had by this time come to a decision. He was beginning to believe once more that his personal presence would certainly influence his men.

"When things have quieted down we will go back to the desert— to the camp."

At this Ezra became tremendously grateful and reinvigorated.

"Thank God for that decision, Barabbas. I have been thinking about it a great deal—and believe me, it is the best thing to do. You won't have much trouble with that fool Juda ben Jacob. The men will be happy to have a man with a strong will over them once more. And perhaps it will be possible after all to strike by summer.

If only you do not doubt yourself, Barabbas, the others will believe in you."

"At any rate we can scarcely count on the Samaritans any more," Barabbas said. "You heard what Manasseh said."

"We will succeed even without the Samaritans. After all, we know we are far superior to the Roman mercenaries."

Barabbas had not so completely regained his self-confidence as to agree with this exaggerated optimism.

"The Romans are better equipped," he replied. "And they are more experienced in fighting in close formation."

Ezra's enthusiasm would not be stayed by such dry military considerations.

"That has always been the case," he said. "But the foreign dogs are nothing but paid mercenaries and do not know what they are fighting for. We fight for our nation, our religion. They fight for money. That is why I believe we can do a great deal even with the number of men we now have. Don't you agree, Barabbas?"

"Yes, otherwise I would not return to camp. But we shall see . . ."

"What is too bad," Ezra continued, "is that this Jesus of Nazareth has won over so many people from the lower classes to his doctrine of patience. But after we have wiped out a few Roman army groups even those people will come over to us. In the end they will realize that salvation can only come by fighting."

Barabbas did not reply. It struck him as odd that Ezra, too, should be thinking of the Nazarene. Why did everyone take this man so seriously? Wasn't it easy to see that he was heading for destruction? There must be something in him that attracts even his enemies, Barabbas thought. Once more a wave of hatred against the Nazarene welled up in him. Raging, he turned and twisted in the straw.

The light from the crack in the floor gradually faded and at last disappeared completely. Night had fallen outside. From above in the house not a sound was to be heard. Barabbas and Ezra fell silent and waited.

It seemed to them that hours and hours had passed before a ladder was let down from above and Manasseh descended to where they sat. He brought them food and some of the renowned wine that grew on the southern slopes of Mount Hebal.

"Another century of legionaries has been posted in the town,"

Manasseh said. "They have abused our priests and occupied our house of worship. It is said that the blood tax will be collected in Samaria also. The legionaries are patroling the streets and have proclaimed that anyone found outside after dark will be arrested and sent to the workshops."

Barabbas and Ezra rose to their feet.

"Are we in a mouse trap?" Barabbas asked.

"It is hard to get out of the town. But you must get away—if they found you here, they might set fire to the entire city."

"We are going!" Barabbas said, and Ezra nodded agreement. "We will try to escape from the city by the way we entered."

"I will guide you," Manasseh said.

"That is more than we can ask."

"Eat and drink—then we will set out. We will have to go by a very roundabout route to avoid meeting up with the Romans."

They ate and drank in silence. Then they followed Manasseh up the ladder into the house, which appeared to be quite deserted, and through the shed into a dark by-street.

Silence overhung the city. The only light came from the direction of the market square, a faint reddish glow from the bonfires the Roman soldiers had started there. The three men could also hear voices uttering indistinguishable sounds—probably the sentinels calling to one another.

Manasseh at first led Barabbas and Ezra out of the city along the same path by which they had entered the night before. Then they made their way westward along gravelly tracks that led through the vineyards of Mount Hebal, until the town itself was out of sight. In the shed of a vineyard that apparently belonged to Manasseh three sacks heavily laden with provisions had been placed in readiness for them. The three men slung these sacks on their backs. Then they began their descent into the broad valley that lay between the Hebal range and Gerizim. Proceeding always by by-paths, they made rapid progress. They did little talking; they were too preoccupied with the road and the not inconsiderable weight of the sacks.

By the time the moon rose they had left the town of Samaria far behind and felt they could afford a brief rest. There was scarcely any danger of discovery here.

"How long do you intend to stay in the caves?" Manasseh asked when they had recovered their breath.

"I don't know, I don't know yet," Barabbas replied. "No longer than is absolutely necessary in any case."

"The Romans will not rest until they have caught you," Manasseh said reflectively.

Barabbas shrugged.

"What does it matter what the Romans want. They'll have a time catching up with me."

"If your own men do not betray you," Manasseh said drily. "You're safe with the Samaritans. But it is said that the priests in Jerusalem want to turn you over to the Romans."

"I don't believe that. I think they're capable of anything, but it isn't to their own interest to turn me over. There are things I might say . . ."

"I'm just saying what I've heard to warn you."

"I thank you for that, Manasseh. I would like to ask you a question. Will you answer me openly and honestly?"

"It is not my way to speak with a double tongue."

"Well then—I know how heavily the hand of the Romans lies upon you. It's partly my fault, as you yourself said. But don't you think the sufferings the Romans are inflicting on you all will in the end incite the Samaritans to rebellion?"

Manasseh shook his head.

"Don't delude yourself with false hopes, Barabbas. We Samaritans are used to being treated badly."

"But will you endure everything?" Barabbas demanded vehemently. "Will you never try to defend yourselves?"

"Don't think we lack the courage, Barabbas. You know too many of our men who have proved the opposite. My brother Eliud, for example. But what sense would there be in fighting? We are too weak. And what would we get out of it if we should help the Israelites to win the victory? Then it would be our turn. You asked for a candid answer and I am giving it to you. If we have the choice of being maltreated by the Romans or trampled by the Israelites, we will choose the Romans. They are the lesser evil; that we have learned from history."

"Then what do you hope for? Every man must have something to hope for. Don't you think your lot will ever be bettered?"

Manasseh fell into a thoughtful silence. After a while he said:

"Yes, Barabbas, a man must have something to hope for. Many

of us have such a hope. We have heard of this prophet of Nazareth. He doesn't preach struggle and violence but patient suffering and love. He himself lives by what he preaches. He does not despise the Samaritans although he is a Jew. On that account many of our people believe he will bring a new era in which the Samaritans, too, will be able to live as they please. What do you think of Jesus of Nazareth?"

Barabbas felt the question like a blow. He . . . always . . . everywhere . . . he . . .

"You ought to be able to answer that question yourself," Barabbas replied sharply. "Let's get going."

They took up their sacks and began walking rapidly through the warm, moonlit night. Gradually the level paths changed their character; they began mounting steeply uphill, descending precipitately into ravines, until toward morning the men stood at the foot of the mountain where the Samaritans worshipped their God. The climb was hard and tiring. Even Barabbas, for all his strength, and even the giant Manasseh were soon panting under the weight on their backs. Ezra, who was much weaker than either of his companions, was soon utterly exhausted.

"Let us hide Ezra's sack in the bushes," Manasseh proposed. One of Eliud's men can fetch it later."

Ezra made no objection. Food did not matter to him; it seemed to him more important that they get on as fast as possible. They hid the sack and continued their journey.

The sky in the east was already flushed with dawn when the three men, after crossing a trackless waste of huge boulders and thick underbrush, finally arrived at a cave whose narrow entrance was concealed by shrubbery. At the entrance one of Eliud's men stood guard. Eliud himself was sent for and came from somewhere in the mysterious depths of the great caverns.

The men exchanged greetings and said little more.

Manasseh took his leave. He intended to return at once to Samaria without resting and promised either to send provisions in a few days or to bring them himself.

Tired out, Barabbas and Ezra lay down to rest. But Barabbas could not fall asleep. After a while he crept from the cave and stole down the road by which they had come in order to fetch Ezra's sack. There was no need for it; he went out of pure restlessness, because he did not want to lie sleepless in the cave, tormented by his thoughts. Slowly, with great caution, he descended the narrow path that led down the mountain. There was a wonderful view over the rolling countryside which lay bathed in bright sunlight. But there was no brightness within him; his heart was filled with bitterness and sorrow.

He was approaching the two wild fig trees near which they had hidden Ezra's sack. As he went toward them he was forced to spread aside with his arms the thick underbrush which in places overgrew the path.

Suddenly he halted. A man was lying across the path. Sleeping? Or dead?

Barabbas rushed up to the man. It was Manasseh, his Samaritan host.

The man was dead. His skull had been split and his chest penetrated by an arrow. The weaponless man had evidently been attacked from ambush.

Barabbas knelt beside the lifeless body trying, without his knowing why, to raise the dead man out of the pool of coagulated blood in which he lay.

As he tugged at the body he received a fearful blow on the head which for the space of a heartbeat knocked him unconscious. But in a fraction of a second he was on his feet again.

The underbrush near the fig trees had come alive. Roman legionaries with drawn swords stood before him, behind him, on all sides. And in the midst of the legionaries, with a knotty club raised high in the air, stood a Jew—one of the men who had escaped from the camp with Joel.

Barabbas was unarmed; he had left his sword in the cave. But he had his two fists, and although he knew he was lost he did not surrender.

With a leap like that of a wild beast he sprang to the side of one of the legionaries and had already snatched the man's sword when the traitor's club crashed on his head for the second time and threw him to the ground.

Once more Barabbas tried to rise, but the legionaries fell upon him and before he regained full consciousness his arms and legs had been bound with strong leather thongs.

He lay still with closed eyes.

"Over," he thought, "all over!"

The thought shot through his head that he had been betrayed by one of his own men. But it scarcely mattered to him now. He wondered that he was still alive. He scarcely felt the pain as the legionaries dragged his heavy body along the stony path to a clearing where they had tethered their horses.

He lost consciousness when they tied his flayed body across the saddle of a pack-horse . . .

16

Juda ben Jacob versus Barabbas ben Ezekiel

THE PROCURATOR THOUGHTFULLY PACED BACK AND FORTH IN HIS PAL-
ace office. At one of the desks sat his secretary, Marcus, the son of
a Roman official and a Jewish woman of Caesarea. The young man,
who bore himself like a Roman and devoted a great deal of care to
his outward appearance, spoke and wrote perfectly Latin, Greek,
Hebrew, and Aramaic. He had also acquired in Greece an excellent general education. The Procurator employed him not only as
a scribe but also as his interpreter; he had no secrets from Marcus.
Pilate often took the advice of his secretary who, though much
younger than he himself, possessed a great fund of shrewdness. His
counsel was always damaging to the Jewish people whom Marcus
hated and despised with all the vehemence of the apostate.

"Take this down," Pilate said, and Marcus set his wax tablet aright
to write down what Pontius Pilate, imperial governor in Judea,
wished to make known to the inhabitants of Jerusalem—the Romans
as well as the Greeks and Israelites.

"Procurator Pontius Pilate invites all inhabitants of Jerusalem and
all strangers who are in the city on the ninth day of April—translate
that into the Hebrew calendar for the Jews—to the games which
will be held in the circus erected by his predecessor, Valerius Grati-
anus. Do you have that?"

Marcus nodded assent.

"What do we have on the program, anyway?"

"First of all there are three lions in the cages," Marcus said. "Three Numidian lions."

"And the opponents?"

"We have a legionary who struck his superior and a Jewish tent-maker who tried to break out of jail."

"Good. Whom shall we set against the third lion?"

"That is hard to say, Procurator. This third lion is a decrepit, cowardly creature. I'm afraid he'll just let himself be butchered without putting up a fight. It would probably be better to make that combat a comic interlude."

Pilate reflected for a moment, then said with a smile:

"That's a good idea. Something to make the crowd laugh. Suppose we name this lion 'Juda ben Jacob'? What do you think of that, Marcus?"

"A marvelous joke, Procurator. The Jews would certainly get the idea and would be furious."

"That would be the point of it. They are furious enough as it is because I've arranged to have these games during their festival week. But your countrymen—I beg pardon, your semi-countrymen—have given me a great deal of annoyance recently. It will be a pleasure to me to give some of it back to them. Can you guess whom I want to oppose to our Juda ben Jacob?"

Marcus smiled knowingly.

"Of course, the joke will be complete only if you oppose him to this fellow Barabbas. Then the Jews would really understand what you mean. 'Juda ben Jacob versus Barabbas ben Ezekiel.' What a show! Have I guessed your idea, Procurator?"

"You never fail, Marcus," Pilate said, laughing. "That was just what I thought. Only I'm afraid it won't work out. They say Barabbas was badly wounded and hasn't altogether regained consciousness yet. Send for the prison overseer."

Marcus went out and returned a few minutes later with the overseer, an African who obviously had some Negro blood in his veins.

"At your command, Procurator."

"Yes. I want to know how Barabbas is. Is he recovering?"

"I think he is."

"I want you to make sure he recovers swiftly, Severus. I wish him to be strong because I want him to face the lions three days from now."

The overseer bowed.

"He will face the lions, Procurator."

"Is he conscious now?"

"Yes. His only wound was a heavy blow on the head which knocked him out for a while. No bones broken."

"Can he walk?"

"Quite well, I think."

"Then send him up here. I want to see him. But in clean clothes. I don't want this room to stink of the sewers for days, understand?"

The overseer bowed and departed.

"I'm really quite interested in the man," Pilate said. "Think of his being so crazy as to measure himself up against the Roman rule. Do you know much about him?"

"Half Jew. His mother was a Samaritan woman. Had a large following for a time. The program of his movement was quite simple: 'Death to all Romans.' But the way it always is among the Jews, they could not unite on this simple program. I think the man wasn't intelligent enough to wangle his way among all the Jewish factions and control the opposing groups."

"A curious nation . . ." Pilate said thoughtfully. "But let us go on. We've settled the three lions. If Barabbas is strong enough to face the lion, that will be the pièce de résistance." (Pilate used a Greek term.) "What else do we have?"

"A tiger."

"Oh yes, I know him. A fine beast. This time I'd like him to face three men. Last time he finished off one man so fast he was obviously bored. Do we have three?"

"We have plenty, Procurator. There are half a dozen waiting for the cross or the galleys."

"Good. Then pick out any three. But wait—are there Jews among them?"

"Perhaps. But mostly Africans."

"No Jews then. We don't want to overdo the joke anyway. Pick out three healthy Africans who can fight the tiger with lance and short sword. Wait a minute—no lance. That would give them too much of an advantage. Just short swords. And what else do we have?"

"Gladiatorial combats, I believe, Procurator. We have a good many professionals among the legionaries."

"And in addition?"

The secretary shrugged.

"Nothing that I can think of . . ."

"The program is a bit slim. Oh well, we can't compete with Rome. We can have only provincial games after all. In any case, Juda ben Jacob versus Barabbas ben Ezekiel would please the Augustus himself. And three men against a tiger isn't bad either. See to it the animals are starved from today on."

A soldier entered and reported that the prisoner was ready. Marcus rose and prepared to leave.

"Stay," the governor said. "I'm not sure I'll be able to understand the man."

"So far as I know he speaks Latin. It won't be Cicero's Latin, I imagine, but still . . ."

"No matter—stay in any case. It may be just as well if you write down the most important matters you hear. I may wish to send a report to Rome."

The Procurator signed to the legionary and the prisoner was brought in.

Barabbas' blood-stained face and hands had been washed and he had been given a clean, white outer garment. His head had been bandaged, the cuts on his back cleansed and covered with plasters. Now, deathly pale and shaking with fever, he stood before the governor, who examined him closely.

"Take the man's chains off," the Procurator said to the soldier who stood beside Barabbas.

The chains were removed. The Procurator gestured again and the legionary left the room.

"So you are Barabbas?" the Procurator said in Latin.

"I am he," Barabbas replied in the same tongue. It was evident that he found it hard to talk.

"Do you know who I am?"

"You are the Procurator."

"How is it you know me?"

"I saw you when you rode into the city for the first time."

"You have lived as a robber and highwayman, Barabbas; it is said you have a number of murders on your conscience."

"I have less murders on my conscience than you. And I have robbed less than you and your soldiers."

It was only with the utmost exertion that Barabbas had managed to speak these words. He swayed and almost fell. To hold himself up he grasped one of the slender white pillars that supported the ceiling of the room.

"You are in a wretched state, Barabbas," Pilate said. "I give you permission to sit down."

"I will accept no favors from you, Procurator," Barabbas said tight-lipped.

"As you please. I would have preferred you to sit down. You must not imagine me so stupid as to believe you are no more than an ordinary highwayman. You would not be standing here if I did not know you had cherished the noble ambition of opposing me on the field of battle. I like to discuss serious matters while sitting."

Barabbas was silent.

"Very well," Pilate continued with a brief smile, "I am not interested in teaching you good manners. Incidentally, Barabbas, it indicates an illogical mind to compare your acts of robbery and killing with mine or those of my soldiers. Any Roman or Greek would understand that acts and actions of the established state power can never be called robbery or murder. But as I said I do not consider you an ordinary criminal. Therefore I ask you this, Barabbas: Is it true that you wished to make war on us?"

"It is true."

"And is it true that in the course of preparing your war you killed legionaries and in other ways made trouble throughout the country?"

"I have killed legionaries wherever I could," Barabbas said, speaking with an effort but firmly.

"You are making everything easy for me, Barabbas. You know, don't you, that by this confession you are pronouncing your own death sentence?"

"I know. And my only desire is that it be executed swiftly."

"I like your pride, Barabbas. However, it won't help you. I cannot promise you that your death will be accomplished very rapidly. I'll come back to that. But first a question: In your—let us say, military preparations, you acted in agreement with the high priest and with the entire priesthood, didn't you?"

"I refuse to answer that question," Barabbas retorted.

"Aha!" Pilate said, taking pains to show Barabbas an ironic rather than an angry expression. "You refuse. You know that I have the means to make even the most stubborn persons talk. But for the present I don't want to do that. I don't need a statement from you, as a matter of fact. The activities of the gentlemen in the Temple are very well known to me. I must say I've never heard of anything more stupid. The only thing that really interests me is this: How could you, who are apparently a reasonable man, get involved with these people?"

"I will not say anything about that either."

"You are taciturn, Barabbas—a worthy virtue in a rebel. Only the priests do not deserve your silence and will scarcely thank you for it. Tell me, then, why did you want to make war on the Romans?"

Barabbas drew himself as erect as he could. Battered and weakened as he was, this giant with his coal-black beard who had to lean against the pillar for support nevertheless gave Pilate the impression that he could pull this pillar down with one arm and make the whole building fall on their heads. His voice rang out clear and strong as he said:

"Because the yoke of foreign rule is unendurable. And because I learned to hate the Romans in the days of my childhood."

The Procurator shook his head.

"It is curious. Why so? Are you a pious Jew? I mean, do you adhere to the laws of your religion?"

"No."

"Then it can scarcely matter to you who rules here. Was it much better for your people under those odd kings you have had?"

"They were our kings."

"That is ridiculous, Barabbas. What were you in those days? A people of shepherds; scarcely any of you knew anything at all about the world. Isn't it better to belong to a great world Power, to be a member of an empire that has placed the whole inhabited world under subjection? Alone you are nothing. With us you might be a nation which would make history."

"We will be such a nation when we have driven you out of our land."

"Perhaps, Barabbas, perhaps, but I don't think you will ever succeed in doing that. Look how I sit here and listen patiently to your arrogant and hate-filled replies. This patience is one of the virtues that has made us Romans masters of the world. You Jews are a thoroughly impatient and unruly people. As far as I know your history, you have only made trouble in the world. The very idea of your One God—this invisible and inconceivable God—stirs up trouble. Don't you think that some day the world will lose patience with you and exterminate the whole pack of you?"

"Before that happens," Barabbas said, biting his lips, "you will be exterminated, at least in this country."

Pilate smiled.

"That sounds like prophecy, Barabbas, and I do not like to dispute prophecies. As a prediction of the outcome of your war it is hardly sensible, since you have lost the game before you began to play. Do you realize that?"

"Yes, I do."

"Do you ask for mercy?"

"Only that you have me killed quickly."

"I like that, Barabbas—it is spoken like a Roman. But I don't know whether I shall be able to grant your wish. That may depend on you. I shall make you a proposition."

Barabbas looked questioningly at Pilate.

"I intend shortly to give games in the circus," Pilate continued. "If you are willing to fight a lion there are two possibilities. Either the lion will win, in which case you need not worry about your future. These lions often kill men in a second. And in any case it would be fitting for you to die battling a lion."

"And what if I overcome the lion?" Barabbas asked.

"That is quite possible, since you are strong and adroit."

"Will you then set me free?"

"No, you know I cannot go so far. But I will have you killed quickly without torture. You will be asked no more questions and spared the pain of slow death. Well—will you fight the lion?"

"Yes, under the conditions you have named."

"Good. That is sensible of you. I'm sorry for you, Barabbas, very sorry. You would have made a good Roman soldier. Why did you have to waste yourself on this preposterous idea of making war against me? It's really too bad."

Barabbas, forgetting his physical weakness in his excitement, glared at the governor with eyes of hate.

"I do not want your pity, Procurator. Keep your promise to me and now have me taken back to my cell."

"Do you long so profoundly for your cell?"

"At least there I see no Romans!"

In a tone of amazement Pilate exclaimed:

"What a capacity for hatred you have, Barabbas. I could almost envy you for it."

He went up to Marcus and whispered to the scribe:

"Have him taken back now. But tell them to give him a clean cell and treat him well. A four-man guard day and night so that he does not try to escape or to take his own life."

Marcus went out and returned at once with two legionaries. Barabbas was placed in chains again. Without a word he suffered himself to be led off.

The legionaries took him by way of a back staircase to the rear part of the palace, on the lower floor of which the prison cells were located. This time they did not throw him into the unlighted, stinking hole where he had first lain. He was given a cell reserved for prisoners of state, a room cut into the rock with a door on the street side and a strongly-barred window. The floor was strewn with straw and, unlike his first cell, was quite dry.

Barabbas was chained to the iron rings which had been inserted in the stone wall, but the chain was long enough to permit him to stretch out on the floor. The soldiers left him quite alone. But in front of the door, which consisted merely of iron bars, the guards paced back and forth, casting searching glances at the prisoner as they passed.

Barabbas had not noticed that he had been placed in a more comfortable cell. After the interview with the Procurator was over, when he was no longer buoyed up by the power of his hatred, he had collapsed completely and was dozing in a state of semi-consciousness. He was too wretched to feel pain; his mind was dulled; he was like an animal waiting in stupefied calm for the death-blow. He took the tonics that were given him, swallowed a jug of wine and had but one desire: to sleep, to sleep. Was it day or night? He did not know. Once it seemed to him that he saw the pale, suffering face of Ezra pressed against the iron bars of his unglazed window; but he felt sure this was a hallucination. And when at last he sank into beneficent sleep he was tormented by delirious dreams. He saw Miriam vanish into the burning house and wanted to run after her, but was paralyzed and could not go to her aid. Then he suddenly saw Jesus the Nazarene sitting with the Samaritan woman at Jacob's Well, but the woman was Miriam and she wore a white cloak as she listened to the Nazarene's words. Once again Barabbas wanted to hasten to her and snatch her away from the Nazarene's perverse doctrines, but his legs would not support him. All he could do was to stretch out his arms and cry, groaning with anguish, "Miriam, Miriam!" But Miriam looked at him as if she did not know him and said, "I belong to him." The soldier on guard heard a fearful series of groans. He stopped at the door and said to his mate:

"The fellow must be having bad dreams."

Then he resumed his pacing.

After Barabbas had been led away, Pilate turned to Marcus who was sitting once more over his writing table.

"What do you say to this fellow, Marcus? I feel sorry for cheating the man. For I have cheated him. If he knew what lion he is to fight he would rather have suffered the worst tortures. I am ashamed of myself, Marcus."

The scribe, who had also been greatly impressed by Barabbas, tried to reassure his master.

"It shows your human greatness once again, Procurator, that you should feel sorry for this bandit. I must admit there is something unusual about him. He could scarcely stand on his feet and yet he refused the chair you offered him."

"Yes," Pilate said, "preferring to die rather than to accept any favors from an enemy. I like that. I have been wondering . . . suppose he had really raised a rebellion and I had suppressed it, would the Senate have granted me . . . ? But no, certainly not a triumph in Rome. Still they would have sent for this splendid beast and looked at him in astonishment. That at least would have been more honorable for me and for Barabbas. Well, it will be interesting to see how he behaves in the circus. Do you think, by the way, that your countrymen—beg pardon, your half-countrymen—will attend the circus? I should think the combat of 'Juda ben Jacob versus Barabbas ben Ezekiel' would attract them."

"No, Procurator, they will not come," Marcus said decisively.

"Why not? I remember that in Caesarea a great many Jews attended the circus."

"The Jews in Caesarea are different from those in Jerusalem. And now with the Passover Festival so close the whole populace is in a state of religious intoxication and nothing would bring them to 'pagan games.' In any case the Jews in general have little taste for bloody spectacles."

"Don't you . . . don't the Jews have any kind of theater?"

"No, the Law forbids it."

"What a barbarian people. They cannot make sculptures—the Law forbids it. They have no shows—the Law forbids it. How can a people live entirely without art?"

Marcus stared thoughtfully at his desk. It was not his custom to say anything good about the Jews, but now there rose to his mind the comparison between his own servile behavior and Barabbas' contempt for death. Somehow he was not inclined right now to be used as a whipping-post for the Jews.

"Not entirely without art, Procurator," he said. "They have their great architecture, the Temple, whose like is not to be found in the inhabited world."

"Well—if you think that is beautiful . . ."

Marcus felt that the encounter with Barabbas had liberated the spirit of contradiction in him. He spoke enthusiastically:

"Beautiful—that might be disputed. But mighty, uniquely powerful. And then they have their sacred songs which stripped of their religious non-essentials make very good poetry. If you're interested, Procurator, one of these days I could work up a translation of the so-called Song of King Solomon for you. It is a tremendous work of art."

"No thank you, Marcus. If I'm not mistaken Joseph of Arimathea has also talked about that piece more than once. I don't think a person of my turn of mind would understand this sort of art. I suppose there is no Jewish philosophy, is there?"

"All the thinking of the Jews begins and ends in God. At least that is how it is supposed to be. From such a point of view, where is there room for a Cicero who believes that philosophy is the instructor of life, the inventor of laws and the guide to virtue? With the Jews all these things come from God."

"A barbarous people," Pilate repeated. "Incidentally, Barabbas' Latin is certainly barbarous enough."

"He probably won't need it much longer," Marcus said drily.

"No, certainly not. But what irritates me is that I must have this fellow who is a real man executed, and cannot get at the high priests and the other instigators. By the way, have you had men keep an eye on that priest Nathaniel?"

"Yes. At present he is at his home, sick. The excitement in Jericho and on the way here seems to have affected his health adversely." Marcus spoke with a malicious light flashing in his eyes.

"That is the only thing about this whole affair that has given me real pleasure. What impudence on the part of the man to complain about being arrested. Next thing you know the high priest will be demanding satisfaction."

"It might come to that, Procurator, if you insist on closing your eyes to everything. You could have them all at your mercy—through information given by Barabbas."

"But that's just what I don't want. Then it would be said we had discovered a full-blown conspiracy and preparations for war against Rome. What do you think they would be saying in Rome about my abilities as a governor? No—I prefer to make the whole affair appear ridiculous. See to it that the joke about Barabbas and Juda ben Jacob is not revealed prematurely. It's the surprise of the circus. I still don't know whether to have Juda ben Jacob and all his men in the desert wiped out at once. It's worth considering."

Pilate nodded to his secretary and slowly strolled toward the living quarters of the palace. Everything—Barabbas, the high priests with their ranks, that fool Juda ben Jacob, even his own joke for the coming games—everything suddenly seemed to him dreadfully boring and disgusting. What a repulsive life one lived here—slowly but surely one became a barbarian oneself.

In a side corridor he came across Mucius the Freedman, overseer of the domestic slaves, dallying with Chloe the slave girl. Pilate beckoned to him.

"You know, Mucius, that I do not permit these things in my house. If I catch you once more, I will reduce you to a foreman in one of the workshops. Chloe will be given twenty-five stripes on the back, and by Balbo. You will be present at the chastisement."

The freedman bowed silently.

Pilate went on. Balbo the African hated the girl—the lover would have to look on while his mistress was whipped by a jealous man. Pretty neat, Pilate thought—too bad I can't very well look in on the scene.

He had reached his library where treasured manuscripts were kept in great chests. And while from the lower rooms of the palace the agonized cries of Chloe the slave girl sounded mutedly in the library, the Procurator buried himself in Plato's *Symposium*.

17 𝕏

Desertion

WHEN EZRA AWOKE FROM HIS SLEEP OF EXHAUSTION HE LOOKED FOR Barabbas but did not see him. He questioned Eliud.

"Went away," Eliud said curtly.

"Down the hill," said the man who was guarding the entrance. No one knew where Barabbas had been going or why.

Ezra set out down the path that Barabbas had taken three hours before. In this way he came across Manasseh's body.

He saw traces of the struggle on the path and in the underbrush, and he also saw the bloody trail that the body of Barabbas had left behind when the soldiers dragged him away. Despair in his heart, he followed this trail until he came to the place where the legionaries had left their horses before they set their trap. The signs were un-mistakable; Barabbas had been captured and taken away.

Unable to think clearly, Ezra followed as fast as he could along the trail the mounted men had left. At the foot of the mountain he saw that the legionaries—for such they must have been—had turned eastward. He followed them without for a moment realizing that he himself would be lost if he fell into their hands.

He reached the road that led from Shechem through Shiloh and Bethel to Jerusalem. It was clear from the hoof prints that the mounted men had turned to the south. Then they must be taking Barabbas to the capital. There he would be judged.

Judged, Ezra thought, killed.

And he himself set out along the road to Jerusalem. Panting for breath he hurried on, feeling neither the weariness in his limbs nor the warmth of the spring day. He shivered with feverish agitation and his teeth chattered. At times he burst into a run and ran until his breath gave out and he fell to the ground. But he soon pulled himself up and continued on his way. How far was it to Jerusalem? Two days' journey it was usually thought to be. No, Barabbas could not wait for him that long. It was afternoon now. On . . . on . . . If he walked all night, he would reach the Holy City by tomorrow. And then?

Ezra did not think beyond that. All he knew was that he must do something to save Barabbas. The work of vengeance must not die with him; the sufferings of the Jewish people and his own sufferings must not go unavenged.

Mounted detachments of legionaries passed him without paying any attention to him.

Were the Romans withdrawing all their troops from Samaria?

Of course. Now that Barabbas was captured the others did not matter. A few outlawed Samaritans who had participated in the attack on the Romans at Jacob's Well might still be lurking about the countryside, but they would not be hunted any longer since Barabbas was caught. The Romans had probably forgotten completely about Ezra, the fugitive from the workshops. Nor would anyone have identified him in this dust-covered pilgrim who tramped wearily along the main highway.

Twilight fell, then night.

Near the town of Bethel Ezra's weakened body gave out completely and he fell to the ground at the side of the road. He would have to rest for an hour before he continued his journey, even if he did not arrive in Jerusalem before daybreak. The thought of food did not even occur to him.

As he lay there with the stars gleaming above his head he tried to think clearly about the situation. The main thing was to find out where Barabbas had been taken. To jail, of course. But there were dozens of jails in Jerusalem. There were the prisons along the walls where those impressed for the workshops were quartered; there were the prisons of the priesthood, the prisons in Herod's palace, and finally the prisons in the Procurator's palace. Probably Barabbas would be taken to the latter since he was a Roman prisoner. They would not put him in the workshops; he was too great a catch for that. But the Procurator's prisons meant death. That must not, must not be.

"I will gather the inhabitants of Ophel around me," Ezra thought—"all the poor and the hungry—and together we will liberate him."

So feverish and ecstatic was his desire to free Barabbas that the impossibility of such a plan never occurred to him. He even imagined that when Barabbas' followers heard of his imprisonment and of the uprising of the men of Ophel they would take this as the signal for a general uprising.

Forging on, toward morning he suddenly found the road barred by a detachment of Roman soldiers who for some reason had elected to rest here. He turned to the left down the side road that led to Bethany. It was a roundabout route, but that did not matter. Bethany! That was where Lazarus of Magdala lived, where he had been given such kindly treatment. He recalled how anxious he had been to flee their kindliness because the charity was the product of their love for the Nazarene. And as he thought about this he was suddenly overcome by ravenous hunger. At first he fought against the thought of once more taking advantage of their goodness. But his hunger prevailed. They would feed him, he reasoned, and unless he had something to eat he would not be able to go on. And he had to go on! When he came to a fork in the road he turned and plodded wearily toward Lazarus' house.

Twilight was already falling when he reached the house, which lay somewhat back from the road. He crept around toward the rear of the dwelling. As he neared the shed at the back he heard voices, and a moment later a young man went up to the well in the yard, drew water and throwing off his tunic began washing himself. At first Ezra thought he was one of the house servants, but as he approached he suddenly recognized the young man.

"Aren't you Jonah?" he asked the man, who was startled by his sudden appearance. "Weren't you a prisoner working in the grain mills?"

"Why, who are you?" the young man retorted.

"Don't you recognize me?" Ezra asked, lifting his kerchief from his face.

The young man took a step backward.

"You are Ezra who escaped!" he exclaimed. And without waiting for a reply he ran to the shed, wrenched open the door and shouted, "Simon, Reuben, come here, quickly, here's someone you know." Then, returning to Ezra, he said, "They are here, too, Simon and Reuben who worked on the same beam with us . . . Ezra, how surprised they will be. How often we talked about you, never knowing whether you succeeded in your escape, although we guessed you had, because the overseers were punished so severely."

It suddenly occurred to the young man that in his joy at this unexpected meeting he had talked too much and asked too little. He looked apologetic and said:

"Are you still a runaway—you look so wretched. What can we do to help you?"

While he was talking Reuben, the small, rather feeble man, and Simon his powerful companion and former fellow-sufferer appeared, recognized Ezra and greeted him heartily. Until Ezra reminded them bluntly of it, they apparently had not given thought to the fact that they were incurring danger to themselves by consorting with a fugitive. Undeterred, they led him into the shed where a large number of men lay on straw, some of them sleeping.

The four men sat down in a corner of the shed. Ezra, frankly admitting his hunger, was given bread and meat. While he ate he in his turn asked questions.

"How did you get away?" he inquired.

"We served our time. They kept us a little longer and treated us even more cruelly because of your flight, but a few weeks ago they released us after all." Simon, who had replied for the other two, spoke calmly and unemotionally about it.

"Then you all had to suffer because of me . . ." Ezra said in dismay.

"It's all over now," Jonah reassured him. "And the way we think about things nowadays, it did us no harm."

Reuben nodded agreement.

"What about you?" Simon asked, looking searchingly at Ezra. "Didn't you want to go to that man Barabbas in the desert?"

"I did go to the desert," Ezra replied slowly. "And I have been with Barabbas. Until yesterday. He has been captured."

There was such despair in these last words that the other men gazed at him with deep sympathy. For a while there was an embarrassed silence.

"Perhaps you do not know," Ezra continued after a time, "how Barabbas already had everything prepared to free us from the yoke of the Romans. Thousands were wearing the Star of David, the badge of the movement. Good soldiers were gathered in our camp . . . But Barabbas made a mistake. He allied himself with the priests. They promised him help, arms and money—and then they betrayed him. Yesterday the Romans captured him and took him to Jerusalem. I must follow him—I must save him."

The three stared at him in horrified amazement.

"You don't know what you're saying, Ezra," Simon said. "How can you hope to free someone who has fallen into the hands of the Romans? You yourself are in great danger. If they lay hands on you, you will be done for."

Ezra made a contemptuous gesture.

"What does it matter about me? And I don't intend to do it alone. I will gather all the poor and hungry and downtrodden in the Holy City around me and together we will free Barabbas from his prison cell."

"You're out of your senses," Reuben said.

"That's what you thought when I made my escape from the workshop. And nevertheless I succeeded, didn't I? Believe me, it is only a question of having the courage to act. Go with me—you too know what it means to groan under the whip lash of the Romans. You have suffered with me, have shared all the humiliation and pain. You must help me to free my master so that he can begin the work of redemption. The hour of vengeance draws near; let us go to meet it. Come with me, friends, come with me and help me free Barabbas!"

Ezra had sprung to his feet as if he wished to start out at once, but neither of the three men stirred. They looked at one another in silence.

"Ah, you are cowards!" Ezra exclaimed. "Because the Romans released you, you have forgotten that they can seize you again whenever they please. You do not want to be free and do not deserve to be."

Simon looked up at him with patient kindness in his eyes. He said:

"You may be right, Ezra; we do not know whether we deserve to be saved. We have sinned a great deal. But we are not cowards.

We simply do not want to spill blood. What would be the difference between us and the Romans if we used the same means as
they—force and violence? Nothing good can come out of violence,
Ezra, remember that."

Ardently, young Jonah spoke up:

"We are waiting for another, for the true liberator, the true redeemer of Israel. With him we shall go up to the Holy City,
tomorrow."

"Who is that?" Ezra asked. "You don't mean . . ."

"Jesus of Nazareth," Reuben finished the sentence for him. "The
same Jesus we spoke of when we were all chained together to the
mill. It is he who carries the salvation of this earth in his blessed
hands."

"Yes," Simon said, "from him there flows that great stream of love
which will bathe all peoples with mercy and grace."

Ezra glared angrily at the wall of the shed to avoid their eyes. Day
had broken and the sleeping men in the shed were beginning to sit
up and glance curiously at the group of four who seemed to be dis-
puting and at the stranger whom none of them knew.

Some thirty men had spent the night in this shed—shepherds,
artisans, and peasants they seemed to be, and of all ages. Some of
them went outside one by one to wash at the well in the yard, others
crouched and prayed, while still others conversed in low tones.

"Have you heard nothing about him, Ezra?" Simon went on after
a lengthy silence. "Haven't you heard about his teachings and his
miracles? All Israel is praising his name."

"Did not Elijah and Elisha perform miracles?" Ezra demanded.
"Yet they did not save Israel."

"Neither of them was the Messiah who was promised to us. But
he is! Now he is going to Jerusalem to take possession of the kingdom that was promised to him from the beginning. And we are
going with him, hundreds now and tomorrow there will be thousands gathered about him. We will be closest to his glory because
we were among the first to believe in him."

Jonah, who was nearest to Ezra's own age, threw his arms around
Ezra as if to shake him out of his gloomy brooding.

"Go with us, Ezra," he pleaded. "Go with him! He will save
Barabbas, for he is the only one who can do it. Not even death itself
can resist him."

Ezra shook his head.

"Even if he could rescue Barabbas he would not do it. There is enmity between them, I know. They once talked together. Barabbas tried to win him over to a union of forces. But even if he wanted to he could not do it. He does not want to fight. How could he free Israel or even Barabbas without a fight?"

Jonah continued his efforts.

"You are talking about something you know nothing of, Ezra," he said. "He loves everyone, even Barabbas. I tell you this: The Master need only lift his hand and his enemies will retreat, for he is the Messiah, the Son of the true God!"

This declaration, spoken in a resonant, utterly sincere voice, moved the hearts of all who heard—except Ezra's. But Ezra sat silent and wretched in his corner, understanding only that he could never, never win over these men. His throat contracted. If these poor men who still bore the marks of the overseers' lashes on their backs would not rise up and fight, who else would?

"The enemy will not retreat from any hand that does not wield a sword," he said bitterly. "How can there be liberation or salvation without fighting? How can you imagine that when you march in at the Damascus Gate with the Nazarene at your head the Romans will simply march out by the Jaffa Gate?"

The figure of a woman whom Ezra recognized appeared at the door of the shed, bathed in the bright light of early morning. It was Martha.

"The Master has sent a messenger and will soon come himself," she called to the men. "Be ready to receive him festively."

Her eyes fell upon Ezra and she came closer to him.

"Aren't you Ezra, the companion of . . ."

Ezra rose.

"I am he. Forgive me for intruding."

"You have joined the disciples of the Master? Welcome!"

Ezra cast down his eyes and replied with some embarrassment:

"No, I have not joined. I was passing here and was hungry and tired. That is why I stopped."

"Do you know that you once almost brought great misfortune down upon our house?" Martha asked.

"I did not know. But if my presence here means trouble for this house I will leave at once."

He started to leave. But Martha called to him:

"Stay. None who is hungry and weary will ever be turned away from these doors. And today especially our house is to partake of the blessing of sheltering the Master—at such a time there must be room for all who knock."

"Thank you, Martha of Magdala. But I cannot stay. I must get to Jerusalem and every moment is precious."

"At least stay to eat with these men before you go. Peace be with you!"

She left. A few moments later tables were set up in the yard and the maids brought bowls of steaming porridge for the guests, who murmured a brief prayer and then took all they wished in small ceramic bowls. In addition to the porridge great baskets filled with still-warm bread stood upon the table.

Ezra was about to leave, but Simon took his arm and led him to a table, saying:

"Take, Ezra, what is given in love."

He did not know whether it was the fragrant odor of the bread that broke his stubborn defiance or the lingering hope that he might yet persuade these men to go with him. In any case he sat down with the others and ate. But no one spoke at the table where he sat. He was a stranger among all these happy people who were filled with joy in expectation of their Master.

Ezra ate little and soon rose to go.

"You really intend to go on to Jerusalem?" Reuben asked as Ezra passed by him.

"I must," Ezra said, drawing his kerchief down over his face.

"Peace be with you, Ezra."

"Peace," Ezra replied curtly and turned away.

Young Jonah followed him and said:

"Believe me, Ezra, the Master will free Barabbas."

Ezra was touched. He did not know why but he suddenly had the feeling that he ought to show his gratitude to this young man.

"You are a good fellow, Jonah," he said. "But I know more about these things than you. You love Rabbi Jesus very much, don't you?"

"With all my soul, with all my heart."

"Then tell him not to go to Jerusalem. The priests intend to take his life. Tell that to Simon and Reuben as well."

If Ezra had thought his words would make an impression upon the young man, he was mistaken.

"Oh, Ezra," Jonah said in the tone of a zealot, "they cannot harm

him. He is mightier than all the priests. He has said: 'If I wished
I would destroy this temple that was made by men's hands and
within three days I would build another made without men's hands.'
You see, Ezra, that is how great his power is. And I tell you again:
He will also strike off the chains from your Barabbas, and save him
along with all men!"

"Peace be with you, Jonah," Ezra said, and left Jonah standing
alone.

As he was making his way past the stables to reach the narrow path
that led across the fields, his own parting words rang in his ears:
"Peace be with you!" For the first time he realized bitterly how ill-
suited these words were to him and to his intentions. Peace? No,
war and more war. There was, there must not be anything else for
him.

Walking slowly and heavily, with dragging feet, he climbed the low
hill to reach the road that led to Jerusalem. Sounds of happy, excited
talk reached his ears. He turned around and saw a small group of
men approaching down the highroad. In their midst walked a man
in a white cloak.

"He," Ezra thought.

For a moment he wondered whether the man might not after all
be able to help him to free Barabbas. Even Barabbas had admitted
that he was a great magician. But Ezra rejected the thought at once.
As Barabbas had said, he and the Nazarene were as fire and water to
one another. Moreover, how could this man help Barabbas, this
man who was also hated by the priests? Ezra began walking faster as
if to flee from his own confused thoughts.

Within two hours he reached the Damascus Gate of the Holy
City. He noticed the Romans guarding the gate but strode on
through without reflecting for a moment that he might be recognized, that the death of slaves awaited him in this city. He walked
past people without noticing them. There were many strangers in
the city already strolling about the streets in the vicinity of the
Temple Mount. They had come early from all parts of the world
for the Passover. A medley of all the languages of the Mediterranean
Basin could be heard. From the Temple sounded the bleating of
the sacrificial animals and the dull resonance of the trumpet calling
the people to prayers and ablutions. The clear sound of horns accompanied the marching footsteps of Roman columns that were

marching through the streets. The Romans were parading a great deal; they hoped to maintain order by impressing populace and visitors with their might. Many an angry glance was cast at the foreign troops, many a curse was muttered in the side streets and many a fist clenched at the sight of the armed men, but those who stood within reach of the lances and swords were silent.

Ezra began looking for the badge with the Star of David among the men he passed on the street, but he saw few of them. A few porters and laborers still wore the badge, but none of the better-dressed people.

Did everyone in Jerusalem already know that Barabbas had been taken prisoner? Was that why the insignia of revolt had vanished?

Ezra thrust has way through the throng in the streets that led to the Temple Mount and continued on toward the Ophel District where stood miserable dwellings, where hunger and need had stamped their sad impress upon the inhabitants, and where the people were always the ones to cry loudest for liberation. Ezra knew them well, these dark, evil-smelling little streets and alleys, for here he had spent his wretched youth, one hungry child among thousands who starved continually. Here, too, he had won the first recruits for Barabbas and here, long after he had become a fugitive, he had always found shelter as safe as that in the desert.

His former comrades would certainly not deny him aid now; this was his intense conviction.

It was close to the fourth hour of the morning when Ezra reached Ophel. The more doors he knocked upon and the more people he spoke to, the more dreadful was the realization thrust upon him that he had come among strangers, among people who had nothing in common with him. The hopes he had placed upon these former friends and comrades—these former members of the movement— vanished into thin air.

Barabbas? The uprising against the Roman yoke? The Star of David? Oh yes, they remembered now. But Barabbas had been captured and would soon be executed; to declare themselves for him now would mean to share his fate. Who would want that? No one, no one!

Yes, they admitted, the hand of the Romans lay heavily upon the unhappy land of Israel. But what could anyone do against the legions, the countless legions? It was altogether hopeless. Besides, while things were bad for the poor under the Roman rule they would be no better under Israelite rule. Weren't the priests even more hard-hearted than the Romans?

What about the Star of David? Oh, certainly, a good many had worn it. But the star had fallen; there was no sense in believing in something that no longer existed. Who knew whether the Romans would not arrest everyone who wore the Star of David? It was better not to be reminded of it, better to deny ever having worn the badge.

In addition to these reasons for their desertion, Ezra found one other. A large part of the inhabitants of Ophel had heard of the Nazarene miracle-worker, of the five thousand who had been fed with a few loaves and fishes. They had heard of the man who healed the sick and had even awakened the dead. And it was in him that they staked their hopes. His followers had proclaimed that he was the Messiah, that he would liberate Israel. Had anyone ever heard of Barabbas' feeding thousands of hungry people or healing the sick? No. Well, then, if it came down to it, they preferred the man of Nazareth to a man who had once made grandiose promises, had kept none of them, and was after all no more nor less than Barabbas the robber . . .

Filled with bitterness, Ezra listened to such talk as this. He found not a single man who was willing to go with him even to seek information or to tell him where Barabbas was imprisoned. At last, however, in one of the low taverns where Barabbas and his men had often hid out he learned that Barabbas had been taken to the Procurator's palace. But even here there were none who were willing to help him.

Toward evening Ezra set out alone, followed by the suspicious glances of guards. From an old beggar he learned where the prisons were and in the gathering twilight he stole by a side-street to the rear of the palace. Here he saw the barred windows of the jail. He hid in the entrance to an old house opposite the palace and whenever the guards had passed by he rushed to the window and looked in, calling Barabbas by name in a low voice. But no one answered.

In his delirium Barabbas saw Ezra's pale, suffering face, but the muted voice did not reach his ears. Ezra remained until dawn before he gave up his efforts and stumbled back to the Ophel district.

In his tormented soul not a spark of hope remained.

18 ✠

A Clever Stratagem

THE CONFERENCE, ATTENDED BY THE MAJORITY OF THE HIGHER priests, which took place on the evening of the last Sabbath before the Passover in the home of High Priest Caiaphas, was a rather unruly affair. The arrest of Barabbas which by now was generally known had evoked considerable anxiety, especially among those priests who had favored support for Barabbas. And the misfortunes of Rabbi Nathaniel in Jericho had caused much concern.

In addition to this there was the Procurator's invitation to the games at the circus. The invitation did not concern the priesthood directly, of course, since it was out of the question for any of the priests to attend the circus. But the puzzling announcement of a contest between Barabbas and Juda ben Jacob indicated that the governor was well informed on recent events. What seemed even more dangerous was that Pilate had not spoken openly about his knowledge. Apparently the Procurator was well aware of the plans of the priesthood while the priests were entirely in the dark about the Procurator's plans. This placed the priests at a considerable disadvantage.

Rabbi Nathaniel had recovered sufficiently to make a report to the conference. He described with painful accuracy his unpleasant experience. One of the priests at once asked the question that was bothering them all.

"Do you think, Rabbi Nathaniel," he asked, "that the Procurator believes your statement that you visited Barabbas for religious reasons only?"

"He set me free immediately after I was brought to Jerusalem," the rabbi replied. "That would seem to indicate that he did not doubt my assertion. But I am not at all sure about it."

No one was sure, since most of the priests realized that their transactions with Barabbas and his men had been handled very clumsily; it was by now well known that they had dealt with the robber, and in addition they had made fools of themselves by taking up with Juda ben Jacob. Each of them inwardly blamed the others and especially Annas, who from the beginning had been the chief advocate of the unsavory alliance.

High Priest Annas was well aware of this sentiment. A malicious smile played around his lips and his hard eyes glanced from one priest to the next.

"I know," he began, "that some of you think we might have gone about this business more cautiously or never have got involved in it at all. I also see anxiety and concern in some of your faces. There is not the slightest reason for such concern. Neither is there any reason for you to rack your brains trying to imagine what that Roman fop knows or guesses. The task that remains is to sever all our relations with Barabbas and his movement. I will undertake to do that myself."

Simon, priest of the first degree, asked a question:

"Do you think Barabbas will inform, high priest?"

"Barabbas is in the Procurator's power," Annas replied, "and there are many ways to make men inform. Perhaps Barabbas will speak against us voluntarily. But what of it? What does it signify? Nothing at all. It is the word of a robber against ours."

"But what if Pilate has proofs?" Simon pressed the high priest.

Annas smiled with scornful superiority.

"If he does he will do his best to overlook the proofs. You do not seem to appreciate the fact that the arrest of Rabbi Nathaniel placed the governor in a distinctly unpleasant position. I think I know why he was in such a hurry to release the good rabbi. Where would he be if he reported to Rome that under his very nose a popular uprising supported by the priesthood was being fomented? The fool would be replaced in no time."

Although the others were generally inclined to respect the aged high priest's political agility, Annas' words nevertheless left a bad taste in their mouths. After all, the whole alliance with Barabbas had been a mistake; that much was clear. It was by no means equally clear that Pilate would let it all pass without taking action. Or had Annas from the beginning intended to use Barabbas only to create difficulties for the Procurator from which the priesthood would profit? Sometimes there were no limits to Annas' cunning. But hadn't he gone too far? It was hard to answer. Annas meanwhile brushed aside the unspoken doubts and anxieties of his fellow priests.

"I see no reason," he said, closing the discussion, "to concern ourselves any more with Barabbas. Not for the present, at any rate. I am far more interested in the matter of the Nazarene. I hear he intends to come to Jerusalem. Have you taken any steps, Rabbi Nathaniel?"

Rabbi Nathaniel gazed at the floor in some embarrassment.

"I have not yet had the opportunity to speak with the man from Kerioth," he said reluctantly. "I was sick abed, as you know."

"What is this man from Kerioth supposed to do for us?"

"He is going to tell us where and when we can arrest the Nazarene without making too much of a stir. We obviously cannot seize him in the midst of a crowd of his followers."

"A little stir more or less does not worry me," the high priest said sharply. "On the contrary. As far as I am concerned, I want as many people as possible to be present when he is taken."

"I see what you mean. But I am afraid our men would be too weak to carry out their task if it should occur to the hundreds who are always around him to offer resistance. We can arrest him only when he is alone or accompanied by just a few of his followers."

"And for that you need the man from Kerioth?"

"He is always with him. But if you know of any other . . ."

Rabbi Nathaniel sounded annoyed. He seemed to be saying, "Do the dirtiest affairs always have to be allocated to me? Try it yourself for once . . ."

The high priest saw his irritation and tried to placate him.

"We know you are doing your best, Rabbi Nathaniel," he said. "But we have also agreed that we want him taken before the Pass-

over. His following is growing; that is proved by the very fact that
he dares to come to Jerusalem at Passover time."

"And what will we do once we have him?" Rabbi Nathaniel asked
with some asperity.

"You don't have any doubts about the verdict, do you?" Caiaphas
interjected.

"Certainly not. But what does our verdict mean? You know as
well as I that we are not permitted to carry out any death sentences."

Annas raised his hand to stop the dispute.

"Let me take care of that. Once the man is in our hands he is
done for. I have good reason to believe the Procurator will not refuse to confirm our sentence. The man must go to the cross before
the Passover."

High Priest Caiaphas straightened up in his seat. At this stage of
his term in office he was beginning to be very sensitive about the
overwhelming power of his father-in-law. His office, after all, was
not a lifetime one, and he knew the Procurator had the power to
depose him if he chose. Caiaphas had restrained himself for a long
time, but he was now beginning to think that his position had been
reduced to a purely nominal one and that his father-in-law had been
playing a dangerous game of late. He decided to seize this opportunity for expressing his own opinion.

"I am not at all sure the Procurator will do as we like," he said.
"I don't know the meaning of this contest in the circus between
Barabbas and Juda ben Jacob—as far as I know Juda ben Jacob is not
in Jerusalem and I don't think the Procurator has captured him as
yet. But even if it should be merely one of his pleasant little jests,
what certainty have we that Pilate will not refuse to confirm the
death sentence because of some technicality of Roman law? If he
does that, we shall have another failure to chalk up beside that with
Barabbas. Two defeats like that will certainly do our prestige no
good."

Annas sensed that the statement of defeat in the case of Barabbas
concealed an attack on himself, since he had been the one to push
the alliance. With an impenetrable expression he turned to his son-
in-law and said:

"For the present I should like to leave in abeyance the question of
whether our alliance with Barabbas has resulted in a defeat for us.
I have my reasons for saying that in this matter I have not acted as

recklessly as some of you may think. In the matter of the Nazarene, which seems to me far more important, I should like to know what you think we can do to make certain that the Procurator will not upset our plans. As I say, I have reasons for thinking he will not, but how can we be sure?"

"By doing what we have always done in such affairs," Caiaphas replied. "By paying a visit to the Procurator. There is no one among us who can handle the Procurator as well as you can."

"I rather think," Annas said, "that I shall have to pay a visit to the Procurator in any case. But at the moment it seems to me a dubious undertaking to ask a Roman for the death of a criminal who is not even caught and whose crime would certainly seem questionable in the eyes of a gentile."

The priest Simon asked for the floor.

"The question is," he said, "whether we need the governor at all. I can imagine that during the trial of a blasphemer and violator of the Temple the rage of the spectators would be so uncontrollable that they would simply take him out and stone him to death, as our fathers would have done, without asking the Roman masters for any sort of permission."

Annas smiled scornfully.

"Rabbi Simon," he said, "you speak eloquently of the rage of the spectators. I admit it can be stimulated if that is desired. We could pay a number of spectators for their righteous indignation and the rest would be carried along. But what about the Nazarene's followers? I imagine they are already too numerous to be stoned all together. And if they could accuse us of the outright murder of their master, his doctrine would not die with him. No—we must make use of orderly legal processes."

High Priest Caiaphas turned to him.

"If that is so, it follows that the governor must be won over from the first and that you must make your visit to him at once."

Rabbi Zadok, priest of the first degree, took the floor.

"I don't know," he said gravely, "but I don't like this whole business. We met to discuss the case of Barabbas and we have spent all our time talking about little else but this fellow Jesus of Nazareth. From all I have heard about the man he seems to me a harmless fanatic rather than a criminal. You say, Annas, that he already has many followers. Possibly he does. But didn't Johannes ben Zacharias have an enormous following? And what happened to it after Herod had his head cut off? It vanished. Probably it would have trickled away even if the man had remained alive. These are all temporary disturbances which are quite natural in a time as chaotic as this. The people suffer severely under the heel of the Romans. In addition the Talmudists have been declaring that the time is fulfilled and the Messiah must soon appear. If the people were free, they would not bother their heads about these fancies. Therefore it is my opinion that we must first shake off the Roman yoke—then the problem of the Nazarene will be solved of its own accord, without trial and without violence."

Annas looked silently down at the table before him. He seemed to be considering his words very carefully and the priests waited in suspense to hear what he would reply. After a rather lengthy pause he said:

"You underestimate the teachings of the Nazarene—and their effect on the masses. His doctrines shake the foundations of the Temple and of our social order. Before we get rid of the Romans—if ever we can get rid of them—our prestige might be so thoroughly undermined that liberation from the Romans would mean nothing at all to us. That is why the question of Jesus of Nazareth is so urgent and why it must be solved quickly."

"I assume," Caiaphas said, "that you are then ready to discuss this urgent question with the Procurator."

"Very well," Annas said, shrugging, "if you consider it unavoidable. However, I don't think the discussion will lead to anything conclusive."

With that the conference adjourned.

Annas at once sent for his litter and had himself borne to the Procurator's palace. It was customary at the palace for the aged priest to be announced at once to the governor and to be spared any long waits. Almost immediately Pilate came to meet him in the great reception hall.

The high priest crossed his arms over his breast, bowed low before the Procurator and in a solemn, singing intonation said, "Peace be with you," speaking in Greek.

Pilate raised his right hand in greeting.

"Peace!" he said. "I am happy to see the high priest—he is welcome. May I ask you to approach."

Annas did so, but he kept to the prescribed distance of seven paces in order not to pollute himself. Pilate might be master of the country, but to Annas he was only a gentile. The governor took note of his action and a mocking smile played around the corners of his thin lips as he invited the high priest of Israel to sit down.

"May I inquire," he commenced the conversation, "what it is that brings the high priest to me? I assume this is not merely a courtesy call."

The high priest's penetrating eyes glided over the Roman's face. He did not like the unusual suavity and politeness he saw there.

"You are right, O Procurator," he said. "I have come for a specific reason. I have received a letter from my son in Rome which has caused me some concern."

"What does your eminent son write?" Pilate inquired, wondering what the high priest had in mind.

"As you know, Procurator, my son at the court of the Augustus has been endeavoring to harmonize the interests of the Roman Empire with those of his native land."

"Highly praiseworthy endeavors," Pilate said.

"In his letter," Annas continued, overlooking the veiled sarcasm, "my son inquires how much truth there is in the rumors that in Judea a popular movement led by a certain Barabbas has already stirred up so much trouble that a number of centuries of Roman legionaries have been killed."

Pilate looked at the high priest in astonishment. What lurked in the back of his mind, he wondered. What had prompted him to be so bold as to bring up the name of Barabbas, with whom he himself was dangerously involved? Momentarily nonplussed, Pilate answered with a forced smile:

"As far as I know, it is my business to maintain order in this country. What has your son to do with it?"

"Nothing, really nothing at all, Procurator," Annas replied. "It merely happens that he is naturally treated as something of an expert on events in Judea and when he is asked questions he likes to be able to give accurate information. A strong popular movement directed against Rome would apparently be somewhat interesting to the court."

Pilate felt the blood rising to his head. Here sat this old man who hated and despised him pretending concern for the opinion of Rome.

Was this pretense a mask for his true dread that he would not be able to wriggle out of the net into which he had fallen when Barabbas was captured? Or was the priest's impudence only a device to sound out the Procurator on his intentions toward Barabbas and to discover whether he meant to take any action against the robber's accomplices among the priests? Well, he would get no satisfaction that way.

"You speak of a popular movement in connection with this fellow Barabbas," Pilate said icily. "I know nothing of any such movement. Barabbas is a murderer and highwayman who committed a number of acts of violence against Roman soldiers, among others. That is all there is to it. I am informed, incidentally, that one of your priests was recently in the company of this robber and attempted to persuade him to leave his evil ways. It was an effort in the best spirit of religion and I am sorry that in the course of his mission he was taken by my men and treated somewhat roughly. You know how soldiers are . . . I repeat my regret for the misunderstanding. I hope the rabbi has by this time recovered from the fright and annoyance he has suffered."

"He has recovered, Procurator," Annas replied. "But much as I appreciate your understanding of our priestly tasks, I am unfortunately compelled to tell you that the affair is not as simple as all that. Rabbi Nathaniel—you have undoubtedly been informed that that was his name—explained his errand as a pious one simply to avoid further brutal treatment from your soldiers."

Pilate sprang to his feet.

"Does this constitute a confession that you made common cause with this robber?" he demanded.

"Certainly you do not think that, Procurator," Annas said quietly. "The priesthood will never make common cause with a rebel. But we have paid considerable attention to this movement, the kind of attention that—to put it mildly—it was your duty to devote to it. We kept up contact with Barabbas in order to undermine the movement from within. But for our watchfulness the movement would have culminated in bloody revolution. Rabbi Nathaniel was the one who kept up the liaison for us."

As was his custom in delicate situations, Pilate paced up and down for a while before answering. For this situation was delicate; he did not doubt that. He was considering whether to remind this high priest, who was openly accusing him of negligence, of his proper place or whether to try to find out what lay behind his arrogance. Pilate decided on the latter course.

"I might," he said with forced calm, "make your intervention in Roman affairs the subject for a very stringent investigation, High Priest Annas. I should also respond to your incredible insolence in reproaching me with neglect of my duties by putting an end to this conversation instantly. Perhaps that would be the proper course. But I am amused by the grotesqueness of your pretending to be the accuser in this Barabbas affair. Will you inform me, High Priest Annas, what factors impelled you to consider Barabbas not an ordinary desert thief but a rebel? And tell me why you let yourselves become mixed up in this—to say the least—perilous game?"

"I did not intend to offend you, Procurator," Annas replied quietly, "and I shall gladly answer your questions. You perhaps minimize the force of the nationalistic spirit in Judaism. I do not. It flourishes in the hearts of all Jews. It is the business of the priesthood to see to it that this nationalistic spirit is not abused and does not become the ruin of the Jewish nation. You were unwilling to see rebellion and—did nothing about it."

"Barabbas happens to be my prisoner, you know," Pilate said ironically.

"Certainly. But he might never have been captured if we had not stirred up trouble in his camp. You forget that Barabbas was betrayed by his own men."

"After those same men had killed a number of legionaries . . ."

"That is just it, Procurator. We realized that a part of the Jewish nation was being driven into senseless killing and seduced into a hopeless popular uprising. We could scarcely take any action against this since you had closed your eyes to the facts. In order to spare the Jewish people a bloody defeat we undertook to clip the wings of the nationalist movement, even though we had to run the risk of being misunderstood by you. However, I understand why Rome may wish to have a clear view of the matter. Up to the present we have saved you considerable inconvenience in this affair. But now that Barabbas is caught I believe it is incumbent upon me to ask you what kind of report I should send to my son in Rome."

So much haughty insolence and so much malicious pleasure was expressed in Annas' face that Pilate lost his self-control. He began to storm at the priest.

"I've had enough of this, High Priest Annas. Even my patience has its limits. I don't believe a word you say. You are simply following the rule that offense is the best defense. You allied yourselves with Barabbas. The enterprise went awry. Fearing I might use this alliance to trip you up, you come here to tell me tall tales about taking over my responsibility; you try to convince me I ought to thank you for your plotting. No, Annas, I am not as naïve as that."

Annas rose.

"I am sorry, Procurator, that I do not find you more aware of your —I repeat, your—situation. I will compose my reply to Rome as I think best."

"Stay!" Pilate said harshly. "What is your price?"

"What do you mean?" Annas asked, sitting down once more.

"I want to know what you demand in return for letting this Barabbas matter be quietly forgotten."

"Demand?" the high priest said in astonishment. "I came, Procurator, with the intention of doing you an additional favor."

"I can imagine," Pilate said sarcastically. "What is this favor?"

"I feel obliged," Annas said quietly, "to call your attention to a movement which seems to me very dangerous."

"Another Barabbas with whom you are keeping up 'contact'?"

"No, Procurator. We have no connections at all with this movement. The man in question is an agitator by the name of Jesus of Nazareth. I take it you have already heard of him."

"Certainly I have heard of the man. But as far as my information goes, he is nothing but a religious zealot who preaches piety and fear of God. He is also said to have worked a number of miracles."

"This man who allegedly teaches piety and fear of God apparently has specific aims of a very different sort. Are you aware, Procurator, that at various times he has desired to have himself proclaimed king of the Jews?"

Pilate waved his hand disparagingly.

"I am aware that his followers have wanted to proclaim him king but that he has always rejected this ridiculous claim."

"Because he did not feel himself strong enough. But now the

situation seems to have changed. The man has the impudence to come to Jerusalem with his following."

"If I am not mistaken many Jews come to Jerusalem for your religious celebration," Pilate objected.

"Certainly, many do come for the Passover Festival. But this Nazarene and his people are not coming here to celebrate the Passover but to stir up confusion and rioting."

Pilate still did not understand what the high priest's hidden intentions were.

"Indeed?" he said, carefully emphasizing that he was somewhat bored. "This Jesus of Nazareth seems to be a curiously clumsy rebel. Far more unskillful than Barabbas. I have been informed that he and his men carry no arms. And the idea that he should come to Jerusalem to pick a quarrel with the Roman legions seems strange to me. Our garrison is strongest here. It would be a very strange procedure indeed."

Annas did not fail to hear the mockery in the Procurator's voice and his hands trembled slightly, but his voice was clear and strong as he said:

"I do not wish to be misunderstood, Procurator. This Jesus of Nazareth is no agitator in the usual sense of the word. He does not work with armed violence, but by a method that in the end is far more effective. That method is sedition, the alienation of men's minds. He takes from the common people, who as you know have little common sense, first their respect for the law and then their respect for all authority."

"You mean respect for the Mosaic law and for the priesthood, if I understand you aright."

"For the state authority as well. The doctrine that all men are equal will inevitably enfeeble your rule as well, Procurator. Yes, I will be so bold as to say that such a doctrine, if it should win widespread adherence, would create considerable difficulties for the Roman Empire as a whole. That is why it is your obligation to see to it that this dangerous agitation is curbed."

Now at last Pilate saw clearly why the high priest had come to see him. Since the affair with Barabbas had fallen through, they wanted to put out of the way a troublesome religious fanatic. And for that purpose they somehow needed his help. He could see the outlines of the barter proposition: "We will not make trouble for you in

Rome about Barabbas if you see to it that this Jesus of Nazareth does not make trouble for us here." The question was, how did the high priest intend to work out the details of the deal?

"And what do you wish to be done?" Pilate asked.

"We will arrest the man. According to the law his crimes are punishable by death. But as you know we need a confirmation of the sentence from you in order to carry it out. And since action against this man is to your own interest, I wish to petition you for this confirmation."

For a moment Pilate gazed silently at the floor. He was infuriated with this old man who had had the unheard-of arrogance to reprimand him, and was now blackmailing him to the bargain. But he recalled what connections the high priest had in Rome and made an effort to remain within the limits of formal politeness. He said:

"The man has violated your laws, you say. That is quite possible —I am no judge of that. But your laws are not our laws. I cannot judge the man by the Mosaic law; my judgments must rest exclusively upon the Roman law. Therefore, I cannot possibly know in advance whether I will find the man guilty or not. What are your charges against him?"

"He has uttered blasphemies against God and the Law!"

Pilate laughed.

"Those are crimes of which you might accuse me, for example. I have little respect not only for your Jehovah but for our own gods as well. And as far as your law is concerned, I have heard that it is an extremely complicated and very vengeful law. I do not believe it is my duty to defend your God or your laws."

The high priest rose again and prepared to take his leave.

"I have another view of this matter," he said coldly. "And if I am mistaken it is also the view of the Augustus, for whom we pray in the Temple, that we should not only feel the power of Rome but enjoy her protection. We have been deprived of the right to execute death sentences passed under our law. But the meaning of this measure cannot possibly be that in Israel everything is permitted which merely is not counter to Roman law."

Pilate bit his lips. This juristic dispute was not to his liking. If he should grant the high priest's thesis, it might end up with his being merely the executive organ of the Sanhedrin. Certainly that would not be in accord with the wishes of the Imperator. He decided to put an end to the conversation.

"It is the Emperor's opinion that we should not intervene in the disputes of your religious sects as long as religious zeal does not endanger the public order," he said.

"But Jesus of Nazareth constitutes a great danger to the public order," Annas replied.

Pilate decided not to let the high priest depart empty-handed.

"I must hear the man myself," he said. "I cannot judge him in advance."

"That is quite natural," Annas said. "All I ask is that you do not forget that this man has permitted himself to be called the King of the Jews. Rome would certainly not like to hear that seditious agitation dangerous to the state is at work among the lower classes of the populace. For the danger is certainly far greater to the Empire than to us. Think of what it might mean if the slaves should take it into their heads that all men are equal."

Pilate bowed.

"I am pleased to find the high priest so solicitous of the security of the Empire. I take it you will have no further cause to worry about the Barabbas affair . . ."

"Nor you," Annas interjected, as if to say that the Procurator need not be anxious about the sort of report he would send to his son in Rome.

"And as far as the Nazarene is concerned, may I remind you that we have a very effective way of dealing with trouble-makers—the cross."

Annas nodded.

"I know, O Procurator. Rome would certainly hold it juster to nail one man to the cross rather than to be forced to erect a thousand crosses, as was the case once upon a time. The Emperor, I am convinced, will certainly be more inclined to approve of the death of one man than of thousands. Thank you, Procurator, for your kind reception. I believe we understand one another. Peace be with you!"

Pilate politely accompanied him to the door, but this time it was he who deliberately kept the seven paces behind the high priest.

"Thank you for your visit," he said, as Annas turned to him once more. "Peace be with you."

He watched as the high priest was taken up in his litter and then he returned to the audience chamber. He could not help feeling a certain grudging admiration for the old man. It was a minor diplo-

matic masterstroke to approach him, the Procurator, with a request
—or rather a demand—in the face of the very real danger that he
might be called to account for the priesthood's intrigues with Barabbas. And the dramatic conclusion the high priest had hit upon was
not bad at all—the open reference to the Spartacus uprising which
had certainly been no glorious page in the history of Rome.

"A sly fox," Pilate murmured under his breath, "but I won't make
things easy for him. One of these days he will regret bitterly that
he ever plotted with Barabbas."

Annas, for his part, was thoroughly pleased with the way the conference had gone. He had maneuvered the priesthood out of an
unpleasant predicament. It hardly seemed important to him to know
what Pilate intended to do with Barabbas in the circus.

"Let the fool have his joke," Annas thought as the litter bore him
through the streets toward the Temple. "He will do what we want
nevertheless."

The streets were still full of migratory peddlers taking advantage
of the influx of strangers. Dozens of lambs which had not been sold
in the Temple yard were lying on wooden carts, their legs cruelly
tied—too weak even to bleat.

"That is the way we must have him . . ." the high priest muttered,
looking at the lambs.

He was thinking of the Nazarene.

19

A Dubious Battle

PILATE, AFTER HIS CONVERSATION WITH THE HIGH PRIEST, WAS MORE than ever determined to make the contest between Barabbas and the doddering old lion the main feature of the games. Although he had shown a certain weakness when confronted with Annas' threats, he was resolved to prove to the priests that he had seen through their intrigues. He also was inclined to think that Annas' version of the relations of the priesthood to Barabbas was something the old man had thought up for himself and that the majority of the priests had placed their hopes in Barabbas up to the moment of the latter's capture. Moreover, Pilate was eager to make of Juda ben Jacob such a butt of ridicule that the grandson of the Maccabean would never again be of any value to the Jews as an insurrectionary leader.

He had charged his secretary Marcus with looking after the health of Barabbas. After the conference with the high priest Pilate crossed the atrium, which was being given its spring cleaning by the domestic slaves, and entered the tablinum in the rear part of the palace where the actual living quarters were situated. As soon as he reached his office he sent for his secretary.

"How is Barabbas?" he asked Marcus as the scribe entered.

"He will put up a good show in the circus, I am sure," Marcus replied. "Fulvius, the young physician who recently came from

215

Rome, is treating him. He bandaged his wounds and has given him
tonics."

"Good. How is the man behaving? Does he talk?"

"No. He has refused to say a word to the guards and does not
even reply to the doctor's questions. He eats what is set before him
and drinks a good deal of red wine—I have ordered that he be given
plenty of it. When he is not sleeping he sits brooding silently. Fulvius says that Barabbas has the strongest body he has ever seen in a
human being."

Pilate smiled. His stern face and compressed lips stood out white
and cruel in the twilight of the room. The thought of seeing this
giant of a man in the circus gave him a feeling of voluptuous pleasure.
He dismissed Marcus, stressing again that he wanted Barabbas to be
in the best possible condition for the circus.

Barabbas did not waste any time wondering why he, robber and
rebel that he was, should be treated better than other prisoners and
be given the food and care his condition required. He lay in a clean,
dry cell, but the chains that fettered him to the rocky wall reminded
him continually that he was a prisoner for whom death waited.

On the sixth morning of his imprisonment the soldiers unfastened
his chains. The Roman physician examined his already-closed
wounds and then he was led away. He thought at first that he was
being taken to trial, but he soon saw that he was being led not into
the palace but away from it toward the inner city. There were few
people in the side-streets through which the small procession of
armed men with the prisoner in the midst made its way. Probably
that was why his jailors had chosen this early hour of the morning.
Where was he being taken? Was he to be executed at once without
trial? It did not matter to him.

He was in fact being taken to the hippodrome, the circus that the
Romans, to the great irritation of the Jews, had built in the center
of the Holy City. Barabbas was placed in a cell secured by heavy
iron bars, a cell used for the criminals who were to fight wild beasts.
He heard the roars of the lions, the hissing and spitting of the great
cats who were also kept prisoner in this place, but the sound scarcely
troubled him. In the desert he had heard mightier roaring.

Once he was inside the cell his chains were removed. There was
no need for them here, and the warders probably intended to give

the prisoner the opportunity to regain the use of his limbs before he entered the arena. The floor of the cell was strewn with straw. Wearily, Barabbas dropped down upon it. The soldiers had locked the barred iron door with heavy bolts. In the corner of the cell was a jug of wine and some bread.

Mingled with the roars of the wild beasts Barabbas heard the bleating of cattle and sheep: sacrificial animals being driven to the Temple. Carts rattled on the stone pavements outside and the sounds of men's voices were audible.

Barabbas paid little attention to the clamor. He was musing about his situation. Here, he thought, his life was to come to an end; in this place he would be crushed by the jaws of a lion. Such a death had often menaced him in his days in the desert. He did not fear death. Did he fear dying? Well, it must happen some time, and this way it would be much quicker than if the Procurator had had him put to torture.

A new thought rose to his mind, one which he had never considered before. What came after death? There was, he knew, a large Jewish sect that denied the immortality of the soul: the Sadducees. That man Joseph of Arimathea, the friend of Pilate and Lazarus, was a member of this sect. But the Pharisees asserted that the soul did not die and that after the death of the body a man's soul would be called to an accounting before the judgment seat of God. It was curious, Barabbas thought, that Jesus of Nazareth who was such an enemy of the Pharisees taught a somewhat similar doctrine.

Perhaps it was true.

But if it were true, the judgment would certainly turn out badly for him, or rather for his soul. For he knew very well that he had not lived according to the laws; if his soul had to pay for his blasphemies it would certainly suffer a thousand times more than would his body in a lion's jaws.

Were there no excuses that he could offer?

As far as the laws went—it was scarcely possible for a man to obey them all. It took years of study just to know them. But there was that simple, unequivocal commandment: "Thou shalt not kill." He had killed, once, ten times, a hundred times over. And the blood he had spilled had by no means been only that of the Romans, of his nation's enemies. And besides . . . But no, there was no sense thinking about these things. Back of these thoughts lay fear of

judgment and that was not the proper mood for a man who wished
to put up a good show before he died. He tried to master the
thoughts that thronged to his mind, but he did not succeed. They
assailed him again and again; every sound he heard seemed to cry
out: judgment, judgment, judgment.

Barabbas felt the perspiration pouring down his forehead. He
swallowed some of the wine, but this did not silence the strange
voices within him. All those who had found death by his hand or by
the hand of his men appeared before him, an endless procession of
pale, dreadful, silent accusers to whom he could offer no defense.
There were faces among them that had been familiar to him since the
days of his childhood, and there were a great many whose features
were vague—those he had killed in battle.

A fearful sense of oppression weighed upon his heart and almost
deprived him of his reason. "I have sinned heavily," he thought,
"I have drunk crime like wine, out of vengefulness and greed for
power. Lord, Lord! how shall I stand before Thee if Thou art truly
the righteous God, how shall I bear Thy punishments if something
of me lives after my body is gone?" What would he have said, that
man of Nazareth who was certainly a prophet? . . . God knows, perhaps he was also the Messiah. He would have spoken of mercy,
surely, of forgiveness for the repentant sinner. Repentant—was he
repentant?

His thoughts whirled chaotically. "I repent, O my God, that I
killed children of my own nation. But Romans? No—I cannot repent of that. And, O Lord, Thou wilt not count this against me, for
they are gentiles, they are enemies of Thy people . . ." But this
thought was immediately followed by the voice of the Nazarene in
his mind: "Love your enemies; do good to them that hate and persecute you." Could anyone do that? No, that required more than
human strength.

He heard the soldiers talking in the corridor outside without understanding what they were saying. He also heard hammering from the
arena—perhaps they were erecting the cross meant for him. Perhaps
the Procurator had changed his mind and instead of letting him fight
the lion was preparing to show his guests the crucifixion of a rebel
and evildoer.

He felt that he did not care. What he feared was not the form of death, but what came—or might come—after death. The thought of judgment was unendurable.

Barabbas grasped the jug of wine and drained it swiftly. He wanted to get himself drunk so that he would no longer have to think. But he did not succeed. He was too innured to alcohol; the wine did not affect him. The shades were still around him. He saw Miriam, screaming, her feet bleeding, rushing with raised arms into the hut; he saw himself drawing the bow and releasing the arrow aimed at the centurion; he saw the man writhing on the ground with the fatal arrow in his throat. Should he not have killed that man? No, God, no, surely Thou couldst not have wanted that of me? And Miriam? She had left her husband on his account. The law provided no mercy for an adulteress; her crime, too, was punishable by death. O God, wilt Thou pronounce her guilty as well when she appears before Thy judgment? No, Thou canst not do that—I am responsible for her—mine is the guilt.

No, there could be no mercy for him.

The animals, disturbed by the noise of the carpenters in the arena and tormented by hunger and thirst, roared incessantly.

He was brought more food and a still larger jug of wine. He ate and drank without knowing what he was doing, nor did he notice the astonishment of his guards who were amazed at his apparent equanimity.

Early in the afternoon Barabbas heard the first spectators enter the circus, but this, too, though it meant that his hour was approaching, did not shake him out of his brooding.

Those who were coming to the circus at this time were Romans, camp followers of the legions that were passing through Jerusalem on their way to the east. These camp followers shouted lustily and made a great clattering as they mounted the wooden steps to the galleries, fought for the front seats and quarreled in spite of their festive mood. Games here were always a festive occasion, and although the hippodrome was a relatively modest wooden structure hardly to be compared with the circus in Caesarea or in the larger cities of the European Continent—not to speak of Rome—in a wretched city like this one these people were grateful for it.

Around the ninth hour the soldiers who were off duty arrived and the middle and higher members of the bureaucracy with their wives,

sons and daughters. At the last moment the Procurator and Claudia
entered at the head of their entourage. For the governor and his
immediate circle a large, roofed, colorfully draped loge had been
erected. The army officers and the higher officials had smaller sec-
tions adjoining the Procurator's box; these were also decorated but
were without roofs. All the other spectators sat on crude wooden
benches which rose above and behind one another around the ellip-
tical arena.

A trumpet blast announced the arrival of the Procurator who wore,
over his uniform of a military tribune, a white toga with purple
edging. Pilate looked very pale. His eyes drifted haughtily over the
multitude, and in acknowledgment of the cheers that greeted him he
lackadaisically raised his hand. Claudia kept her eyes fixed upon her
husband.

Surprisingly enough, there were a number of Jewish guests—people
from Ophel and strangers from the coastal cities, as well as some
Samaritans. All these were people who cared as little about the law
and the priesthood as the priesthood did about them.

Marcus, the secretary, called the governor's attention to this small
group of Jews who sat, huddled together, in an isolated group. Pilate
shrugged irritably. He turned to his wife.

"You received a visit from Mary and from Joseph of Arimathea
today. Did you inform them of my personal invitation to the
games?"

"Yes," Claudia said. "They thanked you but declined. Mary has
a horror of blood and thinks these games are dreadful. Joseph reminded me that their law forbids attendance at such spectacles as
this."

"We do the man an injustice when we say he is not a real Jew,"
Pilate said scornfully. "Theoretically he is a Sadducee and ought
not to be overnice about the law. He is cultured and intelligent as
well, but the man simply cannot get away from his upbringing. Too
bad. But since when is Mary so prim?"

Claudia looked thoughtfully at her husband and answered him
indirectly.

"Mary told me that the great miracle-worker is coming to Jerusalem
to preach here."

Pilate pricked up his ears.

"The miracle-worker? Whom do you mean?"

"Jesus, the Nazarene," Claudia replied. "I, too, am looking forward to hearing him. He is said to be a magnificent speaker."

"To hearing him? You aren't thinking of . . . ?"

"Why not? In Rome and in Athens I heard all the great orators—why shouldn't I do the same in Jerusalem? And I see no reason why you should not also."

Pilate waved his hand as if to dismiss the very thought.

"That is presumptuous of you, Claudia," he said irritably. "I have no objection if you wish to hear him, although I don't understand how you can compare this Jewish artisan with the great rhetoricians of Rome and Athens. You won't even understand him; he speaks the native language. At any rate leave me out of it."

"Mary said she would be glad to interpret for me while he speaks," Claudia replied.

Pilate let his eyes wander over the circus, which was almost filled. After a while he said:

"It is a very tempting offer. But I might say that it is doubtful whether this miracle-worker will have the opportunity to speak publicly in Jerusalem. The priests are preparing a conspiracy against him. He is to be brought to trial."

Claudia blenched. With obvious signs of great emotion she turned her eyes upon her husband.

"Mary says that all the strength of their God is in him. Whoever lays a hand on him . . ."

"In that case why should he have any fear of his opponents?" Pilate asked ironically.

"You must protect him, Pilate!" Claudia exclaimed.

"No," Pilate said coldly, "I will not. I refuse to become involved in the religious disputes of these Jews. And when I see how you all, you, Mary, and my friend Joseph, are under the spell of this man, I am almost inclined to agree with the high priest that this Nazarene is making a nuisance of himself."

Pilate had been so absorbed in this conversation that he forgot that the games could not begin without a sign from him. The spectators were already shifting restlessly in their seats. He suddenly realized this and was grateful for the opportunity to break off the unpleasant conversation with Claudia. Raising his hand he gave the sign for the opening of the games.

Upon the yellow sand of the arena two groups of fencers, six men against six, appeared and engaged promptly in their swordplay. At first they fenced indifferently, but the cries of the spectators spurred on the professional fighters; they lunged more and more furiously and soon blood was flowing on to the yellow sand. The fencers held small round shields for protection, but the darting, thrusting swords were wielded with such speed that they frequently struck home. Soon blood was streaming from the shoulders, thighs, and chests of the naked gladiators. Then two of the fighters, badly wounded, pitched to the ground and rolled in the sand.

The spectators were excited by the smell of the blood, but to Pilate the combat was dull and he ordered it stopped. The gladiators vanished; the two who had been wounded were dragged off.

"Those clumsy idiots ought to be whipped and sent to the workshops," the Procurator growled. "In Rome the public would pelt them with rotten eggs. But this rabble here is happy at the sight of blood; it doesn't matter to them whether the gladiators know their business."

He watched the next contest, between two legionaries who had been condemned to death for striking a superior. One of the two was armed with a sword and a round shield, the other with net and trident. They were two huge, strong, bearded fellows who had been close friends and were now condemned to fight each other for their lives. The victor's sentence would be commuted to the galleys.

They were driven toward one another by heavy strokes of the whiplash and began fighting vigorously at once. Maddened by pain, they battled more and more vehemently. This sort of contest seemed to the Procurator far more interesting than the tame and pedantic dueling of the professional gladiators. Both the men seemed about equal in skill; the man with the sword succeeded in fending off the net and the man with the net evaded the lunges of his opponent. Chance turned the decision. The one with the net stepped into a pool of blood and slipped. Instantly the sharp sword ran the defenseless man through the neck and he sprawled out on the ground.

The victor glanced up at the Procurator's box, saw the lowered thumb and ran his sword once more through his former friend's breast, stretching him out dead on the sand.

The end had come so swiftly that the public again seemed dissatisfied. The spectators felt that the victory had not been won honestly; the victor did not merit the galleys. They whistled wrathfully after him as he was led out of the arena. Pilate smiled scornfully.

"Now they would like to see the victor killed, but slowly, so that they would have some pleasure out of it," he said to Claudia, who had covered her face while the soldier was being dispatched in order not to see the horrid scene.

"I cannot understand it," she exclaimed in a low voice. "How can anyone take pleasure in such an abomination? And how can one provide spectacles like this for the people? It is the worst sort of barbarism."

"Not at all, my dear Claudia," Pilate said. "These games have a profound significance. The ordinary man who is daily cheated and stepped on has a right to see others suffering more than he himself suffers. Besides, for one to see other men die is the strongest proof that one is alive oneself. My awareness of life is never so keen as at the moment I turn my thumb down and so condemn a man to certain death."

"I should not like to live," Claudia whispered, "if others had to die only in order to make me feel alive."

She felt her husband's mocking gaze upon her face.

"A Roman woman shouldn't talk like that, Claudia," he said. "I rather think this reveals the influence of Mary and her Nazarene."

A post was rammed into the ground in the center of the arena. Then a man was led out whose back was covered with welts and half-healed wounds. The man obviously could hardly stand on his feet and would have fallen had the guards not hastily bound him to the post with heavy iron chains which held him upright. The man was pale as death, a picture of utter misery.

"The man is a legionary," Pilate said explanatorily to his wife, "who persuaded two friends to help him attack a centurion and afterwards betrayed his friends. He has been condemned to be torn to pieces by a lion. His two friends must defend him against the lion. Of course, they are armed only with knives. A very ingenious idea, I think."

Claudia did not reply. She felt a sudden horror of this man who considered the tormenting of miserable men "ingenious"; that they might have been guilty of a crime made it no more justifiable.

The two other condemned men were thrust into the arena. Both were very young. They were handed knives and the guards explained to them what they must do. Then the iron bars of a cage opposite the post were raised and a lion stepped out with springy tread.

The glare of the sun after the darkness of its cage seemed to blind the animal. It stopped, lowered its head and blinked. It was a huge, powerful beast; its tail whipped the ground so that sand flew up over the arena wall into the lower rows of seats. It uttered a low roar.

The attention of the public was fixed upon the lion. The beast looked up again, apparently saw the man fettered to the post and stretched. At the sight of the wild beast the two condemned men with their knives had retreated, but behind them stood keepers with burning torches to drive the fighters forward against the lion. The men moved ahead, but hesitated again when the lion roared a second time. They stood frozen until the heat of the torches once again singed their backs.

The public was already growing impatient.

"At the lion, you cowards!" some of the spectators cried, while others encouraged the lion with wild, uncouth shouts. The man on the post had apparently lost consciousness; he hung in his chains with closed eyes.

The drama ended with unexpected rapidity. The lion with one great leap reached the man at the post; the post toppled to the ground and the beast crouched over the unhappy creature, his forepaws digging into the defenseless body, his terrible teeth crunching head and neck.

The two condemned men tried to take advantage of this opportunity. They crept up to the lion and, fired by the roar of the crowd, stabbed at the lion almost simultaneously. But their blows lacked strength; they succeeded only in making two bloody gashes in the yellow hide.

The lion, infuriated, turned on them in a flash and before either could retreat he had stretched them on the ground with two mighty blows of his paws. In the breathless silence of the moment the only sounds that could be heard were the hissing of the great cat and the cracking of bones under the terrible blows of the paws, which were dripping with blood. Before anyone realized how it had happened the two bodies had been reduced to one formless mass.

The fight was over.

The public applauded the lion, which was being driven back to its cage with firebrands and hot irons. Then the remains of the three men were dragged away, the arena was smoothed and fresh sand was scattered to cover the pools of blood.

"You can always depend on the animals," Pilate said to Claudia. "They do their work swiftly and thoroughly."

Claudia did not answer. She was on the verge of fainting; the smell of blood that arose from the arena choked her.

"I guess the business is a little too bloody for you, my dear Claudia," Pilate went on. "But take heart. The next number will be all the more amusing by contrast."

Barabbas in his cell had been paying little attention to the noises. He heard the shouts of the public, but he was too intent upon his own thoughts to wonder what was going on.

Suddenly the iron gate of his cell was raised. Four keepers rushed in, pulled him to his feet, removed his clothes, thrust a wooden club into his hands, and pushed him out. A moment later he found himself in the arena.

In the glaring light he could scarcely see the people who were calling out mockingly and whistling at him. Then he understood. They were going to let him fight the lion armed with this ridiculous wooden club. There could be no doubt about the outcome. So this was the "swift death" that Pilate had promised him. So much the better, Barabbas thought, examining the wooden club in his hand and wondering for a moment whether he ought not to make his end even swifter by throwing away this useless weapon.

On the opposite side of the arena a gate opened and there emerged, pushed and pulled by the keepers, whimpering and spitting desperately, the skeleton of a lion, his pelt worm-eaten, trembling in every limb and obviously three-quarters dead.

A tremendous roar of laughter arose.

"Juda ben Jacob!" hundreds of voices shouted. "Juda the Hero!" "The Great Maccabean!" The laughter swelled to a hurricane and did not let up.

Barabbas, club in hand, stood motionless. Now he realized the full extent of the cruelty and baseness of the game the Procurator was playing with him. So this was the Procurator's intention: to make fools of both Juda ben Jacob and Barabbas himself. There he sat, the tyrant, laughing like all the rest, laughing with the rabble. And the laughter was not meant for him alone or for the scion of the Maccabeans—Pilate was laughing at the entire Jewish nation.

A surge of tremendous fury welled up in Barabbas. For a moment he thought: I have this club in my hand—I can knock down a few of the keepers and they will be forced to kill me."

But the thought vanished, for suddenly he saw on one of the benches, in the midst of the poorly-clad Jews from the Ophel district, a man standing on tiptoe whose flashing eyes sought his. Ah, he knew it well, that gaunt figure, that fleshless face framed in a tangle of hair and beard, those penetrating, questioning, encouraging eyes, that loyalty in the glance. Ezra! And in a moment he heard his friend's familiar voice crying at an ecstatic pitch:

"Kill him, Barabbas! Hail Barabbas!"

Then something very curious happened.

The little group of Jews, among whom Barabbas recognized some faces he knew, rose as one man and began shouting:

"Kill him, Barabbas! Hail Barabbas!"

They shouted so loudly that they drowned out the laughter and howling of the rest of the crowd. Pilate looked toward their section of the gallery with considerable interest.

"Jews from the slum district of Ophel," his secretary informed him.

The crowd tried to shout down the Ophel Jews, but the cries of "Hail Barabbas!" continued to ring loudly through the arena. Again and again Ezra's voice reached Barabbas; he saw his friend waving furiously as if he hoped to inspire Barabbas to act resolutely and rapidly.

A feeling of warmth overpowered Barabbas. He raised his eyes and greeted this loyalest of friends and the others, the poor and the downtrodden, who had not left him in the lurch and who were with him even in death.

Then he looked toward where the lion was being driven forward. The keepers were vainly endeavoring to spur the miserable creature to attack; the lion crouched on the ground and seemed insensible to the lashes. It did not even get up when the torches were thrust repeatedly into its ribs. The arena filled with the stench of singed hair and burned flesh.

Gripping his club tighter, Barabbas strode swiftly toward the group of men who were busy around the lion. The crowd fell silent, watching him intently.

The club whirled through the air and crashed heavily down upon the animal's head. Convulsively the lion turned, stretched out, and lay down dead.

Once again the stands began to howl. Others in the crowd joined in the victory cry of the Jews from Ophel. Shouts of "Well done, Barabbas," arose from many sides, and the mass of the spectators applauded. Those in the Procurator's box were not sure whether the applause was ironical or an instinctive tribute to the majestic strength with which Barabbas had swung the club.

Barabbas threw the club away. He cast one more glance at Ezra and the Ophel Jews, then turned and walked slowly back to the place from which he had entered the arena.

The guards came out to meet him and seized him roughly, although he offered no resistance. Blows rained down upon him as they dragged him away. The keepers were annoyed that Barabbas had ended the contest so quickly. They threw a gray linen tunic over him, chained his arms and legs and pushed him into the cell where he had been kept before.

He felt thirsty. As he reached for his jug, one of the warders kicked it over and the wine spilled out on the floor. There was now no need to save Barabbas' strength for the games. Now he was nothing but a condemned man destined to be executed soon.

A decurion with six men took charge of him to conduct him from the circus back to the prison.

As Barabbas disappeared from the eyes of the spectators, Claudia turned to her husband.

"What will be done with Barabbas now?" she asked.

"I will have him crucified," Pilate said. "I promised him a quick death if he won in the arena."

"Is that what you call a quick death?" Claudia asked, shuddering.

"Yes. I can't exactly make dying a pleasure for him. Death on the cross is comparatively quick. The man has no right to be decapitated—he is not a Roman citizen."

"Why did you subject him to this ignominy?"

Pilate glanced thoughtfully at the arena for a moment.

"I doubt whether it turned out ignominiously for him," he said. "The fellow will go to his death with the plaudits of his countrymen ringing in his ears . . ."

He gave the signal for the continuation of the games.

20

"Arise, Shine,
For Thy Light Is Come, Jerusalem . . ."

THE STREETS AROUND THE HIPPODROME APPEARED TO BE QUITE DE-serted. From the circus the shouts of the crowd and the roar of the wild beasts could still be heard, but after the little party had put a few blocks of houses between themselves and the circus, all was quiet. The afternoon sun shone hotly down upon the city, and when Barabbas raised his eyes he saw white clouds with gilded edges gliding across the blue sky.

Within himself he felt a dulled peace. He realized clearly that the Procurator had intended to humiliate him, but he did not feel humiliated. He saw again Ezra's fanatic expression and heard once more the enthusiastic shouts of the poor Jews of Ophel.

He had to walk slowly; the chains on his legs permitted him to take only short steps. The soldiers were annoyed because they had not been able to see out the games, but they did not take out their irritation on the prisoner by driving him on. Barabbas had impressed them by his behavior in the circus, and in any case they were in no particular hurry. They had to take him all the way back to the prison in the palace, and since they could not return in time to see the remainder of the games it did not matter to them whether they went fast or slow.

As the little group with Barabbas in the midst approached the

220

vicinity of the Temple Mount, the streets became somewhat livelier. In the distance they heard singing without being able to make out what was being sung. The soldiers closed around Barabbas, but this was obviously a needless precaution, since all the people were hurrying ahead, paying no attention to the prisoner and his guards. From the words of passers-by Barabbas heard frequent references to "the prophet" and the "miracle-worker," and now and again the name of Jesus of Nazareth.

Near the avenue that led up to the Temple the way was blocked by a great crowd. The soldiers might have forced their way through this human wall, but the decurion, an elderly and cautious man, apparently decided that under the circumstances this would be too dangerous. Wedged in among such a huge crowd, he and his six men could not have done very much, and even if they got through and brought their prisoner through safely he might very well be punished for leading himself and his men into danger. He therefore decided to make a detour and reach the Procurator's palace by way of side streets.

The decurion spoke a few words to his soldiers and the group turned aside into a street that was relatively deserted. At the entrances to buildings and along the curbs sat the sick and the lame who did not dare enter the crowd; they were absorbed with their maladies and listening silently to the fragments of song that were borne by the spring breeze into this sunless, ugly little by-street.

The singing in the main avenue swelled until Barabbas was able to make out the words:

"Hosannah to the Son of David!"

"Blessed be he who comes in the name of the Lord!"

"Hosannah to the King of the Jews!"

"Hosannah to the Messiah who has come to save his people!"

A crossroad afforded a brief view of the throng in the high street. Barabbas saw festively dressed people with budding branches and twigs in their hands making their way toward the Temple.

He could scarcely believe his ears. This huge crowd—Jesus of Nazareth—King of the Jews—Messiah?

A large procession that was thronging into the crossroad became jammed and for a moment blocked the soldiers' path. They stood still.

Suddenly in the main avenue the crowd grew silent. An old man in priestly vestments, with snow-white hair and beard, had mounted the steps that led up to the side entrance of a house. He stood in full view of the cross street. His fleshless arms were raised and the sun fell upon his wrinkled face. His voice rang out powerfully:

"Thus sayeth the prophet Isaiah: Arise, shine, for thy light is come, Jerusalem, and the glory of the Lord is risen upon thee. For behold, the darkness shall cover the earth and gross darkness the people, but the Lord shall arise upon thee and his glory be seen upon thee. And the gentiles shall come to thy light, and kings to the brightness of thy rising. Lift up thine eyes round about and see: all gather themselves together, they all come to thee: thy sons shall come from far and thy daughters shall be nursed at thy side. Then thou shalt see and flow together and thine heart shall fear and be enlarged; because the abundance of the sea shall be converted unto thee, the forces of the gentiles shall come unto thee."

The powerful voice ceased—the old man dropped his arms and would have fallen had he not been caught by those standing near him. Barabbas heard the old priest's name mentioned. It was Zebulon, priest of the first degree, whom many considered a prophet in his own right because he was known to have spent his long life in worship and fear of the Lord, and in acts of kindness toward his fellow men.

Now the crowd began to shout once more:

"Hosannah to the Son of David!"

"Blessed be the Anointed of the Lord who comes in His name!"

Children were in the procession, strewing flowers along the way and singing, "Hosannah to the Blessed of the Lord."

From the side streets came loud shouts:

"Jesus, Son of David, have mercy on us!"

"Jesus, Son of David, take pity on us!"

And then he himself came.

He sat upon the back of a young, light-grey donkey, his white cloak hanging down on both sides of his mount almost to the ground. It seemed as if he were gathering up all the light of the sun and reflecting it with redoubled force. His glowing eyes looked tenderly and mildly over those thousands of people who were paying him such ecstatic homage.

Then his eyes met those of Barabbas, who still stood with the guards at the intersection.

Barabbas felt a quiver pass through his tortured body. He did not know what it was that overcame him, but he had the feeling that he too, like these crippled and diseased people near by, should cry out: Jesus, Son of David, take pity on me! But his throat contracted and from his lips came a broken, helpless stammering.

It all took place in the fraction of a second. Then Jesus had ridden past the intersection and was out of sight.

He was followed by bands of disciples, people from Galilee who had come to Jerusalem for the Passover, and a multitude of the inhabitants of Jerusalem who, hearing of his coming, had hastened to meet him and honor him.

"Hosannah to the Son of David!"

"Blessed be he who comes in the name of the Lord!"

Everyone followed him and the crush in the side street slowly cleared up. The soldiers once again began leading Barabbas toward the Procurator's palace, this time walking somewhat faster than they had before. But even as they arrived at the gates of the palace Barabbas could still hear the singing of the rapturous throng and the cries of "Hosannah to the Son of David!"

When the prison overseer took charge of him, Barabbas was quickly shown that the period of relatively humane treatment of him was over and done with. He was thrown into one of the underground holes which was coated with filth and in which moisture dripped from the stone walls. Then he was chained to the wall and the chain drawn so short that he could scarcely stretch out on the remnants of rotted straw that represented his bed. When he asked for water he was kicked in the ribs by one of his jailers.

When he was left alone Barabbas attempted to set his thoughts in order.

First of all there was this fear within him—not of death but of what might come after death. What was the source of such thoughts? All his life he had never troubled about this problem, and now he found himself fearing the judgment. Why, why?

What had happened in the circus . . . No, that was dead and gone, blotted out as if it had never been. It seemed like a dream dimly remembered upon waking.

But the other thing, the thousands in the streets, the triumphal entry of the prophet of Nazareth . . . For it had been a triumph! "King of the Jews!" "Son of David!" What did it all mean? Had the Nazarene finally resolved to take over the rule of all Israel? And what would the Romans do? Was this triumphal entry a surprise assault—had it been deliberately undertaken at a time when the majority of the foreign rulers were enjoying their bloody games in the circus? Had the guards at the gates been overpowered by the masses? Were those festively-dressed people carrying arms under their clothing?

For a moment this thought stunned him. He felt not a touch of envy that it had not fallen to his lot to complete the work of liberation; he even toyed with the idea that the Nazarene's great mass following would set him free. Then he rejected the whole idea. It was simply not possible, he told himself; Jesus of Nazareth would never adopt methods of violence. He recalled the Nazarene as he had seen him at the head of the procession. In the darkness of his cell the features of the remarkable man were luminously present to him—close, very close, the radiant eyes filled with sympathy and kindliness. "What am I thinking of?" Barabbas asked himself in fright. "What is happening to me?"

He recalled the night in Magdala. All the rabbi's words revived within him in the silence and darkness of this cell where the volume of air scarcely served to fill his lungs. They were harsh words, and his heart burned with shame that he had listened to them so tamely. What an uncanny power this Nazarene possessed. "Since that night in Magdala he has been affecting me, trying to change me," Barabbas thought tormentedly, "and I have become weaker than I was. Since then have I not shunned the shedding of Israelite blood? In the circus did I not spare the Roman lackeys? And this idea of judgment after death—that came from him also. And at his entry—was I not also tempted to cry out with the others: 'Hosannah to the Son of David, the Messiah!'? What a downfall!"

The more Barabbas thought about it, the more vehemently his pride resisted the idea that he had fallen prey to the man's wiles. He recognized how ridiculous was his conjecture that the Nazarene had conquered Jerusalem. He had seen him after all, their eyes had met and there had even been signs of recognition in his glance when he saw Barabbas bound, guarded by Roman soldiers. Would not a sign from the real liberator have sufficed to drive away the soldiers and remove his chains? No, he was not the liberator; only the stupid, blinded mob was capable of believing that the Messiah, the conqueror of Israel's enemies, would ride unarmed into Jerusalem on the back of an ass. Barabbas reproached himself bitterly. "I was wrong for running after him," he told himself, "wrong in offering him an alliance, wrong in not fighting vigorously from the beginning this strange weakness I had for him, wrong in not killing him that time at Jacob's Well. It was a betrayal of my aims to permit this man to preach love and patience when I knew so well that only struggle and violence can possibly bring freedom."

His aims? What aims could a man have who would be dying within a few hours or days? "There are no longer any aims for me," Barabbas thought. "But others will come after me, with more luck than I have had. A sorcerer blocked my path—I was too weak. But others will go on to the end and remain strong; what will come on earth will not be a deadly peace but the force and violence which that magician claims must be renounced. And whatever he does or says, his words and deeds will vanish in the wind, for they are built upon weakness and not upon strength."

Finding consolation in this thought, Barabbas fell asleep. In his dreams he saw himself riding on horseback, triumphantly entering Jerusalem, while beside him rode Ezra crying: "Hail Barabbas, King of the Jews, Messiah!"

Ezra, almost immediately after the end of the ludicrous contest between Barabbas and "Juda ben Jacob," had left the circus. He hoped to catch one more glimpse of Barabbas, but failing to find the proper exit at once he came too late. There was a burning bitterness within him at the insult offered Barabbas by his being given an almost lifeless corpse for opponent; Ezra was more ashamed than Barabbas himself had been. With Barabbas out of the arena he felt it impossible to go on breathing the same air as the Roman masters for another moment. The games in themselves disgusted him. To give and receive wounds in honest combat, to kill or be killed, was a man's task. But to tear men to pieces for entertainment and amusement seemed to him a crime against nature.

Outside the hippodrome Ezra found the streets deserted until he reached the main thoroughfare. There he saw people hastening ahead toward some unknown goal. He joined them in the irrational hope that somewhere in the city a rebellion had begun. But when he saw what the excitement was about he felt bitterly disappointed.

It was a severe blow to him to see the populace rejoicing at the entrance into Jerusalem of the man from Nazareth.

It was something Ezra could not understand. He had always considered the Nazarene an opponent of Barabbas and had felt the doctrine of loving-kindness, patience, and forgiveness to be ridiculous and undignified as well as harmful to the cause of the Israelite nation. Why were these people jubilantly cheering the man as though he were a liberator?

His heart filled with gloom, Ezra watched the parade with the Nazarene in the midst march toward the Temple Mount. The Hosannahs of the thousands found no echo in his embittered soul.

What fools these men were! With half their number he could have broken open all the jails in Jerusalem. A few hundreds of them would have sufficed to free Barabbas. And here they were running after the man who asked them to love even their enemies!

He saw the Temple servants carrying off the lifeless body of an old man in priestly vestments. From bystanders he learned that the man was Zebulon, priest of the first degree, and many of the people remarked how fortunate he had been to breathe out his long life "before the face of the Messiah." All this talk made not the slightest impression upon Ezra. Slowly he went on, avoiding the stragglers who were following Jesus. Unwittingly his feet bore him in the direction of the Procurator's palace to which, he suspected, Barabbas had been returned.

A litter was borne swiftly past him. For a moment he thought he glimpsed the pale face of the Procurator within, but he thought he must be mistaken, for the Procurator would certainly still be sitting in his ornate box watching men being torn to bits and human blood flowing like water.

But it was in fact the Procurator.

The laughter in the circus had slowly abated after Barabbas was taken out, and the poor Jews from Ophel who had so loudly shouted their sympathy for him began to fear they might be rounded up and punished; they hastily left the circus. The keepers cleared away the dead lion's body. Before the next number began Pilate turned to Claudia.

"It seems to me, Claudia," he said, "that you did not enjoy my little joke. Forgive me, Jerusalem is not Rome. I know this is only a provincial show. But I had a definite purpose in mind when I made Barabbas fight the lion. I hope those conspiratorial high priests understood it."

"How long is this entertainment to go on?" Claudia asked impatiently.

Just then a centurion in command of the palace guard entered the box and raised his arm to salute the Procurator.

"What news, Publius?" Pilate asked lazily.

"There is a riot in the streets, Tribune," the centurion replied nervously.

"I hope, Publius, that this was a slip of the tongue. There was a riot in the streets, you mean. What sort of riot?"

"Crowds of people are marching from the Damascus Gate to the Temple Mount."

"What sort of crowds?"

"They seem to be Jews, Procurator."

"And what are they doing?"

"They have a man in their midst who is riding on a donkey. They keep calling to him and seem to be paying homage to him."

"What are they saying?"

"I do not understand the barbarous language of this country, Tribune. I have been informed that they are singing a hymn of praise to a certain Son of David, and they are also singing something about a king of the Jews."

"How are the people armed?"

"They are not armed at all. They are carrying palm branches in their hands and strewing flowers along the street."

Pilate laughed.

"Is that what you call a riot, Publius? I hope there has been no interference with these people. They are marching toward the Temple Mount, you say?"

"Yes, Procurator. By now the procession must have reached the Temple Mount."

"Very well, Publius. Let the high priests worry about that kind of riot. As long as the Jews carry palm branches and sing we have no reason to bother them. In fact, we will do well to keep away, if only to avoid the filth they always bring with them . . . Have any of them molested our men?"

"No, Procurator. They are behaving very peaceably."

"Good. See to it that the cohorts are held in readiness in any case. These Jews are so unpredictable. But don't interfere with the people in the streets. Clear?"

"Yes, Procurator."

The Procurator saluted carelessly and the centurion withdrew. But indifferent as Pilate had seemed, he was too much of a soldier not to be aware of the potential menace in the words "King of the Jews" and "Son of David."

Below in the arena preparations were going on for another sword contest.

"Do you think that fool Juda ben Jacob is actually going to do something after all?" Pilate murmured. The question was directed more to himself than to his wife. But Claudia replied:

"It must be Jesus of Nazareth; his followers intended to celebrate his entry into Jerusalem," she remarked.

Pilate sat erect. This he had not thought of, but it was quite possible that Claudia was right and the thought disturbed him more than he was willing to admit even to himself. These Jews were capable of anything! Come to think of it, what he had said before about Jews singing and carrying palm branches was a mistake. Just the opposite would be true. As long as they behaved rebelliously and stubbornly like Barabbas, or with concealed enmity like the high priest, there were ways of handling them. But what if they marched under the banner of love and mildness? Was there not a greater peril implicit in such behavior against which he was powerless?

The Procurator beckoned to his secretary.

"See that my litter is made ready, Marcus," he ordered. "I had better go back to the palace. There's no knowing what may happen."

Marcus bowed and left the box. The governor turned to Claudia.

"There are only three more numbers on the program, Claudia. I will send the litter back for you. Don't forget, in my absence you are the *domina* here and have the decision as to life or death. Since you are so preoccupied with the Nazarene I am afraid you will grant life to them all. Do so if you wish; it doesn't matter to me. I want to look into this trouble in the streets."

He strode swiftly out of the box and entered his litter.

"Proceed quietly and by the shortest route to the palace," he ordered. "Come along too, Marcus, I may need you. If this Nazarene should happen to try any tricks, we will be ready."

The litter-bearers carried their burden quickly through the city. Pilate saw only the stragglers behind the thousands who had participated in the Nazarene's entry into Jerusalem—the sick, the aged, and the crippled. The only sign of the great crowd that had passed by was the debris of branches, buds and flowers that had been strewn in the thoroughfare.

As soon as he reached the palace he called for reports from his various commanders. He learned that the Nazarene, followed by a great throng, had entered the square before the Temple and had spoken to the people there. There was little definite information on just what he had said; the captains of the guard had merely noted that his words did not seem to be inciting the people to any action. He had spoken a good deal about love of men and that the time was fulfilled and humanity would soon be freed of the curse of sin.

"Do you understand what that means?" Pilate inquired of his secretary.

Marcus shrugged.

"He is evidently putting himself forward as the Messiah," he said thoughtfully. "There are a number of passages in the sacred books of these people which might be interpreted to mean that the liberation of the people of Israel is to come at the present time."

"Liberation? From Rome?"

"I don't think so, Procurator. The books deal with a spiritual, not a political liberation. But the interpreters don't agree; every one of them interprets the writings as he chooses. You know the Jews assert that they have a special contractual relationship with their God, but that they still have to atone for an old sin and that is to be done by the Messiah, a person sent by their God. When that happens the chosen people of Israel will rule the entire world through their belief in a single God. You can interpret that as you choose, of course."

"Crazy fanatics," Pilate murmured thoughtfully. "Do you think this Nazarene's movement is dangerous?"

"Dangerous to the priests, certainly, and to himself," Marcus replied.

"The priests are as a matter of fact hot on his trail."

"Naturally. He is filching their hold on the minds of the Jews. And besides he's ruining their business."

"I've been hearing about these matters for a long time, but—I admit it frankly—I don't understand the whole affair. Are you familiar with the man's doctrine?"

"Just the ordinary gossip I've heard about it. It's the kind of doctrine that would be very comforting to the poor and the slaves, promising them a better life in the other world if they keep the commandments, that is, if they love their fellow men."

"Joseph of Arimathea told me about that. What do you think of it, Marcus?"

"It depends—from what point of view do you want to consider it?" Marcus said evasively.

"From the point of view of Rome, of course," Pilate replied.

"From that point of view the doctrine has elements that are both useful and subversive. A nation that wishes to rule the world might well find it salutary for its subjects to leave off caring about their welfare on earth and to expect a better life only in an unknown other world. On the other hand, it is dangerous to have people get it into their heads that they are all equal before their God. They might begin to wonder why they are not equal before their earthly masters."

"Do you think the doctrine can spread very widely in Judea?" Pilate continued his interrogation.

"Here as everywhere the poor are in the majority," Marcus replied.

"I have heard that this Nazarene has performed a number of remarkable miracles."

"The Jews are a highly superstitious people," Marcus said. "Even in the simplest things they imagine they see supernatural forces at work. I have seen none of those miracles personally. But a few minutes ago I saw a good many cripples and diseased persons in the streets who had not been healed by the miracle-worker."

A courier entered with the message that the people in front of the temple had started to disperse and that Jesus of Nazareth had vanished.

"It doesn't look much like insurrection," Pilate remarked. "But we'll double the guards in the streets tonight and break up any gatherings of considerable size. The Nazarene should be kept under surveillance—I don't want to hear again that he has vanished." He turned to Marcus. "Is there any other business?"

"Barrabas has been brought back to the prison," the secretary replied.

"Good. I will have him brought to trial in a few days. Come to think of it, the man was really disappointing. A rebel, an insurrectionist with a weapon in his hand, and he contented himself with knocking a dying cat over the snout. If I had his strength, I would have killed a few of the keepers. Oh well, I'll have him crucified on the Passover. I want to give him a good tall cross so that plenty of Jews will see him hanging there."

"I wonder, Procurator, whether such spectacles accomplish their purpose," Marcus said. "Martyrs always win popularity."

"I'm willing to grant popularity on the cross to any rebel," Pilate replied smilingly, and dismissed his secretary with a wave of his hand.

21 ✠

A Letter from Rome and a Reply

THE PROCURATOR WAS IN A VERY BAD HUMOR.

Two days after the Sabbath cold weather had unexpectedly returned. An icy wind blew from the northeast; it was almost as cold
as it had been in winter. Pilate was chilly. He could never get used
to these sudden changes in the weather.

In addition he had heard from Claudia that she had visited the
man of Nazareth twice, accompanied by Mary of Magdala. His wife
had tried to tell him something about the Nazarene's doctrines, but
he had refused to listen. Today, when she had again started to talk
about this Jewish preacher, he had left the room, gone to his study
and was now pacing back and forth to keep warm.

He was also thinking of a letter he had received from Rome and
which had contributed mightily to his ill humor. The letter read as
follows:

FROM SENATOR TULLIUS APER TO THE MILITARY TRIBUNE AND
GOVERNOR OF JUDEA AND SAMARIA, PONTIUS PILATE.

Greetings! If I were to wait, my friend, until you sent me news
of yourself, even a few wretched lines—by all the gods of Rome
and Greece I would probably wither away like the summer grass
while waiting. You, my dear Pilate, are so lazy it is almost offen-
sive. Or, master of style that you are, has your sojourn among the

241

barbarians already robbed you of your ability to wield the stylus? Or else—are you so comfortable in that curious province of yours that you have simply forgotten your old friends?

I cannot answer these questions, but I wish to heap burning coals on your head and therefore send you by Centurion Lepidus Cancer—a good and handsome youth, incidentally—this epistle from which you may learn first, that in spite of your silence you still have good friends in Rome and, second, that the province you administer is at the moment extraordinarily favored in high, or rather the highest, circles. Perhaps it would be more correct to say that the interest of those circles is devoted less to the province than to its natives.

The Imperator, who has always had a weakness for the odd and curious, has just acquired a Hebrew bodyguard. In addition there is a young man—I can no more spell the name than I can pronounce it—who is a kinsman or son of the Jews' pontifex maximus and who has the ear of the Augustus in a really astounding fashion. He and a whole crew of Jewish scholars—and by Jupiter what a curious race they are!—come to the palace almost every morning, and if I am correctly informed these barbarians have talked the Augustus into such a respect for their God that he is thinking of erecting a Temple to him right here in the middle of Rome. This young man, whose father must be known to you, has also obtained permission for the Jews who live in Rome to erect houses of worship dedicated to their God on the other side of the Tiber. Our priests are quite wrought up about the matter. They fear the obviously increasing influence of the Hebrews. And not without reason, my friend Pilate, for a Jewish physician succeeded recently in curing the Augustus of a kidney stone. In return the Augustus had such a stone fashioned in gold and has placed it in his temple. Hebrew is all the rage at the moment—I will not entrust to the waxen tablet all the bad jokes that are being bandied around about this, and particularly about the kidney stones.

But while these matters may strike you at first glance as a sign of my weakness for gossip, I think you will recognize that they are not without significance for you. To stand at the head of such a highly-favored province imposes certain obligations, which is why I am informing you of these matters; you will draw the necessary conclusions for yourself.

From all that I can gather from my friends in the palace, I believe the Augustus is very well informed about your relations with the dominant group in Judea—the priests, I assume. He also seems to have been told that these relations are not altogether friendly—a fact I can very well understand. How could you endure these odd and, so I hear, extremely arrogant persons? But there are a good many intriguers in Rome who envy you your position and consider it so profitable that they would not shrink from playing along with the machinations of the Jews. You are wise enough, my friend, to direct your behavior accordingly.

I had to inform you of this because it may be of importance for your future career. I will say nothing about other affairs in Rome—in punishment for your long silence. Just this: during the years you have been away in the east we have become considerably madder and—more keen on so-called vice than we used to be. Sometimes I really don't know whether to pity you or envy you for being unable to take part in our pleasures.

My best greetings to the noble Claudia!

Farewell.

Pilate was able to read fluently between the lines. Watch out, his friend was saying, or they may complain about you to the Augustus and that will mean the end of your public career. If until now he had felt himself master of Judea, he must now acknowledge that his power had certain limitations. He ruled to the extent that High Priest Annas permitted him to rule. Obviously the priesthood did not feel altogether secure. In spite of the insolence with which Annas had broached the matter of Barabbas, the Procurator knew that the priests were worried about their relations with the robber and with the grandson of the Maccabean. But there could be no doubt now that Annas had been writing to Rome for some time.

Pilate ceased his pacing and went up to the desk where his secretary was writing.

"I am dissatisfied with you, Marcus," the Procurator said.

The secretary looked up at Pilate.

"May I ask the reason, O Procurator?"

"There are too many letters going to Rome for my liking. Too many letters in Hebrew and Aramaic, understand? So far as I know my order to inspect all letters still stands. Is my order not being carried out? The ports are under our control and we have enough soldiers to search every suspicious person or courier. It seems to me there is negligence afoot here and I am not inclined to let it go unpunished."

"If I am not mistaken, Procurator, you are concerned about High Priest Annas' letters to Rome?" Marcus asked.

"Those and others. But you are right—primarily the high priest's letters."

"I have learned," Marcus replied, "that the high priest has frequently received letters brought by Roman officials and has answered them through those same officials. We did not presume to search Roman functionaries who were arriving or leaving here."

"In the future see to it that it is done," Pilate said. "And I do not desire the high priest's letters to reach the addressee."

"This is the first time you have expressed such a desire, Procurator."

"It should not have been necessary for me to specify," Pilate said irritably.

"Your wish will be fulfilled. But may I ask you to give me express permission to proceed against the messengers with the utmost severity and without consideration of their station?"

"That goes without saying. If I had loyal and intelligent servants, it would not be necessary for me to say all this."

Marcus said nothing and once more bent over his work. Pilate resumed his pacing.

"Damnable country," he mused. "And on top of everything else I have to go easy in order not to fall into disfavor with Rome."

He suddenly thought of Barabbas. That was one affair he ought to settle, he thought. There was nothing standing in the way of his passing judgment on the man. From what Annas had said the priests would have no objection; in fact they would probably be glad to be rid of a troublesome potential witness against them. The Nazarene now—they did seem to consider him a good deal more important. Well, he would see. One thing at a time.

"Get Barabbas up here," he said to Marcus. "I want to get that business over with for good."

Barabbas was lying on the rotting straw. Since his chain was drawn so short that he could not even stand up, he had been lying thus since the combat in the circus. His condition was pitiable.

The brown smock they had thrown over him in the circus reeked with filth. Since he had been lying in this hole he had been given nothing to eat but a few crusts of mouldy bread and water every second day. For two days now he had been feverish and dazed. When he was not dozing apathetically he had hallucinations. He saw himself at the head of a mighty army battling the Romans. In these chaotic dreams blood flowed copiously—Roman blood. He had given orders to see to it that not a single Roman in Jerusalem escaped with his life, and his soldiers were faithfully carrying out these orders.

Now two of his keepers entered the cell and detached his chains from the wall. Then, with blows and kicks, they dragged him to his feet, and although he could hardly stand he was pushed out into the corridor. Here they took off the brown smock and poured cold water over him. It did not cleanse him very thoroughly, but it was refreshing. Then he was given a dirty undergarment, chained again and pushed into the corridor leading to the interior of the palace. Here he was placed in charge of two soldiers who held their noses at the sight of him and burst into laughter.

"You pigs!" one of the soldiers snapped at the warders. "Do you imagine we're going to take the fellow before the Procurator in this condition?"

There was a sharp exchange of words between the soldiers and the jailers. Then more water was poured over Barabbas, he was dried and this time given a linen tunic that was fairly clean. After this second washing the soldiers took him in hand and led him up to the Procurator's office.

Pilate was standing in the center of the room when the soldiers thrust Barabbas in at the door. The Procurator scarcely noticed the wretched condition of the man, his deathly pallor and his weakness. His eyes were used to the misery of others; and this, moreover, was a man who was in any case condemned to death. He did not have Barabbas' chains removed. Scarcely interested in the reply, he asked the routine question:

"Do you wish to have a formal trial?"

"My only wish is that you keep your promise and have me killed quickly," Barabbas replied, and his voice rang out more forcefully than could have been expected, considering his condition.

"Then you waive a hearing of witnesses who might perhaps testify to facts or circumstances which would mitigate your crimes?"

"I waive it."

"You confess to having committed murder?"

"Yes."

"And you committed highway robbery?"

"Yes."

Pilate turned to Marcus, who had been writing down the questions and answers.

"Since he confesses we need no witnesses. You need merely enter the confession and the sentence."

He turned again to Barabbas:

"My finding is as follows: The Jew Barabbas is by his own confession guilty of murder and highway robbery. Incidentally, how many murders have you committed?"

"As many Romans as I could lay my hands on."

"Do you regret these acts?"

"I regret only the fact that I also killed Jews."

"The priests would be pleased to hear that, but it doesn't interest me. Would you care to offer in extenuation that you committed murders of Romans at the instigation of the priests?"

"At no one's instigation."

"Very well. Continue, Marcus: the Jew Barabbas is sentenced to death on the cross. Have you anything else to say, Barabbas?"

"I wish the sentence to be carried out at once."

For the first time Pilate looked his prisoner squarely in the eyes. What he saw there was not the savage defiance of the first hearing but an infinite weariness, the desire to get his forfeited life over with quickly.

"Dying means nothing to you, does it?" he asked.

"It is better than being a Roman prisoner."

"Do you believe in a life after death? As a Jew you ought to believe in that."

"I do."

"It must be a painful thought. You will certainly go to the place of eternal punishment which you call hell."

"Perhaps."

"Do you imagine it will be better there than in a Roman prison?"

"I don't know," Barabbas replied, and now his eyes flashed with their old fire. "But I hope to meet you again there."

Pilate laughed—he liked this reply.

"I see there is still some venom left in you. I am sorry that you will have to curb your impatience for a few days. I want your friends to have the pleasure of seing you hanging on the cross on the Festival day. In three days!"

He turned to the soldiers.

"Take him away. I will appoint the hour of execution later."

Barabbas was led out. He did not glance again at the Procurator; he was so worn out by hunger and thirst that he scarcely noticed when he was cast into another cell, this one slightly drier than the last had been. He was once more chained close to the wall and his request for water and bread was ignored. Again he fell into that twilight state in which he was capable of no organized thought.

The Procurator stood at one of the tall windows and looked down at the square in front of the palace. There had been a light fall of sleet; the stone pavement looked almost as if it were covered with snow. A litter was borne across the square—Claudia's. He saw Claudia and Mary of Magdala get out.

"Probably they've been up to the Temple Mount again to hear the preaching of the man from Nazareth," Pilate reflected, frowning. Mary of Magdala no longer had any time at all for him, he mused, and grew hot wtih rage. "By the gods," he muttered, "if it weren't that I would be doing the priests too big a favor, I myself would have the man seized to get him out of the way. Perhaps the galleys would be the proper place for him."

Embittered at the world in general and at Judea and its inhabitants in particular, he left his study and went to the living quarters. Before he left he said curtly to Marcus:

"I will have a letter to dictate to you later. Wait here for me."

The secretary nodded and continued working. He, too, had liked Barabbas' reply that he hoped to meet the Procurator in hell, and Marcus chuckled to himself as he thought of it. He made up his mind to give Barabbas the benefit of having his verdict put down in well-polished phrases.

Pilate hesitated for a moment, wondering whether he should not go to Claudia's rooms at once in order to see Mary there. But he felt that he had to take his irritation out on someone first or he would burst. He listened to see whether the domestic slaves were up to anything, but not a sound was to be heard. In his living room, which adjoined the library, he found the slave-girl Chloe busy filling the braziers, which had been burning all day long. There was no reason to object to it, but now even this effort to make him more comfortable annoyed him.

"Let that be!" he shouted at her. "You fill the room with smoke and stench, but it doesn't warm it."

Timid as a scolded child, with lowered eyes, the young slave girl left the room. This, too, irritated him. Why had she not replied? Then he could have scolded her again or had her whipped, and so relieved himself.

He tried to read but could not. Again and again his thoughts returned to his sensation that he was isolated and deserted, that neither Claudia nor Mary cared at all about him. This man of Nazareth had turned them both against him, he thought. He could not understand why they persisted in running after that Jewish beggar. He let half an hour pass, then he overcame his hesitation and hastened toward Claudia's apartment.

In addition to Mary of Magdala he found Joseph of Arimathea with his wife. When Pilate entered the room Joseph arose and greeted the Procurator with friendly courtesy.

"I am pleased," Pilate said with forced cordiality, "to find here friends who have not visited frequently of late. Greetings, Mary, and you too, Joseph—it does me good to see you both."

"You're very kind, Procurator," Joseph said, bowing. "The noble Claudia asked us to keep her company for a while."

"I hope I am not intruding," Pilate replied. And then he asked abruptly: "Aren't you interested in inquiring after the health of your old friend Barabbas? I had a talk with him a while ago."

"You are jesting, Procurator," Joseph said gravely. "You know very well that Barabbas is not our friend. But since you speak of him—may I inform you that in part of the Jewish populace there is a certain resentment on account of Barabbas."

"Do you mean that for an admission that the Jews harbor sympathy for a murderer and robber?" Pilate asked with pretended amazement.

"Not that, Procurator," Joseph answered quietly. "But people felt that making a spectacle of Barabbas in the circus was humiliating to all Jews."

"I hope it will prove a salutary lesson for the priests. In any case the question of Barabbas is settled for good. He will die on the cross in three days. He will be on view, so to speak, during the Festival days.

"Horrible!" Mary exclaimed, covering her eyes with her hand.

"How so?" Pilate asked. "The man was a murderer many times over. You should praise me for passing judgment, Mary. An eye for an eye and a tooth for a tooth, as your sacred writings say."

Mary felt the governor's mocking gaze on her face, and suddenly this huge, ornate room seemed narrow, bare, and cold as a tomb to her. In a low voice, with bowed head, she said:

"Only God has the right to judge men. It is our duty to love them."

Pilate laughed; his laughter sounded shrill and forced.

"The Augustus would certainly thank me kindly if I threw up my magisterial duties. It seemes to me that all this confusion in your minds comes from the preaching of this Nazarene to whom you listen so diligently."

"Confusion?" Joseph exclaimed. "Nothing could be clearer and less confused than what the Master preaches. Nothing is simpler than the commandment to love God and one's neighbor."

"Clear? Simple?" Pilate repeated inquiringly. "It doesn't strike me that way. If you only consider it, this love of neighbor destroys the power of the emotion of love. For if love breaks up into so many parts, there cannot be very much left for any single individual."

Mary's eyes glowed.

"Love is like a light," she said with deep sincerity. "Thousands and tens of thousands of other lights can take their flame from it, and yet it remains what it is; it is not diminished by giving of itself. For the light comes from God."

These words were followed by silence, as if it were impossible after them to revert to ordinary polite conversation. Claudia sank back in her chair and let her veiled gaze drift off into the remote distance. Joseph clasped his active hands in his lap and stared down at the floor. But the Procurator looked astonished at the girl whose deep emotion was evidenced by her heavy breathing; she sat with eyes directed upward as if she had received illumination from above.

"How beautiful you are, Mary," the Procurator thought, but he was unable to put this profane thought into words in the pure air that had been created by Mary's outburst.

During this silence the overseer of the slaves entered the room, went up to Claudia and whispered a few words to her.

Claudia appeared to be delighted.

"Some rose seedlings have just arrived from Latium," she said, turning to Joseph. "You remember, Joseph, I spoke to you about them. I intend to plant them in big wooden tubs in the atrium. Would you like to come with me and see them?"

Joseph bowed assent and rose. He and Claudia followed the overseer out. Pilate and Mary remained alone in the room.

The light was already fading. From the atrium they could hear voices without being able to make out the words. Mary, absorbed in her thoughts, had scarcely noticed that she was alone with the Procurator. But now she felt the man's ardent glance and turned to him.

"Mary," he murmured, leaning toward her until he was almost touching her, "I've been waiting and wishing for a long time to have a moment alone with you like this. I have had a great deal to say to you."

His eyes made her uneasy and she looked at him in wonderment, startled by his words and still more by his constrained tone.

"I am not hard to find," she said, forcing a smile.

"You are—for me, Mary. I cannot very well ride out to Bethany, and even if I did, how could I know whether I would be successful in finding you alone? And since you have been in Jerusalem I would probably have been able to find you only among the disciples of this Nazarene. You see, what I have to say to you, Mary, cannot be said before others. Don't you know that I love you, Mary?"

The girl's face revealed mingled amazement and dismay.

"I may not, I will not hear these words," she whispered.

"Why not, Mary, why not? A few months ago you liked coming to see us; you called me 'friend' and in your eyes I thought I could read a warmer feeling. Now your eyes are cold. Can't you love, Mary?"

"Not the way you mean, Procurator?"

"How am I to understand that? I know what a horror you Jews have of adultery. But I don't mean it that way, Mary. Claudia is wise and generous; she has never been anything more to me than a motherly friend and she would be the last to condemn me for loving you because she also loves you. Nothing stands in the way of my

breaking the bond that links us only formally and making of you the
first lady of the East. And I love you, Mary, do you hear—I love
you."

Mary's cheeks were hot and flushed.

"Do you imagine," she said, "that I would be so base as to take
away the husband of a woman whom I honor as a friend? No, you
can't think that of me. But it isn't that alone, Procurator. I shall
never belong to any man."

These words were spoken quietly, but with great emphasis. The
Procurator looked his bewilderment.

"What are you saying, Mary? You don't mean that!"

"I do mean it," she said in a clear, fervent voice. "I certainly do
mean it. I must say this to you: Anyone who has had the happiness
to be struck by a ray of that merciful sun which is in His eyes is hal-
lowed forever and casts off all earthly desires."

At these words Pilate started and trembled. His face paled and
his eyes glowed with wrath.

"So that is it," he growled. "The man of Nazareth. Do you love
him?"

Mary winced at the question. But then she looked up into the
face of the governor, who was quivering with emotion, and said
quietly:

"Love . . . the word is wrong in the sense you mean it, Pilate. He
is so incomparably far above me and all of us, so utterly removed
from all earthly things, that no such thought, no bold desires, could
touch the soles of his feet. I love him—yes—as I love the sun that
warms me, as I love the earth that sustains me, as I love the clear
stars of the heavens . . . No, I love him more than sun, earth, and
stars—I love him who is above all other things as I love God, in
deepest humility. That is how I love him!"

She had clasped her hands over her breast and her shining eyes
seemed to be looking into another world.

"The Messiah!" Pilate exclaimed hoarsely. "In what wilderness
are you wandering, Mary? You were so cool and wise; you walked
so sensibly along the paths that life had laid out for you. And now
along comes a man who knows how to speak eloquently and you
forget riches, culture, your own beauty; you throw yourself at the feet
of a vagabond. You are losing yourself, Mary."

"Oh no, Pilate," Mary said firmly. "On the contrary, I have found myself. I had been following the path of vanity and arrogance and egotism. I wasted my days in idle play and idle thoughts until he revealed to me the profound meaning of life."

The Procurator's lips twisted in mockery.

"The profound meaning of life . . . You certainly know more than I do if you know the meaning of life. To me it seems altogether meaningless."

"Because you look for it where it is not, Pilate. You look for meaning in pomp and power and splendor, in all the things outside yourself that lure your senses."

"Well, where is the meaning of life to be found?"

"In yourself, Pilate, in your own soul. God kindled the flame in you as in all men, but you have smothered it as we all do. But your soul is good, Pilate, and it will be illuminated through him."

Standing before Mary, Pilate threw his head back and coldly demanded:

"Why did the man come to Jerusalem? Don't you know he is in deadly peril here?"

"You see, Pilate," Mary said pensively, "you are good, although you do not wish to admit it even to yourself. You sent us a warning through Claudia, and Lazarus spoke to him about the danger he would face in Jerusalem. But he said that he must go on his way to the end without deviating a hairsbreadth from it. What is to happen to him is not in the power of men . . ."

"That remains to be seen," Pilate said, walking over to the window. He knew that there was no use in continuing the conversation; Mary's faith was unshakable.

Claudia and Joseph returned from the atrium, still talking about the roses, for Joseph himself was an amateur plant breeder, but both noticed at once that something had happened between the Procurator and Mary. Claudia guessed what it was and threw Pilate a glance that seemed to say, "I warned you." She hurried over to Mary and placed her hand graciously on the girl's hair.

"It's late, Mary—we must be going," Joseph said.

After brief, flurried goodbyes the guests took their leave. As Mary got into the litter she said softly to Joseph:

"I feel he will do everything in his power for Him, Joseph . . ."

As soon as their guests were gone, Claudia asked Pilate:

"Did you have a talk with Mary?"

"Yes," Pilate said.

"And?"

"It is hard to understand this oriental fanaticism. I am going to have a look at this—this Messiah."

"I saw him today," Claudia said. "He is not an ordinary man. One feels something divine in him."

"A mortal God, I suppose. At least it's something new."

"Do not mock, Pilate. Perhaps you are closer to the truth than you imagine."

"I am not mocking," Pilate replied. "But I do want to keep my wits about me. Now will you excuse me, Claudia; I must write a letter to Rome."

He strode rapidly out of the room. Marcus was waiting for him, but he dismissed the secretary curtly, took up the wax tablet and began writing in his own hand:

FROM THE PROCURATOR OF JUDEA AND SAMARIA, MILITARY TRIB-
    UNE PONTIUS PILATE, TO SENATOR TULLIUS APER.

Greetings. Thank you for your letter, my friend, which I received today. If you knew what my frame of mind is in this horrible country, you would not reproach me for my long silence. It is no kindness to a friend to write letters filled with wailing and complaints.

It is very useful to me to know what is going on in Rome. I am well aware that a son of High Priest Annas, the spiritual head of the Jews, is in Rome and has been admitted to the presence of the Augustus. But I did not know that he and his coterie had been so successful in calling the attention of Caesar to themselves and their affairs. I know well their ability to worm their way in wherever there is some profit in it for them. Apparently they are favored by the fact that the Augustus always shows preference to those religious cults which are distinguished by their oddity and their differences from the cults of the Occident. That, of course, is a penchant concerning which it is not appropriate for us to form any opinion.

But as for my governing my relationships to the religious heads of the Jewish people here in this country with an eye to developments at the court of Caesar, I must, my dear Tullius Aper, decline to let such favors influence the conduct of my rule. Those who know Rome as well as you and I know how swiftly moods change there. Those who have the ear of the Augustus today may find themselves in the galleys on the morrow. The humors of the Divine One are unpredictable. But government must be permanent, power must be lasting, Rome must remain unshaken. And for that reason it is the duty of a governor to keep in mind the maintenance of the imperial power and not to be distracted by moods and whims and infatuations.

To apply these generalities to my particular case: I would be committing a grave wrong against the Empire if, just because the Hebrews happen to be the darlings of Rome at the moment, I should slacken the reins here and curry favor with the priesthood. Just the contrary! It is then my duty to make it quite clear to those slippery gentlemen that the cordiality the Augusus shows them in no wise detracts from the unconditional rule of Rome.

It is impossible, my friend, to give you in a short letter a clear account of the political conditions of this country. Here politics is so intricately interwoven with religion that one never quite knows what is political maneuvering and what religious fanaticism. I have at hand two examples which will serve to give you some small conception of the difficulties of my position as governor.

Some time ago a man named Barabbas began making himself conspicuous in an unpleasant manner. He had been a robber and a murderer. As long as his activities were restricted to securing the necessities of life for himself and his band at the expense of rich Jews, I had no reason to pay more attention to him than to any other criminal. It never occurred to me to make an affair of state out of a policing problem. This man, however, who hated the Romans, took advantage of the latent longings for national liberation and played himself up as the coming "liberator of Israel." I should inform you that the Jews have enjoyed national liberty several times in the past and are filled with a strong urge to regain it. It would be a mistake to underestimate the vigor of this desire, a still greater mistake to persuade oneself that laxity, compromise, and amicable treatment could ever make so fanatical and barbarous a people understand Rome's good intentions.

On the other hand, my dear Tullius Aper, it would be equally

mistaken to create the impression that Rome's power stands on
such weak legs that we must worry about every robber and murderer who has nationalistic pretensions. Without too much effort
I could have had the man and every one of his followers captured
and tried. There is ample wood for crosses in this country. But
I do not have excessively large military forces at my disposal, and
the example of Pretorian Varinius who was defeated by Spartacus
the Slave at the foot of Vesuvius appeared to me far from tempting. And although I certainly cannot be accused of soft-hearted-
ness, it seems to me a moot question whether Licinius Crassus
with his mass crucifixions at Potelia did harm or good to the prestige of Rome. I prefer, my friend, to deprive these political agitators of the aureole of liberating heroes, to stamp them as ordinary
criminals and make them butts of ridicule. Instead of running to
Rome with alarmist pleas for more soldiers, I had this Barabbas
arrested as a robber and murderer at the proper moment and made
a comic figure out of him at the circus. He will die on the cross
in a few days. His movement has been scattered to the winds
and his followers are happy that I permitted them to scatter and
run like a herd of frightened goats.

I may also add that these same Jewish priests who with hypo-
critical submissiveness have won the confidence of the Augustus
were in league with this fellow Barabbas and did not break off relations until I had the man captured as a robber. That, my dear
friend, will give you some idea of the diplomatic skill that is necessary to govern this country; no one at the court seems to have any
conception of it. You might, if occasion offers, put this matter in
the proper light at court.

Now for the second example. Although these Jews are split up
into many sects which hate and are perpetually warring with one
another, all of them believe in a prophecy contained in some sacred writings of theirs that some day a man will come along and
"save" the Jewish people. They call this man who is to come the
Messiah. To me it is not quite clear just what the Jews mean by
"salvation." I think they deliberately confuse the issue when
they assert that the Messiah will free them from their "sins"; just
how this is to be done is hard to conceive. Probably they are too
cunning to admit plainly that they expect this Messiah to drive
us out of the country.

A number of different Messiahs have already appeared, and one of these Herod Antipas recently had decapitated. Once again it was not my business to pay any particular attention to such prophets, although, as you well know, prophecies create a great deal of confusion and often result in the release of unsuspected energies. One must always be on guard.

For some time now a Jewish artisan has been going about whom many Jews seem to think is the "real" Messiah. I won't bore you with what the man preaches. Suffice it to say that this Jew—unlike the Barabbas I mentioned above—tells the people to exercise patience and to love their neighbors and—again in contrast to Barabbas—promises them a better life in a mystical heavenly kingdom. As far as that goes, the man is not worth mentioning from our point of view—he is simply one more preacher in a country overrun by wild-eyed preachers. Nevertheless, I cannot close my eyes to the fact that this man—his name is Jesus and he comes from Nazareth—has acquired many adherents among the lower classes of the populace and as a result has evoked vigorous hostility from the Jewish priesthood; the priests are demanding that he be crucified. Frankly I don't wonder at their annoyance, for this man Jesus—who is said to be an extremely clever orator—denies their authority in religious matters and thus shakes the foundation of their influence over the masses.

Now for me the question that arises out of this idiotic contention among the Jewish sects is this: Am I the guardian of the business of this arrogant priesthood? Has Rome any interest in defending one clique of Jews against another?

To this, my friend, you might reply: Keep on good terms with the people who have the ear of the Augustus; evade any conflicts which threaten the existing order. That is easy to say. But to me the interest of Rome is pre-eminent. And it seems to me that it is not to the interest of Rome for me to act as a willing tool of a priesthood whose prestige nowadays depends largely on the presence of our legions. Isn't it better to show these priests that Rome stands above parties? Is it not better to let the priesthood feel that we hold their power in the hollow of our hand?

Believe me, my dear Tullius Aper, I am not in the least concerned with this man who is causing the Jewish priests so many headaches. In fact I am repelled by his talk of "the equality of men," which might lead the filthiest slaves to think they are men. I intend to keep my eye on him. But as long as the man does not agitate against us—and he certainly has not been doing that!—and merely makes trouble for these priests, I don't intend to do the priests any favors.

I have written at such length about this, my friend, because it may happen that these Jewish sycophants at the court will complain about me again. Make the people whom it concerns realize that I know best how to preserve the prestige of Rome and that I will not barter with Roman justice.

As far as my personal affairs are concerned, let me assure you that not for a single day have I felt really happy in this so-called "Holy City." The country is terrible, the city is terrible, the people are terrible. Just imagine, for the last few days it has been as cold here as it is in the dead of winter in Italy. When I call to mind that in Latium it is spring, that there is sunshine and warmth, that the people there speak a beautiful tongue, that I have so many dear friends there, I would like best to pack at once and leave this unpleasant and inhospitable country which offers me nothing but work and constant annoyance. But it would not be proper for an old soldier to abandon his post.

I beg you to write to me again soon. Word from a friend is always the best consolation in my loneliness. And, of course, it is always worth my while to know what is going on in Rome.

Goodbye for now, my dear Tullius Aper.

Pilate laid aside the stylus and sighed.

"Words . . . words . . ." he murmured to himself. "What use are they to me?" A bitter smile settled in the corners of his mouth.

In his heart he understood what it was he was doing. He was preparing to prove that the greatest sacrifice of love is renunciation. Never had he loved Mary of Magdala more than when he resolved to save the man of Nazareth.

22 ❧

Another Prisoner

SINCE THE DAY IN THE CIRCUS, EZRA HAD HAD NO INFORMATION ABOUT his leader. It was rumored that Pilate intended to grant Barabbas his life in reward for his "victory" in the arena. The fact that nothing was heard about Baarbbas' execution strengthened Ezra's hope that this rumor was based upon some truth. But of what use would it be, Ezra reflected, if Barabbas were sent to the galleys? Then he would never see him again.

There was another hope that he clung to. Perhaps the Procurator would sentence Barabbas to the workshops. Then he might escape as Ezra himself had escaped. And with the knowledge that Barabbas was in reach, a popular uprising might still take place and liberate him. It would not be the first time in history that the people had rescued its leaders. Ezra was altogether unwilling to believe that Barabbas was lost.

He meditated on the Nazarene a good deal. It was on the day of the circus games that Ezra had heard him speak for the first time. Uncertain of what to do and despairing for his leader, Ezra had joined the stragglers who were streaming toward the Temple Mount to hear Jesus of Nazareth. He saw Jesus mount one of the gigantic square blocks near the Temple gate from which the trumpet fanfares were sounded at the prescribed times. The Nazarene stood above the heads of the crowd, white and glowing in the light of the setting sun; he raised his hand and in the silence that suddenly ensued he began to speak.

Ezra heard his words of peace, love, patience in enduring suffering, hope in the Father whose divine mercy embraced the whole world, and in spite of himself his hate-filled heart was warmed. When he became conscious of the fact that the Nazarene's words had touched him to the depths of his soul, he hurriedly made his way out of the rapt crowd. His flight was prompted by the same feeling he had experienced in the house of Lazarus: fear of kindness. "I am lost," he thought, "if I abandon myself to this man, like these others who have patiently accepted their destiny. I must get away . . . away . . ."

Swiftly he strode out of the main gate of the Temple yard, where the sick and crippled had gathered that day. There were lepers among them, too, standing together in an isolated group and crying, "Jesus, Son of David, take pity on us!" The faith of all these unfortunates was tremendously impressive. "All of them are expecting to be healed and saved by him," Ezra thought. And once again the idea occurred to him, "Why should he not rescue Barabbas? He raised Lazarus who was already dead to life—what is more difficult, to open the door of a prison or the portals of death? And is not Barabbas, too, committed to death?" Ezra considered whether he ought to seek out the Nazarene and plead for his leader. But he rejected the thought. How should he, how could he free Barabbas? If this multitude who followed him carried swords instead of palm branches; if instead of listening to the words of that gentle man they would launch an assault upon the hirelings of the Roman rulers— then Barabbas might be freed. But the man was against violence, and prisons could not be opened with palm branches.

Nevertheless Ezra continued to think frequently of the Nazarene as he hopelessly drifted in the neighborhood of the Procurator's palace, or sleeplessly twisted and turned on the straw in the disreputable tavern where he had found shelter. Five days had passed since he had heard the Nazarene; for five days and nights Ezra wrestled with the question of whether he should not, after all, look to the miracle-worker of Nazareth for the salvation of Barabbas and for his own salvation. The fifth night he could no longer endure the tavern. Restlessly he slunk about Barabbas' prison, carefully avoiding the soldiers who at regular intervals paced their rounds. A cold wind was sweeping through the streets; black clouds scurried jaggedly across the sky, momentarily obscuring the moon. He did not succeed in approaching the window through which he hoped to catch a glimpse of Barabbas. Finally he gave it up and walked slowly out of the city, without any particular goal, busy with his own tormenting thoughts.

When he came to the bridge across Kedron Brook he saw, along the road that led from the Mount of Olives into the town, a large procession carrying many torches. At first he thought it was a century of Roman soldiers and turned off the road in order not to encounter them. But when they came closer he realized that they were not Romans but armed Temple officers who were marching along with loud shouts.

Soon he made out at the head Nathaniel, priest of the first degree, several lower priests, and some Levites. They were followed by torchbearers; then came some of the regular Temple guards who carried swords and spears. These were market apprentices and butchers—a rude folk who were used for all the lowest tasks. Torchbearers ran along the sides of the procession and torchbearers brought up the rear. In the middle the Temple officers were leading along on ropes a prisoner whose hands were tied behind his back and who seemed to be walking with great difficulty. Repeatedly the Temple officers struck him in the back and sides with the hafts of their lances, accompanying the blows with furious curses and insults.

"What a stir to make about one prisoner," Ezra thought wonderingly. At that moment the prisoner raised his face to the light of the waning moon and Ezra started in amazement.

The prisoner was Jesus of Nazareth.

His hair and beard were matted; his pale face expressed silent, submissive sorrow, but there was also an aura of dignity and nobility.

At first Ezra saw only the submissiveness and the sorrow, and the sight filled him with dismay. He had long known that the priesthood and the Pharisees were hostile to the Nazarene, even that they had set a price on his head. He knew how the high priest had tried to persuade Barabbas to kill the Nazarene. But the fact that they had not been able to harm him was precisely what, during these days of alternating doubt and hope, had made Ezra dream that this man with his special gifts might be the one to save Barabbas.

And now?

Five days ago Jesus of Nazareth had ridden into Jerusalem like a conqueror with a great retinue. Where now were all his followers? Where were the thousands who had cried, "Hosannah to the Son of David!"? Alone, deserted by all his companions, in the hands of his worst enemies, cursed and abused, this "prophet" was being taken into the city bound hand and foot—a picture of misery and human impotence.

Ezra felt icy shudders coursing through his body.

This man, then, was not a great sorcerer, not a miracle-worker, for otherwise he would not have fallen into the hands of his enemies. But if that were so, he was also no prophet, he was also not the Messiah and Saviour; his words had no more force than the words of a slave. Despair cut deep into Ezra's soul; he felt suddenly as if he had been whipped and beaten. Overpowered by a strange weakness, he had to lean for a moment against an olive tree to remain on his feet. Something akin to hatred for the man of Nazareth rose within him. Had he not for days toyed with the thought of asking this man to rescue Barabbas; he might have sought and found ways to do it himself. Now he had lost days, precious days, while Barabbas languished in the Roman jail.

The procession had passed. Near the bridge Ezra thought he recognized a few persons following hesitantly. Perhaps these were the disciples, the friends of the man of Nazareth. But why, if it were they, had they not protected their master? It would not have taken many men to frighten off the cowardly rabble whom the priests had sent to take him. Or was it that they, too, no longer believed in the prophet who had not known how to take advantage of the moment when he had thousands and tens of thousands following him?

Without knowing why he was doing so, Ezra followed some distance behind the torchlit procession.

It passed the governor's palace. Here the Temple servants were careful not to make too much noise. Then the leader of the procession, Rabbi Nathaniel, turned to the left. For a moment Ezra thought with astonishment that they were bringing their prisoner to the Temple, but he soon realized that he was mistaken. After passing the old wall the procession turned again to the right and reached the upper city where, from streets and alleys, a large number of per-

sons who had apparently been waiting joined the procession and remained in it until it stopped before the home of High Priest Annas.
The doors of the house were wide open and inside all was brilliantly
lighted; obviously the delivery of the prisoner was expected.

Ezra, with a number of others, passed through the doorway into
the great reception hall of the house. The high priest came forward
and conversed excitedly for a while with Rabbi Nathaniel. Then he
had the prisoner brought before him and for some moments looked
at him in silence. Ezra could see the expression of scornful triumph
on the face of the high priest. He saw Annas address a few words to
the prisoner, but the high priest spoke so low that he could not make
out what had been said. However, he heard clearly the answer that
Jesus of Nazareth gave; it resounded throughout the large chamber:

"I spoke openly to the world. I even taught in the synagogue and
in the Temple, whither the Jews always resort, and in secret I have
said nothing. Why then do you ask me? Ask those who heard me
what I have said to them."

There was a moment of hushed silence, an involuntary tribute not
so much to the words as to the clear, ringing tone of voice in which
they were spoken. Then one of the Temple guards who stood near
him slapped his face and growled:

"Do you answer the high priest so?"

Jesus turned his smarting face toward the man and replied:

"If I have spoken evil, bear witness of the evil. But if I have
spoken well, why do you strike me?"

The high priest took Rabbi Nathaniel aside once more and they
conferred briefly. Then the rabbi turned to the Temple officers
and said a few words to them. The men, as if they were suddenly
in a great hurry, turned the man of Nazareth around and dragged
him toward the door. As he passed, Ezra was unable to see his face,
for he walked bowed as if he were bearing a heavy burden.

Ezra followed along after the procession, which was once more
headed by the rabbi, the priests, and the Levites. He caught a
glimpse of the high priest emerging from his house and climbing
into his litter to follow.

Ezra was now walking in the midst of the rabble who had joined
the Temple officers and their assistants in the streets. Absorbed in
his own despondency, he nevertheless heard in the murmured conversations the imprecations against the Nazarene and expressions of

The wish that this agitator had come to the end of his seditious career. The people discussed what form of death the court would prescribe, and the majority regretted that the ancient penalty of stoning could no longer be invoked, for if such a sentence were passed, they, too, would be able to take an active part.

The procession reached the huge mansion of High Priest Caiaphas, whose business it was to administer secular justice while his father-in-law Annas supervised religious affairs. Here, too, the procession, which had swelled considerably on the way, was evidently expected. Priests and Levites were waiting at the door, and these hastened into the house presumably to announce the delivery of the prisoner.

Here, too, Ezra succeeded in entering the house and made his way into the hall where the Sanhedrin was already assembled—only Annas was still missing. On the raised platform sat High Priest Caiaphas, the priests of the first degree, and the eldest of the other rabbis. But not all the seats were occupied—apparently a large minority of the priests was unwilling to take part in this nocturnal judgment.

Now High Priest Annas entered, was greeted respectfully by his son-in-law and the other priests and, leaning on Nathaniel's arm, mounted the steps to the judges' seats and sat down beside Caiaphas.

The Temple officers had meanwhile thrust the prisoner close up to the platform and stood around him in a semicircle. The crowd from the street pushed forward as far as possible, but were forced by the Temple officers to line up along both walls, so that a broad aisle was left clear in the center. Ezra found himself on the side of the reception hall which led, between great stone columns, into the inner court of the house. Fires had been laid in this court and both Temple officers and some of the household servants were warming themselves at these. Some of the spectators left the hall and went into the court to warm their hands, but Ezra remained to hear the proceedings.

The trial was slow in beginning. The priests conferred, looked at the prisoner and seemed to be exchanging remarks about him.

At last High Priest Caiaphas opened the trial by asking the prisoner whether he was Jesus of Nazareth.

Jesus confirmed that he was.

Then one of the priests of the first degree rose and read aloud a sort of indictment which Ezra could not wholly follow. It spoke of crimes against the law, of perverting the people into disobedience of the Commandments, and of blasphemy.

Afterwards several witnesses were led in to testify against the accused. Ezra could not quite understand what these men were saying. He heard, or thought he heard, that the judges deduced from their testimony grave accusations against Jesus. But all of the witnesses offered as the chief point in their testimony the alleged statement of the accused that he could destroy the Temple and build it up again in three days. Even Ezra, untrained in legal phraseology as he was, realized that all these people framed their denunciations in the same words; they had obviously been coached. Each time a witness finished testifying, the high priest turned to the accused and asked:

"What have you to say to that?"

But Jesus was silent.

"Why doesn't he speak out, why doesn't he answer them?" Ezra asked himself. "It would not be hard for him to answer these ridiculous charges. If he doesn't speak, he is lost."

Ezra was outraged at the man for, as it seemed to him, deliberately inviting conviction. He forsook the trial chamber and went into the court where the Temple officers were standing around the fires and drinking wine out of huge jugs. They had been joined by some of the men who had arrested Jesus of Nazareth and were now discussing the events of the capture. One of the blasphemer's disciples, they said, had attempted to resist and had actually raised his sword and cut off the ear of one of the officers. But the Nazarene had picked up the ear which lay on the ground and touched it to the officer's head, healing it at once, and then he had reproached his aggressive disciple. The man to whom it had happened was standing by the fire; his ear was examined but there was no trace of a wound and the bystanders refused to believe the story in spite of the oaths of the men who claimed to have seen it with their own eyes.

Among the outsiders who had sidled into the court was one man whom a Temple officer suddenly accused of being a disciple of the prisoner; his pronunciation had betrayed him as a Galilean. But the man loudly averred that he did not know Jesus of Nazareth. Ezra looked at him and recognized him as one of the guests he had seen at the Nazarene's side entering Lazarus' house in Bethany. A sense of revulsion overcame him; would he, he asked himself, deny Barabbas in so cowardly a fashion? "No," he told himself, "I would stand by him. But what do I care about these people?" He turned and went back to the hall.

There the hearing of witnesses had been concluded. High Priest Caiaphas rose from his seat and stepped to the center of the platform, just above the accused who stood below him. In a raised voice he demanded:

"You have heard what these witnesses say against you. Will you answer nothing?"

But Jesus held his peace. Hands tied behind his back, he stood with face lifted up to the high priest, but not a word passed his lips. The priests looked tensely down on him. Some of them were half standing, leaning forward on the judges' bench, trembling with excitement.

Caiaphas stretched out his arms and cried in a solemn voice:

"I adjure you by the living God—tell us, are you the Christ, the Son of God?"

For a moment there was perfect silence in the room. Then the voice of the accused rang out:

"You have said it. Nevertheless I say to you, hereafter you shall see the Son of Man sitting on the right hand of God's power and coming in the clouds of heaven."

At this the high priest seized his own ornate vestment and rent it from top to bottom, crying in a high-pitched voice:

"He has spoken blasphemy; what further need have we of witnesses? You have heard his blasphemy—what do you think?"

The priests had all risen from their seats and now they shouted in unison:

"He is guilty unto death . . . death . . . death!"

The trial was apparently over. While Rabbi Nathaniel descended from the platform, the two high priests and the other members of the Sanhedrin left through a back door. Nathaniel said a word to the Temple officers who were holding Jesus by the ropes with which he was bound, and then he rapidly strode out of the main entrance to the hall.

The Temple servants pulled the condemned man around, pushed him, struck him, and spat in his face. One of the men standing behind him threw a filthy kerchief over his eyes and then slapped him in the face, saying:

"If you are the Christ, prophesy: Who is it that struck you?"

The other officers burst into laughter, but Jesus remained silent and walked straight toward the door. Probably, Ezra thought, he would now be thrown into jail until the morrow. Jesus raised his head only once, and Ezra saw his sorrowful glance directed at the disciple who had denied him. This disciple was leaning against one of the pillars which separated the hall from the court. When the Nazarene's eyes met his, he seemed to sag as if he were bearing an insupportable burden, and quietly he slunk toward the exit.

Ezra followed. All were leaving now and the household servants were already beginning to extinguish and remove the lamps that hung from the ceiling and along the walls.

When he reached the street, the group with the condemned Jesus was already out of sight, but Ezra heard the Temple officers noisily berating and reviling the Nazarene in a near-by side street.

Ezra drifted slowly back to the Ophel district, intending to go to the tavern for a few hours' sleep since the stars were already paling in the east and dawn was near.

The people who had been with him in the hall were scattering in all directions. They seemed highly pleased by what they had seen. Ezra could not help reflecting that many of these people had probably followed the Nazarene when he entered the city, and many of them must have shouted hosannahs. If his own disciples denied him, why should the populace who scarcely knew him behave any differently?

Then Ezra's thoughts turned once more to his own sorrow and his own despair. Once more he realized clearly that there was no longer the faintest hope for Barabbas. Perhaps the Romans had already quietly done away with him. What then? What was he, Ezra, going to do with himself, with his life?

When he reached the tavern, he lay down on the straw and tried to sleep. But sleep did not come to help him forget the wretchedness and despair in his own heart.

He heard the cocks crowing the arrival of morning, he heard heavy footsteps on the pavement, the bleating of animals being driven to the slaughter, and the oaths of the drivers. At the same time he was assailed by a frightful hunger. He could no longer remain on his miserable bed; he rose and staggered out into the cold, early morning air.

He went to the market where the peddlers were laying out their wares and begged a couple of stale loaves of bread and a half-rotted onion. Then he sat down on the curbstone and while he consumed his pitiful meal he considered what he should do during the day.

Should he continue his senseless, purposeless haunting of the Procurator's palace? He could learn nothing there about the fate of Barabbas. Could he help Barabbas to escape? No one had ever yet escaped from the palace prisons. And how, alone and himself a hunted criminal, could he even make the attempt? Would it not be better to leave the city and return to the desert where at least it was possible to breathe freely? But the mockery of Juda ben Jacob in the circus had proved that the Romans knew the priests' plans. Probably the Procurator had already sent his soldiers to destroy the camp. He, Ezra, had only a few friends left among the men in camp; the others would probably not even accept him, even assuming that the camp was still in existence.

Suddenly he recalled blind old Eliazar and his goats. Yes, Eliazar would give him some help. But perhaps he was no longer alive? Ezra could investigate; it would give him something to do. There was no sense in his sitting around here waiting for Barabbas; nothing but a miracle could save his leader now. And Ezra did not believe in miracles. How stupid he had been ever to dream that the Nazarene would perform a miracle for Barabbas!

If he remained in the city, there was the ever-present danger that sooner or later he would be recognized by some Roman soldiers. Then he was done for. He was by no means strongly attached to life, but he also did not wish to suffer the slave's death on a Roman cross. And even if he should find none of his old comrades in the desert, there were still the friendly shepherds; he need not go hungry as he was doing here in the Holy City. Some day the Jews would certainly rise up against their oppressors—and when they did Ezra wanted to be there.

But even though he thus recognized the necessity for leaving Jerusalem, his obsession carried him in spite of himself past the Temple Mount, where the streets were filled with a bustling throng, to the Procurator's palace. He had no idea what he should do there, but something urged him to pass once more by the place of Barabbas' imprisonment, as if it would be easier there to take a silent farewell of his leader.

It struck him as curious that there were so many sizable groups of
Jews standing around in the broad square before the palace, in spite
of the earliness of the hour. The people stood in clusters conversing in low voices. The palace guards had also been struck by the
size of the crowd; the centurion in charge had doubled the number
of his guards on duty and was keeping a close watch on the scattered
groups.

Ezra, who connected everything that happened around him with
Barabbas, feared for a moment that this hour had been appointed
for the public execution of his leader and that these swarms of the
curious had already gathered to witness the spectacle. But when he
reached one of the groups he heard them talking about Jesus of Nazareth, not about Barabbas. He heard that the high priests and the
other members of the Sanhedrin had just met to pass formal sentence
upon the agitator and blasphemer, and that Jesus of Nazareth
would then have to be turned over to the governor for him to carry
out the sentence. Many of the Jews were indignant that it was
necessary to ask the Roman for permission to execute the man. The
general opinion was that the Sanhedrin would promptly pass a death
sentence, and everyone seemed to think such a verdict perfectly
justified.

Ezra was disgusted to find among all these people not one who
had any qualms about the justice of sentencing the Nazarene for
imaginary crimes.

"Why do you want him killed?" he asked the people standing near
him. "I heard the trial; they were unable to prove that he committed any crimes at all. The priests and the Pharisees want to get
him out of the way because he had a large following. But is that any
reason for killing a man?"

This expression of opinion aroused a great deal of indignation.
But the men did not dare speak too loudly because of the presence
of the Roman guards, some of whom understood the native language.

"Are you another one of the Nazarene's men?" one of the Jews
demanded hotly. "If you don't keep your mouth shut, we'll call
over the guards and have you arrested."

"You are a fool!" Ezra said contemptuously. "I am not one of his
followers. You are all fools or rascals or both. I am a poor devil
like yourselves. What do we care what the priests and the rich have

against this man? Are you being paid to stand here and help along the priests' dirty business?"

"What concern is it of the Procurator's what we do with a blasphemer?" another man growled.

"He is not a blasphemer, you blockheads," Ezra said urgently. "He is a man who wanted to help the poor, like Barabbas who is also a prisoner of the Roman dogs. Do you want to kill all those who try to help you?"

The anger of the group subsided. Some of the men appeared thoughtful.

"What has happened to Barabbas?" one man asked. He had undoubtedly been wearing the Star of David up to recently, Ezra guessed.

"I don't even know whether he is still alive," Ezra replied. "If you were men, you would see to it that Israel regained its freedom. Instead of standing here crying for the Nazarene's blood, you ought to force the Romans to release Barabbas."

Some of the men thought the talk was growing dangerous and dropped out of the group. Others warned:

"Take care that the guards don't hear you."

Ezra spat contemptuously and also left the group. He went into a side street from which he could see the prison windows. These people disgusted him. He did not know why he had spoken up for the Nazarene, for he cherished a grudge against the man for having caused him such painful disappointment, and because Jesus had silently permitted the high priests to abuse him. But he was unwilling to let this rabble in the square, the same people who had also deserted Barabbas, have their triumph and their pleasure in watching the execution of a man who had cured so many of their sick and crippled kin.

For a long while he leaned against a post at the entrance to a house, gloomily brooding. A tumult in the square roused him, and curiosity drove him to see what was happening.

The crowd had meanwhile swelled considerably and by now filled almost the entire square with the exception of a broad area immediately in front of the palace which the guards, with drawn swords, were keeping clear. A litter was borne toward the palace gate and from it emerged Simon, the priest of the first degree, who addressed a few words to the crowd. The criminal, Jesus of Nazareth, he said, had just been sentenced to death by the Sanhedrin and would be executed in the course of the morning.

A shout of applause greeted these words.

Amid the jubilant cries of the mob Simon, followed by two Levites, ascended the outside staircase to the Procurator's office.

23 ✡

Claudia Has Bad Dreams

LIKE EZRA, THE PRIESTS HAD ALSO HAD NO REST DURING THE LATTER part of that night. By dawn they were once more assembled in Caiaphas' home to pronounce formal sentence upon Jesus of Nazareth. It had to be done betimes because a number of the members of the Sanhedrin had duties in the Temple which began early, and because, in addition, there was a general desire to see the sentence executed that very day. The Passover began in the evening and they wanted to have everything over and done with by then.

The sentence had been determined even before the Nazarene's arrest. Without much ado the formal pronouncement of the death sentence was rendered.

But now came the real difficulty. Only the governor could carry out the sentence, and the Sanhedrin was well aware that the crimes for which Jesus had been sentenced to death would be in the eyes of the Roman ridiculous trivialities for which the man would not even have to be punished mildly.

Rabbi Simon, by common consent the most glib-tongued of the priests of the first degree, was given the commission of informing the governor of their sentence and transmitting to him the high priest's request to execute the sentence. Presumably Rabbi Simon would be rendered unclean by entering the governor's palace on the eve of

271

the Passover, but someone had to do it and the rabbi seemed to be not at all disturbed by the prospect of being barred from Temple duties during the Passover.

He was at once carried from Caiaphas' house directly to the Procurator's palace. The litter was followed by two Levites—since this was an official mission, a certain amount of ceremonial pomp had to be observed.

On the way through the city Rabbi Simon announced to the people in the streets the joyful tidings that the evildoer had been condemned to death. Now he stood with his two Levites in the anteroom of the palace. The guards had called the centurion whose watch it was, and the centurion asked the priest's errand in a surly fashion.

"I have an important message for the Procurator on behalf of the Sanhedrin," Rabbi Simon said.

"You might just as well have come at midnight to ask to see the Procurator."

"I might," Rabbi Simon said sternly, "but I wish to see him now." He had no intention of being polite to this underling; in fact, he wanted to make the man feel that he was here as the representative of the priesthood and would not deal with subordinates.

"The Procurator cannot be seen at this hour," the centurion said.

"Then go to him and tell him the emissary of the Sanhedrin urgently wishes to speak to him."

The centurion considered for a while and then left the room. Perhaps it was really something important, he thought; he did not want the governor to have cause to reprimand him for delay in an important matter. At the same time the governor did not like being disturbed so early.

The centurion went to inform the governor, but he did not hurry. It was some time before the Procurator appeared.

Pilate was highly annoyed. In the first place it was a shameless piece of rudeness, he felt, to bother him at this time of day, and in the second place it was still cold, which always put him in an ill humor.

He greeted the rabbi curtly and invited him into the audience hall where he brusquely asked him what he wanted. The two Levites remained behind in the anteroom.

"The Sanhedrin, O Procurator," Rabbi Simon began, bowing, but not too low, "wishes to transmit to you as representative of the great Augustus its greetings and respects."

"Thank you," the Procurator replied. "And what does the Sanhedrin want of me at this unusual hour?"

Rabbi Simon was nonplussed by the direct question. The Procurator was certainly not behaving very courteously. He began to fear for the success of his mission.

"The Sanhedrin has a request to make of you, O Procurator," he said. "We have arrested a state criminal, an agitator, perverter of the people and blasphemer who pretends to be the Messiah and has had the people proclaim him king of the Jews. By our law he is guilty of crimes punishable by death and the Sanhedrin has passed the death sentence. Accordingly the Supreme Council of the priests requests you to confirm and carry out the sentence."

"Is that all?" the Procurator asked frigidly.

"That is all," Rabbi Simon said. "The case is perfectly simple and clear. The Sanhedrin has tried the man and both by his own confession and the testimony of the witnesses he is guilty unto death thrice over, not only by our law but also by the Roman law. Death is the penalty for rebellion under the Roman law also, as far as we understand it."

Pilate glowered at the rabbi, who had spoken with great fervor.

"How well you understand the Roman law," he said contemptuously, "is clear from your request. According to you the imperial governor has nothing else to do but take your orders and carry them out."

"I did not mean that at all, O Procurator," Rabbi Simon said placatingly. "I merely wanted to say that this agitator would be condemned to death by the Roman law as well. All that the Supreme Council asks is that you provide a century or so of your military to execute the sentence or at least to supervise the execution."

The governor's mouth twisted in a mocking smile.

"So that is all you ask? Splendid. You make the arrest, conduct the trial and pass sentence, and permit me to play the executioner. No, emissary of the Supreme Council, it isn't as simple as that. If the Sanhedrin wishes this criminal—if he is one—to be executed, send him to me. The only kind of sentence I intend to carry out is one that I have passed myself.

Pilate rose from his seat; the rabbi did likewise.

"Consider, Procurator . . ."

Pilate angrily interrupted him.

"No, there is nothing to consider. The right to punish is mine, and therefore the right to judge. If you have anyone against whom you wish to bring charges in my court, do so. I have no more to say."

Rabbi Simon bowed again, lower this time, and prepared to continue the argument. But Pilate forestalled him.

"No, I will not hear another word. Carry my greetings to the Sanhedrin, but tell that august body that if they harm a hair of the man they accuse, they will find out that Rome is wholly able to crush the arrogance of a priesthood which is getting too ambitious to run things by itself. You are warned. I am informed that hundreds of people are standing in the square in front of my palace. If the Council hopes to use the crowd to exert pressure on me, you can tell them they have miscalculated. I know only too well how 'public opinion' is created. And I have soldiers enough to round up this hired rabble and send them all to the workshops. Goodbye."

Rabbi Simon had no choice; obviously he had to leave before he was thrown out. He bowed low once more and turned toward the anteroom. At the door he encountered Joseph of Arimathea coming in. The rabbi hastily retreated three steps in order not to come too close to the hated Sadducee. Pilate observed the scene with sardonic amusement.

Joseph of Arimathea entered and greeted the Procurator. He was obviously extremely excited; his face was pale, his hair and beard uncombed and his cloak dragged along the floor.

"You know what has happened, Procurator?" he asked.

"Certainly. They have arrested your Nazarene, condemned him, and I am supposed to carry out the sentence."

"Are you going to do it, Procurator?"

Pilate looked thoughtful.

"I don't know. I first want to see this prophet of yours. The priesthood will have to be content with my passing my own sentences. They are going to bring the man before me."

Joseph of Arimathea sighed with relief.

"Thank you, Procurator," he said. "Once you have heard him yourself, he will be free. Permit me to take my leave now and bring this message to the disciples, who are terribly concerned about the Master."

"In your place I would not be in such a hurry," Pilate said. "I have not promised to free the man."

"I know, Procurator. But if only you take him away from the priests, we do not fear for him. We know and trust your sense of justice."

"Thank you, my friend Joseph," Pilate said, inviting Joseph with a gesture to take a seat. "Sit down. I want to ask you a few questions before you go. The affair is not as simple as you seem to think. Perhaps your answers can help me reach a decision."

Visibly impatient, Joseph of Arimathea sat down and looked questioningly at the Procurator. Pilate remained standing in front of him and asked:

"Do you think these priests are scoundrels, Joseph?"

"Oh no," Joseph replied forcibly. "They are extremely honorable men. They pray, fast, and obey the law."

"Don't be evasive, Joseph," Pilate said with a disparaging wave of his hand. "Don't make this thing hard for me. I am not talking in academic terms. If these men are so God-fearing, why do they persecute the Nazarene—who you assert is innocent—with such hatred?"

Joseph understood his Roman friend too well to expect him to comprehend fully the great sense of truth that he knew Jesus to possess. He could not expect the cynical Pilate to grasp the Master's lofty ideas. Therefore he tried to explain the priesthood's hostility to the Nazarene on a practical plane.

"It is a question of prestige and influence, Procurator, which they, of course, call God's prestige and influence. As Jesus says, 'The scribes and Pharisees sit in Moses' seat.' And they believe that they alone possess the keys to wisdom. Whoever questions that commits a crime in their eyes against the divine order and they hate him with all their souls. Now then there comes this man of Nazareth who says: There is only one law, that of love. And he says: You need no priests and no Temple to be with God; all that is required of you is that you respect all men, even public sinners and gentiles, for they are all children of the one Father whose kindness is infinite. But where would the priests be if all men were held equal? He teaches gentleness while they want to rule by sternness and harshness. How can they help hating him? Now if you will excuse me, Procurator . . ."

Joseph of Arimathea arose, but Pilate showed no signs of being ready to let him go.

"This doctrine of the equality of all men seems dangerous to me, too," Pilate said thoughtfully. "But where would we end if we took seriously the fancies of all these warring sects and punished heresy by death? The priests with their stubborn adherence to the letter of the Jewish law have also caused me no end of trouble. Whatever I wanted to do for the good of the country they objected to, invoking the law of your Moses. I would think twice before letting myself be made an instrument of your vengeful laws . . ."

Joseph perceived that the Procurator's dislike for the priests was greater than his concern for Jesus of Nazareth, whom he evidently considered simply one more of the many Jewish religious fanatics. He said:

"Do not, Procurator. If you do it, they will put the whole responsibility for the act upon you."

Pilate shrugged.

"That does not bother me. What does one man's life matter? But I do want to protect the political authority against the pretensions of religious fanaticism. We shall see who is the greater threat to Rome's political authority, this Nazarene or the priests. But one more question, Joseph. Why did the priests conspire with Barabbas while they persecute the Nazarene to death? Barabbas was also interested in seizing power."

"I don't know what the priests intended to do with Barabbas," Joseph replied. "But, you see, Barabbas proclaimed the very ideas upon which the power of the priesthood rests: violence, hatred, harshness, mercilessness, impatience, arrogance, idolization of one nation and one race, killing and warfare. Perhaps they thought they could employ Barabbas as a willing tool because of this basic agreement with them. But Jesus of Nazareth preaches the opposite of all these things. Now do you understand, Procurator, why they could be for Barabbas but had to oppose Jesus of Nazareth?"

"What you say about Barabbas sounds accurate," Pilate said. "I have given that man his hearing—his case is settled. Now I shall hear the other one."

"Will you permit me to leave now, Procurator. My friends are waiting with the greatest impatience . . ."

"Yes, go now, Joseph—I understand your haste. Come to see me soon."

Joseph of Arimathea rushed out. Pilate remained alone. His rough dismissal of Rabbi Simon had given him great satisfaction, but, on the other hand, he could not help realizing that he was being placed in an embarrassing situation. To be sure, he wanted to release this Nazarene . . . But was that what he wanted in reality? Had he not lifted Joseph up with excessive hopes? The Nazarene was almost as repugnant to him as the priests—in fact, if he considered the matter in the proper light, more so. For he was truly a corruptor of the people and an agitator—there was not the slightest doubt about that. Claudia was the finest proof of it. If an intelligent, cultivated Roman woman surrendered to his influence, why should not these simple, uncultured Jews do so? And Pilate could not think of Mary of Magdala without feeling intense hatred for the Nazarene. But if he condemned the man, he would lose Mary for good; then she would despise him as a cowardly murderer. And he would lose Joseph as well, the only man in this country with whom he could occasionally have an intelligent and interesting conversation. On the other hand, Rome looked upon the priests as the pillars of the existing order. The Augustus was friendly to them. Was he going to ruin his career on account of an eccentric Jewish artisan? Where was the solution? Pilate paced furiously back and forth, but nothing occurred to him. Finally he sent for Marcus— that half-Jew could always provide an ingenious idea. Perhaps he would know what to do in a case like this.

But just as Marcus entered, a great uproar arose in the square before the palace. The governor hastened to the window.

He saw the square swarming with people. Approaching the palace along the main avenue was a procession of Temple officers, led by a number of priests. In their midst walked a bound prisoner, dressed in a torn cloak and a soiled, trailing tunic.

Pilate realized that he was not to be given much time for considering the question. The priests had evidently thought the matter over and had decided to deliver the Nazarene up to him.

The crowd was shouting incessantly. Pilate could not understand the Aramaic words, but he guessed that they were crying imprecations upon the prisoner. The procession could scarcely force its way through the throning mob; the people spat at the prisoner and tried to beat him with sticks, so that the Temple officers were forced to protect him.

Marcus, too, had stepped to the window.

"What is that rabble down there shouting?" Pilate asked him.

" 'Death to the agitator! To the cross with the blasphemer! Crucify the rebel!' "

"That last is addressed to me," Pilate said. "But is this really the notorious Jesus of Nazareth, this frail, beaten, filthy person?"

"I don't know, I've never seen him," Marcus replied. "But it must be he. They are leading him to the courthouse. I guess you will have to judge him, Procurator."

"I'm afraid so—I see no way out of it. Consider what can be done, Marcus. I don't want to do the priests the favor of having the man killed just because they want his death, but as for releasing him— well, I don't want to do that either."

Before Marcus was able to reply, a legionary entered and reported that a prisoner had been brought to the courthouse. The soldiers had taken charge of him at the door and conducted him into the court, where he was now awaiting trial.

"We will go there," Pilate said, signing to his secretary to follow him.

They passed through a tunnel connecting the palace with the adjoining courthouse and climbed the steps into a rather small, unadorned hall which contained only a raised seat for the governor. In the center of the hall, before the judgment seat, stood Jesus of Nazareth, guarded by four soldiers. The door was left open, for the Jewish prosecutors and witnesses had remained outside in order not to be defiled.

Pilate glanced at the prisoner. If the Roman had been accustomed to pity, this defendant would have struck him as eminently pitiable. It was easy to see that he had been severely maltreated. His swollen face was splotched with blood, his hair and beard were not only tousled but large handfuls of both had been torn out; worse yet, the man was covered with excrement that his tormentors had thrown at him. His bluish-red hands, greatly swollen, were tied so tightly that the cords had cut into the flesh; his feet were covered with coagulated blood.

Jesus had cast down his eyes and did not seem to have noticed the entrance of the Procurator.

"Remove his bonds!" Pilate ordered the soldiers. Then he stepped to the door.

Rabbi Nathaniel, a number of other priests and the witnesses stood at the foot of the short flight of stairs that led up to the entrance. The priests bowed to the governor.

"How dare the Sanhedrin send me the man in this condition?" Pilate cried indignantly. "You have already pretty much arrogated to yourselves the right to carry out your death sentence."

"Pardon, Procurator," Rabbi Nathaniel replied. "The rage, the bitterness of the populace—we do not have at our disposal sufficient armed men to prevent the excesses of the people, which we, of course, regret."

"I intend to investigate that question," Pilate said with an angry gesture. "What accusation do you bring against this man?"

Rabbi Nathaniel opened his prosecution. He described Jesus of Nazareth as an agitator who had let himself be proclaimed king of the Jews. He asserted that Jesus had forbidden the payment of taxes to the Augustus and had won a great following by pretending to be the Christ, the Messiah, the liberator and ruler of the people of Israel whom God was to send. He presented witnesses who could testify to all he had said and concluded by averring that the witness merited death by the Roman law as well as the Mosaic law. Then, speaking in Aramaic, he called upon the witnesses to come forward and testify. With a contemptuous gesture Pilate refused to hear the witnesses and retired into the hall.

"You have heard what these people say against you," he said to Jesus. "Are you the king of the Jews?"

Jesus turned to him and asked in turn:

"Do you say this thing of yourself, or did others tell it to you about me?"

Angrily, Pilate shrugged his shoulders.

"Am I a Jew? Your own nation and the high priests have delivered you up to me; what have you done? Did you really try to set up a kingdom of the Jews?"

Jesus answered:

"My kingdom is not of this world. If my kingdom were of this world, then would my servants fight that I should not be delivered to the Jews."

The governor looked at the man in astonishment. His reply that his kingdom was not of this world confirmed Pilate in his previous opinion that the man was a harmless fanatic whom the priests in their jealousy were trying to get rid of. But he wanted to make absolutely sure and so he asked again:

"Are you a king then?"

"You say that I am a king," Jesus answered. "To this end was I born and for this cause came I into the world that I should bear witness to the truth. Everyone that is of the truth hears my voice."

"Truth . . . what is truth?" Pilate said, more to himself than to the defendant. Then he turned once more toward the door. The soldiers had meanwhile driven the mob back; only Nathaniel and his companions were standing by the steps. Between them and the crowd stood legionaries with bared swords.

"I find no fault in this man," Pilate called out to the priests.

An angry murmur arose in the mob, swelled and at once died away when fresh squadrons of legionaries thrust their way between the mob and the group of priests.

But the accusers would not admit defeat. Nathaniel began a résumé of his charges, adroitly and repeatedly pointing out that the defendant was a rebel not only against the law of Israel but against Caesar himself. His voice rose to such a pitch that Jesus within the hall could not help hearing every word of the charges. Again and again Pilate turned to him and asked:

"Do you hear? What do you answer to that?"

But Jesus remained silent.

"What kind of man is this?" the governor wondered. "Why doesn't he defend himself? It would not be difficult for him to expose these patent lies. Has the man read Zeno the Stoic and introduced some of that oriental fatalism into his doctrine? Yet he seems to be unlettered."

He concluded that the Nazarene's behavior was one more example of the peculiar nature of this incomprehensible Jewish people.

While these thoughts were running through his mind, Pilate heard Nathaniel bellowing:

"From Galilee to the heart of Judea this man has gone up and down sowing sedition among the people; it is only due to the alertness of the sons of Israel that no rebellion has arisen in the nation."

Marcus, who was standing behind the governor, whispered in his ear:

"Do you really want to get the man off your hands, Procurator?"

"Yes, if possible," Pilate whispered back.

"It is possible. The man comes from Nazareth. Galilee is under the jurisdiction of Herod. Send him to him."

"Where is Herod now?"

"He has come to Jerusalem for the Festival and is at his palace now."

Pilate took his secretary's advice at once. He gestured to Rabbi Nathaniel to be quiet and asked:

"Did you not say that this Jesus comes from Nazareth?"

"Yes, Procurator."

"Nazareth is in Galilee, is it not?"

"Certainly. And it was in Galilee that he first began stirring up the people."

"Then I see no reason why you have brought him to me. The governor of Galilee is in Jerusalem—it is his duty to judge Galileans. I shall send the defendant to King Herod. He is of your own faith and one of your own people—perhaps he will more easily understand the charges you are making against this man."

Nathaniel bit his lips. He was not at all pleased by this turn of affairs. He perceived at once the cleverness of the Procurator's stratagem. Pilate was certainly aware that Herod, the king and governor of Galilee, was bitterly hostile to the high priests and to the priesthood in general and would gladly seize any opportunity to upset their plans. The Procurator himself could more easily be persuaded to condemn Jesus than Herod.

He tried to avert this disaster.

"Admittedly the man was born in Galilee," he said, "and he also preached there, but his chief crimes were committed in Judea and therefore he should in all justice and law be judged here."

"You have heard my decision, rabbi," Pilate said sternly. "The defendant will be taken to the governor of Galilee."

Pilate turned away and retired into the hall with his secretary. There he ordered Marcus to have the defendant sent to Herod under heavy guard. A company of legionaries was called in and Pilate emphasized to the captain of the company that the rabble must not be permitted too near and that he must allow no abuse of the prisoner. Marcus wrote a few lines to Herod, explaining the circumstances, and then Jesus was led out.

African soldiers with lashes ran along the sides of the marching column, keeping the mob away. The rabble growled, the priests withdrew and the square gradually cleared.

"That was a brilliant idea, Marcus, my boy," the Procurator complimented his secretary as they returned to the palace. "Now let them do what they wish with the man. As for me, I must say he disappointed me. Why didn't he speak up? Don't these Jews customarily defend themselves when they are brought to trial?"

"They certainly do, Procurator. Vigorously. You ought to look in on a secret Jewish trial some day; it would amuse you. They are ingenious talkers. This fellow Jesus, too, is said to be a very fine and flowery orator."

"That makes the business all the harder to understand. The little he said was confused nonsense. A kingdom not of this world . . . Meaningless. Do you think, by the way, that Herod will condemn him?"

Marcus smiled.

"Certainly not, if I know Herod. In my note I particularly emphasized that the Sanhedrin was anxious to have a death-sentence. It will amuse him to annoy the priests by refusing."

"I don't mind, as long as they leave me out of it. Let the Jews settle their disputes among themselves. But it is curious how many people the priests got together to give weight to their cause."

"The populace is fickle as a woman of the streets," Marcus said. "Undoubtedly there were a good many in that mob who were former followers of the Nazarene. Besides, a good deal of money pours into the Temple treasury, and some of it can be doled out again if need be."

"Perhaps there were some of Barabbas' men there," Pilate replied. "They were enemies, weren't they, this Jesus and Barabbas?"

"Yes," Marcus said. "But actually both of them wanted to help the Jews, each in his own fashion. It has become a habit among the Jews to kill their prophets."

"I imagine all peoples kill their prophets," Pilate said pensively. "Remember Socrates . . ." He left his secretary and retired to his apartment to warm himself somewhat at the charcoal braziers. He had scarcely lain down on the couch when Claudia entered the room.

"You have had business so early," she said.

"Do you know what it was about?"

"I inquired. These terrible men have arrested their prophet and condemned him to death. You did not confirm their sentence, did you?"

Claudia sat down on a chair and looked mournfully at the floor. Her red-rimmed eyes betrayed recent tears.

"Does the fate of this Jew mean so much to you?" Pilate asked.

"I saw him last night in a dream—bound and beaten—it was horrible. I suffered frightful anxiety. Save him, Pilate—it will bring evil down upon our heads if you let him die."

Pilate was offended by his wife's imploring tone, but he managed to restrain his irritation.

"Pull yourself together, Claudia," he said. "It isn't proper for you to get into such a state about a Jew." He paused and then added casually, "Wasn't Mary with you—to interpret your dream?"

"Yes, Mary has been with me."

"I thought so. Mary is in love with the man."

"What a horrid thing to say, Pilate. And how ill you know Mary. You don't realize what the Messiah means to her. Can't you feel, Pilate, that this is more than a question of an ordinary man?"

"Messiah? He looked very strange for a Messiah. There was nothing but a man standing before my judgment seat, a very wretched man. I cannot understand the fuss that has been made about him. Every week we crucify two or three Jewish agitators. If I refuse to have this man of Nazareth crucified, it will not be because I consider him in any way out of the ordinary or divine, but because I think him a harmless fool whom you and Joseph and Mary—I don't know why!—have asked me to spare. But I'm glad I've got the man off my neck now by sending him to Herod. This business is beginning to bore me."

"But then Herod will sentence him," Claudia protested.

"Herod will not do what the Sanhedrin wants; that is what I told myself. Anyway, these Jews who seem determined to see one of their number hanging on the cross in time for their Festival will have the pleasure of seeing Barabbas there. I hope that will satisfy the kindhearted populace of Jerusalem."

He arose and was about to leave the room when one of the household slaves entered to report the presence of the centurion of the guard. Pilate admitted him.

"Well," the Procurator asked, "has anything happened to the prisoner?"

"No, Procurator, he must be in Herod's charge by now. It is something else. There is a messenger from High Priest Annas outside who wishes to know whether you will receive the high priest."

Pilate was so surprised that for a moment he was unable to reply. The high priest who had seen him only a few days ago wished to speak to him again—it was inexplicable.

"Inform the high priest that I shall welcome his visit," Pilate said finally. "Report to me again when the high priest arrives."

"Strange, isn't it?" Pilate said, turning to Claudia. "High Priest Annas hates me like the plague and has always avoided meeting me whenever he could. And now he has come to see me twice in a week. Can you possibly imagine what it means?"

"I am afraid it has some connection with the Master," Claudia replied. "He will request you to carry out their sentence after all."

"Nonsense," Pilate said. "He knows I don't intend to have anything more to do with that affair. Let him apply to Herod. That old plotter need not imagine he is going to change my mind."

Pilate turned to go. Claudia took his hand and said in a voice trembling with anxiety:

"Terrible things will happen to us if you yield. I feel that, Pilate. Save him . . . !"

With unusual tenderness Pilate stroked his wife's hair.

"I will do my best, Claudia," he said.

He had a profound feeling of uneasiness as he went out to meet the high priest.

24

Christif or Barabbas

"I SEE, PROCURATOR, THAT YOU ARE SURPRISED AT MY COMING," THE high priest opened the conversation, "but extraordinary events necessitate extraordinary measures."

"I am unaware of any extraordinary events," Pilate said coldly, taking a seat opposite the high priest.

"There is no use, Procurator, in not looking the facts in the face," Annas said. "The arrest of this Jesus of Nazareth is an extraordinary event."

"Perhaps from your point of view," Pilate retorted. "In the nature of our relationship, we must consider events in Jerusalem from very different points of view."

"Certainly, Procurator, we are not friends."

"Have you come to remind me that you have done everything in your power to make life in Judea unpleasant for me? You might have saved yourself the trouble. I am keenly cognizant of that."

"No, Procurator," Annas replied quietly, "that is not the purpose of my visit. But let us talk about that candidly. You are governor for the Augustus who has conferred his favor upon us, but you know little of the people you must govern. Oppressors despise the oppressed—that is a law of nature that we cannot alter. But I must tell you this: Although you with the legions at your command hold the power, that does not mean that we cease to be a nation."

Pilate was well aware that the high priest had not come to him to discuss a theoretical question, and under other circumstances he would have urged his visitor to come to the point. But since he also knew that the high priest had come to speak about Jesus of Nazareth, he was more than eager for circumlocution. He would bring up the matter of the Nazarene a little later, he thought, and perhaps would catch Annas off guard.

"You know my views on that subject, high priest," he said. "It would be better for the Jewish nation to assimilate itself into the great Roman community."

Annas stroked his white beard thoughtfully and looked at the Procurator with something that verged on pity in his eyes.

"No, Procurator, we are Jews and we wish to remain Jews. In our two thousand years of history we have often been a subject people ruled by foreign overlords. Our forefathers were under the thumb of the Babylonians and Assyrians, and today where are Babylon and Assyria? But the nation of Israel lives, and even if today it has lost its liberty, it exists and will remain. But we, the priests, are the leaders of this nation, whom the commandment of our God and the law of our God has given into our hand."

"That may be," Pilate said. "I know well that you derive your power and your law from your God. It is not the custom of Rome to dispute the legality of established authorities in the lands of the empire, so long as those authorities can really control the people. The events of the last few weeks have fostered in me considerable doubts precisely on this point. Do not those recent events indicate that you no longer have your hand on the helm? I am referring, of course, to the cases of Barabbas and Jesus of Nazareth."

"I see, Procurator," the high priest said, "that you hasten to bring the issue forward. That makes my task easier. As far as Barabbas is concerned, I hope that I have explained that affair fully to you. Does not his case prove most conclusively that the nation is what we make of it? Was it not I who called your attention to the fact that we gave Barabbas temporary support. Why did we do so?"

"In order to make difficulties for me," Pilate replied with affected candor.

"It is not as simple as that, Procurator. You see, our people have only one God and believe in Him alone. But they also wish to have a *patria*. They have always desired a fatherland and will always desire it. Barabbas promised it to them. But it was foolishness in the man to imagine he could contend successfully against your legions. Therefore it was our duty to guard the people against this foolishness. We succeeded in obtaining control of the movement. We kept the people obedient to the law and they turned away from Barabbas."

"I am not so sure of that, high priest. You played with fire too long."

"The fire has been extinguished. But now—mark well what I say, O Procurator—along came this Jesus of Nazareth and attempted to shake our power over the souls of the Israelite people; he declared that the law was antiquated and feeble, and all in all he agitated in a manner that gave us cause for the gravest concern."

"Those are your worries, high priest," Pilate said.

"Not so, O Procurator; those worries necessarily concern also the governor of the noble Augustus. For if our power is shaken, who is to keep the Israelite nation within its prescribed limits? The legions, do you say? Perhaps for the moment. But consider this: What would Rome say if, in addition to the war against the Parthians, which as you know is costing many lives, there took place an insurrection among the people of Israel? The legions would suppress the uprising; we realized that full well when we considered the case of Barabbas. But, Procurator, the Augustus would scarcely think highly of a governor under whose rule a province which is dear to Caesar's heart rose in rebellion."

"Thank you, high priest," Pilate said mockingly. "I am happy to find you so watchful over my welfare."

"You mock, Procurator," Annas responded, "but you ought not to look with suspicion upon every suggestion that comes from us. There is one point at which our interests touch. We—you and I— represent the state power. In this land you have power over men's bodies, I over their minds. Consider the doctrines of the man of Nazareth from that point of view. He asserts that all men are equal, that men must love one another. That is pleasing to those who are ruled—quite naturally. But can it also be pleasing to the rulers? What would you say if your slaves should come to you and inform you: 'Procurator, we have decided not to serve you any longer, for we are men equal to you in every respect.' Why should you be certain that the ideas of this Nazarene can only be implanted in the minds of Jews and not in the minds of your own slaves as well? We want to forestall a revolution which could be equally dangerous to us and to you Romans. The idea of rulership must be defended against millions of subjects. In such a struggle, is not our petty personal enmity a crime against the common cause? And in view of the inflexible requirements of the situation, can the life of one man, which is all I ask of you, be given even a moment's consideration?"

Pilate glared gloomily at the floor. This high priest certainly made his position clear. But to admit that the rule of Rome could be endangered by one wretched fanatic seemed to him a ridiculous confession of weakness.

"I consider it impudent," he said, "to compare the world dominion of Rome with the conditions of your own power."

"Do not, Procurator, underestimate the force of seditious ideas," Annas replied with some vehemence. "I repeat: In the interests of Rome, as well as in our own interest, that man must be swept aside before his doctrine spreads beyond Galilee and Judea to becloud the minds of the lower classes and so do even greater harm than it has already done."

"I have already decided this matter. I sent the man to the governor of Galilee because he is a Galilean. Decide between you what is to be done with him."

The high priest raised his hand as if to brush aside this suggestion.

"Between us? Herod Antipas, who still calls himself king, is not one of us. He is a rotten limb on the trunk of Israel. He will let that agitator go scot free simply because it is we who are bringing the charges. I can tell you what will happen: He will send the Nazarene back to you. And justly. For the blasphemer ended by preaching his pernicious doctrines in the territory that is under your jurisdiction, and therefore you must be his judge."

"You have already judged him!"

"By our law. In so doing we have not anticipated you. There is nothing in what we did to imply that you should confirm our judgment and execute it. I know we cannot order you to do anything. You will judge him yourself and sentence him yourself not because we want it, but because the welfare of your empire requires it."

"We shall see what Herod decides," Pilate said, rising. The high priest rose also, crossed his arms upon the bejeweled gold plate over his breast and bowed, saying:

"I do not doubt that you will have to decide for yourself. Farewell."

Pilate accompanied him to the door where the high priest entered his litter. When the rabble which had once more begun to fill the square recognized the high priest's equipage, it broke into resounding cheers.

Pilate remained in the reception hall in a highly disagreeable mood. All this fuss about a Jewish carpenter because he dared to interfere with the priests' sacred business! But what the high priest had said about the danger of the man's doctrines to the Empire itself continued to trouble the governor, although he would not state so to himself. He could not wholly repress the thought of Rome. Nevertheless he was still convinced that he would not do what the high priests demanded. Three times during his governorship they had rebelled against him; three times they had demanded that Rome recall him and twice they had almost succeeded. They hated him as a Roman and they hated him personally—why should he now do them this favor which would only increase their power? He did not care about the defendant, but he was determined to make the Sanhedrin feel his control.

The centurion of the guard reported to the governor that the prisoner had been turned over to Herod's soldiery. The report was belated because the high priest's visit had prevented him from notifying the Procurator at once. Even as the centurion spoke, a tremendous uproar once more arose in the square in front of the palace. Herod's soldiers were bringing the prisoner back. The mob received him with curses and insults, but the Roman guards blocked off part of the square to keep the mob at bay.

Pilate sent for Marcus.

"Now we are in for it," he said. "Your advice was not so good after all, Marcus. We are no further than we were before. What next?"

A wax tablet was brought in to him. Herod wished to inform the Procurator that he had given the prisoner a hearing, but that it was not within his power to judge him since there were no charges against him in Galilee. As far as he could learn the man had done nothing in Galilee which merited death or any other punishment at all.

Pilate threw the tablet on the table and beckoned to Marcus to follow him to the courthouse.

Jesus had been taken in charge by Pilate's soldiers and was once

more standing before the judgment seat. At the entrance to the
courthouse Nathaniel and his men were standing once more, and
the rabbi began his prosecution immediately, repeating the allega-
tions he had already made several times.

When he had finished his speech, Pilate replied:

"You have brought this man before me as a perverter of the people.
You have made your accusations against him, but I found no fault
in him. The governor of Galilee has also found him not guilty.
But perhaps he has broken your laws—for that I will have him
scourged and then release him."

The priests and Pharisees in the crowd who understood Latin
acted as interpreters and translated these words for the rest. The
mob responded with a tremendous shout of rage and indignation.

"Well-drilled rabble," Pilate said to Marcus. "Do you think they
have all been paid?"

"The priests would never spend so much money," Marcus said
smilingly. "Many of them have been paid, many must believe he
is really a criminal, and most of them simply enjoy the prospect of
seeing someone crucified."

"Wouldn't it be the simplest thing to let the legions clear the
square?" Pilate asked.

"There are thousands of people here and in the side streets. It
might be too dangerous. But I can suggest one possible way out of
the difficulty."

"Let me hear it."

"You have the custom of releasing one criminal to the Jews at the
Passover. What is to prevent you from condemning this Jesus and
then pardoning him?"

"But suppose they don't want to accept him?"

"Then let them choose between him and a real criminal."

Pilate reflected.

"Perhaps there is a chance there. But whom shall I present to
them for alternative? At the moment the only important criminal
I have is Barabbas. And how do you know for certain that the rabble would not rather see him pardoned instead of the Nazarene?
Possibly Barabbas still has some following among the people, even
though the priests have abandoned him."

"Unsuccessful and fallen leaders don't usually have any following
among the people," Marcus said.

"I'll try it anyway."

Marcus did not reply. He was not at all sure of the outcome of this trial, but it also did not seem to him to matter much one way or the other whether the life of this Nazarene was saved.

Outside the tumult had subsided. Pilate once more went to the door.

"It is the custom," he said to Rabbi Nathaniel, "that I release one criminal to you at your festival. I therefore give you the choice: either Jesus, who calls himself your king, or Barabbas the murderer. Decide for yourselves."

When the governor's words were communicated to the crowd, a new wild uproar arose, in which Pilate could distinguish only the one word: "Barabbas!"

When the noise had died down, Rabbi Nathaniel cried to Pilate: "You hear the answer of the people. They want Barabbas."

Pilate, infuriated at the turn his experiment had taken, exclaimed: "Then I shall show you what you are asking for!"

He retired into the court and said to Marcus:

"Have Barabbas brought up here. Perhaps they will come to their senses when they compare that murderer with the harmless and innocent man there."

Marcus shrugged and departed.

While he waited for Barabbas to be brought up, Pilate paced restlessly back and forth in the courtroom, now and then glancing at the accused, who still stood without moving in front of the judgment seat. Herod had had a white cloak thrown over the man's bespattered clothes, but Jesus' face, hands and feet still bore traces of the abuse he had been subjected to.

"If only he would speak up," Pilate thought. "To me or even to that rabble out there. He has the gift of speech; everyone says so. Or does he want to sacrifice himself? It would not be a new idea. Did not Epimenides the Wise sacrifice himself to purify Athens? There have been a large number of such men who immolated themselves for the sins of the community—but what did they ever achieve? In Curium, in Cyprus, in Terracina, every year a man threw himself into the sea to atone for the sins of his fellow men—and have men become any better for it? But for whose sake does this man want to offer up himself? For the priests who intend to kill him anyway? For the Jewish masses who have betrayed and deserted him?" It

did not even occur to Pilate that anyone might want to sacrifice himself for the whole of humanity. For truth then? There was no
such thing as truth. Why did he not speak? He would certainly
be able to change the temper of this incited mob? Or—was he such
a weakling that he had completely lost his head in the face of
danger?

But Jesus stood silently before the judgment seat . . .

The secretary had hastened to the prison and informed the overseer of the order to bring Barabbas to the courtroom.

Barabbas had been lying dully on his straw. He had spent the
past few days in a kind of twilight state, interrupted only when he
was given water and a little food. He was not permitted to starve
to death because his life was being spared for death on the cross.
As for Barabbas, he had written off his life, and if in his delirium
an occasional flash of hope appeared, it hardly pierced the dense veil
obscuring his conscious mind.

When the keepers unchained him from the stone wall and pulled
him to his feet, he felt convinced that he was now being taken out
to be executed. In the darkness of his cell he had had no means of
knowing how many days had passed since he was sentenced, but
he did not even think of that. Now, he was sure, the hour of death
had come for him.

Since he could scarcely stand, he was brought a cup of wine which
he drained at one draft. He was given a superficial washing and
conducted through a long tunnel that led beneath the Procurator's
palace to the courthouse.

His eyes fell first upon Jesus, and he awoke at once from his daze.

He saw the man whom he considered to be a great sorcerer and,
in his heart of hearts, a prophet; he saw him bound and smeared
with blood, and his only thought was that the Romans had arrested
him because he and his following had begun to be dangerous to them.
The scene when Jesus had entered Jerusalem accompanied by the
jubilation of the populace returned vividly to his mind. And now
—now he, too, had been overcome like Barabbas himself; he, too, was
a mere prisoner, perhaps already condemned to death like himself.

Something within Barabbas broke down; he became aware of his
unconscious, repressed faith in this prophet. Now for the first time
Barabbas felt that in all the time since the man had first appeared
he had been moving in a circle around him; that he had tried again

and again to break through the magic circle and approach Jesus. Since he had met this man he had been too weak to take another human life; since he had met him he had really believed Jesus was the Messiah. How could he have been so mistaken, how could he have believed for an hour or even for a moment in such an illusion? For here was the answer to all the questions he had been asking himself about Jesus of Nazareth. Here stood the man, defeated and condemned to death like himself, no conqueror, no king, no Messiah—merely a defenseless Jew who had in all probability been sentenced to die on the cross. Within Barabbas there surged up an overwhelming contempt bordering on hatred for the man of Nazareth. It seemed to him that his own fate was somehow the fault of Jesus. Yes, certainly, if this fool with his confusing sermonizing about peace had not turned such numbers of people away from Barabbas himself, all Israel might have gathered about him and a united people would have driven the Romans from the land and won their freedom. It struck Barabbas as the bitter irony of fate that he and the Nazarene should meet once more in the last hour for both of them.

He was not given much more time to reflect upon fate. Pilate ordered Jesus and Barabbas to be led to the door and shown to the people.

To the left stood Barabbas, filthy, in torn clothing, his hair and beard besmeared with the dirt of his cell, his lips compressed, his eyes glaring with hatred at the crowd: a symbol of savage power in spite of his chains.

To the right stood Jesus of Nazareth. He, too, bore the traces of the maltreatment he had received, but he seemed to be surrounded by an aura of truly royal dignity; a radiance shone from his marred countenance and his eyes, which were also directed at the crowd, bespoke kindness, love and forgiveness.

A murmur arose in the crowd at the sight of these two men who stood beside one another like day and night, like the forces of darkness and radiant love.

Now Pilate stepped in front of the two.

"Here you have Jesus of Nazareth, whom some of you also call the Christ and the King of the Jews, and whom I find guilty of no crime. This man is Barabbas the murderer, who stole your sheep and slaughtered your shepherds. Now choose!"

Pilate had a keen eye for crowds. In Rome and Athens he had
learned to observe the faces of a throng, and as governor he had often
had the opportunity to draw conclusions from the expressions of the
masses whom he was addressing. At this moment he felt absolutely
certain that the crowd favored Jesus of Nazareth. He saw their eyes
upon both men and he thought he saw that the crowd recognized
the difference and would choose the better of the two. Their faces
spoke for Jesus. He continued to have this impression while his
words were being translated. But scarcely did the mob understand
what Pilate had said when the tumult broke loose once more:

"Release Barabbas! We want Barabbas! Barabbas!"

The secretary translated what they were shouting, though this
was scarcely necessary. Rabbi Nathaniel murmured a few words to
those standing beside him, other priests had mingled with the crowd,
and like a chorus of demons the people screamed:

"Release Barabbas! Barabbas! Barabbas!"

As the raucous shouting began, Pilate had turned deathly pale.
A curious feeling arose in him; he began to fear this unpredictable
mob which seemed to have become totally mad. He raised his hand
to indicate that he wished to speak.

The uproar subsided.

"I find that Jesus of Nazareth has done nothing deserving of
death," he cried to the crowd. "What do you wish to be done
with him?"

At once the diabolic chorus began:

"Crucify him, crucify him, crucify him!"

Pilate stepped back and said to Marcus:

"I can't understand it. A few days ago they greeted him joyously
as the son of David and now they are howling for his death. Jesus
or Barabbas—I did not think the choice would be hard for them to
make."

"It is not hard, as you see, Procurator. They are wholeheartedly
for Barabbas."

"Yes, but why, why?"

"To them Barabbas is the patriot, the martyr whom the foreigners
are persecuting. Jesus is a rebel against his own nation, a radical
who wishes to destroy the law of Moses and the Temple. In short,
one is a national hero and the other a traitor to his nation. I really

should have foreseen that. Forgive me, Procurator; my advice doesn't seem to be very good today."

"I could not advise myself any better," Pilate said. "We had to make the experiment. I guess that whenever the masses are faced with the choice between good and evil they will always choose evil."

Outside the chorus was still chanting: "Crucify him, crucify him! Release Barabbas, Barabbas!"

Barabbas stood motionless between his guards, stunned by what was going on around him. When his name had been mentioned for the first time, he had not understood what it was all about. Only gradually had Pilate's words penetrated his consciousness and he had realized that the people were being asked to choose between him and Jesus of Nazareth. Then his heart had almost burst with excitement. A sense of warmth arose within him such as had marked the happiest hours of his popularity, the times when he had gone forth to recruit for his army of liberation and the mob had cheered him loudly. He could not believe that Pilate who had condemned him to death, Pilate who had humiliated him, Pilate who knew how Barabbas hated him—that Pilate the Roman would grant Barabbas the leader of a Jewish rebellion his life and release him just because a few thousand Jews shouted his name in front of the courthouse. This presentation of himself and the man from Nazareth to the crowd seemed so improbable and incredible that Barabbas was inclined to believe it was all a dream of his.

Of course, it must be a dream; the thought that had been tormenting him during all these days of imprisonment was now being grotesquely turned and twisted in his dreams. Often Barabbas had asked himself what would happen if every Jew could be asked in a great popular plebiscite whether he would prefer to have Barabbas or Jesus of Nazareth for his leader. He had never been able to answer this question to his satisfaction, though of late the feeling had grown in him that if it came to a choice the people would decide in favor of Jesus. At such moments of doubt Barabbas had consoled himself with the thought that no such plebiscite could ever come about. It had occurred to no one to ask the people, and it would be foolish to think of anything of the sort, for what the masses needed was not a free choice but the imposition of a strong will. And now— what a mad dream!—Pilate was asking the very question: Jesus or

Barabbas? And—what a miracle!—the mob was turning away from this weakling who deceived it with gentle words, was turning away from this false Messiah toward the man of strength who had promised liberation through battle and violence. It was too good to be true, Barabbas thought.

Pilate cast one more glance at the two men and summoned up his energies for one more attempt to free Jesus of Nazareth from the grip of this faithless and insane mob.

"I will have him scourged," he said to Marcus. "Perhaps that will placate this incomprehensible mass hatred."

"Perhaps," Marcus replied, shrugging dubiously.

Pilate ordered the soldiers to return Barabbas to his cell and to take Jesus into the courthouse yard and have him whipped in the presence of all the people. Then he left the courthouse precipitately and fled to his office. But even there he heard the howls of the mob which had made its way into the yard to watch the scourging of the Nazarene.

When Barabbas was seized roughly by the soldiers to be taken back to his cell, it dawned upon him with tremendous impact that he had not been dreaming and that his fate was still linked with that of the Nazarene. He tried for a moment to catch a glimpse of the mob, in order to read in someone's face the answer to the questions that were whirling through his mind, and his searching eye fell upon the face of Ezra. Ezra stood in the forefront of the crowd and his eyes seemed to be trying to draw Barabbas' glance. Their eyes met. But for once Barabbas did not see in Ezra's gaze the flame of love and enthusiasm that he had seen there so often, nor did he see the flashes of hatred with which Ezra ordinarily looked upon the enemy. Instead Barabbas read in Ezra's eyes mingled fear and doubt, and he turned hastily away.

Then he was led out and the mob pushed its way into the courthouse yard. The shouts and imprecations of the crowd gave way now and then to the crack of the lashes upon the body of Jesus of Nazareth.

Ezra, who had been in the crowd all this time, sat down on a stone. He had seen and heard everything, and he knew that he, too, had been asked to choose between Jesus and Barabbas. With the others he had shouted, "Release Barabbas," but he was unable to join in when the mob began to chant, "Crucify him!" For suddenly, to his own amazement, he had experienced a surge of sympathy for the prophet. With every fibre of his being he desired Barabbas to be freed, but some powerful emotion within him resisted the thought that the life of Barabbas was to be bought by the death of the Nazarene. He could not have said what was the source of this sudden sympathy for Jesus, but his soul convulsed with pity as he watched the man being scourged. He knew that among the thousands who stood there howling like madmen scarcely any of them knew as he did what it felt like to be beaten in such a manner. Ezra saw himself in Jesus of Nazareth; he saw in him all the righteous and innocent men who had been tormented and lashed and hounded to death because they believed in truth and justice. And then he suddenly saw in the victim the man who had raised Lazarus from death and for whose sake Lazarus and his sisters had saved his, Ezra's, life. And he saw in him the man who had spoken kindly words to the Samaritan woman, the man who was forgiving to sinners and who felt only love even for Barabbas. He saw in him the embodiment of all that was good in man and all that was divine; he saw in him the promise that had been made of the people of Israel, the Redeemer, the Messiah. It came upon Ezra in a sudden illumination; all at once he felt certain that Jesus of Nazareth was the Messiah and that no matter what humiliation he might have to endure, what sufferings he might pass through, he would not die and he would save Israel.

But—the thought crept into his mind—what would happen to Barabbas? If Jesus were crucified, Barabbas would be released, or was Jesus being scourged only that he might be released afterward? Then that would mean death for Barabbas. A voice within him whispered: "You cannot be for both Jesus and Barabbas . . . You must decide between them—either Jesus or Barabbas—either love or violence." Ezra felt that his heart was constricted by an intolerable pressure. He could scarcely breathe. And wringing his hands he murmured an answer to the inner voice: "Lord, help me; I am a weak human being; I cannot decide. I am for Christ and for Barabbas both; I want both of them to live, for both of them desire the good of the nation whose son I am and for whom I live."

How horrible were the shrieks and laughter that accompanied the scourging of Jesus, more horrible than the blows of the lash. Would this torment never end? Would that holy man not only be scourged but beaten to death? God, O God, do not let it happen! Ezra prayed, throwing himself on his face.

Suddenly the uproar ceased, but the silence was followed at once by howls of mocking laughter, as if all the devils of Hell had been let loose. From within the courtyard and from the mob in the square came loud cries: "Hail, King of the Jews! Hail, King of the Jews!" And again the roar of diabolic laughter rose up.

Then the mob poured out of the yard and back into the square. Apparently Jesus had been taken away.

What had happened was that the soldiers had snatched the exhausted Nazarene away from the scourgers, who had draped an old, tattered purple robe over him and placed a crown of thorns on his head.

The legionaries returned Jesus to the courthouse.

The secretary hurried to the palace to fetch the governor. On the way to the courthouse he informed Pilate of what had taken place.

When Pilate entered the courtroom, even he trembled at the sight of the Nazarene.

Jesus of Nazareth, now clothed only in the filthy, ragged purple robe, was so covered with bleeding wounds that there was not an uninjured spot visible on his body. His face under the crudely-woven crown of thorns was also encrusted with ribbons of coagulated blood. He was a picture of unspeakable wretchedness.

Pilate ordered the soldiers to lead him to the door to be shown to the crowd.

"Behold," he cried loudly and incoherently, "a man!"

Marcus sensed what the Procurator wished to say. Pilate was anything but a sentimentalist, but in the face of the terrible thing that had been done to the Nazarene he had become inarticulate with horror; he was too shaken to frame more than this phrase; he was incapable of elaborating all he really meant: "Are you not horror-struck to have done this to any man? Here is a man like yourselves, and you have caused him to be beaten so shamefully that he scarcely resembles a human being any longer. Do you not repent? Is not this enough for you?"

And to this unspoken plea Pilate added aloud:

"I find no fault in this righteous man!"

At once the clamor of the mob arose afresh.

"Crucify him, crucify him!" they shouted, and the priests who were among the crowd incited them to shout louder.

Rabbi Nathaniel, bellowing to make himself heard above the uproar, said:

"By our law he must die, for he made himself the Son of God."

"Then take him and crucify him yourselves," Pilate cried, sick with abhorrence.

"You know we may not do that," Rabbi Nathaniel screamed.

The governor ordered Jesus brought before him once more and asked:

"Whence come you?"

But Jesus did not answer.

"Why do you not speak to me?" the governor demanded. "Do you not know that I have the power to crucify you or to release you?"

At this Jesus turned his face toward the Procurator and answered:

"You could have no power at all against me, except it were given you from above; therefore he who delivered me to you has the greater sin."

Pilate did not understand what Jesus meant by this. From the square he could still hear the cacophonous howling: "Crucify him, crucify him!" Such a wave of mob hatred was surging up against the walls of the courthouse that the Procurator felt he could scarcely remain there a moment longer. He wanted at all costs to get the matter over with. Just as he was striding to the door to order the soldiers to clear the square by force, he heard Nathaniel shouting:

"If you let this agitator go, you are not Caesar's friend, for whoever makes himself a king speaks against the Augustus himself."

The words rang like a thunderclap in Pilate's ear. "Not Caesar's friend?" Did he dare let that be said of him?

"He is your king," Pilate cried. "Why do you ask that I crucify him?"

But Rabbi Nathaniel and the priests who were close enough to distinguish what the Procurator had said shouted with one voice:

"We have no king but Caesar."

Pilate blenched when he heard these words. He felt that he had made a fateful slip of the tongue. If all that had taken place here was reported to Rome, the Augustus would learn that the governor of Judea had permitted a king of the Jews to be proclaimed and that the Jewish priests had had to remind him that there was only an

Emperor in the Roman Empire. If such a version of the story reached Rome, Pilate was lost. And Pilate knew that the priests would find ways to smuggle their report out of Jerusalem. With this thought he made his decision: it was better for the Nazarene to die than for Pilate himself to be ruined.

He went over to the judgment seat from which the decisions of the court were announced to the people. There he ordered a vessel of water to be brought in, and while Jesus was once more led to the door Pilate ostentatiously dipped his hands in the water, stating:

"I am innocent of the blood of this just person."

But the people shouted:

"His blood be on us and on our children."

The governor shuddered with horror at the madness of this mob. With a hasty movement he broke the wand and let it fall to the ground.

This was the sign that Jesus was condemned to death.

The mob went wild with jubilation.

The governor fled back to his palace without another glance at the Nazarene. He was horrified by what he had done and raging with impotent fury against the priests who had driven him to it. Already he could not understand how he had permitted the death sentence to be extorted from him, in spite of his firm intention. He felt oppressed by shame, tormented by disgust for this city, this nation, himself. What most revolted him was not that he had sentenced an innocent man to death—what did one human life matter? —but that he had been tricked by the priests.

Marcus had followed him, since there were several orders of a practical nature to be issued. Pilate pulled himself together; there was no need for his secretary to see how utterly wrought up he was by the trial. He issued the orders:

"The cross that was prepared for Barabbas will be used for Jesus of Nazareth."

"And the inscription?" the scribe asked.

"Write: Jesus of Nazareth, King of the Jews."

"The Sanhedrin will hardly like that," Marcus ventured.

"Never mind! That's just why I want it. And see to it that Barabbas is released."

25

Loneliness

WHEN PILATE PRONOUNCED THE DEATH SENTENCE UPON JESUS OF Nazareth, Ezra's hope that Barabbas would be released became almost a certainty. If the governor granted one of the popular demands, he would certainly not refuse the other.

In spite of this conviction, Ezra was incapable of feeling the joy which would have been natural after so much suffering and despair. He saw Jesus standing at the door of the courthouse, drenched with blood, bowed down with incredible torture and humiliation, and now condemned to the death of slaves. And Ezra groaned to think that Barabbas' freedom had been purchased at such a price. When the mob howled: "His blood be on us and on our children," Ezra shuddered. He had a premonition of the dreadfulness of the crime that was here being committed, and he knew that he could not join these madmen who were howling for the blood of the Nazarene. It almost seemed to him that Jesus of Nazareth was dying solely for Barabbas, and he was incapable of feeling joy over this sacrifice.

In a state bordering on mental paralysis, he prepared to receive Barabbas, his friend and leader, when the rebel chieftain was let out of the prison. "He looked wretched," Ezra thought, "I will have to tend him for a while and make him rest." He imagined that Barabbas would be released from the near-by prison gate, and he decided to go there and wait until his leader came out.

But he did not turn and enter the narrow side street. It was as
if he were chained to this place of horror, as if a higher power had
imposed upon him the duty of witnessing the tragedy to the bitter end.

He saw how Jesus, who had been clothed in his own robes again,
was led out of the courthouse and down the steps into the square
where, amid the insults and imprecations of the rabble, a cross of
such huge dimensions was placed upon his back that he almost sank
down under the burden. He saw the procession form which was
to take the condemned Jesus to Golgotha: the priests at the head.
Even High Priest Caiaphas had come in his litter to the square and
was now being borne in the midst of the priests along the street that
led to the place of execution. Between the priests and the detachment of soldiers under the command of a centurion who were escorting the prisoner, members of the mob had pushed their way. Jesus
himself could scarcely be seen. Just one of his arms and the point of
the cross swayed above the helmets and lances of the legionaries.
Behind the priests came the main body of the mob, again and again
breaking into cheers.

It had not at all been Ezra's intention to join this frightful procession, but he could not help himself; he felt compelled by a power
outside himself.

The procession moved very slowly. Jesus, wholly exhausted from
the beatings and the loss of blood, fell to the ground thrice under
the weight of the cross. The Roman soldiers took pity on him and for a
time permitted another Jew to carry the cross for him. But the mob
was dissatisfied to see the man of Nazareth relieved of his burden
and shouted such abuse at the soldiers that they at last gave in and
replaced the cross on Jesus' shoulders.

At the tail end of the procession was a smaller group of soldiers,
between whom walked two criminals, also with crosses on their shoulders, who were condemned to die at the same time. But no one
paid any attention to them.

Shortly before the procession reached the top of Golgotha there
was a halt. The priests had noticed the inscription attached to
Jesus' cross and, turning to the centurion, had demanded that it be
changed. The centurion refused and advised them to speak to the
Procurator, who had given the order for the wording. The priests
promptly sent a message back to the palace.

On Golgotha the terrible act of crucifixion was accomplished without delay. The executioners who had accompanied the legionaries were practiced at their trade. Ezra heard the dull thud of the hammers that drove the nails through the hands and feet of the victim, and his heart almost stood still at the frightful sound. Then he saw the cross raised and the tormented body of Jesus hanging high above the mob. Almost immediately the two other, smaller crosses were raised to the right and left. Above the head of the Nazarene stood the words:

JESUS NAZARENUS REX JUDAEORUM

Pilate had refused to accede to the priests' request that the inscription be changed. He had ordered the messenger to say to the high priest:

"What I have written, I have written."

Now, led by High Priest Caiaphas and Rabbi Nathaniel, the priests went up to the cross. What they said to the man on the cross Ezra could not make out because of the howling of the mob. The rabble pressed closer and closer to the cross. A veritable blood-madness seemed to have overcome them, such as frequently happened in the circus when a man or an animal did not die as quickly as the mob desired. They screeched incessant insults at the "false prophet," "despoiler of the Temple" and "blasphemer."

There was a small group standing, huddled together, to one side—women, among whom Ezra recognized Mary of Magdala, who appeared utterly stricken with sorrow, and one of the disciples whom he had seen with Jesus approaching Lazarus' house in Bethany.

Ezra had not approached the cross. He, too, stood to one side, his heart aching with pity. He did not understand the feeling that had overcome him; all he knew was that his sympathy was not for Barabbas but for this man on the cross.

At last the priests departed in a body, surrounded by the jubilant crowd which seemed to feel that a great victory had been won. The scene grew calmer beneath the crosses. Ezra, too, intended to join the throng returning to the city. It was about time he looked for Barabbas, who would certainly have been released by now. But Ezra seemed rooted to the spot. It was his duty, he felt, to hasten to Barabbas who, deserted by all and weakened by his incarceration, would certainly need him. Yet he could not go.

The priests and the mob descended from Golgotha into the city
to prepare for the beginning of the Passover. The priests, with High
Priest Caiaphas at their head, went to the home of Annas, who had
not wished to attend the execution, to inform him of what had taken
place. There they congratulated each other on their success.

Annas was borne in his litter to the Temple, to make an offering
of thankfulness to the Lord. But as he went toward the Sanctuary
of the Temple, the veil was rent from top to bottom . . .

At this same hour Joseph of Arimathea climbed the outside staircase to the governor's palace. He walked wearily. He had been on
Golgotha and had tried to console the weeping women, though without himself feeling that anything in the world could console him.
The events of the past few hours had pierced him to the heart.

What more was there for him in the world?

Jesus, the Messiah, the Son of God, hung on the cross, killed by
his enemies, a mockery to the mob which a few days ago had hailed
him. All was over!

"If I were a Roman," Joseph thought, "I would cast off this life
that has become without hope or purpose, just as that disciple who
betrayed the Master, Judas of Kerioth, did but a few hours ago. But
I am no Roman, and the thought is unworthy of one who sat at
the feet of the Master."

When, pale, disheartened, ill to the depths of his soul, he entered
the governor's room, he saw Pilate sitting before a brazier of glowing
coals.

Pilate scarcely turned his head in answer to Joseph's greeting.

"You have come to reproach me," he said hoarsely. "I did not
keep my promise. I delivered Jesus up to the priests, I had him
scourged and crucified . . . I know what you want to say, and what
is worst, I can find no excuse for it all. I was simply defeated by the
priests at every turn."

Joseph nodded somberly.

"I did not come to talk about things which can no longer be al-
tered," he said. "I have come with a plea."

"Yes?"

"I want to ask you to permit me, when it is all over, to take the
Master from the cross and bury him in my own tomb."

"Yes, of course! Why should I refuse you that?"

"I feared his enemies would even wish to seize his body. Their

hatred is so infernal that it would probably reach beyond death itself
if it could."

"I saw this hatred, Joseph, and never in my life could I have imagined anything so diabolic. I will give orders that you be permitted to bury him undisturbed. Is he . . . is he . . . ?"

"No, I do not think it is over yet. You can see the cross from
your window—it is high enough."

Pilate almost screamed as he covered his eyes with his hands.

"No, I don't want to, I don't want to see it."

"Thank you, Procurator. Peace be with you."

Joseph of Arimathea left. The Procurator did not look up; he
stared into the smoking brazier while slowly, slowly, the coals turned
to ashes. Then he called for a fresh brazier.

The slave-girl, Chloe, brought it, set it down before the Procurator
and started to leave the room.

"Stay," Pilate commanded. "I don't want to be alone. Do you
know what has happened today, Chloe?"

The girl nodded; her eyes were red with tears that she had shed
over her mistress, who lay in her room in an agony of sorrow.

"Then you know—all the world knows it. Do you believe in
gods?"

"Yes, lord."

"You are fortunate. I believe in nothing. I do not even believe
I will be forgiven if I burn incense and bring sacrifices to the gods.
Do you understand that, Chloe? But no, how could you understand?
I wish I could escape myself, I wish I could ask forgiveness, but I
can only wrestle with myself and endure what is unendurable. If
only I could wipe this day from the calendar. But it is burned into my
mind; what has happened remains and will remain for all time.
Pilate is a cowardly judge. So cowardly that he cast off his Roman
pride and bowed to the blackmail of the priests and the shouts of the
rabble. Why did that happen? Am I afraid of Rome? Of the
priests? Of the mob? The Augustus is far away. If I wanted I
could drive all this horrid nation and its priests into the desert. And
yet I cringed before them. Craven . . . craven . . . but why am I
craven? I don't know. But, Chloe—I think it had to be, so that
the face of the world should not be changed. These do not seem
to be the times for heroism; the age has the men it needs, the judges
and priests, and the murderers as well. Barabbas and Annas and

Pilate and the people! In such a world there is no room for him; it is necessary to nail him to the cross so that he does not change the world. This world is made for murderers, not for prophets. Do you understand that, Chloe?"

The girl was terrified by this outburst; with bowed head she stood before Pilate, who stared at her with wide, almost delirious eyes.

The centurion who had been in charge of the soldiers on the way to Golgotha entered, saluted and said hoarsely:

"It is done, Procurator. The sentence has been carried out."

Pilate looked at the man.

"How did he behave?" he asked.

The centurion, a young man with a frank, open face, responded to the Procurator's beckoning finger by approaching.

"I have seen many men executed," he replied, "but none who went to his death with so much tranquillity, so much dignity. So must Socrates have died!"

Pilate did not speak; he was breathing heavily.

"I have posted a guard there," the centurion continued, "so that the mob will not make the death agonies even harder for him, and also to protect a few people who are standing at the foot of the cross."

Pilate looked up inquiringly.

"Then he has friends who have not deserted him?"

"His mother, one of the disciples, and a few other women, among them Mary of Magdala."

Pilate rose from his couch.

"Three human beings . . ." he said, sighing and speaking to himself rather than to the centurion. "Three who are faithful to him unto death. That is really a great many. I don't know, centurion, whether when I die three persons will stay by me to the end. You do not know either—no one knows."

The centurion, astonished, decided it was time to withdraw.

"Have you any more orders, Tribune?" he asked.

Pilate did not have a chance to reply, for at that moment the walls of the room seemed to rock and a great underground rumbling was heard.

Chloe screamed:

"The earth is shaking."

The centurion, too, had turned a shade paler.

"What is the matter with you two?" Pilate exclaimed, looking at

each of them in turn. "The earth is shaking? Ridiculous. It must
be a thunderstorm."

At once there followed a second and then a third earthquake; and
this time the underground rumbling was in fact as loud as thunder.

"The earth is shaking!" This time it was the centurion who
exclaimed.

He had scarcely spoken the words when all the light vanished and
the room became pitch-dark.

Chloe fell to the floor and clapped her hands over her face.

The sudden blackness gave way to a pale, gloomy light. Pilate and
the soldier stood like phantoms in the darkness of the room.

Then the blackness descended again, and then pale light. Once
more came the alternation of utter darkness and light, and then the
pallid light remained. From the street shouting and wailing could
be heard. Then the decurion who had been left to guard the cross
rushed into the room and threw himself at the Procurator's feet.

"What does this mean? Are you a soldier, to writhe like an old
woman at my feet. Stand up and speak like a man."

The decurion rose somewhat sheepishly.

"Forgive me, Procurator. But if you had seen what I saw . . . !"

He paused, shaken by the recollection.

"Well, what did you see?" Pilate snarled. "Stop muttering like an
idiot and speak up."

"I had my men form a circle around the execution ground, facing
outward with lances fixed, in order to protect the man on the cross
and the women below it from the mob, who were already beginning
to gather stones. The rabble shouted insults, but in the face of the
lances none of them dared to throw the stones, although they were
already poised to do so. The man on the cross was silent except for
low moans . . . Then it seemed to me he was praying. It was not
until the last agony began that he screamed out in despair. Then,
Tribune, then it was as if a quivering passed through his flayed body;
he seemed to grow, together with the cross, to gigantic size. Light
radiated from him and clear and loud as the sound of trumpets his
voice rang out: 'It is finished. Father, into thy hands I commend my
spirit.' Then his head drooped—he was dead. But the radiance
remained. The women wept; the mob fell silent. And of my soldiers—veterans, mind you, Tribune—more than half of them had
turned their heads toward the cross and fallen to their knees, as I

myself did. Then the ground began to quake under our feet. The
light vanished—just the cross and he who hung on the cross shone
out in the darkness."

"Women!" Pilate said contemptuously.

"The mob fled. Then the light returned. Twice more the shaking of the earth and the darkness and illumination was repeated.
And something within me or outside of me forced me to cry out:
'Truly this man was the Son of God.' Then I took my soldiers and
returned here on the double. The streets are filled with terrified
people. The rocks on Mount Golgotha burst; cemeteries have
opened; the people are running about like a herd of cattle startled by
lightning and shouting: 'The dead are rising.' The whole city is in
the grip of horror . . . Tribune, I was present when the Augustus
died—but here in Jerusalem a man has been crucified who stood
closer to the Divine than Octavian."

"Silence!" Pilate commanded. After a pause he said curtly: "Go."
The decurion saluted and left. Pilate turned to the centurion.

"I have decided it is time the cohorts are relieved. The supersti-
tion that runs rampant in this country has turned them into old
wives and makes them see ghosts in broad daylight. That man and
the whole maniple of men who were guarding the cross with him
will be transferred to the north this very night, understand?"

The centurion looked at the floor shamefacedly—he, too, had been
impressed by the old soldier's tale.

"I don't know . . ." he stammered.

But Pilate angrily interrupted him.

"You don't need to know anything. Your business is to keep your
mouth shut and obey. Go!"

The centurion saluted and departed.

Chloe was still cowering on the floor, her face contorted and her
eyes filled with tears.

Pilate began to pace. Speaking to himself rather than to Chloe,
he said:

"There you have it. They will cry, 'The man on the cross was
the Messiah, the Son of God.' When he died miracles took place,
the earth trembled, the sky was darkened. But what I say is: folly,
folly! Hasn't the earth ever trembled before, where there was no
Messiah hanging on the cross? Hasn't the sky ever been darkened
because clouds obscured the sun? No, by all the gods I don't believe

in—I won't permit my sane mind to be cozened by all your silly fantasies. He was guiltless, you say? I, too, found him without guilt. And yet he had to die. Why? The Stoic says: Fate. That ends the case. It was his fate to die in this fashion. A human life? Even the best and noblest is worth no more than a brief moment's thought. He died and so he is dead—what more is there?"

Shouting and wailing could still be heard from the street, but Pilate thought he also made out voices crying the name of Barabbas.

"That's it," he said, "there's the answer. The one had to die so that the other might live. Fate. Has it any meaning that a Barabbas should live and a Jesus die? It must have a meaning. Everything has a meaning. Send Marcus in to me, Chloe."

The girl cast a shy, questioning glance at the Procurator and slipped out of the room. Almost at once the secretary entered. The room was still dimly lit by a sallow glow. Marcus was pale and excited; his hair, usually so carefully combed, hung in a tangle around his beardless face.

"Have you heard, Procurator?" he cried. "The . . ."

Pilate interrupted him.

"Yes, I've heard all about it. All the idiocies that are being talked about, all the ghost-stories the rabble is retailing. The earth is trembling, the sun has been darkened, the dead are resurrected— miracles upon miracles."

"And even now the moon stands blood-red in the sky," continued Marcus, taking the governor's words in earnest, "and the curtain of the Temple has been torn in two so that the people can see into the Holy of Holies."

Pilate looked wide-eyed at his secretary. He seemed to be quite stunned.

"Tell me, Marcus, do you really believe all these things?"

The scribe bowed his head and did not reply.

"I have always," Pilate continued, "thought you an unusually intelligent fellow, Marcus. I am afraid I was mistaken. Apparently you do not differ from your countrymen. You think yourself superior because your mind has soaked up Greek culture, but the first thing that happens to which your logic can find no answer knocks you head over heels and makes you believe in supernatural forces. A few tremors of the earth, a few dark clouds, and you throw your reason overboard. You are actually no more sensible than the stupid

populace who associate these natural phenomena with the execution
of Jesus of Nazareth. I expected you to behave more intelli-
gently . . . Why has Barabbas not been released?"

The secretary made an effort to pull himself together. The governor had never before treated him with such contempt and he was
afraid he might lose his position.

"Pardon, lord," he said. "I thought it might be wiser not to release Barabbas at once. The Jewish populace is all stirred up—who
knows whether in their present excitement they might not suddenly
decide to make Barabbas their leader again."

Pilate reflected. Then he said:

"I have also been a little worried about that. But I gave my word:
Barabbas must be released. The rabble who seem to rule this country are already shouting for him. But keep him under surveillance.
As soon as he leaves Jerusalem he is to be killed, quietly and without
leaving any clues. Is that clear?"

"Yes, Procurator," Marcus said zealously. "I will have him killed
by a Jew."

"Good. But outside the city, so that we don't have any more
tumult. I've had enough uproar for the day."

Marcus went down to the prison and ordered the warden to release
Barabbas at once.

Barabbas had been returned to his cell and chained to the wall
again. He could not imagine what this meant. What had happened? Pilate had allowed the people and the priests to choose between him and Jesus of Nazareth; they had asked for him and had
demanded the cross for the other. Had the Procurator nonetheless
changed his mind? Had he broken his promise?

Curiously enough, as long as Barabbas had looked forward to certain death, it scarcely mattered; life had meant nothing to him. But
now that some prospect of life had appeared, he trembled with fear
of death and every moment that passed in uncertainty was an age of
frightful mental torment to him.

He felt the trembling of the earth and heard the underground
rumbling, but, of course, he knew nothing of the obscuring of the
sun, for eternal darkness prevailed in his cell. Sweat poured from his
brow and every time he heard sandals slapping against the stone pave-

ment of the corridor his heart contracted with fear—was he to be led
to his death or were they bringing him freedom?

But the footsteps went past each time—no one seemed at all concerned about him. It must be night by now, he thought. Perhaps
the Passover had already begun, and surely they could not execute
him during the holiday.

What had happened to Jesus of Nazareth? Barabbas summoned
to his mind the image of the man as he had seen him in the hall of
the courthouse. He could not understand how it was he had ever
let this terribly broken-down specimen of humanity disturb his plans,
how he had ever been so weak-willed as to be influenced by the
Nazarene's words and deeds. So that was the end of this preacher of
love, kindness and mercy: the populace demanded his death. "Poor,
foolish idealist," Barabbas thought, not with sympathy but with the
contempt that the strong feel for the weak.

Once more he heard footsteps in the corridor.

Choking with anxiety, Barabbas got to his knees, which was all
the chains allowed him to do. Yes—this time the footsteps were not
passing by. Two keepers, one bearing a torch, entered his cell.
Barabbas quivered. Now at last he was facing the question: life or
death?

They brought him life.

The keepers removed the chains from his arms and legs and kicked
him until he staggered to his feet. Then they drove him out into
the corridor. There they pointed to a basin of water, with which he
could wash, and threw him a bundle of clothing—his own, but
crumpled and soiled. They waited until he was dressed, then led
him to the outer door. A heavy bolt was pushed aside, and a moment later Barabbas stood on the street. Behind him the door
clanged shut.

Free! For a moment he could not believe it. Was this reality or
another of his deliriums?

The street was deserted.

Twilight was already falling. Barabbas tried to take a few steps,
but he was so weak that he had to sit down on a curbstone. He had
eaten nothing all day.

Why was there no one in the street? Knowing nothing of all that
had taken place that day, he could not understand the silence and
emptiness of the city. He knew nothing of the changes that had

taken place in the hearts of the people, nothing of the terror that had made the inhabitants of the city crawl into their houses like frightened animals, nothing of the frightful thought that had but a short time ago assailed the members of the afternoon's vociferous mob—the thought that the Righteous One's innocent blood which they had so wantonly called down upon their own heads was already becoming an intolerable responsibility.

Barabbas imagined that the Passover celebration had already begun; the people, he reasoned, would be sitting in their homes by now and eating the Passover lamb, thanking God for their ancient liberation from Pharaoh.

"Liberation . . ." He uttered an involuntary groan. Ah yes, today was the celebration of liberation; today men were celebrating not only the past but the present, the liberation of Barabbas, the leader and future liberator of the people of Israel from the Roman prison. But why was there no one here to meet him? Why had they all disappeared, all those thousands who had stood before the courthouse shouting his name, demanding his liberation? Why at least was there not a group of the people's delegates waiting at the prison door to invite him to their homes, invite him to share the Passover Feast with them? Where, at least, was Ezra? Why was he not there?

Where should he go now, since Jerusalem seemed to have turned against him once more. Was it only another dream that thousands of people had been shouting his name, while now not one of them was anywhere about? But yet he was in fact free; his chains had been removed; he no longer lay on the filthy floor of the cell . . . Therefore it must have been true that Pilate was forced by the people to release him. But why this dreadful silence in the streets? Where was the population of Jerusalem?

Unsteadily, Barabbas staggered through the silent streets toward the Ophel district. He headed toward the low-class tavern where he had formerly spent many nights in hiding. He wanted above all to see people, someone, anyone.

There were a few men who knew him in the tavern, but their greeting was hesitant. The proprietor gave him something to eat, but without any trace of his former alacrity. The atmosphere of the place was cheerless; the men sat gloomily in corners saying nothing to one another.

"What's the matter with all of you?" Barabbas at last burst out in exasperation. "Does it make you so unhappy to see me free?"

For minutes no one answered him. Then one of the men said: "Jesus of Nazareth has been crucified."

The words fell upon him like a shower of icy water. Barabbas shivered. He felt a sense of abandonment and loneliness such as he had scarcely endured even in his cell.

Then Ezra came in.

He seemed not at all surprised to find Barabbas here. He greeted him with some warmth, but his eyes seemed to be looking upon things far away and his voice sounded strange and weary, as if it were not his but another's.

"What's the matter with you, Ezra?" Barabbas asked. "You're so different—what has happened to you?"

"I have seen the Messiah crucified," Ezra said dully, turning away from him.

"The Messiah?" Barabbas exclaimed. "Do you mean that poor devil, Jesus of Nazareth?"

A long-drawn out cry was wrenched from Ezra's throat; it became a sobbing exclamation.

"He was the Messiah, he was the Messiah! And they nailed him to the cross. He died for you, Barabbas—for you, for me, for all of us."

"You've gone mad, Ezra," Barabbas said.

Ezra drew himself erect. The tears were flowing over his face, but his eyes sparkled. With a warm, kindly, almost blissful expression he looked in to Barabbas' eyes and said:

"He was the Son of God, Barabbas, and he saved you as well as others. You will understand—all will understand it some day."

Without a word Barabbas turned away from his friend and went out into the dark night that covered Jerusalem.

26 𝕏

Hate's Apostle

BARABBAS WAS DETERMINED TO LEAVE THE TAVERN AND SHAKE OFF
Ezra for good. This change in Ezra, the desertion of his truest comrade, Ezra's preposterous devotion to the dead and "finished" Nazarene, caused Barabbas greater pain than the pangs of his worn and
exhausted body. The disillusionment he had met in the tavern was
the final blow. Physical and mental distress merged into so overwhelming a weakness that his legs refused to support him. A few
steps from the door of the tavern he fell to the ground unconscious.
He was not aware when Ezra came out and bent over him, nor when
the men in the tavern carried him back; he felt nothing of the care
and anxiety in Ezra's mind while Barabbas slept without interruption for twenty-four hours.

When he awoke at last he saw Ezra sitting beside his bed.

"What happened to me?" Barabbas asked. "I left this place
and . . ."

"Yes, Barabbas," Ezra said, "you wanted to escape. But you were
still too weak. You must not try to escape from me. I love you,
Barabbas, perhaps more than ever. For now I know how you suffer
and how much you need love."

Barabbas was alienated at once by these words. For the first time
he noticed how much Ezra had changed outwardly. Since Barabbas
had last seen him Ezra's hair and beard had turned completely grey,

but his features were peaceful in a way they had never been before and his eyes, which used to glare with inexhaustible hatred, now held a mild gleam.

"Love . . . love . . ." Barabbas murmured. "There is death in that word. You see where it brought Jesus of Nazareth. You have been infected by him and are as soft as a woman, Ezra. You are no longer a warrior."

"Yes, Barabbas, I am," Ezra replied quietly. "I have become a warrior for goodness and love. I have seen that love is better for humanity than hate, and that kindness is better than violence."

"We no longer understand each other," Barabbas said, and he fell silent.

This discussion was followed by others of a similar nature. The result was that Ezra decided to separate from Barabbas. He would go to the northeast part of the country, he thought, where the shepherds pastured their flocks in the borderland between the desert and the cultivated countryside. There he would try to find work and a livelihood. In Jerusalem he could stay no longer; he had a horror of the city and did not want to remain there a day more than necessary. For the present Barabbas needed care, and Ezra had to obtain food for him. But as soon as Barabbas was well again he intended to leave.

Barabbas, too, was considering what he should do. When Ezra informed him of his intention, Barabbas suggested that they start out together.

"I will be frank with you, Ezra," he said. "I have no thought of settling down as a peaceful shepherd. I'll go along with you for a while and then I'll strike out into the desert. It's quite possible that I'll be able to find at least a part of my band again. The next attempt at revolt I'll prepare better than this one. And it will succeed. I shall liberate Israel, Ezra."

"I no longer believe in the method of armed violence, Barabbas. It can mean the ruin of Israel. Can't you abandon the idea of fighting? Can you not make peace at last with God and with yourself?"

"I hate the Romans more than ever. I can never make peace so long as a single Roman stands on the sacred soil of our country. And I do not believe in their invincibility—now less than ever. You yourself were a witness when Caesar's governor quailed before the will of the priests."

"It would have been better for himself, for our nation and for all mankind if he had not made himself an accomplice of that killing," Ezra said thoughtfully. "The blood of the Messiah will come down upon them all . . ."

The fourth day after Barabbas' release they departed. They left the city in the early morning and took the road toward Jericho. The weather had completely changed; it was a warm, bright, and spring-like day. Barabbas still walked with difficulty; his powerful frame had not yet wholly recovered from the maltreatment of the prison; but his set face reflected gloomy determination and an iron will. Ezra, too, was in poor physical condition. His soul had been terribly buffeted in these last few days, since it had been revealed to him how he had wasted his life and how he had heaped great guilt upon his head. Barabbas walked by his side like a shadow out of the past, and Ezra wondered whether he could ever in his life altogether free himself of that shadow.

By afternoon they were tired out. They reached a crossroads where Barabbas saw, resting in the shade, a man he thought he recognized. He stood still.

"Peace be with you. Are you not Ephraim?"

The man rose and approached. He peered for a moment in apparent bewilderment and then recognized Barabbas, who was worn to a shadow of his former self.

"And you are Barabbas. Peace."

"Where are your comrades?" Barabbas asked.

Ephraim, a youth whose beard was barely sprouting, shrugged his shoulders.

"How should I know? Most of them have probably made their way to the seacoast cities by now."

"What has happened to my army?" Barabbas snapped at the man in a tone that seemed to imply that Ephraim was responsible for all that had happened.

He might well have grasped how times had changed by the manner of the young man's reply. Ephraim looked at Barabbas with a touch of pity.

"Your army?" he drawled. "Army? It doesn't exist. One fine day we chased Juda ben Jacob and his lackeys out of the camp—he is said to have fled to Syria. And then everyone ran around in confusion and finally they all pulled out. You were not there, nor Ezra.

We heard the Romans were coming to break up the camp. We were in no condition to put up a fight. And we had heard you were captured and would undoubtedly be put to death by the Romans. So first a few and then whole bands slipped away. What should we have waited for? We were already beginning to run out of food. I imagine I was the last man who left the camp."

"What about blind Eliazar?" Ezra asked.

"He probably isn't doing very well. They slaughtered his goats when the camp ran out of food."

"But then he will die of starvation," Ezra exclaimed.

Ephraim looked down at the ground, slightly embarrassed.

"How shameful!" Ezra said. "Is he all alone? How long has it been?"

"I left three days ago, and as I say I was the last to leave."

"How could you leave the blind old man alone there?" Ezra asked reproachfully.

Barabbas turned irritably to Ezra.

"What does it matter—the old man lived long enough. This is no time to worry about useless graybeards."

"I was altogether useless when Eliazar fed me and saved my life," Ezra said. And in a low voice he added, "No man is useless. I will go to find Eliazar."

"What do you intend to do?" Barabbas asked Ephraim, paying no more attention to Ezra.

"I'm also going to one of the port towns," Ephraim answered.

"We will sit down with you," Barabbas said, "and you can tell us about the camp."

But Ephraim shook his head.

"There's no more to tell. And I must be getting on. The sun is already declining—I was just about to start when you came along. Peace be with you!"

He turned swiftly down the road that led westwards. It was obvious that he did not want to stay with Barabbas, or that his conscience was troubled—at any rate, in a moment he had vanished from the sight of the two men.

"Let us rest here," Barabbas decided, and he sat down in the bushes with his back to the wooded copse that ran along the road. Without a word Ezra sat down on a stone near the road, facing Barabbas.

Barabbas sat frowning. What he had heard from Ephraim interfered with his plans. What was the use of going into the desert if the camp was broken up and none of his men were there?

Ezra for his part was thinking of blind Eliazar. He resolved to proceed to the camp as fast as possible to save the poor old man from starvation. He would have preferred to continue on the journey at once, for he felt now that he no longer had any ties with Barabbas.

While he was considering the matter, he suddenly heard a rustling in the woods and looked up. He saw a man hidden behind the bole of a tree, in the act of bending a bow.

"Beware!" he shouted at Barabbas. "Murder!"

As he cried out he jumped up and rushed toward the man in the woods.

Barrabas heard the hissing of an arrow and a heavy thud behind him; he rolled over and saw Ezra lying at full length on his back, an arrow protruding from his chest.

Springing to his feet, Barabbas dashed at full speed into the woods from which the arrow must have been shot. But his efforts were in vain; he found no trace of the assassin. At last he gave up the search and, panting for breath, he returned and fell to his knees beside Ezra.

The arrow had penetrated deep into the left side of Ezra's chest. He lay unconscious, with closed eyes. He was still breathing stertorously, but his lips were flecked with a bloody foam.

Barabbas dragged him to the edge of the road and tried to pour into his mouth a few drops of wine he had in a skin. He realized clearly that the arrow had been meant for him; Ezra now lay dying in his stead. At that moment he understood that he had thrust away this one friend who had remained loyal to him, loyal to death, and now it was too late for him to show his repentance.

Down the road came the thud of hoofs and the tramp of heavy footsteps. Barabbas paid no attention; he scarcely heard the sounds.

A party of travelers approached. The man riding at their head caught sight of Barabbas and Ezra beside him in the grass, with the shaft of the arrow protruding from his chest. He reined in his horse and dismounted.

It was Joseph of Arimathea.

As soon as he approached them he recognized Barabbas and the dying Ezra. He gestured for his followers to stop and then asked Barabbas, who had not yet looked up at him:

"What has happened?"

"You can see," Barabbas replied sorrowfully.

"I see Ezra—is he dead?"

At the mention of Ezra's name Barabbas glanced up at the speaker and recognized Joseph.

"Not yet," Barabbas said. "But you can see how he is—there isn't any hope."

"He is still breathing. But how did it happen?"

Barabbas pointed to the woods.

"From ambush. It was meant for me. The Roman probably had his regrets about releasing me."

Joseph of Arimathea knelt beside the unconscious man, uncovered his chest and listened carefully to his breathing and heart beat.

"He can't be saved," he murmured. "But this is no Roman arrow. It's too short and the barb is too broad. You can see that by the size of the wound."

Barabbas did not reply.

Meanwhile Lazarus, Mary, Martha, and some of their attendants had joined the group. Lazarus and his sisters, as well as some of the others, recognized Ezra, and they felt deep pity for this man who had suffered so many discomforts and defied so many dangers, only to succumb at last to the arrow of an assassin.

"Can't anything be done for him?" Mary asked.

"I'm afraid not," Joseph of Arimathea replied.

Just then Ezra opened his eyes and gazed in astonishment at the large group standing around him. A faint smile of recognition passed across his white face.

"Peace!" he said in a barely audible voice. He attempted to sit up, but fell back helplessly. His left hand moved toward his heart and touched the arrow, but the smile did not vanish from his lips.

"You must not move, Ezra," Joseph said. "You are sorely wounded—worse than you were when you came to us that time. Here, take a drink of this—it will strengthen you and you will feel the pain less."

Ezra tried to drink from the skin that Joseph held to his lips, but it was almost impossible for him to swallow.

"Enough," he said. "It won't help. It will soon be over. I wish to thank you, Joseph—I thank you all. You have always been very kind to me . . ."

"Is there anything you wish that I can do for you?" Joseph asked.

Ezra seemed to be trying to remember something.

"Eliazar," he whispered, and closed his eyes.

"What does he mean by that name?" Joseph asked Barabbas.

"He is speaking of a blind old man who was left behind in my camp and will undoubtedly starve—if he has not already starved to death."

"How can he be located?" Joseph asked.

Barabbas explained briefly.

"I will look for him and try to find him as soon as possible," Joseph said.

Ezra seemed to have heard these words, for he opened his eyes once more and whispered, "I thank you." Then he again sank into unconsciousness.

"He has only seconds to live," Joseph said to Barabbas. "Would you like to come with us?"

"Where are you going?" Barabbas asked.

"We are going to Galilee; the Master has preceded us there."

Barabbas looked at him without understanding.

"What master?"

"Jesus whom we call the Christ!" Joseph replied, bowing his head as he pronounced the name.

"But he was crucified," Barabbas said.

"He has risen, as he prophesied," Joseph said calmly, and Lazarus added:

"He has been truly resurrected and has appeared to Mary and Simon and two other disciples who were going to Emaus. And he gave orders for us to follow him to Galilee. Some of the disciples are already on their way there."

For a moment the words sent Barabbas' mind reeling. Had all these people gone mad? Who had ever heard of a man returning from death? But yes, this Lazarus who stood before him had been dead, and by some magic the Nazarene had brought him back to life . . . But how could any man who was already dead bring about his own resurrection?

Sheer unbelief was manifest in his face. Barabbas smiled at such unreason.

"You don't believe us," Mary said. "But I tell you I saw him with my own eyes and he spoke to me. For he is truly the Son of God and the Saviour of the world!"

During this conversation no one had paid any attention to Ezra. Now Mary observed that his eyes were open and his face illuminated by a radiance that seemed to come from another world.

And his lips whispered:

"Jesus, Son of God, have mercy on me!"

Then his eyes closed once more; but the expression of blessed peace remained.

"He received the message of salvation and took it to his heart in faith," Mary said softly to her brother. "The Lord be praised. See how peacefully he lies there, like one sleeping."

Barabbas had heard Ezra's words and his face contorted into a terrible frown.

"You still have not answered my question, Barabbas," Joseph said. "I asked whether you would like to come with us?"

Barabbas threw his head back defiantly.

"No, Joseph of Arimathea. There can be nothing in common between you and me."

"You are rejecting the greatest of blessings," Mary said to him. "You would have the opportunity of seeing Him."

At this Barabbas broke out into savage laughter that echoed horribly back from the wooded copse. He seemed to have a hysterical seizure—all the unbelief, the hatred, the hardness of his heart burst out of him, and he laughed wildly, insanely, unable to stop himself.

"Fools, fools!" he cried when he had caught his breath. "What fools you are. Resurrected. Expects you in Galilee. A man who had thousands following him and yet was too weak to defend himself against his enemies!"

He looked down at Ezra. Joseph of Arimathea also saw that Ezra was nearing his end. Ezra groaned and waved his arms. His eyes were open and gazing straight at Barabbas; he panted for breath and fresh bubbles of bloody foam rose to his lips.

Barabbas gripped his hand.

"Can I do nothing for you, Ezra, my friend?"

The dying man's eyes looked at him with tenderness, and the trace of a mournful smile could be detected around his blood-stained lips.

"Thank you," he whispered. "I am going now, Barabbas . . . I am going to Him. For believe me: He lives. And love is still stronger than hate . . ."

A quiver passed through his body and his eyes glazed.

Ezra was dead.

But his face reflected a peace that was like a light from the other world.

With bowed head, murmuring silent prayers, Joseph of Arimathea and his companions stood around the dead man. Then Joseph said to Barabbas:

"We will look for a place to bury him. You are too weak to do it yourself, Barabbas . . ."

Barabbas stood up beside the body of Ezra and stretched himself to his full height, so that he looked more like a giant than ever before. It seemed as if all his old strength had returned, as if he were once more that Barabbas who had been the idol of the masses and whom thousands had feared throughout Judea. His eyes flashed rage and hatred as he stood squarely over Ezra's body—as if to protect it from an enemy—and said to Joseph of Arimathea in a voice that resounded far beyond the small circle of his hearers:

"Hearken, Joseph of Arimathea, I am not too weak and I shall bury Ezra myself. For he was my friend and he died for me. But let me tell you this: Your Nazarene is also guilty of his death, as he will be guilty of the death of all who believe in his trumpery about love. Love? Do you not see that love means suffering and death? Do you think I have never loved? I loved my mother—she died abandoned. I loved a woman—she had to die for that love. I loved Ezra—he had to die for me. Men love—but why? Only to suffer? Don't you see where love leads? Hasn't the man on the cross shown you that? I am saved from weakness, Joseph of Arimathea, because I preach hatred and violence, and these will always be stronger on this earth than love. I don't know what lies before me in this land— but the seed I have sowed will germinate and the day will come when hate will seize all man's souls so powerfully that no living creature will survive to stand in its way. Your Nazarene preached love. I preached hate. He is dead, I live. In this world hate will always survive love, for hate is stronger than love and violence stronger than goodness. The struggle is decided between me and Jesus of Nazareth. We can never approach one another. And now go your way—leave me alone with my dead!"

Joseph of Arimathea had blenched at this terrible outburst of vindictiveness. Lazarus, Mary, and the others also stood rooted, not knowing what to do. Then Joseph signed to them and turned away. The others followed him. Swiftly the group vanished toward the north.

Barabbas gazed after them for a while; then he set about looking for a place to bury Ezra. Near the edge of the woods he found a trench already dug; evidently it had been intended for him. He carried the lifeless body to it and laid Ezra in. Unconsciously he placed his friend so that the eyes looked north, and not toward the Holy City. For he sensed that Ezra's hope was not in Jerusalem and the Temple, but in the resurrected Saviour who was now in Galilee. Then he closed Ezra's eyes and set about finding stones to protect the body from wild beasts. It was difficult work for him in his weakened condition, and it was night before he had completed the burial mound for his friend.

Then Barabbas sat down at the head of the grave and covered his head in the sign of mourning.

"And love is still stronger than hate . . ."

These last words that Ezra had spoken echoed again and again in his mind. "Poor Ezra, how dearly you paid for your love for me," he thought. "And if it is true that Jesus of Nazareth loved even me, has he not also paid dearly for his love?"

His whole life passed before him. His dreary youth, never brightened by love; the torment and depression of his early manhood. On how many doors had he knocked in vain? How often had he been rejected, how often mocked because of his birth. No, he thought, he had not been a man until he had come to a realization of his physical strength, until he had begun to take by violence what was otherwise denied to him. And he had been happy, really happy, for the first time when the lust for power overcame him and bore him upwards. Only in power and violence could there be joy, and only in strength success, Barabbas said to himself, not noticing that he was speaking these words aloud, almost shouting them. He did not hear himself blurt out to the night air:

"There is only one thing in the world that is worth living and fighting for, and that is power. And power can be had only by violence. And the truest and strongest servant of violence is hate."

And in a wild ecstasy Barabbas shouted at the top of his lungs: "Jesus of Nazareth, the struggle between you and me will go on forever."

The thousand voices of the night replied to Barabbas: the hoarse barking of the jackals, the brief yelp of the fox, the hoot of the owl in the trees, and the high-pitched chattering of the smaller animals.

In the east, over the desert, far beyond the Jordan, a streak of light appeared. Dawn was breaking.

Barabbas rose. In his soul was the darkness of night, on his brow defiance and his eyes glared hatred.

And he went out to the road and marched off down the road— apostle of hate for all ages and all nations.